"Do you attempt ruin often?" he asked.
Charlotte gestured to the sofa and took a place half a yard to Sherbourne's right.

"I like you," she said. "Somewhat. A little. I don't dislike you."

"My heart pounds with joy to hear it. I don't dislike you either."

Thank the gods of porcelain and silver, the tea cart rattled loudly as somebody pushed it along the corridor. Sherbourne thus knew to fall silent rather than expound about why he didn't dislike Miss Charlotte Windham rather a lot.

A footman steered the tea cart into the parlor, and a maid came along to assist with setting the offerings on the low table before the sofa. The polite fussing gave Sherbourne a chance to consider possibilities and theories.

His mind, however, usually reliable during daylight hours, failed to focus on the facts as he knew them.

Charlotte Windham was seeking her own ruin. What the devil was she about?

HIGH ACCLAIM FOR GRACE BURROWES

"Sexy heroes, strong heroines, intelligent plots, enchanting love stories...Grace Burrowes's romances have them all."
—Mary Balogh, *New York Times* bestselling author

"Grace Burrowes writes from the heart—with warmth, humor, and a generous dash of sensuality, her stories are unputdownable! If you're not reading Grace Burrowes you're missing the very best in today's Regency romance!"
—Elizabeth Hoyt, *New York Times* bestselling author

NO OTHER DUKE WILL DO

"Compelling, sympathetic characters and a rare blend of passion and humor result in another exquisite gem from a master of the genre. Gorgeously done."
—*Library Journal* (starred review)

TOO SCOT TO HANDLE

"A well-plotted, beautifully written story made all the more satisfying by its delightful secondary characters."
—*Library Journal* (starred review)

"Top Pick! Burrowes's delightful plotlines, heartfelt emotions, humor, and realistic, honest characters have turned her Windham series spinoffs into a fan favorite...a gem of a read. 4½ Stars."
—*RT Book Reviews*

THE TROUBLE WITH DUKES

"The hero of *The Trouble with Dukes* reminds me of Mary Balogh's charming men, and the heroine brings to mind Sarah MacLean's intelligent, fiery women...This is a wonderfully funny, moving romance, not to be missed!"

—Eloisa James, *New York Times* bestselling author

"*The Trouble with Dukes* has everything Grace Burrowes's many fans have come to adore: a swoonworthy hero, a strong heroine, humor, and passion. Her characters not only know their own hearts, but share them with fearless joy. Grace Burrowes is a romance treasure."

—Tessa Dare, *New York Times* bestselling author

"*The Trouble with Dukes* is captivating! It has everything I love in a book—a sexy Scotsman, a charming heroine, witty banter, plenty of humor, and lots of heart."

—Jennifer Ashley, *New York Times* bestselling author

"Exquisite writing, outstanding characters, a gorgeous romance, and a nail-biter of an ending. *The Trouble with Dukes* is the definition of a perfect historical romance!"

—Fresh Fiction

"Readers who enjoy Tessa Dare will embrace...this affecting and clever tale."

—*Booklist*

ALSO BY GRACE BURROWES

A ROGUE OF HER OWN

WINDHAM BRIDES #4

GRACE BURROWES

FOREVER
New York   Boston

Copyright © 2018 by Grace Burrowes

Excerpt from *Rogues to Riches* #1 copyright © 2018 by Grace Burrowes

Cover illustration by Chris Cocozza. Cover hand-lettering by Jen Mussari. Cover design by Elizabeth Stokes. Cover copyright © 2018 by Hachette Book Group, Inc.

Forever
Hachette Book Group
1290 Avenue of the Americas, New York, NY 10104
forever-romance.com
twitter.com/foreverromance

First Edition: March 2018

Forever is an imprint of Grand Central Publishing. The Forever name and logo are trademarks of Hachette Book Group, Inc.

The publisher is not responsible for websites (or their content) that are not owned by the publisher.

The Hachette Speakers Bureau provides a wide range of authors for speaking events. To find out more, go to www.hachettespeakersbureau.com or call (866) 376-6591.

ISBNs: 978-1-5387-2891-8 (mass market), 978-1-5387-2892-5 (ebook)

Printed in the United States of America

OPM

10 9 8 7 6 5 4 3 2 1

ATTENTION CORPORATIONS AND ORGANIZATIONS:

Most Hachette Book Group books are available at quantity discounts with bulk purchase for educational, business, or sales promotional use. For information, please call or write:

Special Markets Department, Hachette Book Group
1290 Avenue of the Americas, New York, NY 10104
Telephone: 1-800-222-6747 Fax: 1-800-477-5925

To my great, big, wonderful, irksome, impressive, bothersome, and—most of all—loving family.

ACKNOWLEDGMENTS

When I completed the original Windham Family series, I did so wondering if I'd have a chance to write happily-ever-afters for Uncle Tony and Aunt Gladys's four daughters. Being unmarried Windhams, they kept me up at night. Thanks to my editor Leah Hultenschmidt and the whole team at Grand Central Forever for being such a pleasure to work with on the Windham Brides series. (Though I do think we should have planned a project team meeting at a Welsh Castle...just sayin'.)

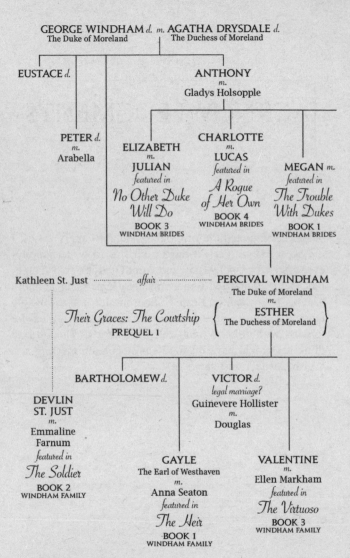

GEORGE WINDHAM *d.* *m.* **AGATHA DRYSDALE** *d.*
The Duke of Moreland   The Duchess of Moreland

EUSTACE *d.*

ANTHONY
m.
Gladys Holsopple

PETER *d.*
m.
Arabella

ELIZABETH
m.
JULIAN
featured in
No Other Duke Will Do
BOOK 3
WINDHAM BRIDES

CHARLOTTE
m.
LUCAS
featured in
A Rogue of Her Own
BOOK 4
WINDHAM BRIDES

MEGAN *m.*
featured in
The Trouble With Dukes
BOOK 1
WINDHAM BRIDES

Kathleen St. Just ⋯⋯⋯⋯ *affair* ⋯⋯⋯⋯ **PERCIVAL WINDHAM**
The Duke of Moreland
m.
ESTHER
The Duchess of Moreland

Their Graces: The Courtship
PREQUEL 1

BARTHOLOMEW *d.*

VICTOR *d.*
legal marriage?
Guinevere Hollister
m.
Douglas

DEVLIN ST. JUST
m.
Emmaline Farnum
featured in
The Soldier
BOOK 2
WINDHAM FAMILY

GAYLE
The Earl of Westhaven
m.
Anna Seaton
featured in
The Heir
BOOK 1
WINDHAM FAMILY

VALENTINE
m.
Ellen Markham
featured in
The Virtuoso
BOOK 3
WINDHAM FAMILY

GRACEBURROWES.COM

WINDHAM *Family Tree*

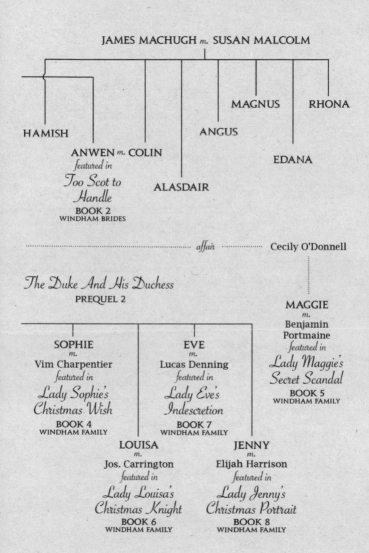

JAMES MACHUGH *m.* SUSAN MALCOLM

HAMISH

ANWEN *m.* COLIN
featured in
Too Scot to Handle
BOOK 2
WINDHAM BRIDES

ALASDAIR

ANGUS

MAGNUS

RHONA

EDANA

·············· *affair* ·············· Cecily O'Donnell

The Duke And His Duchess
PREQUEL 2

MAGGIE
m.
Benjamin Portmaine
featured in
Lady Maggie's Secret Scandal
BOOK 5
WINDHAM FAMILY

SOPHIE
m.
Vim Charpentier
featured in
Lady Sophie's Christmas Wish
BOOK 4
WINDHAM FAMILY

EVE
m.
Lucas Denning
featured in
Lady Eve's Indescretion
BOOK 7
WINDHAM FAMILY

LOUISA
m.
Jos. Carrington
featured in
Lady Louisa's Christmas Knight
BOOK 6
WINDHAM FAMILY

JENNY
m.
Elijah Harrison
featured in
Lady Jenny's Christmas Portrait
BOOK 8
WINDHAM FAMILY

Chapter One

"Heed me, Miss Charlotte, for mine is the only offer you're likely to receive, no matter that your uncle is a duke. I am a viscount, and you shall like being my viscountess very well."

Charlotte Windham had no choice but to *heed* Viscount Neederby, for he'd taken her by the arm and was nearly dragging her along Lady Belchamp's wilderness walk.

"My lord, while I am ever receptive to knowledgeable guidance, this is neither the time nor the place to make a declaration." Never and nowhere suited Charlotte when it came to proposals from such as Neederby.

He marched onward, simultaneously walking and pontificating being one of his few accomplishments.

"I must beg to differ, my dear, for receptive to guidance you most assuredly are not. Married to me, your sadly headstrong propensities will be laid to rest. My duty and pleasure as your devoted spouse will be to instruct you in all matters."

His lordship sent her a look, one intended to convey tender indulgence or a disturbance of the bowels, Charlotte wasn't sure which.

"Might we circle back to the buffet, sir? All this hiking about has given me an appetite."

Neederby finally halted, though he chose a spot overlooking the Thames River. What imbecile had decided that scenic views were a mandatory improvement on Nature as the Almighty had designed her?

"Were you being arch, Miss Charlotte? I believe you were. I have appetites too, dontcha know."

Neederby fancied himself a Corinthian, as accomplished at all the manly sports as he was at tying a fancy knot in his cravat. Hostesses added him to guest lists because he had a title and had yet to lose either his hair or his teeth in any quantity.

In Charlotte's estimation, his brains had gone missing entirely.

"I haven't an arch bone in my body, my lord. I am, however, hungry." The occasion was a Venetian breakfast, and Charlotte had intended to do justice to the lavish buffet. The roaring water more than ten yards below the iron railing had carried away her appetite.

"One hears things," Neederby said, wiggling his eyebrows. "About *certain* people."

Charlotte heard the river thundering past and edged back from the overlook. "I have no interest in gossip, but a plate of Lady Belchamp's buffet offerings does appeal."

His lordship clamped a gloved hand over Charlotte's fingers. "What about *my* offerings? I'm tireless in the saddle, as they say, and you're in want of a fellow to show you the *bridle* path, as it were."

Equestrian analogies never led anywhere decent. Charlotte escaped Neederby's grasp by twisting her arm, a move her cousins had shown her more than ten years ago.

"I'm famished, your lordship. We can return to the buffet, or I'll leave you here to admire the view."

Neither option could salvage Charlotte's morning. The gossips would claim that she had taken too long on this ramble with his lordship, or that she'd returned to the party without his escort, both choices unacceptable for a lady.

As the only remaining unmarried Windham, Charlotte had earned the enmity of every wallflower, failed debutante, matchmaker, and fortune hunter in Mayfair. The little season brought the wilted and the wounded out in quantity, while Charlotte—who considered herself neither—longed to retire to the country.

Neederby moved more quickly than he reasoned, and thus Charlotte found herself trapped between him and the railing.

"When anybody's looking," he said, "you're all haughty airs and tidy bonnet ribbons, but I know what you fast girls really want. Married to me, you'd be more than content."

Married to him, Charlotte would be a candidate for Bedlam. "I need breakfast, you buffoon, and I haven't been a girl for years. Get away from me."

Charlotte also needed room to drive her knee into his jewelbox, and she needed to breathe. His lordship took a step closer, and Charlotte backed up until the railing was all that prevented her from falling into the torrent below. Her vision dimmed at the edges and the roaring in her ears merged with the noise of the river.

Not now. Please, not here, not now. Not with the biggest nincompoop in all of nincompoopdom flinging his marital ambitions at me.

The thought had barely formed when Neederby was abruptly dragged three feet to the right.

"Sherbourne," his lordship squawked. "Devilish bad taste to interrupt a man when he's paying his addresses."

Lucas Sherbourne was tall, blond, solidly built, and at that moment, a pathetically welcome sight.

"If that's your idea of how a gentleman pays his addresses," Sherbourne said, "then I'd like to introduce you to my version of target practice at dawn."

"His lordship was *not* paying his addresses," Charlotte bit out. She clung to the rail in hopes of remaining upright, and yet, she needed to get away from the precipice.

Sherbourne peeled her fingers free one by one and offered his arm. "Then I misread the situation, and his lordship merely owes you an apology."

Sherbourne glanced at the river, then at Neederby, as if measuring angles and distances. Charlotte's heart was beating too fast and her knees were weak, else she might have managed a dignified exit. Instead, she held fast to Sherbourne's muscular arm—needs must—and conjured a mental image of her grandmother Holsopple's fancy tea service.

"My apologies," Neederby muttered, yanking on his waistcoat. "I'll wish you good day, Miss Charlotte."

He turned his back on Sherbourne—a lord's privilege where a commoner was concerned, but rude treatment of a lady—and stalked off in the direction of the next scenic view.

Sherbourne switched positions, so he stood between Charlotte and the railing. "If you were any more pale, I'd be measuring you for a winding sheet. Come sit."

On some other day or in some other place that offered no dratted scenic vista, Charlotte would chide him for his peremptory tone.

"Your store of flattery is wanting, Mr. Sherbourne." She

could not possibly sit on the bench he'd led her to. "The prospect does not appeal."

"The prospect of being seen in my company? Perhaps you'd prefer the pawing and snorting of Lord Nettlebum, or one of his equally blue-blooded—"

Charlotte waved a hand. "The prospect of the river. So far below."

Sherbourne glanced past her shoulder. "A long leap, I'll grant you, but hardly...Are you about to faint on me, Charlotte Windham?"

The curiosity in his tone—no outrage or dismay—had Charlotte standing straighter. "And fuel the talk already circulating? What do you take me for?"

Sherbourne was a social upstart, but he was a wealthy, single upstart who had the good fortune to be neighbors with the Duke of Haverford in Wales. That fine gentleman had recently married Charlotte's sister Elizabeth, and thus Sherbourne was a *well-connected*, wealthy, single upstart.

Also a pest, but not a fool.

Charlotte watched him adding facts and observations, and coming to the logical conclusion.

"Have you taken any sustenance?" he asked. "The buffet line was long earlier. Perhaps a spot of tea would appeal?"

"A spot of tea would be heavenly. Thank you."

That Sherbourne would be both kind and discreet was miraculous. Later, Charlotte might find the resolve to resent him for both—why had *he* been the one to interrupt Neederby, why not some meddling cousin or devoted auntie?—but for now, she was grateful simply to leave the river's edge.

* * *

"Writing to one of your sisters again?" Julian St. David, Duke of Haverford, asked his duchess.

Elizabeth had taken over the tower room known as the Dovecote for her personal corner of Haverford Castle. She set aside the page she'd been working on and rose to hug him.

"I've missed you, Haverford."

He'd been gone less than three hours. "I've missed you, too. I promised Sherbourne I'd keep an eye on his acres, and that requires the occasional glance in the direction of his property. His steward isn't exactly an advertisement for modern agricultural practices."

Elizabeth remained in Julian's arms, and that was fine with him, for he loved to hold her. They'd met when she'd attended his summer house party. From the first day, Elizabeth had begun setting Haverford Castle and its owner to rights.

Now that she was the chatelaine, the property boasted a lot fewer musty old books, also a lot less dust and mildew. Windows had become spotless, carpets once again had luster, and not a single chimney dared smoke.

Being a duke had never been such a comfy, pleasant undertaking, while being Elizabeth's husband...

"I'm in need of a nap," Julian said. "Cantering all over the shire tires a fellow out."

"You need luncheon first. Napping with your duchess requires stamina."

"Point to the lady."

A tap sounded on the door, and Julian admitted a footman bearing a tray. As usual, Elizabeth had anticipated her spouse's appetites, not merely his desires.

She settled beside him on the sofa and let him fix the tea. Then she let him feed her a piece of shortbread, *then* she let him kiss her until he was more or less lying atop her, the tea growing cold.

"We have a perfectly lovely bed," Julian said. "Why am I compelled to accost you on sofas, benches, and picnic blankets?"

"I made the overtures on the picnic blanket," Elizabeth said, stroking a fingertip over his eyebrow. "I've grown fond of picnic blankets."

Julian was fond of her, and he hadn't expected that, not so soon, not so...profoundly. He loved Elizabeth, he respected her, and God knew he desired her, but the pure, friendly sense of liking they shared was as precious as their passionate sentiments. She had become his confidante, his sounding board, his advisor, and most of all, his *friend*.

And his lover, of course. "We'll picnic after we nap," he said, giving his wife room to breathe.

"We'll nap after we've done justice to the tray," Elizabeth said, using Julian's shoulder to pull herself upright. "I'm worried about Charlotte."

Hence, the whirlwind of letters flying among the three married Windham sisters. Various cousins participated in the epistolary storm, for the ducal branch of the Windham family had no less than eight healthy offshoots, all happily married.

And all, doubtless, also *worried about Charlotte*.

"Is this a different sort of worry than you had for her before we married?" Julian asked around a mouthful of shortbread.

"My anxiety is worse, because I am married. We're all married, except for Charlotte. That can't be easy. Did you just put butter on your shortbread?"

"I must fortify myself for this *lengthy* nap you're planning."

"Fortify me with both butter and jam," Elizabeth said. "Will you be wroth with me if I've done a bit a matchmaking?"

He would never be wroth with her. "You can make a match for Charlotte by correspondence?"

"I'm a Windham. Matchmaking is my birthright, according to Uncle Percival and Aunt Esther."

These relations of Elizabeth's, the Duke and Duchess of Moreland, were a deceptively charming older couple who'd likely brought about half the unions in Mayfair.

"You're a St. David now," Julian said, passing her a slice of shortbread slathered with butter and jam. "Thus, I am your accomplice in all things. At whom have you aimed Cupid's arrow?"

"I didn't aim it, exactly. Charlotte is so very contrary that I instead warned my aunt that of all men, Lucas Sherbourne ought not to be shoved at Charlotte. She seemed to notice him at the house party this summer, which for Charlotte, is tantamount to a mad passion."

"You have a bit of raspberry jam on your lip." Julian kissed the relevant feature. "Scrumptious."

"If Sherbourne is steered away from Charlotte," Elizabeth went on, "then she might favor him with the occasional glance."

"My thoughts complement your own, for I've written to Sherbourne that he is not, under any circumstances, to contemplate a courtship of Charlotte Windham. Hold still."

Elizabeth gave him an amused look—she'd hold still only if she jolly well pleased to, of course—and set down her teacup.

Julian dipped his finger in the jam pot and drew a line of preserves along her décolletage. "Is this one of your favorite frocks?"

"Is the door locked?"

"Yes." Out of recently acquired habit.

"This is my least favorite dress in all the world."

Julian stood and shrugged out of his jacket, then undid his cravat and sleeve buttons. "We must earn our rest."

"We'll need to hire another seamstress at the rate I go through dresses."

Julian ran his tongue over the jam adorning Elizabeth's right breast. "I'm ever mindful of the necessity to economize. We could simply dispense with clothing when we're at home, and save both time and money."

Elizabeth swiped her finger through the jam on her left breast, then pressed raspberry sweetness to Julian's mouth. "I vote we dispense with your clothing right now, Your Grace."

Julian seconded that worthy motion and had coaxed Elizabeth out of her shoes and stockings when it occurred to him that he was not especially worried about Charlotte Windham. Charlotte had scolded the Duke of Wellington for hiding in the card room at her aunt's ball, and His Grace had meekly spent the rest of the evening standing up with wallflowers.

Julian was, despite all common sense to the contrary, concerned for Lucas Sherbourne. Sherbourne was a commoner, overly confident, and out of his depth socially among London's elites. He was also dunderheaded enough to do something truly unforgivable, like propose to Charlotte without even attempting to court her.

* * *

The look in Charlotte Windham's eyes had inspired Lucas Sherbourne to interrupt Lord Neederby's forlorn hope of a proposal.

Sherbourne had had the privilege of studying the lady over the course of a three-week house party earlier in the year, and he'd seen her amused, anxious, disdainful—Charlotte Windham did an exquisitely convincing disdainful—exasperated, mischievous (his favorite, though rare), and in many other moods.

She'd never once looked frightened, but cornered by Lord Nitwit's matrimonial presumptions, she'd been approaching panic.

"You will please endure my company for the length of the buffet and at least thirty minutes thereafter," Sherbourne said as he escorted Miss Windham to the Belchamp gardens.

"You will please, for the sake of your unborn children, refrain from giving me orders, Mr. Sherbourne."

Splendid. Miss Windham was feeling a bit more the thing.

"Heaven forefend that I do more than offer you a suggestion, madam. I'm merely asking for the return of a favor. I spared you the effort of tossing his lordship into the river. You will spare me Lady Belchamp's devotion. She's been eyeing me as if I were her favorite dessert."

Miss Windham smiled, her merriment mostly in her eyes. "Her ladyship gambles imprudently, and thus wealthy, generous bachelors are her favorite sweet."

Most redheads were striking enough with green eyes, but Charlotte Windham's eyes were blue. They were the first feature of hers Sherbourne had noticed, and while her eyes were everything a lady's should be—pretty, slightly tilted, framed by perfectly arched brows—they were also many other things a proper lady's eyes should not be.

Bold, direct, intelligent, and—this intrigued Sherbourne—subtly unhappy. Why would a woman who claimed a close connection to not one but *three* dukes have cause for complaint about anything?

"You would toss me to her ladyship's tender wiles and enjoy my discomfort," Sherbourne said. "Though I suspect you'd rescue me before my cause was hopeless."

"Or I'd rescue her ladyship. You are not the tame gentleman you impersonate."

"Thank you. One fears that a charade perpetrated too earnestly will become reality." With Charlotte Windham, Sherbourne could only be honest. She'd verbally skewer him for wasting her time with flattery or flirtation.

"Or one fears that such a charade will drive one mad," Miss Windham muttered.

Well yes, though Sherbourne hadn't considered that a creeping sense of unease would also plague Miss Windham, who had more titles on her family tree than Wellington had battle honors.

For Sherbourne, this year's little season had acquired the unwelcome rigor of an expensive finishing school. The Duke of Haverford had decided to turn up cordial after years of polite disdain, and thus Sherbourne had arrived to London with something of a sponsor.

Haverford had sent word ahead to his auntie-in-law, the Duchess of Moreland, that Sherbourne was to be taken in hand, and Sherbourne hadn't had a decent night's sleep since arriving to town. Haverford would be made to pay for that kindness, assuming Sherbourne survived the next three weeks.

"If you don't enjoy all the socializing, waltzing, and gossiping," Sherbourne said, "why not remove to Kent, or wherever the family seat is, and spare yourself the aggravation?"

"My time is not my own, Mr. Sherbourne. I'm the sole

remaining marital project in my family, and the Windhams are a large family."

"Visit your sister Elizabeth. Wales is lovely in the autumn, and bachelors who are up to your weight are virtually nonexistent there." With the exception of himself, of course.

Miss Windham gave a slight shake of her head as they approached the buffet. "Try again, sir."

Ah—he'd spoken in the imperative. "Have you considered a visit to Haverford Castle? I'm sure the duchess would love to have your company."

"Better, but still a preposterous suggestion. Their Graces of Haverford are newly wed, and a newly wed Windham is a happily preoccupied creature."

Preoccupied? If His Grace of Haverford's besottedness was any indication, both halves of the couple were seldom fully clothed.

Sherbourne was about to direct Miss Windham to try the apple tarts, but caught himself. "Would you care for some apple tart?"

Had he not seen Miss Windham's smile for himself, he would never have believed the benevolence of her expression. Her smile suggested that at some point, Charlotte Windham had been a very sweet girl. That sweet girl would have been spared Lord Neederby's oafish overtures, because even a clodpate such as he would have kept a worshipful distance.

"What do you fancy besides the apple tart?" Miss Windham asked, passing Sherbourne a second plate. "Peckish men are seldom good company."

They moved down the table, with Miss Windham filling the plates Sherbourne held. The breeze was achingly soft, as early autumn breezes in southern England could be, and the guests had settled about the terraces and walkways in couples and small groups.

Miss Windham had chosen basic fare: slices of beef, small squares of cheese, buttered bread, and half an apple tart. Not for her, the rich desserts or pretty confections, while Sherbourne loved fancy treats.

"You're not eating much," he said.

"My digestion is still a bit tentative." The lady surveyed the lawn as if deciding where to position her cannon. "Let's enjoy the sun."

How did a woman enjoy the sun, when she was expected to wear a bonnet and carry a parasol, in addition to covering every inch of skin save her hands—the occasion was a meal out of doors—and her face?

"Excellent choice," Sherbourne said. "If we sit in the sun, we'll also avoid the company of females overly concerned about the perils of freckles."

The sweet smile made a fleeting return. "You're welcome, though I'll thank you to defend me from any fortune hunters between bites of apple tart."

They settled on a bench and were soon consuming their meal.

"Was it Neederby's addresses that upset your digestion or the height of the overlook?" Sherbourne asked.

"You heard him. I shudder to speculate why he'd think his horseman's talk could put a lady in a frame of mind for amorous advances."

For Sherbourne, the connection was easily grasped. "Care for some of my raspberries?"

She frowned at her food. "I thought the raspberries were to go on my plate."

Sherbourne held out his plate to her. "My mistake, I'm sure. Profound apologies."

He was *nearly* flirting, trying to make her smile again, and that was...that was nothing to be concerned about. What else did one do at such an inane gathering?

Miss Windham spooned most of the raspberries onto her plate. "Mistake corrected. At least Neederby didn't liken marriage to gardening. Poor Lord Helmsford considers himself a botanist, and by the time he'd discoursed about bees, fruits, and pollen, I wasn't sure if his objective was turning a profit from his orangery or securing the succession. These raspberries are luscious."

"Helmsford proposed to you?" Helmsford was an ass, even for an earl.

Miss Windham licked the tip of her thumb. "He proposed the first time five years ago, then again last week."

Helmsford could go to the devil, for all Sherbourne cared, but that small gesture—Charlotte Windham licking a dab of raspberry from her thumb—lit a flame of imagination in Sherbourne's mind.

Charlotte Windham was intelligent, honest, pretty, and enduring one stupid proposal after another. Sherbourne esteemed her greatly, as the cliché went, and also genuinely.

How would she react if Sherbourne offered her a sensible proposal?

Chapter Two

Charlotte got through the meal with Sherbourne partly by correcting his manners, which were in truth perfectly adequate, and partly by delivering pointed stares to the hopeful young ladies, prowling matchmakers, and merry widows sashaying by.

She'd left Sherbourne in the company of her cousin Valentine, who'd doubtless report to the family that Charlotte had strolled down the garden path with Neederby and returned on Sherbourne's arm.

Thank the heavenly intercessors for the quiet of the ladies' retiring room.

For the next three weeks, Charlotte would be dragged about from one entertainment to another. After the weather turned cold and hunt season started, she'd be free of London until next spring.

Three weeks—four at the most—and she could choose between Papa's estate in Hampshire, or Uncle Percival's family seat in Kent. Charlotte nodded to the maid sitting on a stool in the corner, let herself into one of the little closets intended to provide privacy, and settled on the cushioned bench.

Four weeks was 28 days, 672 hours, or 40,320 minutes. She was working on the seconds when chattering voices filled the silence.

"Well, *I* heard that Minerva Fuller *had* to marry Captain Baumrucker, and that explains her *immediate* remove with him to the north. You, girl—fix my hair."

Nanette Monmouth had been Minerva Fuller's bosom bow for much of the season. Charlotte rustled her skirts as a warning—gossiping in the retiring room was a tyro's mistake, and Nanette had finished her second season.

"Well, I heard that Charlotte Windham is *ruined.*"

That would be…Miss Cynthia Beauvais, also recently graduated from her second season.

"Captain Baumrucker is in my cousin's unit," Lady Ivy Fenton said. "The weavers up north are discontent, and the army has been dispatched to keep the peace."

Smart woman, and she didn't put on airs.

"What do you mean, Charlotte Windham is ruined?" Miss Monmouth asked. "My brother says she's an Original. Is she ruined-ruined, or has she been scolding His Grace of Wellington in public again?"

"She was teasing him," Lady Ivy said. "My mama overheard the whole exchange."

"Ouch! You stupid girl!" The sound of a hand smacking flesh brought the gossip to a momentary halt.

"At Haverford's house party this summer," Miss Beauvais said, "Miss Charlotte was observed to suffer poor digestion. The ruse of a megrim was put about, but I know of only one cause that renders an otherwise healthy young lady prone to casting up her accounts."

The problem had been bad ale, or nerves. House parties were a circle of hell even Dante had lacked the courage to describe.

"The dress Miss Charlotte has on today did strike me as a bit loose," Miss Monmouth observed. "She was definitely pale when I saw her clutching Mr. Sherbourne's arm."

"She wore a walking dress," Lady Ivy replied. "Mr. Sherbourne is something of a challenge for us all."

Do tell.

"Even if he's common as coal and rough around the edges," Miss Beauvais said, "no man with so much lovely, lovely money is too great a challenge, according to my mama. I doubt even he would put up with Charlotte Windham's waspish tongue and haughty airs."

Haughty again? Did polite society really have such a limited vocabulary?

"She's a Windham," Miss Monmouth said. "They are quite high in the instep, but Charlotte Windham needs ruining. None of us will have a chance next spring if she's still being invited everywhere."

So don't invite me, please don't invite me. Charlotte's prayer was in vain, of course. As the last unmarried Windham, she'd become her Aunt Esther's de facto companion, and even prayer did not stand much chance against Her Grace of Moreland's wishes.

"I see no harm in admiring Miss Charlotte's fashion choices," Miss Beauvais said, "even if they are curiously loose about the waist and bodice."

"I'm leaving," Lady Ivy informed her companions. "As you plan this assassination, please recall two things: First, in a few years, you might stand in Miss Charlotte's slippers. She warned me away from that dreadful Mr. Stanbridge, and for that I will always be in her debt. Mama had become convinced of his worthiness."

"Whatever happened to Mr. Stanbridge?" Miss Monmouth asked. "He was a fine dancer."

Stanbridge had developed a pressing need to admire the glories of ancient Rome after Charlotte had sent him an anonymous note, totaling his debts of honor such as she'd been able to winkle them from her cousins. Stanbridge's illegitimate daughter was kept in near penury, while her dashing papa wooed decent women by day and scandal by night.

Charlotte had used her best imitation of Uncle Percival's handwriting and threatened to reveal the sum of Stanbridge's debts to Lady Ivy's papa.

Alas, a compulsion to travel had overcome Mr. Stanbridge's version of true love.

"Who cares about Mr. Stanbridge?" Miss Beauvais asked. "We must look to our futures. Miss Charlotte Windham was pale this morning, and did anybody notice that she started her walk with Lord Neederby but returned to the buffet with Mr. Sherbourne?"

"His lordship has the loveliest hair," Miss Monmouth said. "I would adore to muss it up, but it's already so adorably mussed."

"I wish you both good-day," Lady Ivy said, "and leave you with one final thought: Charlotte Windham's uncle is the Duke of Moreland, one of her sisters is married to the Duke of Murdoch, another to the Duke of Haverford. I need not enumerate the cousins and in-laws she's connected to, any one of whom could ruin you without saying a word. And then there's Her Grace of Moreland to consider."

Another silence stretched, this one respectful, if not awed.

The door opened and closed.

"Poor Lady Ivy," Miss Monmouth said. "She's getting long in the tooth, and one can't quite call her pretty."

While the blond, dimpled Miss Monmouth was all that was ugly about polite society. Had Charlotte not already suffered Neederby's proposal by the river, she might have marched forth, smiled brilliantly at the two young fools—they were still more foolish than malicious—and been about her business.

But marching forth took bravado, and her stores of that staple were depleted.

"Let's see if Miss Charlotte has turned loose of Mr. Sherbourne," Miss Beauvais suggested. "She must be luring him on for an eventual set down. She does that, you know. One must admire her skill even if she's not very nice."

They went tittering and conniving on their way, though theirs was not the first such conversation Charlotte had overheard. She remained on the tufted bench, more dispirited than she'd been since watching Elizabeth and her duke drive off to Wales.

"They're gone, miss," said a soft voice. "Best come out now before the next batch arrives."

Charlotte pushed to her feet, smoothed her skirts, and unlatched the door. The maid sat on her stool, her left cheek bright red.

"Thank you," Charlotte said, fishing a coin from her skirt pocket and passing it to the girl. "You should put some arnica on that cheek when you have a moment."

The maid smiled wanly. "The young misses are slappers, but I do fancy the vales."

Pennies, hoarded up against the day when a young miss decided a maid must take the blame for a spilled bottle of ink or something even more trivial.

Charlotte hadn't such a desperate need of pennies, but what resources would she have when her family's influence, or the common sense of a Lady Ivy, was no longer adequate to protect her from ruin?

As she left the retiring room, a dangerous question popped into her head: Did she even want that protection? Her sisters were all married, and their reputations were safe.

For Charlotte, ruin was becoming perilously hard to distinguish from rescue. She had the odd thought that none of her family would understand her reasoning, but Lucas Sherbourne—blunt, common, ambitious, and shrewd—would grasp her logic easily.

* * *

The more Sherbourne considered offering marriage to Charlotte Windham, the more he liked the idea. Many a debutante married on short acquaintance, provided the suitor met with her family's approval.

Those debutantes didn't often marry a Welsh nobody, though, regardless of the nobody's wealth. Nonetheless, a letter sat on Sherbourne's desk from no less exalted a dunderhead than Julian, Duke of Haverford. Sherbourne's neighbor hinted, in a roundabout, ducal, indirect way, that Charlotte Windham was in need of marrying.

"I must determine what I have that can tempt the lady into looking with favor upon my suit," Sherbourne informed his cat.

Solomon went about his ablutions, licking his right paw

and swiping it about one black ear. The feline sat on the sideboard in the front foyer, occupying a gold tray intended to hold the day's correspondence.

"Elizabeth Windham is keen on books—and on being married to His Grace of Haven't-a-Clue—but all I know about Miss Charlotte is that she's a highly skilled archer and does not suffer fools."

Sherbourne checked his appearance in the mirror over the sideboard. He loved fantastically embroidered waist-coats for town attire—the only spot of color gentlemen's fashions allowed—but his valet had advised moderation.

"I hate moderation," Sherbourne muttered, tilting his hat a half inch on the right. "Better."

Solomon yawned, showing every toothy detail of his mouth.

"Same to you. I'm off on reconnaissance."

Which for Sherbourne meant presenting himself on the Duke of Moreland's doorstep. Sherbourne's townhouse was larger but lacked the profusion of potted heartsease on his portico.

Before he could raise his hand to use Moreland's brass knocker, the door opened.

Charlotte Windham stood before him in a fetching ensemble of soft green with a snug cream spencer. Her bonnet was a small-brimmed straw hat, and her reticule was a beaded confection that caught the midday sun.

"Oh, it's you, Mr. Sherbourne."

He tipped his hat, though her greeting was a bit lowering. "Who else would I be?"

"I was just going out."

"Not without an escort, you weren't. Might I offer myself in that capacity?"

Behind Miss Charlotte, a white-haired butler stared

across the foyer as if the conversation were being conducted on somebody else's front stoop in some other hemisphere.

"I'm merely off to visit a cousin. No escort—"

The butler cleared his throat. Loudly.

"Indulge me," Sherbourne said, because clearly, Miss Charlotte had been prepared to strike off across town on her own. Even he knew that was not the done thing.

"I've changed my mind," she said, taking Sherbourne's arm and dragging him into the house. "Hodges, a tray in the blue parlor, please."

"Very good, Miss."

Hodges shot Sherbourne a look that promised doom to any caller who put his boots up on the furniture—or his hands on Miss Charlotte—and made a silent exit down the corridor.

"This way," Miss Charlotte said. "If you're here to curry favor with Moreland, you'd be better off accosting him at his club. Her Grace is occupied at the modiste's, which means you're stuck with me. You have two cups of tea, stay fifteen minutes, bore me to tears with chatter about the weather, then take your leave."

"I came to see you, even if you do mistake giving a man orders for making small talk."

She preceded him into a blue, white, and gilt parlor. A bowl of daisies graced the windowsill, and a lady's work basket was open on a hassock.

"I'm simply reviewing the protocol with you. Her Grace has spoken well of you, which means you'll have to blunder badly to ruin your reception by polite society."

Miss Charlotte had left the door open, but she'd also assured Sherbourne that her aunt and uncle were not home. Had she done that on purpose?

"Were you attempting to blunder, Miss Charlotte? Leaving the house without an escort?"

She untied her bonnet ribbons and tried to pluck the hat from her head. Some hairpin or bit of hidden wire got caught in her coiffure, and the hat was thus stuck, half on, half off.

"Blunder by walking two streets from my own door without a chaperone, you mean? Drat this hat."

"You're making it worse."

"A gentleman wouldn't notice."

How could Sherbourne not notice skeins of glossy red hair cascading around the lady's shoulders? He moved close enough to grasp the bonnet.

"Hold still. I'll have you free in a moment."

"My objective was freedom. You've forced me to reschedule my outing."

Sherbourne liked knowing how things worked, how parts fit and functioned together. Miss Charlotte's bun had been a simple affair involving a chignon and some amber-tipped pins. To get the hat untangled, he had to loosen the chignon, which meant taking off his gloves.

"You were intent on larking about the streets of Mayfair on your own," Sherbourne said, sliding a pin from her hair. "Being a woman of blindingly evident intelligence, you know such behavior will cause talk."

"Maybe I was off to meet a lover."

Another pin came loose, and he slipped it into his pocket. "Had you been intent on a tryst, you would have worn a plain cloak and bonnet, carried a market basket, and slipped out the back door. What is that scent?"

"Orange blossoms, mostly. You've undone me."

He passed her the hat upside down, the pins piled in the crown. "You're welcome."

Though the sight of her left him undone too. Miss Charlotte was in a temper about something, and that put color in her cheeks and fire in her eyes—more fire than usual. Her hair fell nearly to her waist and shimmered in the sunshine streaming through the windows.

She was lovely—though she seemed oblivious to that fact, and to the impropriety of having her hair down while a gentleman paid a social call.

"I have come to a decision, Mr. Sherbourne," she said, stalking across the room. "Perhaps your arrival was meant to modify my choice."

"A gentleman aids a lady at every opportunity." Or some such rot.

Miss Charlotte set the hat on the piano bench, stuck two hairpins in her mouth, and used both hands to bundle her hair up.

"I have decided to be ruined," she said around the hairpins. "It's either that or endure more years of being resented by the debutantes, proposed at by the dandies and prigs, and flirted with by the fortune hunters."

"I'm sorry. My ability to translate the hairpin dialect is wanting. Did you say something about being ruined?" Deciding to be ruined, as if she'd decided to be a Roman centurion at a masked ball.

She twisted her hair this way and that, not braiding it, but looping it around itself and shoving a pin here or there. The whole business stayed up and looked as if some maid had spent an hour arranging it.

"I'm missing a hairpin."

"How can you tell?"

"Because I count my hairpins, and this set was a gift from my aunt Arabella when I made my come out two hundred and forty-seven years ago."

"Might we discuss your attempted self-ruin instead of your fashion accessories?"

She gave him a look. If he'd been eight years old, he would have produced the hairpin from his pocket, blushed, and stammered his remorse. He was past thirty and would keep that hairpin until the day he died.

"You want to discuss my *failed attempt* at ruin," she said.

"My apologies for interfering with your schedule. Do you attempt ruin often, and might we sit while we don't talk about the weather?"

She gestured to the sofa and took a place half a yard to Sherbourne's right.

"I like you," she said. "Somewhat. A little. I don't dislike you."

"My heart pounds with joy to hear it. I don't dislike you either."

Thank the gods of porcelain and silver, the tea cart rattled loudly as somebody pushed it along the corridor. Sherbourne thus knew to fall silent rather than expound about why he *didn't dislike* Miss Charlotte Windham rather a lot.

A footman steered the tea cart into the parlor, and a maid came along to assist with setting the offerings on the low table before the sofa. The polite fussing gave Sherbourne a chance to consider possibilities and theories.

His mind, however, usually reliable during daylight hours, failed to focus on the facts as he knew them.

Charlotte Windham was seeking her own ruin. What the devil was she about?

* * *

Charlotte had hoped the ritual of the tea service would soothe her, but there Lucas Sherbourne sat, in morning attire that featured a waistcoat embroidered with more gold thread than some high church bishops wore at Easter services.

How could one be soothed when beholding such masculine splendor? His attire was distinctive, but so too was the sense of animal instincts prowling close to the surface of his personality. Sherbourne was alert, heedful of both danger and opportunity even in a duke's drawing room. With him on the premises, Charlotte would never be bored, never feel invisible.

"You might not dislike me," Charlotte said, checking the strength of the tea, "but many others find me...irksome. How do you take your tea?"

"Milk and sugar. I would have thought the shoe on the other foot. You find most of humanity irksome, if not most of creation."

"People usually can't help themselves when they are tiresome or ignorant. They do the best they can, that doesn't mean they're likeable. More sugar?"

"That's enough, thank you. Too much sweetness destroys the pleasure of the experience. Get to the part about being ruined."

"A lady can be ruined by flouting convention, such as by walking unescorted from the home of one family member to the home of another, traversing two entire streets on her own in broad daylight in the safest neighborhood in London. Mind you, the maids, laundresses, and shopgirls manage many times that distance without losing their virtue, but let's not impose a foolish consistency on the rules of proper decorum."

Sherbourne held his tea without taking a sip, which was

mannerly of him, because Charlotte had yet to serve herself.

"A lady taking a short walk on her own would cause a few remarks," he said. "I doubt she'd be ruined."

Charlotte had planned to test her wings with a small but public gesture—a pathetically tame adventure, and yet, she'd felt daring as she'd put her hand on the door latch and prepared to negotiate the wilds of Mayfair alone.

"I was starting with a modest exercise in ruination. I doubt full-blown impropriety is within my abilities."

"For which your parents are doubtless grateful. Aren't you having any tea?"

"I prefer mine quite strong. Another path to ruin is to simply go mad."

Sherbourne set down his teacup. "Charlotte Windham, you are the sanest woman I know. Who has afflicted you with this case of the blue devils?"

A hundred jealous debutantes and presuming bachelors had contributed to Charlotte's low mood. So had a horde of happy, well-meaning, married relations.

"Viscount Neederby spoke to my papa before my parents left for Scotland. Papa's letter arrived this morning, asking me to give the boy a chance."

Sherbourne got to his feet. "Neederby is not a boy."

"Nor is he a man in any sense that could merit my esteem, and yet, I was supposed to give him a chance." The betrayal of that, and the lack of staunchly supportive sisters to commiserate with, had pushed Charlotte from a blue mood to a black mood.

What was the distance from a black mood to melancholia or some other form of mental instability?

"You are understandably upset, but why seek ruin? Windhams are nearly unruinable."

Full-blown impropriety had no appeal, but perhaps...?

"If the right people came upon me in a torrid embrace with the right sort of man, I'd be ruined." Charlotte took a sip of Sherbourne's tea, which was perfectly hot, sweet, and strong.

He crossed his arms, regarding her as if she'd proposed building a bridge across the Channel. Fine idea—if daft.

"Have you ever been in a *torrid* embrace, Miss Charlotte?"

Charlotte rose, because that was not a question a lady answered sitting down. "I've never so much as said the word *torrid* aloud before, but the plan has merit. I thought I could put up with all the matchmaking, be the family project for a few years, then the doting aunt, but I'm alone now."

The admission hurt as Papa's ridiculous letter had not. Papa was simply being a papa—half blind, well-meaning, fallible.

But the aloneness... In less than a year, all three of Charlotte's sisters had married well, and to men who lived very far from London, Kent, or Hampshire. The Moreland townhouse, always spacious, was now a maze of empty rooms and silent reproaches.

"You'll be much more alone if you're ruined," Sherbourne said. "You'll be packed off to some distant cottage, the only people to visit you will be other outcast women, some of them so poor they'll impose on your hospitality for months. You won't like it."

Well, no. To be smothered by family was unbearable, but to be abandoned by them...

"I'm prepared to endure a kiss or two in the interests of broadening my options. Vauxhall should serve for a location, which means—"

Sherbourne moved so he stood immediately before Charlotte. "Shall I kiss you?"

Though he'd asked permission—to kiss her—the question was far from polite. The whole discussion was outlandish, for that matter, and Sherbourne's tone was pugnacious rather than flirtatious.

"Why?"

"You think some dashing cavalier can buss your cheek and earn you a holiday in Kent for the next six months. Room to breathe and rest from the blows this year has dealt you. A buss to the cheek won't cause any stir whatsoever. Your family will brush it aside, the witnesses will recall it as a harmless indiscretion on your part, a daring presumption from the gentleman."

He was right, drat him clear back to Wales. "I must do something, Mr. Sherbourne. The present course is unsupportable."

"Kiss me."

Charlotte never, ever complied with orders given by men, but she occasionally compromised. In this case, she closed her eyes, raised her chin, and wondered if truly her reason hadn't already departed.

"You kiss me," she said.

Sherbourne obeyed her.

* * *

I must learn to discuss the weather.

On the heels of that thought, Sherbourne had another: Charlotte Windham could teach him to prattle on about the weather more proficiently than any titled dandy had ever discussed anything.

She looked bravely resigned. Her face upturned, lips closed, shoulders square.

Sherbourne started there, rubbing his thumbs over her shoulders, learning the contour and muscle of them.

"Relax, Charlotte. This is a kiss, not a tribute to your posture board."

She opened those magnificent blue eyes. "Then be about the kissing, please, and dispense with the lectures."

Sherbourne kissed her cheek and slid his hands into her hair. "A kiss is generally a mutual undertaking. You might consider putting your hands on my person."

Her hair was soft, thick, and at her nape, warm. She smelled of orange blossoms with a hint of lavender.

"There's rather a lot of you," she replied. "One hardly knows where one's hands might best be deployed."

Deployed, in the manner of infantry or weapons. "Surprise me."

Surprise him, she did. She put her right hand over his solar plexus, the softest possible blow, and eased her fingertips upward, tracing the embroidery of his waistcoat. Her left arm went around his waist, getting a good, firm hold.

As her hand meandered over his chest, Sherbourne touched his lips to hers. She neither startled nor drew back, so he repeated the gesture, brushing gently at her mouth.

Charlotte reciprocated, like a fencer answering a beat with a rebeat. Sherbourne drew her closer, or she drew him closer. She might have been smiling against his mouth.

The kiss gradually became intimate, wandering past playful, to curious, then bold—the lady tasted him first—to thoughtful, then on to daring. By the time Charlotte had sunk her fingers into Sherbourne's hair and given it a stout twist, he was growing aroused.

He stepped back, keeping his arms looped around Charlotte's shoulders. "That's a taste of torrid, a mere sample. A lovely sample, I might add."

"You torrid very well, Mr. Sherbourne. May I prevail on you to ruin me?"

Charlotte felt wonderful in his arms, real and lovely. She neither put on the amorous airs of a courtesan or a trolling widow, nor endured his overtures with the long-suffering distaste of a woman eyeing his fortune despite his lack of a title. He'd kissed a few of both and had thought those were his only options.

"I would rather not ruin you," he said, stepping back. "I am far more interested in marrying you."

The softness faded from Charlotte's eyes, and Sherbourne was sorry to see it disappear. He'd put it there, with his kisses, and now—with his honest proposal of marriage—he'd chased it away.

"If you're jesting, Mr. Sherbourne, your humor is in poor taste."

"I'm entirely in earnest. Look at the facts logically, and you'll see that marriage to me offers you much more than being ruined would."

He expected her to laugh. Charlotte was as blue-blooded as he was common, and she'd been turning down proposals for years. His reconnaissance mission had gone badly awry—wonderfully, badly awry—and proper society set a lot of store by courting protocols.

Which did not include torrid kisses during an initial call.

"Shall we sit?" Charlotte said. "Not that my knees are weak, of course, but the tea will grow cold."

Sherbourne's knees were weak.

He sat, taking the enormous, torrid liberty of positioning himself a mere fifteen inches from his possible future wife.

* * *

"Have I been at the modiste's long enough?" Esther, Her Grace of Moreland, asked her spouse.

Percival, Duke of Moreland, consulted his pocket watch. "By my calculations, you've only just arrived there, and I've barely opened the newspaper at my club. Do we approve of Sherbourne or not, my love?"

The Welsh upstart had come striding along the walk, handsome as love's young dream, but sadly lacking in flowers, French chocolates, or proper taste in waistcoats. Percival and his duchess had seen Mr. Sherbourne on their doorstep—the ducal suite afforded an optimal spying perspective—and modified their plans accordingly.

Her Grace took a sip of chocolate. She was a surpassingly lovely blonde of mature years, her proportions those of a goddess, her social power greater than the sovereign's. At present, she was barefoot and tucked next to Percival on their cuddling couch.

"We give Sherbourne a chance, Moreland. I thought Elizabeth and Charlotte would have each other for company, but then Haverford stole a march on us, and there's Charlotte."

"The last of the regiment," Percival said. "Most soldiers would rather perish defending the colors than be taken prisoner."

Her Grace kissed his cheek, a half-amused, half-exasperated sort of kiss. After more than thirty years of marriage, Percival was a proficient interpreter of his wife's kisses.

"Marriage is not a military campaign, sir. What flag is Charlotte defending? She's a dependent female approaching spinsterhood. Her future might include a modest household of her own, if her papa can be talked into it. For the most part, she'll be a traveling auntie if she remains unmarried. Her sisters and cousins will think they're being kind, inviting her all over the realm, but Charlotte will be confronted over and over with Windhams in love."

Percival delighted in the state of his family, when they weren't driving him daft. "But Sherbourne? His dearest aspiration is to pile up coin to flaunt at his betters."

Percival approved of a man improving his station through hard work, ambition, and good fortune, but Sherbourne was...

Running around in public wearing waistcoats that should have blinded the tailors who'd created them.

"What does it say about me, Esther, that I've begun to think exactly like my father?"

"Your father was a wonderful man who knew a love match when he saw one. We give Sherbourne a chance— Haverford spoke well of him—but twenty minutes with Charlotte is as much chance as any proper gentleman should need to leave a good impression."

Charlotte could leave a bad impression in less than thirty seconds, unfortunately.

Percival rose and offered his hand to his duchess. "Twenty-three minutes, to be exact. I was once a bachelor, you know. Twenty-three minutes in the hands of an enterprising young fellow is a very great chance indeed."

Esther toed on her slippers, a pair of gold house mules lavishly adorned with silk flowers.

She patted his lapel. "You simply want to intimidate poor Sherbourne, but you forget, he's been neighbor to Haverford for years. A duke will not overawe him, not even the Duke of Moreland."

"You have it all backward, Esther. I feel it my duty as

a gentleman to rescue the poor sod if Charlotte has taken him into disfavor."

"Gracious. I hadn't thought of that."

The duchess invariably moved with perfect dignity, and yet, she beat Percival to the door.

Chapter Three

Had Charlotte been asked, she would have said that kissing could be a pleasant undertaking, albeit unsanitary in its more intimate incarnations. Noses tended to get in the way, and if one wore spectacles as some gentlemen did, those created even more awkwardness.

But kissing Sherbourne...

Such a large, unsubtle man had no business trading in tenderness. He'd teased his way past Charlotte's expectations and tickled awake dreams more suited to a woman ten years her junior. Sweet, silly, naughty dreams...

Then he'd gone and ruined everything—except her—by proposing marriage.

"Explain yourself," Charlotte said. "As I foresee the life of a spinster, I'll have independent means, freedom to occupy myself however I choose, and..." And the freedom to discreetly aid those most in need of assistance.

Charlotte couldn't say that of course. She didn't admit of those activities to even her family.

Sherbourne poured a cup of tea. "Freedom and independence. Do go on."

"I'll also have a lively and interesting circle of friends." Aunt Arabella had had that, though she'd been a widow rather than a spinster before joining the herd of Windhams thundering up the church aisle this year.

Sherbourne added milk and sugar, stirred the tea, and passed it to her.

"Your independent means," he said, "will likely be a charitable trust arranged by your papa, brothers-in-law, or your uncle. Those funds will be controlled by the trustees of their choice, not yours, and once your male relatives are gone, you will be completely at the mercy of the trustees."

Was that how it worked? Charlotte was not much interested in legal matters, but she would ask a cousin who had read law, for controlling her own money mattered.

"Having a husband oversee my expenditures is preferable?"

"Your settlements will spell out which funds remain under your exclusive control as pin money, and will provide that should you be widowed, you and you alone will manage your finances. One item I have in adequate supply is coin."

"One item you lack is delicacy, Mr. Sherbourne." This cup of tea was not as hot as Charlotte preferred, but it was fortifying and perfectly sweet.

"Precisely. I lack delicacy, which is why you should marry me."

His command of a tea service was excellent, his shoulders were broad, his logic eluded her. "I'm to subject myself to a husband's supervision rather than be pitied for failing to secure any spouse at all?"

Sherbourne set the teapot down rather too hard on the tray. "Nobody would dare pity you."

Charlotte wanted to believe him, but too many tittering, gossiping, spiteful conversations prevented her. *He* did not pity her, and that meant more than it should.

"All spinsters are pitied, Mr. Sherbourne. We're supposed to pine away for lack of children to wait upon or a husband to serve, when in fact, our greater sorrow is that we could become a burden on the parish."

"Many married women have no children and see little of their spouses, but I hope our union would be fruitful. I like children, and think you'd make a marvelous mother."

How casually he flung compliments at her. "Why?"

"Because you are fierce. Your children would be fierce, and if they're to help shape the future of a realm threatened by a profligate imbecile on the throne, they'll need to be fierce."

The destruction of the entire nation didn't concern Charlotte. She was focused instead on lives left in tatters thanks to heedless young men. She liked that Britain's fate concerned Sherbourne, though, even if his politics were the nearest thing to blaspheming under Uncle Percival's roof.

"You see us married and filling the nursery, Mr. Sherbourne, when I have yet to consent to even a courtship."

He held up the plate of teacakes for her. "Would you *like* to be courted?"

Charlotte chose a cake draped in orange glaze and tried to focus on the question rather than on the lazy heat in Sherbourne's blue eyes. He'd kissed her passionately, with the door open and the house full of servants. How would he kiss late at night, tucked beneath the covers with his wife?

Charlotte took a small bite of her sweet.

"Your expression is far from a resounding yes," Sherbourne said, selecting a lavender cake and popping the whole treat into his mouth.

Part of Charlotte yearned to be courted, for the petty pleasure of flaunting Sherbourne at all the nincompoops who had presumed she'd be delighted with their offers.

At all the debutantes who'd spread unkind gossip about her.

At all the matchmakers who'd regarded Charlotte as the sole reason their daughters hadn't taken.

At all the Windhams, who'd be surprised at her choice, and even a little worried.

Especially at the Windhams.

"You shouldn't gobble the whole teacake at once," she said. "Take a genteel bite, then put the rest back on your plate as you chew."

"Genteel bites leave crumbs everywhere. Shall I court you, Miss Charlotte? I'm sure you could instruct me on the particulars."

Charlotte wanted to be courted, to be flirted with, to be given indulgent looks by married couples, while she earned envious sighs from the unmarried ladies.

Such longings were foolish. She didn't love Sherbourne, and he didn't love her. She'd be the only Windham in the history of Windhams who had failed to attract a love match.

"You shall not court me," Charlotte said. "Such a farce would have no point."

Sherbourne held up the plate of cakes for her again. She chose a slice of shortbread this time and got crumbs all over her lap while nibbling genteelly.

"The lady's wishes should be controlling," he said. "I'd enjoy squiring you about for a few weeks, but I applaud your pragmatism too."

"Mr. Sherbourne, what on earth are you—?"

He kissed her, a friendly smack on the lips. "A special license it shall be. I'll apply tomorrow."

"Mr. Sherbourne! A special license will not in any way—"

He kissed her again, more lingeringly. "Please, Charlotte? I'm not hopeless, and I will honestly try to make you happy."

Her inclination was to flounce away and leave him on the sofa with a signature Charlotte Windham set down. A laugh, a wave, a witticism.

But he was *asking* her to marry him. Not flinging an offer at her as if she should be desperate to become his wife. Perhaps this was what her version of matrimony needed to look like—pragmatic, with an element of attraction, but no delusions, no flummery.

"I must have time to think about this," Charlotte said. "To think about the settlements."

She'd surprised him, which pleased her.

She'd surprised herself. Mr. Sherbourne was not the dashing swain of her fervent, girlish dreams, but he fixed her tea the way she liked it, didn't put any value on small talk, and kissed intriguingly even with the door open.

He didn't strike Charlotte as the type to hover about his wife, though he would be very mindful of the finances. In short, he had *possibilities*.

By the time Aunt Esther joined them five minutes later, claiming to have confused the day of her appointment—as if the Duchess of Moreland couldn't keep the days of the week straight—Charlotte had decided only that she must have at least three days to consider Sherbourne's proposal.

Three days was not long to ponder a decision that would

affect Charlotte's entire future, but 4,320 minutes was an eternity to wait before she could sample another one of Sherbourne's kisses.

* * *

Sherbourne suspected that the London newspaper had been invented so that men dining alone at their clubs had a fig leaf to drape across their pride. A fellow poring over the financial pages while consuming his steak could make the food—necessary for the life of every species—look like the afterthought crammed between more important undertakings.

Sherbourne refused to indulge such a fiction. A good steak was worth appreciating. Too many hardworking subjects of the crown rarely had that privilege.

He thus sat in unlordly splendor alone at a table by the window, the passing scene on the street holding his interest between bites of fine English beef. The days were growing shorter, but the nights had yet to acquire a true chill. The thoroughfares of St. James were thronged as the sun set and the mood of the neighborhood shifted from work to play.

Directly across the street were two discreet brothels, indistinguishable from their genteel neighbors but for the volume of masculine foot traffic coming and going through their doors. Young men mostly, well dressed, and—based on their expressions as they emerged—well pleasured.

In a just world, the ladies would be well compensated for putting up with the young fools, though Sherbourne knew from long experience that the world was not just.

"Good evening, Sherbourne. Might I join you?" Quinton, Earl of Brantford, pulled out the chair across from

Sherbourne. "Presumptuous of me, but when Parliament sits, one must resort to desperate measures to avoid the politically impassioned."

A waiter was already crossing the room, cutlery for a second place setting in his hand.

"Brantford," Sherbourne said, gesturing with his wineglass. "How flattering, to be elevated to the status of a desperate measure. By all means, join me."

The waiter organized silver in a precise pattern on the linen tablecloth, then whisked a table napkin across Brantford's lap and poured his lordship a glass of the expensive vintage Sherbourne had planned to savor over the next two hours.

"Humor makes so many situations more bearable," Brantford said, sipping his wine. "That is decent potation, if I do say so myself."

Brantford had a title and means. His family seat was in the north, and his holdings included coal mines. Sherbourne had made it a point to acquaint himself with aristocrats who held mining shares, or—like Brantford—owned mines outright.

In recent weeks, Sherbourne's status among proper society had shifted from politely excluded to cordially tolerated. Now an earl—albeit a presuming one—had singled Sherbourne out for a shared public meal.

"The Duke of Moreland favors that wine." Moreland had sponsored Sherbourne's membership at this club, and dropping a ducal association into the conversation seemed prudent, though Sherbourne had no idea how His Grace preferred to wash down a steak.

"Moreland's duchess has polished her former cavalry officer to a high shine," Brantford replied, "though she's had decades to do it. I hear you have some interesting commercial ventures in train over in Wales. I admire initiative in a man, or in a woman, for that matter."

Brantford smiled at his wine, as if recalling a lady of recent and intimate acquaintance. He was attractive, his blond locks arranged à la Brutus, and his blue eyes complemented by a sapphire cravat pin.

Sherbourne sat back—the steak was overcooked—and signaled the waiter.

"Are you having a meal," Sherbourne asked, "or was conversation your aim?" Conversation that Brantford had turned to business with all the subtlety of a hound on the scent.

"I'll have the usual," Brantford said to the waiter. "Conversation is always part of a civilized meal. I know mining, Sherbourne, while you're about to sink your first shaft. We can benefit each other, if you're amenable to taking on a partner."

The partner Sherbourne wanted to take on—Charlotte Windham—had until the day after tomorrow to give him an answer to his proposal. If she agreed to marry him, settlements would require an immediate outflow of cash into the keeping of the lady's relatives.

Had Sherbourne so boldly broached a commercial matter, he'd have been labeled an encroaching mushroom, ill-mannered, grasping, and—the death knell of a gentleman's reputation—*not good ton*. The same gauche overture from an earl was supposed to be flattering and admirably direct.

Sherbourne took a sip of hearty claret, the wine's smoky-sweet notes lingering nicely.

An investor who brought both funds and expertise to a business undertaking was worth considering, even if that investor did have a title and wore a waistcoat that made a nun look stylish by comparison.

"I'm willing to listen," Sherbourne said, as the waiter placed a rare steak before his lordship, "but our discussion can wait for a more private setting."

Brantford took up his knife and fork. "You must be joking. One's club is the holiest of holies, Sherbourne. Why do you think the fashionable impure have set up shop across the street? No one in this establishment would dare mention who was seen paying them a call, much less who was in his cups or betting too heavily. Behind these walls, discretion is assured."

Sherbourne had it on the very best authority that discussing business in a social setting was inexcusably bad form. Charlotte could explain why a club wasn't a social setting, though all that transpired here was gossip and indolence.

"If I'm to take on an investor," Sherbourne said, "then that individual will be privy to my ledgers, my budgets, my financial plans for the mine, right down to the last farthing. Anybody who'd discuss that level of detail where a competitor might lurk at the next table is a fool."

Brantford speared his steak, which swam in a pool of thick, red juice. "You come close to insulting your betters, Sherbourne." His tone was amused and chiding.

"You come close to disqualifying yourself as a possible business associate, Brantford. I will not sacrifice common sense for the sake of traditions I have little reason to trust."

Brantford sliced off a bite of meat. "A modern sensibility, and one of which I approve, though not too loudly. Tell me about your mine."

The mine was still mostly sketches, estimates, and schedules. "Every geological indicator bodes well for good quality coal immediately beneath the surface. No other mines operate in the valley, so finding labor should be easy, and we're close enough to the sea that transport of the product will be cheap."

"Who's your engineer?"

"Hannibal Jones."

"Good man, though you must be paying him a fortune to have enticed him away from Waxter." Between bites of steak, Brantford continued his interrogation. His questions were intelligent and kept to the polite side of prying. From the nods and occasional greetings sent the earl's way, Sherbourne deduced that his lordship was well liked and well known.

Though the aristocracy did not air their linen before outsiders. Brantford could have fought duels with half the men in the dining room, and Sherbourne would never hear a word about the contests, much less about any underlying provocation.

"So," Brantford said, helping himself to more wine, "shall we engage in a bit of commerce, Sherbourne? I'm casting about for new investments, and I can send my man of business around to have a look at those ledgers you mentioned."

"If you and I become involved in the same venture, I'll be dealing with you, not your toady. Intermediaries introduce delay and error, to say nothing of their own little agendas and schemes."

Sherbourne's ambitions were tempered by pragmatism. He aspired to become accepted by polite society, which was not the same as included. To achieve his goal, he'd have to remain at least modestly wealthy, which his family had managed to do for a half-dozen generations.

To ensure that his sons had a chance to continue that tradition, Sherbourne could not afford a fool for an investor, no matter how well connected or titled.

Brantford set his plate aside, the steak only half finished. The dining room had filled with lesser titles, younger sons, and a smattering of old, quiet money. Sherbourne was gradually putting names with faces—or with entries in Debrett's—but most of these men had likely gone to school with Brantford or even now sat with him in the House of Lords.

Why wasn't Brantford investing with one of them?

"Times change," Brantford said, "and you're right that subordinates are not always the most efficient means by which to accomplish a goal. You may bring the relevant documents—"

Sherbourne shook his head. "I'm not hauling my confidential information all over Mayfair like some tinker come to repair your pots. *You* have approached *me* about selling you an interest in a venture likely to be very profitable. The least you can do is take a stroll to my doorstep and pass an hour in my study."

An investor wasn't strictly necessary, but the right sleeping partner, as such an associate was termed, could create options, especially now when marriage settlements would reduce Sherbourne's reserves. With an influx of capital, Sherbourne could develop the mine more quickly, other investors were more likely to contribute, and subsequent projects—for Sherbourne always had subsequent projects—would benefit from the connections formed in the mining venture.

Even so, Sherbourne would not yoke himself to a simpleton, not for any amount of coin or goodwill.

"Where is your doorstep, Sherbourne?"

He provided a direction several doors up from the Albany, the most prestigious lodging a bachelor could claim in London.

"Then perhaps next week I'll take that stroll." Brantford filled his wineglass yet again, then shook the last drops—the dregs—into Sherbourne's glass.

A blatant gesture in the direction of *my cock is bigger than your cock*, confirming once again that England was owned and run by a pack of overgrown schoolboys.

Nonetheless, Sherbourne had formed no particular opinion of Brantford as an individual, which was to say, he hadn't affixed to his lordship any of the labels that applied to most titled men of means: buffoon, parasite, idiot, disgrace to the species, hound, well-dressed incompetent.

Though Brantford expected Sherbourne to await a possible call on a day yet to be disclosed, on the slim chance that a business association might result.

Sherbourne simply lacked the humility to accommodate the earl, so he provided Brantford instructions, much as Charlotte Windham would have.

"I am a busy man, Brantford, with many demands upon my time. I haven't the luxury of idling about like some blushing debutante who hopes you'll get around to asking her for a minuet. I conduct business in a businesslike manner or not at all. You either make and keep an appointment with me, or you find another project to grace with your coin."

Brantford studied him while laughter erupted from a table that included two earls, a baron, and a ducal heir. Sherbourne hadn't raised his voice, hadn't attracted notice in any way, but he'd reached the limit of his manners.

"And that," Brantford said, a slow smile breaking over his features, "is why your endeavors are notoriously profitable. Shall I come by Tuesday at two of the clock?"

Better. "Two o'clock will suit."

Brantford rose and extended a hand. "Until next we meet. A pleasure, Sherbourne."

That gesture was as unexpected as Brantford's smile. Sherbourne rose and shook hands—without smiling—but when he reached the street he did toss his hat into the air and catch it on the end of his walking stick. He had enormous work to do before he was accepted by polite society, but that achievement would come closer to fruition if an earl became involved in the mining venture.

And if Sherbourne were accepted, then his children might find themselves not merely tolerated, not simply accepted, but *included* among the best families in the realm.

Provided he could equip them with the right mother.

* * *

Hour by hour, Charlotte was talking herself into accepting Lucas Sherbourne's marriage proposal. He would provide well. His property marched with the Duke of Haverford's, meaning Charlotte would be neighbors with her sister Elizabeth.

Sherbourne wasn't stupid, arrogant, or idle, as Charlotte's previous suitors had been.

She took another turn down the stable aisle, the horses eyeing her as they munched their hay.

She could mail bank notes from any location, provided she had a little discreet assistance from a loyal staff.

"I'm not being entirely fair," she informed Her Grace's bay gelding. "Mr. Sherbourne is quite bright, confident without being an ass, and he brings a sense of energy with him as some women wear a signature scent."

He was also attractive.

"Attractive," Charlotte admitted to her own chestnut mare, "is not the same as handsome."

Handsome was commonplace. Every ballroom in Mayfair was full of handsome. Lucas Sherbourne commanded attention—one wanted to know where he was, what he was about, because he was no respecter of meaningless conventions. His movements, thoughts, and decisions were unpredictable.

Witness, he'd chosen Charlotte Windham for his bride.

"So you're visiting the stables in the grand Windham tradition." Her Grace of Moreland, silhouetted in the stable doorway, cut a dash in a fine blue driving ensemble. "Would you like to tour the park with me today?"

Sherbourne wouldn't be caught dead gossiping under the maples at the fashionable hour. "No, thank you, Aunt."

The duchess stroked a gloved hand over the mare's nose. "Are you avoiding anybody in particular or the whole lot of them?"

"The whole lot. I have been taken into dislike by several of last season's unclaimed blossoms. I'm leaving them a clear field. What do we know of Lucas Sherbourne?"

"Come outside and we'll talk." Her Grace chose a bench in the sun, the afternoon light bearing that blend of mellowness and sharp contrast unique to early autumn. "I have consulted with Aunt Arabella and a few of her friends, because Mr. Sherbourne is something of a puzzle."

"You read the history books, so to speak." The duchess was clearly not surprised that Charlotte was curious. Would she be surprised if Charlotte became Mrs. Lucas Sherbourne?

"When His Grace of Haverford put in a word for Mr. Sherbourne, I decided some research was appropriate, and the tale is interesting. Mr. Sherbourne's grandfather, Optimus Sherbourne, was engaged to marry a daughter from the Haverford ducal line. She fell in love with another, and Optimus took the slight badly. He married a banker's daughter, became appallingly wealthy, and set about ruining the successor to the Haverford title."

"His attempt at a feud failed," Charlotte said. "The St. David family thrives, and Haverford Castle is lovely." If quaint. Elizabeth would soon have all in hand, though.

"Optimus didn't expect to bring down a ducal family at one go," Aunt said. "He raised his son Alcestus to take over the task, and the present Mr. Sherbourne was apparently brought up in the same tradition. Thank the good celestial ministers that Mr. Sherbourne and Haverford have settled their differences. Some say the Sherbournes have a head for business; others declare them vulgar and vengeful."

Lucas Sherbourne was robust rather than vulgar, and Charlotte would never judge another person who had legitimate grounds for vengeance. Had she the means, she'd have wreaked vengeance on a certain titled dandy years ago.

"What do you say about Mr. Sherbourne, Aunt?"

Her Grace's driving habit was a soft periwinkle wool, the hems draping over smart black boots. She fussed with skirts that were tailored to arrange themselves into graceful folds even while hanging in the wardrobe.

"Mr. Sherbourne is not the average climbing cit," Aunt Esther said, "and you never were a marriage-mad henwit. Do you fancy him, Charlotte?"

Yes. "He doesn't put on airs."

"Your uncle wishes Mr. Sherbourne wouldn't put on such remarkable waistcoats."

"I like those waistcoats. They remind me of our Scottish relations in their kilts. Only a confident man wears such noticeable attire."

A groom brought out Aunt Esther's phaeton from the coach house.

"Only a confident man will do for you, Charlotte Windham. I've admired your fortitude, you know. Perhaps Mr. Sherbourne is your reward for years of not settling for a nincompoop."

Charlotte rose to walk her aunt to the vehicle. "When you say that word, it sounds so much more disgusted. I gather Uncle Percival wouldn't object to Mr. Sherbourne paying me his addresses?"

"His Grace would of course consult with your parents and with you, but he wouldn't call Sherbourne out simply for having excellent taste as a suitor. Try not to overthink the situation, Charlotte. If you like Lucas Sherbourne, then get to know him better and see what develops. Our menfolk will ensure that your settlements are handsome. You determine whether the fellow suits you."

Aunt patted Charlotte's shoulder and nimbly ascended to the bench.

As the phaeton clattered out of the mews, Charlotte wandered across the alley into the back gardens of the Moreland townhouse. Aunt and Uncle would reconcile themselves to Charlotte's interest in Lucas Sherbourne, and thus Mama and Papa would too. This was good to know, for Charlotte didn't fancy battling all of the elders over her choice of husband.

Though battle them, she would, *if* she accepted Lucas Sherbourne's proposal.

The garden was going bedraggled about the edges. The chrysanthemums offered an occasional splash of purple, while the hedges were yellowing, the maple losing its leaves.

The garden was tired, and so was Charlotte. Tired of a

life without friends, without kisses, without a household of her own. The weariness alone would not have daunted her, but she was also bored and lonely. Bored enough to consider daft schemes such as getting herself ruined.

What *had* she been thinking?

"He'll do." Mr. Sherbourne's kisses would more than do. The decision felt both bold and right—right for Charlotte, if not for the typical romantically inclined Windham.

"Excuse me, miss. Are you Charlotte Windham?"

A young woman stood at the garden gate, close to the wall, as if she dared not set foot on private property. Her cloak was plain brown wool, and the unevenness of her hem suggested repeated mending. Her bonnet was a mere straw hat, no fancy ribbons or even a silk flower for adornment.

"I am Charlotte Windham. Who might you be?"

"My name is Miss Sharon Higgins. They said you'd help me."

Charlotte had been contemplating marriage to Lucas Sherbourne with a combination of glee, anxiety, and excitement—for she had all but decided to accept his suit. Now this—another delicate situation arising without warning. Judging from Sharon's pallor, the situation was desperate as well as delicate.

As such situations always were, though Charlotte hadn't been called upon to assist in this manner for months.

"When was the last time you had something to eat?" she asked.

"Yesterday, I think. Will you help me? They said you would."

They would have been the other maids, the laundresses, possibly a seamstress or even the vicars at the humbler London churches.

"Of course, I will help you. You're eating for two now, so the first order of business is to find you some sustenance."

The woman wilted against the wall. "Thank you, miss. Thank you."

"No tears, please," Charlotte said, leading the way back across the alley. "We have much to discuss, time is of the essence, and you'll need your wits about you."

Sharon cried anyway, and—as usual—Charlotte's wits were the only ones available to prevent what could all too easily become a tragedy.

Chapter Four

"Gold or silver?" Turnbull held up two waistcoats, both heavily embroidered. The sunlight streaming through the bedroom window revealed them for the works of sartorial art they were.

"I'm paying a courting call," Sherbourne said, "though you are sworn to secrecy. I want to look like a man who can be trusted with the last prize in the Windham marital vault."

Turnbull said more with silence than most bishops could communicate in an entire sermon. On one occasion, when he'd been extremely disappointed with his employer, he'd turned in his notice. The memory still gave Sherbourne nightmares.

"If you are off to plunder treasure from a ducal family, wear the gold. By all means, the gold, sir. An earring wouldn't go amiss either, and a clean cutlass—no blood—though I venture to say that an eye patch might be a bit too much."

Not the gold, then. "If you were about to ask for Charlotte Windham's hand in marriage, which waistcoat would you wear?"

Turnbull returned both the silver and the gold to the wardrobe and stood with his back to Sherbourne while surveying the other possibilities. A Scottish marquess with military inclinations had come across Turnbull on a Caribbean island, bought his freedom, and taken him home to the Highlands. Either Turnbull had grown weary of the northern cold or life as valet to the Scottish marquess had given him an appetite for challenges.

Turnbull's wages were exorbitant, his knowledge of etiquette and fashion beyond price.

"This one," Turnbull said, laying a rather dull choice across the bed. "She'll be intrigued by the uncharacteristic subtlety."

And his scolds were exquisite.

"The embroidery has neither gold nor silver threads," Sherbourne said. "It's boring."

"On a burgundy velvet waistcoat lined with black silk, I see purple, red, green, and white embroidery with teasing dashes of yellow and orange. By your standards, it's a bouquet of gentlemanly understatement, and there's not another like it in all of London."

The pattern was a paisley intertwining of flowers, vines, and leaves, a bouquet in truth. "You say there's not another like it in all of London?"

"If the Deity is merciful, there isn't another like it in all the world."

Turnbull would not allow Sherbourne to go abroad in anything other than the first stare of fashion, despite his commentary on the occasional waistcoat.

"Fine, then, subtlety for the suitor. I'll likely have to

toss back the congratulatory tot with old Moreland, and he wouldn't know a splendid waistcoat if his duchess modeled it for him."

That thought brought to mind Charlotte Windham wearing the gold waistcoat and nothing else. Thank heavens she wasn't inclined to a tedious courtship.

"You are assured of the lady's acceptance?" Turnbull held out a hand for Sherbourne's dressing gown.

"As assured as any man can be where the ladies are concerned. She likes me but not too much. I respect her and will provide for her as lavishly as her good taste allows. She'll bring connections and polish to the union, and I'll give her children. I think a ruby for today's cravat pin. The biblical connotations are quite the clever association, if I do say so myself."

She is more precious than rubies, and all the things thou canst desire cannot be compared unto her.

"No jewels when calling during daylight hours, sir. Will you make the young lady happy?"

"I've promised her I'd try," Sherbourne said, passing over the dressing gown, "but that's about as much of a swain as I can honestly be. Charlotte deals only in honesty, for which I'll doubtless worship her before our first anniversary."

When Sherbourne had been dressed from top hat to toes, he had to admit that Turnbull's suggestion, as always, had been perfect.

"I look like a sober London gent until one takes a closer look. The waistcoat is subtle, you were right."

"Thank you, sir, and what flowers will have the honor of accompanying you on this most important call?"

The call was a formality, a gesture to Charlotte Windham's pride, though a gesture Sherbourne was pleased to make. Demanding that he wait three days for an answer was her prerogative, one of few a lady could claim. Polite society loved its little rituals, and Sherbourne loved the idea of marrying a duke's niece.

He was also—this did not sit entirely well with him—*fond* of Charlotte, and more than fond of the fire she brought to even a brief kiss.

"I had hoped," Sherbourne said, shifting the angle of his top hat, "that you, as the most competent valet in all of creation, would have the matter of flowers well in hand."

"If I were choosing the bouquet, I'd equip you with saffron," Turnbull said, holding out a pair of white kid gloves. "The message it symbolizes is 'beware of excess.'"

"Symbolism is involved? I have no patience with symbolism, Turnbull. I'm not philosopher, I'm a suitor."

"Snapdragons, then. Very colorful."

And likely very expensive, given the time of year. Sherbourne pulled on his gloves. "What do they symbolize?"

Turnbull closed the doors to the wardrobe with priestly solemnity. "Presumption."

Turnbull was never wrong.

With a single word, he'd given Sherbourne pause. Charlotte Windham was closely connected to three dukes. A brief review of her family tree also revealed a marquess, a marquess's heir, four earls, and a smattering of courtesy lords.

And Sherbourne expected Charlotte to settle for a Welsh commoner? "I do like the woman—rather a lot—and I'll be faithful and considerate. She'll never want for anything, and Charlotte's the managing type. She won't be bored with me."

Turnbull sighed like a weary, disappointed godmother.

"I'll do my best, Turnbull."

"A bouquet of snowdrops, speedwell, and jasmine awaits you in the foyer. Good luck, sir."

Coming from Turnbull, the good wishes were ominous. Sherbourne straightened the angle of his hat and prepared to become an engaged man.

* * *

"Esther, refresh my memory. What does speedwell signify?"

Her Grace joined Percival at the window overlooking the front walkway. "Fidelity. The snowdrops are for hope, and jasmine—if that's what Sherbourne is carrying—is for grace and dignity, presumably Charlotte's grace and dignity, and her suitor's fidelity and hope. A tasteful combination."

Love's handsome delight stood on the front steps, back to the doorway, as if taking a moment to rehearse a speech or a proposal.

"Young people today are so precipitous."

Esther kissed the duke's cheek. "Says the man who couldn't make it through a house party without offering for me. I hope Charlotte accepts him."

"If he's here to propose, then he's jolly well courting my wrath. I've heard not a word from Mr. Sherbourne about paying his addresses, esteeming Charlotte greatly, and all that other folderol. Even I asked your papa's permission."

Esther gave him an amused look.

Well, yes. He'd asked her father's permission after gaining Esther's notice, to put matters delicately. Her intimate notice.

"I was an idiot," Percival said. "Charlotte is a sensible girl."

"Charlotte is not a girl, my dear. She's done it again."

Percival wasn't sure what *it* was, but he didn't care for the worry in his wife's eyes. He drew her down beside him on their cuddling couch.

"Done what? Cut her hair? I don't favor the mannish styles, but hair grows back."

"Percival, she's taken on another poor soul. I saw the whole business from my parlor window yesterday afternoon. I'd tooled away for a round of gossip in the park but had forgotten my reticule, so I stopped out front and came back up here to remedy my error. A more bedraggled creature never set foot in our garden, and within the hour Charlotte's maid was off to return a book to the lending library."

Oh, damn the luck. "By way of a pawn shop?"

"Precisely. Another pair of earbobs, a bracelet, perhaps even a locket, sacrificed to buy coach fare for a complete stranger."

A complete stranger who was doubtless with child and without husband. "Charlotte's charitable impulses are nothing to be ashamed of."

The duchess rose and Percival remained sitting. Her Grace needed the whole of the parlor for pacing purposes when she was in a passion, and nothing confounded her more thoroughly than her sole remaining unmarried niece.

"Charlotte doesn't merely purchase them coach fare to whatever village they came from," Esther said. "She decks them out in widow's weeds, buys them a ring, manufactures letters from their supposed deceased spouses...I suspect the bulk of her spending money is cast upon the same waters, ensuring the same women have funds to raise their children. I'd commend her thoroughness, except that her scheme strays perilously far from traditional concepts of charity."

In other words, Charlotte didn't talk about helping the less fortunate, she took action. "I can increase her allowance."

The duchess whirled on her husband, her skirts nearly knocking over the hearth set. "You most certainly cannot, Percival. She'll spend every penny on wayward laundresses or straying chambermaids. I would far rather you encouraged Sherbourne's suit."

"Charlotte deserves more than a preening Welsh nabob with a penchant for gaudy waistcoats. If more people had her ingenuity and practical sense of generosity, we'd not be hearing of corn riots and Luddites."

Esther took out a handkerchief and polished the base of the brass candlestick on the mantel. "Do you recall Lord Hennessey's youngest boy?"

When the Duchess of Moreland took to dusting, the topic was worrisome. "The fair Adonis? Hard to forget a man cursed with such a name, even if he was a good-looking young devil. At one time, I thought he'd earned our Jenny's notice."

"Be glad he was nothing more than an aesthetic curiosity for Jenny. He got the Wapshot girl in trouble. Her mama whisked her off to tour the great capitals—which everybody knew the Wapshot family could ill afford—and a child was born somewhere in the vicinity of Rome."

The duchess had an intelligence network that beggared description. Decades in polite society resulted in a web of connections more complicated than even German royalty could fathom.

"Charlotte and Miss Wapshot were cordial as I recall." Charlotte hadn't made any real friends in recent years, but as a younger woman, she'd been cordial to others near her age.

"Precisely," Her Grace replied, taking a swipe at a second candlestick. "Adonis was found in the fountains behind Carlton House, dead drunk and wearing not one stitch of clothing. His curls had been shaven off, and his legendary physique was revealed to be a result of well-tailored padding."

"I recall the talk now—the hilarity. I hadn't known about the Wapshots' daughter." That put a different light on what had appeared to be the sort of prank young men played on each other when they weren't waving dueling pistols about.

"Lady Hennessey was beside herself," the duchess said, rejoining her husband on the couch. "A note had been tied about the young man's...tied where he was likely to find it: Provide for your offspring or next time you'll wake up missing more than your curls."

Percival managed not to guffaw—barely. "And did he?"

"Assuredly, though the young woman is still ruined and always will be."

True enough. Men were castigated for sowing wild oats, but suffered serious criticism only if they did so without providing for the resulting progeny.

"You suspect Charlotte had a hand in this mischief?"

"I know not how, but yes. The Wapshots have no sons, and Mr. Wapshot would never undertake such folly. Do you recall a Mr. Charles Aldman?"

Percival took his wife's hand. "Banker's son. He was cutting a dash several years ago, though I haven't seen him about for the past few seasons."

"He got a maid with child. Charlotte shot his hat off his head at some archery tournament, and the hat, along with his hairpiece, landed at his hostess's feet. He acquired the nickname Baldman."

No more cutting a dash for Mr. Aldman. "Charlotte has devilish good aim."

"Charlotte has devilish poor sense. Viscount Dearing

got an arrow in the fundament at the last tournament Charlotte was invited to."

"Another chambermaid?"

"I did not inquire, but if I'm invited to a social gathering that includes an archery contest, I decline out of concern for the profligate rakes of proper society."

A truly proper society ought not to have profligate rakes, much less an abundance of them.

"Why are you telling me these anecdotes now, Esther?" Percival inquired not to accuse his wife of withholding intelligence, but because the duchess had reasons for speaking and reasons for keeping silent.

"I had hoped Charlotte was done being the conscience of Mayfair's randy bachelors. I haven't known her to take on a charitable project for months, and Arabella said Charlotte's behavior at the summer house parties was exemplary—for Charlotte."

"You hoped to marry her off before her schemes came to light."

"I still do."

"Then we must wish Mr. Sherbourne luck."

And courage, to go with the speedwell and snowdrops in his bouquet.

* * *

"He's here, miss," Tansy said. "Give your cheeks a pinch, and do try to let him finish his speech. Gentlemen set great store by their courting talk."

Tansy Luckett was Charlotte's lady's maid, and she looked honestly pleased to be sending Charlotte to greet Mr. Sherbourne. Perhaps Tansy was tired of trips to the pawnshops.

"*I'm not hopeless* isn't much of courting speech," Charlotte replied. Though the other part—*I will honestly try to make you happy*—had haunted her.

She checked her appearance in the mirror: hair in a tidy bun, dress reasonably free of wrinkles, smile nowhere in evidence.

"He's had three days to pretty up that sentiment," Tansy said, "though I've always admired a man who can get his point across with few words. You do look pale."

Charlotte had been up late penning love letters from a man who didn't exist. She had managed a half dozen progressively ardent epistles to Miss Higgins before falling asleep at her desk. Even the most skeptical parents ought to be convinced by Charlotte's prose, particularly when she'd also equipped the lady with a gold ring, widow's weeds, and five pounds that "dear Mr. Wesley" had managed to put aside for his wife before he'd fallen so tragically ill— or been struck down by a runaway fishmonger's wagon.

Mr. Wesley's various sad fates had all begun to blend together.

Five pounds was a pittance to some, and yet, the lordly bounder who'd got Sharon in an interesting condition had spared her exactly two shillings and a warning never to contact him again.

"Mr. Sherbourne brought you flowers," Tansy said.

"Roses?" Red roses were the symbol of true love, though never had Charlotte been offered roses.

"Nothing so predictable. Go down and see for yourself. Best of luck, Miss."

Tansy was small, but she packed a substantial push. Charlotte left the safety of her room and took a moment at the top of the steps to gather her resolve.

If she married Lucas Sherbourne, she'd remove with

him to Wales, where she'd bide for months if not years before returning to London. From Wales, Charlotte could maintain her correspondence with the various Mrs. Wesleys, but where would London's unfortunates go for help if Charlotte left town? The foundling hospitals were a dodgy bet and usually full. The Magdalen houses were little more than an excuse to make a profit by working hopeless women to death.

Nobody *helped*. Many sniffed and passed judgment. Even more took advantage of women who'd already been exploited. Some politely regretted the plight of gullible young ladies, but *nobody helped*.

If Charlotte accepted Mr. Sherbourne's proposal, she wouldn't be able to help anymore either.

She did not pinch her cheeks—what would be the point? By the time she reached the formal parlor, a maid was already wheeling a tea cart down the corridor.

"We won't need the tea tray, thank you," Charlotte said. "Mr. Sherbourne's visit will be quite brief."

The maid bobbed a curtsy. "Very good, Miss."

Charlotte tried for a dignified gait as she entered the parlor, neither hurried nor reluctant, but she was no duchess, and she almost tripped on the carpet fringe.

"Mr. Sherbourne, good day."

He stood by the window, the sunlight burnishing his blond hair to gold. He was a Viking in Bond Street tailoring, and Charlotte was about to send him back to his long boat.

Why must he be such an attractive Viking?

"Miss Windham." His bow was correct and his waistcoat quietly exquisite.

"Shall we be seated, sir?"

He gestured to the sofa, and Charlotte took a seat. He sat immediately beside her, not a decorous half-yard away.

"The butler stole my flowers. I suspect he's examining them for a torrid note. How are you?"

In want of torrid notes. "A trifle anxious, to be honest. I'd like another kiss." She'd like a lifetime of kisses where Sherbourne was concerned, but she'd have to make do with two.

"Putting the cart before the horse, are we?"

"Putting the kiss before the discussion. That waistcoat is tastefully glorious."

He rose and held out a hand. "Now I'm anxious. My valet told me you'd approve of my ensemble. I worry that he was right on several other counts."

Whatever that meant. Charlotte put her hand in Mr. Sherbourne's and was drawn to her feet. "I want a truly, impressively, memorably torrid kiss."

"Inspecting what's on offer?"

"You are a who, not a what, and nobody has made any offers today. Please kiss me."

He frowned at her, as if she were a painting that hadn't quite turned out as the artist had intended.

"We should lock the door, my dear."

I will never be your dear, more's the pity. "You came bearing flowers. For that unprecedented act of bravery, we'll have a few minutes of privacy."

"Nobody sends you flowers?"

"Mr. Sherbourne, do the words 'Please kiss me' exceed your comprehension?"

He smiled, and Charlotte stared at his cravat. A gold pin nestled among a wealth of blonde lace, with the smallest ruby winking from the depths. For a moment, she wavered—not about the kiss, which she was determined to have—but about refusing his proposal.

He had significant means and as his wife, Charlotte might be able to aid many women…or she might be able to aid none at all. A wife was her husband's property, and if Lucas Sherbourne disapproved of Charlotte's priorities, his word on the matter would be final.

Then some friendless young woman, helpless and despondent, might die as a result of his whim.

"So solemn." He drew his finger down the center of Charlotte's brow. "So serious. One can't travel the distance from solemn to torrid in a single leap." He touched his lips to hers and drew back a quarter inch. "Now you."

She heeded his suggestion for this would be the last, most torrid kiss of her life. She kissed him, her lips landing on the corner of his mouth, though that hadn't been her target. He waited, and she corrected her aim.

He tasted of peppermints. Charlotte moved closer, the better to trace the curves and swirls of his waistcoat.

"When you do that..." he muttered, looping his arms around her shoulders. He kept a small distance between their bodies, which Charlotte took as evidence that he liked her hands on his torso.

His heartbeat was a steady tattoo. When Charlotte teased her tongue along his lips, that rhythm might have accelerated.

Her heart was certainly beating faster.

Matters after that grew blurred. At some point, Mr. Sherbourne wrapped her in a snug embrace, which gave her permission to do the same with him. He was wonderfully solid in her arms, kissing her even as she pressed closer, and then he lifted her off her feet.

He sat on the sofa with Charlotte in his lap, and a kiss that had been passionate turned consuming. Charlotte tasted him deeply, and if he hadn't been wearing so many blasted clothes, she might have lapped at him as a cat laps up cream.

He *did things*, with his tongue, with his body, that shocked and delighted, and with his hands...

His hands were a revelation. Where he touched her, Charlotte became sensitive—her face, her neck, her wrists. His caresses were confident and unhurried, which was the most breathtaking, maddening aspect of the whole encounter.

"I hate that I don't know how to...to..."

He brushed her hair back. "To arouse me?"

Arouse was another word Charlotte hadn't spoken aloud. "Tease you, as you're teasing me. It's not fair."

She was cradled in his lap, the sofa's armrest supporting her back. The position was undignified, intimate, and far more comfortable than she'd imagined.

"Simply walking across a room, you arouse me, Charlotte Windham." He sounded no happier about that admission than Charlotte was to be refusing his proposal.

For she would, any minute now. Before she made that sacrifice, she snuggled closer. Mr. Sherbourne obliged her with a snuggle of his own—she *had* aroused him—and for a moment, Charlotte grieved what could not be.

Passion, affection, closeness that went beyond what Charlotte knew of sexual mechanics to a sort of friendship she'd never envisioned. But then, what woman could imagine Lucas Sherbourne?

Charlotte would be imagining him for the rest of her life. "I've decided not to marry you."

Mr. Sherbourne went still.

"You do me great honor," she went on, for that was how this was done, "but we would not suit."

He set her aside, not roughly, but firmly. "Of all women, I never took you for a hypocrite."

He was entitled to a fit of pique; he was not entitled to insult her. "I am not a hypocrite. I meant what I said. I cannot marry you, and we would not suit." She was lying, and she was telling the truth.

He ran his hands through his hair, bringing order where Charlotte had sown chaos. "We would suit like a lit taper suits tinder. You simply can't bear to marry a man who lacks a title."

"What?"

"I'm a commoner and always will be. You can't reconcile yourself to marrying down."

Charlotte had braced herself for politely wounded male pride—every unsuccessful suitor had had his pride—not for righteous indignation.

"My decision has nothing to do with a lack of title on your part. I am a commoner, as are all of my siblings and cousins save one, and he was born out of wedlock."

"Your siblings are titled nonetheless, while I am a mere mister, not even an honorable."

And Charlotte was not her siblings. "You are very honorable. If I were to marry anybody, it would be you. I'll see you out before either one of us says something regrettable." Charlotte regretted turning him down.

She did not regret kissing him.

He rose. "No need to see me out. I lack a title, but I do possess the ability to find the front door."

Charlotte got to her feet as well, lest he be seen stalking from the parlor in high dudgeon.

"Mr. Sherbourne, I will accompany you to the door. You will bow over my hand, I will curtsy, and what has passed between us in this room will remain private. Women turn down proposals every day. We're fickle creatures and our whims are of no moment."

He pulled on his gloves. "You are neither fickle nor whimsical, and you don't turn down proposals every day."

"I turn them down, nonetheless." With appalling regularity, but he doubtless didn't *offer* proposals, ever, and thus a frisson of guilt threaded through Charlotte's regret. "I am sorry Mr. Sherbourne. Any woman would be lucky to have your esteem."

His perusal was brooding, but at least he wasn't dashing off in a temper. "If you mean that, then why reject my suit? If some other man has a claim on your affections, I'll concede the field, of course. Otherwise, I'm prepared to be generous with the settlements. I'll be a decent and faithful husband, and you'll have a sister biding not a thirty-minute stroll from our home."

He was genuinely perplexed, and Charlotte's heart was genuinely, and very inconveniently, breaking. Fidelity didn't characterize every marriage, or even most society marriages, but Lucas Sherbourne would keep his vows.

"I wish you joy, Mr. Sherbourne. Shall I see you to the door?"

"For a woman wishing me joy, you look like you're about to cry."

Why must he turn up perceptive now? "Tears are soon dried."

"Charlotte?" He was calm now, or worse than calm, he was focused. She'd become a puzzle for him to solve, and his scrutiny was more than Charlotte could bear.

She cupped his cheek against her palm, and went up on her toes to give him a farewell kiss. He held her hand with his own and kissed her back with a tenderness that tried Charlotte's resolve to the utmost.

One more embrace, just one more…

A breeze wafted past Charlotte as she bundled closer to the man she'd never marry.

"What on earth is afoot here?" The Duchess of Moreland's question cracked like thunder across Charlotte's awareness. For a moment, she held on to Mr. Sherbourne simply to remain upright.

Sherbourne stepped back, but kept his hands on Charlotte's arms until she was standing independently.

"Charlotte Windham, explain yourself," Her Grace snapped. "And you, Mr. Sherbourne, taking unseemly liberties under the guise of paying a social call. Is this how you repay my welcome?"

Uncle Percival stood at Aunt's elbow, a portrait of the outraged patriarch. "Sir, you will step away from my niece."

"Uncle, Aunt, please calm yourselves. Mr. Sherbourne was about to leave, and I…"

Two people whom Charlotte loved very much were regarding her with heartrending dismay. If she explained that she'd just refused Mr. Sherbourne's proposal, then kissed him as if he were her every wish come true, they'd be hurt and angry past all bearing.

"Mr. Sherbourne," said the man himself, "was about to ask a servant where to find you, sir, for Miss Charlotte has done me the great honor of indicating that she'd welcome my addresses, were I to gain your permission to court her."

Charlotte's heart thumped against her ribs, as if she stood on a high precipice and couldn't make herself step back.

"You'd like to court our Charlotte?" Her Grace asked.

Oh, Aunt…no.

"I'd like to *start* by courting Miss Charlotte."

"Charlotte?" Uncle Percival asked. "I cannot believe the tableau that greeted us. If you were in any way coerced, then courtship, much less marriage, is out of the question and Mr. Sherbourne will return to Wales, permanently."

Mr. Sherbourne was watching her, waiting for her to see him effectively banished from England through no fault of his own. She couldn't do that, couldn't make him pay for her lack of caution. Of all women, she refused to see an innocent party ruined simply because she'd stolen one more kiss.

"I was in no way coerced, Uncle. I apologize for upsetting you and Aunt. I am very fond of Mr. Sherbourne, though that is no excuse for how I've behaved."

"The fault is mine," Mr. Sherbourne said, with a credible rendition of bashful chagrin. "I apologize to Your Graces as well."

Aunt Esther reached for Uncle Percival's hand, suggesting that Charlotte had rattled a woman who thought nothing of scolding King George himself. Uncle Percival tucked her hand over his arm and rested his palm over her fingers.

"Apologies accepted," he said. "Don't let it happen again. Mr. Sherbourne, you will spare me a few minutes in the garden when you've bade my niece a *proper* farewell."

"Yes, sir."

"Leave this door open," Aunt Esther said. "For the sake of my nerves and Mr. Sherbourne's continued good health, you will leave this door open."

They left, and Charlotte took a seat on a chair by the hearth rather than on the sofa where she'd—

"Did you mean it?" Mr. Sherbourne asked. "I'll not have it said you were forced, Charlotte. You either tell your family you were having a small adventure with a willing bachelor, or you become Mrs. Lucas Sherbourne. Don't lead me around Mayfair by the nose only to reject me several weeks hence."

"My family would be disappointed in me for that small

adventure." Then they would ruin Lucas Sherbourne without even trying. The invitations would disappear, the greetings would become perfunctory, civilities would be withheld.

A man who'd done nothing wrong would make a hasty departure for Wales, like a chambermaid who'd been turned off without a character for refusing the lord of the manor's advances.

Sherbourne's disgrace would be Charlotte's fault.

"Make up your mind," Mr. Sherbourne said, "and know that if we marry, I will be a husband to you in every way that matters. Ours won't be a match based on affection, but neither will it be a union of appearances. Choose carefully, Charlotte, and I will honor your decision."

Chapter Five

Sherbourne could honor Charlotte Windham's decision, but could he honor *her*?

This question plagued him even as he knocked on the Earl of Westhaven's door two days after becoming an engaged man.

Charlotte had kissed him like every bachelor's naughty dream, then flung his proposal...well, not flung it in his face, but handed it back to him like a wrinkled, damp, handkerchief.

He had no title, no illustrious family history, no impressive coat of arms, no family motto beyond "Make money, and sneer at the titled fools." Of course she'd refused him. He'd been a fool to expect otherwise.

Only when she'd stood to lose her family's respect had she agreed to become Mrs. Lucas Sherbourne.

Sherbourne lacked aristocratic antecedents, but he had pride, and thus he'd insisted on negotiating the settlements with the Earl of Westhaven in person. His lordship was the ducal heir, and apparently the financial brains of the Windham family.

"Mr. Sherbourne, welcome," said a liveried butler. "His lordship awaits you in his study."

Sherbourne passed over his hat and walking stick and followed the butler down a corridor that boasted not one cobweb, not one speck of dust or smudged mirror. Those mirrors had been placed to catch and reflect sunlight, giving the house an airy, pleasant quality at variance with the priggish butler.

"Mr. Lucas Sherbourne to see you, my lord." The butler presented Sherbourne's card on a silver tray.

Westhaven bore a resemblance to both of his parents. He had Moreland's height, the ducal nose, and lean build, and the duchess's green eyes and chin. His hair was chestnut, and he exuded about as much hospitality as an elderly cat welcoming an invasion of noisy children into the library.

"Sherbourne, good day."

A lordly perusal followed. Sherbourne had endured many such inspections, and he perused Westhaven right back.

"You had a reputation for brawling at school," Westhaven said after the butler had withdrawn. "Aunt Arabella says you were cheerfully dedicated to the ruin of a neighbor of longstanding—which neighbor is married to my cousin—and now you demand that the settlements be negotiated in person rather than through the good offices of the diplomatic intermediaries whose job it is to tend to these matters. Don't expect many concessions, Sherbourne."

Sherbourne took a moment to look over the earl's study.

The desk was tidy to the point of obsessive organization, from the gleaming silver pen tray to the immaculate blotter, to the sealed correspondence sitting in a neat stack in another silver tray.

"Cheerfully dedicated to the ruin of a neighbor..." Sherbourne replied. "Interesting, and here I thought I'd cheerfully awaited repayment of debts decades overdue. May I remind your lordship that Haverford and I have made our peace? Perhaps you and I should change the subject. Discussing another man's finances strikes me as ill bred."

Now came the lordly reassessment, which from Westhaven meant a twitch of the ducal proboscis and a narrowing of green eyes. "Quite. Please have a seat."

As a former schoolyard brawler, Sherbourne took that seat at one end of the sofa rather than perch before the altar of Westhaven's desk like a supplicant. With the toe of a boot, Sherbourne flipped up a fringe of the carpet as he sat.

"Charlotte is dear to us," Westhaven said, taking a wing chair. "We will expect a generous contribution to her settlements, and I have a very specific figure in mind for her pin money."

Delightful. The royal *we* had a Windham counterpart.

"Charlotte is dear to me as well," Sherbourne said, "and as pleased as I am to pass the time of day with you, I'd rather spend my afternoon with her. Perhaps you'd share that specific figure before sunset?"

A footman interrupted, bearing a fortune in silver on a tea tray. The next five minutes were spent testing Sherbourne's manners, though in fairness to Westhaven, the cakes were excellent and the tea strong. Some hosts served Sherbourne the day-old cakes and the used tea leaves, as if he'd not know a stale sweet when he bit into it.

Westhaven set about an interrogation that was doomed to brevity. Sherbourne's family consisted of one crotchety great-uncle on the maternal side. His residential real estate was one modest dwelling of twenty bedrooms, the former dower house to Haverford Castle. He did not wager on cards or horses, or make stupid bets on the book at White's.

"You would have me believe you are a dull fellow," Westhaven said. "I cannot credit that Charlotte Windham would yoke herself to a drudge."

To an *untitled* drudge. "We drudges tend to redeem ourselves in important regards. I will keep the lady in comfort and style, for example, and I won't insult her with a string of mistresses whom I flaunt at the theatre before her friends. I will never break my neck riding to hounds half-drunk out of sheer boredom. I won't gamble away her pin money merely to impress the fellows. I don't trifle with the help. Might we discuss figures, my lord?"

"Charlotte is forthright," Westhaven said. "One shudders to think what sort of children the two of you will raise."

Sherbourne set his teacup beside the tray, not on it. "We will raise well-loved children, if the heavenly powers grant us offspring, and *we* will raise them. They won't be packed off to public school from infancy for the ritual starvation and torture that passes for aristocratic education. Nor will they be banished to the fourth floor until the age of six, at which time they'll be permitted to parade through the parlor twice a week spouting Latin and sums."

Westhaven set Sherbourne's teacup on the tray. "The parade was nigh daily, if you must know, and started when I was four. My father was a military man and in some ways always will be."

Hence the immaculate desk, the pens laid neatly in the

tray, and the compulsion to subject all new recruits to parade inspection.

"I brought a set of figures," Sherbourne said. "I'd like to discuss them with you."

The door burst open, and a small boy cantered—he did not run, he cantered—across the carpet. "Tally ho! Tally ho! Reynard is making for his covert!"

The boy came to a halt, confusion in eyes the same shade of green as Westhaven's. "Excuse me, Papa. I thought you met Uncle Valentine for lunch on Mondays."

"Uncle Valentine is working on the final movement of a new sonata," Westhaven said, gathering the boy into his lap. "You know how he is about finales."

The child was utterly at home roosting on his papa's knees. "He's awful. Aunt Ellen says so, then she kisses him. We have company."

"We do. This is Mr. Sherbourne. He's a friend of Cousin Charlotte's. A good friend."

Well, no he wasn't. He was her *fiancé.* "Greetings, young sir."

"I'm a viscount, but not the real kind," the child said. "Cousin Charlotte doesn't like to climb trees, but she can do sums in her head even better than Papa. Her favorite cakes are lemon, which is capital, because I don't care for lemon."

Sherbourne would have bet his walking stick—if he were to bet anything—that Charlotte had no particular fondness for lemon cakes, though for this nephew, she'd have told that lie.

"I hear something," Westhaven said, cocking his head. "Do you hear it?"

The boy scrambled off his father's lap. "Is it a fox? Do you hear the wily Reynard making designs upon our biddies? Foul dastard! You shall not menace our biddies! Tally ho! Pericles, Tally ho!"

Westhaven rose to close the door behind the first flight, pausing to smooth the carpet fringe Sherbourne had flipped.

"His brother prefers shooting expeditions in the garden. God help the pigeons if the boy ever learns to aim his sling-shot."

Foul dastard? That was not a small boy's oath. "Westhaven, have you been riding to hounds in the parlor?"

His lordship resumed his chair, crossing one ankle over the opposite knee. "When my wife goes calling, I some-times take it upon myself to entertain the children. About those figures?"

Sherbourne extracted a sheaf of papers from his breast pocket and passed them over. Westhaven drank another cup of tea while he studied the proposed settlements.

"Can you afford this, Sherbourne?" The question was merely curious, which was all that saved Westhaven from wearing tea on his tidily knotted cravat.

"My cash reserves are not where I'd wish them to be," Sherbourne said, "though most would envy me my sol-vency. I've lately taken on a charitable project of consid-erable proportions, invested in a new mining venture, and otherwise committed liquid assets. I never involve the re-sources of my bank in personal obligations, nor do I allow the other directors or owners to do so."

"That charitable project would be Cousin Elizabeth's lending libraries," Westhaven said. "I've heard something about them."

Part of making peace with the duke next door had been indulging the Duchess of Haverford's passion for lending libraries. Sherbourne had purchased a fortune in books—

from His Grace—and in essence forgiven the rest of Haverford's indebtedness.

The decision had seemed prudent at the time, though Sherbourne dreaded his meetings with the duchess. She was so very enthusiastic about her causes—and about her damned duke.

"The short answer is that I can afford the settlements proposed. If I acquire a sleeping partner or two for my mining venture, I'll have more latitude, but those figures are within my means. If there's one asset I bring to this union, it's the ability to assure Charlotte of a comfortable dotage."

"She'll have a comfortable dotage with or without you, Sherbourne. The Windhams take care of their own." Gone was the doting master of foxhounds and in his place sat the prosy ducal heir.

"Review the figures, your lordship. I'm prepared to negotiate within limits, but you will please assure me that Charlotte's funds will be managed by you or one of your brothers, not by some paunchy solicitor whose attachment is to Charlotte's coin rather than her welfare."

Westhaven popped a tea cake into his mouth—the whole thing at once. "I will manage the funds personally, or in conjunction with my sister, the Countess of Hazelton. Her ladyship's skill with investments goes beyond genius. She will like you, though her version of liking can leave a fellow feeling as if he's been mauled by a lioness. One makes allowances. She's married to Hazelton, after all."

Sherbourne resigned himself to further study of the Windham family tree. No other lord of his acquaintance would liken his sister's approval to an attack by a wild creature, and yet, Westhaven conveyed genuine affection for the lady.

"I'll await your response to my proposal," Sherbourne

said, rising. "My thanks for the hospitality. I have one question for you."

"Ask." Westhaven wrapped two tea cakes in a table napkin and slipped them into his pocket, then got to his feet.

"Do you hoard food?"

"Of course not. Those are for the hunt breakfast."

Westhaven loved his son, which reassured Sherbourne as signed settlement agreements would not have.

"Who is Charlotte's best friend?"

Westhaven paused with his hand on the door latch. "Her best friend *now*? She was thick as thieves with the Porter girl, but that was years ago. The poor thing left town amid some talk, and I gather Charlotte has kept mostly to the company of her sisters since then. Why do you ask?"

"I'd thought to make the acquaintance of Charlotte's friends." To learn what he could from them about a woman he was likely to spend the rest of his life with.

"Ah, now, there I can offer you a bit of marital advice," Westhaven said, with more enthusiasm than the topic warranted. "*You* be Charlotte's friend and allow her to be yours. The other part is lovely of course—connubial bliss is more than a cliché—but be Charlotte's friend."

The aristocracy was prone to eccentricity—foxes under the sofa, for example. "I'll be her husband, once you approve those settlements. Good day, my lord."

Sherbourne left the earl's townhouse with much to ponder. Westhaven was a lordly prig, a ferociously devoted father, a loyal brother and cousin, and a conscientious minder of the family fortunes.

Also besotted with his countess, if gossip was to be believed.

Sherbourne was *not* besotted with Charlotte Windham, but one admission she'd made gave him peace where their union was concerned: *If I were to marry anybody, it would be you.*

If Charlotte was honest—and Sherbourne believed she was—then her objection was not to him personally, but to marriage in general. He wasn't overly fond of the institution himself, which boded well for their expectations of each other, if not for their connubial bliss.

* * *

"The only possible risk is that he might from time to time be somewhat cash poor," Maggie, Countess of Hazelton, said. "The same ailment afflicts half the titled families in the realm."

"Sherbourne is *poor*?" Charlotte couldn't keep the dismay from her tone.

"Far from it," Maggie replied, taking off a pair of gold-rimmed spectacles. "We would never allow you to entertain his suit if he were without means. Sherbourne's worth is impressive. He owns majority shares in a bank, shipping ventures, and numerous mercantile establishments. He owns an entire school in the Midlands and built a hotel last year in the Lakes that was booked to capacity all summer."

"May I see the figures?"

Westhaven had given Charlotte a summary version of the negotiations: Sherbourne had met or exceeded every item on the Westhaven's list—unasked.

His lordship hadn't seen fit to explain to Charlotte what the list of demands had entailed. If Sherbourne had been negotiating settlements on behalf of a cousin, *he* would have ensured that she grasped every detail, down to the penny.

"Charlotte, I understand that you're nervous," Maggie

said, pouring herself a third cup of tea. "But you needn't fret about the settlements. Sherbourne assured Westhaven that every aspect of his proposal was within his means."

"You have doubts." Charlotte certainly had doubts, an entire queasy tummy full. She'd sent Tansy to the post with next month's payments for the various Mrs. Wesleys, but Tansy wasn't coming to Wales. Charlotte would need to establish alternate arrangements almost as soon as she arrived at Sherbourne Hall.

"I have reservations," Maggie said, "but then, I've become averse to risk since the boys came along."

The boys were at present with their papa in the park, flying kites, sailing boats on the Serpentine, and otherwise enjoying a pretty autumn day. Would Sherbourne take time for outings with his children?

And good gracious, Charlotte blushed to think of how those children would be conceived. Sharing passionate kisses was all well and good—also safe. Never had a child resulted from intemperate kisses alone. This marriage would involve far more than kisses, though, Sherbourne had made that clear.

"I need pin money, Maggie. Lots and lots of pin money."

Her ladyship was a formidable redhead nearly six inches taller than Charlotte. The countess had a regal air, despite having been born on the wrong side of the ducal blanket.

"The sums proposed are generous to a fault, Charlotte. Why do you need more?"

"I just do. Sherbourne has never had a wife before, and he can't very well waltz into his club and ask the nearest viscount how much a well-born missus costs these days. He won't know enough to quibble over the figure for pin money."

Pin money was Charlotte's to use as she alone saw fit—even Sherbourne had defined it thus—and yet, deceiving him made her uneasy. Telling him the truth regarding the various Mrs. Wesleys was impossible. Not yet. Not before the wedding, and possibly not after.

Maggie lifted the pot as if to refill Charlotte's cup, but Charlotte hadn't taken more than a polite sip. Her ladyship set down the teapot and gave Charlotte an uncomfortably protracted perusal.

"Charlotte, you were seen by Their Graces in a most passionate embrace with your prospective spouse. If you don't care for him, say so now."

That interrupted farewell kiss had not been the *most* passionate Charlotte had shared with Sherbourne.

"I respect the gentleman greatly, but hardly know what to expect from marriage to him." After Charlotte's initial refusal of his suit, how could their wedding night be anything but awkward? "He was compelled by honor to propose to me, and that is not the best foundation for a successful marriage."

"Would you like a crumpet?"

"No, thank you." Did polite society have nothing better to do than swill tea and consume sweets?

"If honor compelled him to propose, what compelled you to accept?"

The same inconvenient honor. "I was tired of turning down buffoons. Mr. Sherbourne is a surpassingly sensible man and he doesn't put on airs."

"You're saying he suits you."

Charlotte wanted to bolt away from the conversation, but Maggie was family, and as the oldest female cousin, she'd always been something of a confidante.

"I hope he suits me. I still need more pin money."

"Then we'll reduce his contribution to your dower account."

He had offered settlements at the limit of what Maggie considered prudent. Why? "Reduce them by as much as you can without insulting him. I have no wish to beggar my husband."

"You won't," Maggie said, munching on a crumpet. "He's merely in the same position as most of the best families, though his wealth is tied up in commercial assets rather than land. He has a substantial income, and he's reinvesting much of it in his mining venture. New businesses typically require capital and attention before they become profitable. He also refuses to treat his bank as his personal treasure trove, which is commendable."

Maggie reviewed with Charlotte the terms of the proposed agreement, paragraph by paragraph, but Charlotte couldn't focus. The numbers stuck with her of course, but the endless, convoluted words...

"You're woolgathering," Maggie said, some thirty minutes later. "With a wedding in less than a week, you're entitled."

By special license, of course. The stated reason was to allow the ceremony to take place at the Moreland townhouse, but the real reason was Her Grace's nerves.

"I'm preoccupied," Charlotte said, the grandmama of all understatements, surely. "I wish I knew what to expect. Mr. Sherbourne and I aren't that well acquainted. I know hardly anything about him."

Maggie patted her hand. "Marriage is an adventure for two. Look for the good in him, the same as you would with any friend. Give him your loyalty and the benefit of the doubt, find things to laugh about together, and don't worry if the early days are a bit bumpy. That's part of it."

What about the wedding night? What about those moments under the covers when the two became as one flesh?

"Maggie, the whole business makes me...anxious."

Panicked, in truth. Charlotte was about to take vows with a man who believed she didn't respect him, and who very possibly didn't respect her. How in all creation was she to get through the wedding night?

"If you're anxious, that's good. Marriage is an enormous step. One shouldn't take it lightly." Maggie left off studying the garden. "They're back," she said, rising and gathering her skirts. "I can hear them coming up the alley. We must greet them and hear all about their adventures."

Charlotte rose slowly, keeping a hand on the back of her chair. "You'll see the settlements modified? More pin money, less invested in the funds?"

"Of course, though I think you're daft. You're also a bit pale, but then, this has been an exciting week. Come along, my dear, and prepare to be regaled with tales of dragons and wizards."

Charlotte followed Maggie back into the house, more relieved than she could say. The wedding night was still a looming ordeal, but at least she'd weathered tea on her ladyship's third-floor balcony without serious embarrassment.

* * *

"We found Cousin Charlotte's friend in the park," the Earl of Hazelton said. "Much to the delight of all concerned."

Hazelton, a dark-haired brute with northern antecedents in his speech, was being ironic.

"Charlotte, good day," Sherbourne said, as Hazelton—in broad daylight and with minor children looking on—kissed his countess on the cheek. "Won't you introduce us?"

In the park, Hazelton hadn't stood on ceremony. With a toddler grasped by the hand and a very small child clinging to his back, he'd marched right up to Sherbourne and demanded to make the acquaintance of Cousin Charlotte's friend.

Charlotte looked pale and pretty in a sprigged muslin walking dress that was several years out of date, judging by the waistline. She recited the introductions with a haste that verged on uncordial.

"May I walk you home?" Sherbourne asked. "I'm sure Hazelton can see to my horse."

"I'd be happy to," Hazelton said, slipping an arm around his countess's waist, for pity's sake.

"We'll wish you good-day, then." Sherbourne offered Charlotte his arm. She hadn't consented to his escort, but her pallor, her quiet, and the way she retied her bonnet ribbons—twice—suggested she might welcome a respite from all this marital affection.

Nonetheless, much cheek kissing and hugging was required before two women who'd probably seen each other every week for the past fourteen years could part. They'd see each other again in a few days, though Charlotte had agreed to leave for Wales immediately after the wedding breakfast.

"Did your cousin terrify you with lurid tales of the wedding night?" Sherbourne asked as he and his intended started down the alley.

"She dodged discussion of wedding nights in any sense."

Which meant Charlotte had, indeed, raised the topic. "This bothers you." Was that why Charlotte was pale? "We needn't consummate the marriage until we're home in Wales, if you prefer." The words were out, spoken by some idiot with pretensions to gentlemanly consideration—or cowardice.

"Will putting the business off make it any easier?"

The business. She referred to consummation of solemn vows, the first joining of man and wife, as *the business*.

"Delaying the wedding night will allow for the occasion to be more private. I don't fancy making my debut as your lover at some noisy coaching inn."

Charlotte's pace slowed as they approached the street. "You don't?"

He did, he did, he most certainly did. The traveling coach was another possibility, and quite comfortable.

"One wants to make a good first impression."

Her smile was hesitant. "Are you *nervous*, Mr. Sherbourne?"

He was attracted to her, but on another level, he was uneasy. Charlotte had chosen him over scandal, making them reluctant partners at best—a marriage not of cordial convenience, but of pure expedience.

"We will have decades of married life to share a bed. Why hurry into the situation when we could instead choose the moment that best pleases us both?"

The *situation*? The ailment of vocabulary Charlotte suffered was apparently contagious.

Charlotte lowered her voice despite the racket provided by the nearby street. "Part of me wants to get the consummation over with."

And part of her dreaded the occasion. *Splendid.* They walked along, two people bound for marriage and possibly for perdition.

"Did your cousin review the settlements with you?"

"In detail. I'm asking for more pin money but less in the funds. Nothing would do but Maggie must have this discussion with me on her favorite third-floor balcony."

Why more pin money, and what did a third-floor balcony have to do with—?

Sherbourne's bedroom was on the third floor of his manor house and had a lovely balcony. This did not bode well for the wedding night, even in Wales. The rest of their walk home was made without conversation. Apparently, Charlotte's pallor resulted from tea on a third-floor balcony, not worry over the wedding night.

Though she was worried, and thus Sherbourne was worried. Ye gods, marriage was making him daft before he'd even spoken his vows. That Charlotte's cousin hadn't respected her fear of heights was disquieting, but that Charlotte wanted more pin money was . . . a problem.

What could she possibly spend lavish pin money on in rural Wales?

And how would he come up with yet more coin for the bride who was marrying him only to avoid disgrace?

Chapter Six

"Everything Lucas Sherbourne touches turns to gold." Quinton, Earl of Brantford, was certain of this happy conclusion. "Papa-in-law disapproves of him on that basis alone. Says new money should never be trusted."

"His lordship sets great store by tradition." Meyerbeek wrapped a stack of papers in a folder and tied it with red ribbon. Brantford's man of business was large and bluff, though he took care with the papers, ribbon, and bow.

Lord Halstead also set great store by his daughter, whom Brantford had married a good five years ago—or was it six? Possibly seven. Veronica was a mousy little thing who had yet to produce a single infant. Other than that, she was an untroublesome wife who'd brought beautiful settlements to marriage.

Though an earl without an heir was not a man to be envied.

"Dear papa-in-law has yet to put his financial house in order," Brantford said, because Meyerbeek had doubtless heard the gossip, and ignoring the obvious would only fuel speculation. "When the inevitable happens, I hope to be in a position to prevent scandal for my in-laws."

Which scandal would, of course, wash up on Brantford's own shores.

"Very noble of you, sir." Meyerbeek tied up another set of papers. "You are well on your way to a handsome fortune. Nonetheless, I must echo his lordship's caution where Mr. Sherbourne's new coal mine is concerned."

Meyerbeek's penchant for caution was as reliable as Veronica's appointments at the milliner's. The woman was addicted to buying hats.

"You don't trust Sherbourne?" Behind the closed doors of Brantford's private office, he could pose that question to a subordinate. In the clubs, nobody would dare be so blunt when Sherbourne's bank held mortgages on a number of titled estates.

"Mr. Sherbourne's integrity as a businessman is above reproach, from what I've gathered. He doesn't engage in sharp practice, doesn't go back on a contract signed and sealed, but the mining operation is different."

Mines were simple businesses. One dug a hole, excavated valuable ore, and got paid for it. Miners grumbled about low wages, and the occasional mine collapsed, but England's appetite for coal was insatiable and thus the profit was reliable.

"Different how?" Brantford asked, keeping his seat behind his desk.

"The Duke of Haverford is Sherbourne's neighbor and soon to be connected to him by marriage. Haverford is only supporting this mine because Sherbourne has promised to run it as an example of the most enlightened business practices. The workers are to have decent housing, no children will be employed below the surface, that sort of thing. Very *forward-thinking*, if you take my meaning."

Progress was good and usually went hand in hand with profit. Forward thinking could be troublesome.

"All the more reason," Brantford said, "that Sherbourne should ally himself with somebody who can be the voice of wisdom in the face of Haverford's fanciful notions. His Grace is a fine fellow, but like my papa-in-law, he clings to land rents, flocks, and herds as the only acceptable sources of income."

"Those aspects of our economy remain vitally important." Meyerbeek tapped his hat onto his head. "Might I suggest, if you do invest in Mr. Sherbourne's mine, that you pay a call on your business partner in Wales and inspect the works yourself? Haverford lives in the immediate area and would take your involvement more seriously if you showed the flag, as it were."

Wales had decent shooting, and Veronica didn't exactly need her husband underfoot during the little season.

"I'll consider it. My thanks as always for your efforts, Meyerbeek."

Meyerbeek went on his way, folders tucked in a plain black leather satchel. Brantford waited a suitable interval—one did not perambulate about Mayfair with one's man of business—then timed his own departure so he'd be only a few minutes late for his appointment with Sherbourne.

Sherbourne's butler was all anybody could wish for in an upper servant, and the townhouse was appointed in elegant, if slightly overstated, good taste. Brantford's host greeted him in a room that might have been any lord's estate office—ancestors scowling down from portraits on the walls, carpets thick and recently swept—but for the plethora of correspondence in four different trays on the desk.

"You *are* a busy man." The letters Brantford could see all bore a recent date. Sherbourne was also, apparently, a man who didn't let his affairs go untended for long.

"I said as much," Sherbourne replied. "Please have a seat."

A seat facing the desk was a novel perspective, putting Brantford uncomfortably in mind of frequent interviews with his papa when deportment at university had been disappointing.

Sherbourne likely knew this. He didn't know enough to ring for tea, though, which was a shame when the man could maunder on at such tiresome length about a damned coal mine.

"You have a solid grasp of the venture you're undertaking," Brantford said, "and the terms you propose for my role are agreeable, in principle. When can you reduce them to writing?"

Sherbourne opened a drawer, produced a sheaf of papers, and passed them across the desk.

"You'll find four copies, two for you and two for me. I've signed them all. My staff can witness your signature, if you're inclined to invest."

A conundrum presented itself: Sherbourne's quaint insistence on doing business face-to-face had proved useful. Brantford liked knowing that he wasn't engaging in commerce with some vulgar cit, liked knowing exactly where Sherbourne would dwell when in town. He liked seeing proof that Sherbourne was industrious and conscientious about his affairs.

For Sherbourne to insist on an appointment on his terms and on his turf was a petty stratagem, but tolerable. This notion of signing a legal document on the spot, though...not the done thing.

"I'd need time to read every word," Brantford said. "I mean no slight to you, of course, but any scribe can make a mistake or misinterpret his master's directions."

Sherbourne rose and withdrew a key from a japanned box on the mantel. "I wrote out all four copies myself. As contracts go, it's brief and to the point." He wound the clock on the mantel, which would typically be a butler's job.

The hour approached three, and at four Brantford was expected at a cozy little household off of Cavendish Square. A gentleman kept a new mistress waiting at peril to his exchequer.

"Let's have a look," Brantford said, smoothing out a copy of the contract. "Though perhaps you'd be good enough to order us a tea tray while I read?"

His objective was to get Sherbourne out of the room, because a bit of judicious reconnaissance was called for.

Sherbourne merely tugged on a bell pull twice.

Well, damn. Lucas Sherbourne was no fool, an oddly cheering realization. Brantford's money would be safe in Sherbourne's hands, and that was the larger concern. Besides, the terms on paper weren't exactly binding on a peer of the realm, despite what the courts might lead the common man to believe.

Sherbourne resumed his seat behind the desk and took up the first of the items stacked in the nearest tray.

"You're soon to be married, I hear," Brantford said a few minutes later. In all the world, was any soporific more effective than lawyerly prose?

Sherbourne didn't even look up from his reading. "Miss Charlotte Windham has looked with favor upon my suit."

"You can't fool me, Sherbourne. You're no more smitten with your bride than I am with the prospect of Lady Deerwood's card party tonight."

Sherbourne set the letter aside, shot his cuffs, and folded his hands on the blotter. "Did you just insult my *fiancée*?"

Oh, dear. The lower orders could be high sticklers, witness the proliferation of etiquette manuals they consulted on everything from social calls to funerals.

"I insult neither you nor your lovely bride, Sherbourne. I insult the institution of marriage. I have years of experience with holy matrimony that you have yet to acquire. Allow me my crotchets, hmm?"

Sherbourne resumed reading. "If your experience of marriage has been disappointing, then you insult yourself, for I know a gentleman would never slander his wife."

Brantford resumed reading, mostly to hide a smile. Sherbourne was precious, in his ferocious propriety and his unrelenting focus on business. The clubs were buzzing about his upcoming nuptials, wondering how and why he'd become engaged to the formidable Charlotte Windham.

Money had doubtless played a role. As a bachelor, Brantford had observed Miss Charlotte from the safe distance of the men's punch bowl. She had an air of discontent, and at an archery tournament her aim was notoriously unreliable.

Or rather, too accurate. Perhaps the Windhams had paid Sherbourne to spirit the lady off to Wales.

"That reminds me," Brantford said, giving up in the middle of the paragraph about indemnifying and holding harmless. "I'll want to inspect the works firsthand. I'm told it's sound business to have a look oneself, rather than rely on—what is the word?—toadies?"

Sherbourne's smile was cool. "You'd travel out to Wales to see the mine?"

Brantford would travel out to Wales to do some shooting, pay a call on His Grace of Haverford, and avoid several tedious weeks of card parties while Veronica bought out the milliners' shops.

"Seems prudent to have a look at where my money's going," Brantford said. "This is your first mining venture, while I've seen many. I understand Haverford has tried to hamper the operation with quaint notions of lavish housing and exorbitant wages for the workers. We'll soon enlighten His Grace about how business is done."

Sherbourne set a silver standish on Brantford's side of the desk. "We will do no such thing, unless you sign those contracts now. I leave for Wales immediately after my wedding, and work on the housing at the mine started last month. We'll sink the main shaft before St. Andrew's Day."

Brantford chose a quill from the three in the standish. He wasn't about to give himself a headache reading two more pages of heretofores and however-exceptings. A difference of opinion on a business matter was settled amicably or not at all. Only fools or those already afflicted with scandal resorted to the courts.

"A moment," Sherbourne said as Brantford dipped the pen. "We need witnesses."

Good God. "As you please, Sherbourne, but I draw the line at allowing you to count my teeth."

A butler and clerk appended their signatures as witnesses, then departed without a word.

"Thus do we become partners," Brantford said, extending a hand. "Shall I take my copies with me?"

Sherbourne shook hands—briefly. "Your copies will be delivered when I have a bank draft from you. When we both have signed copies, and only then, I'll deposit your bank draft, as described on the last page of the agreement. Until the consideration has been exchanged, we have no enforceable bargain under the law."

"You do like to belabor the details, don't you?" Sherbourne would be a terror with subcontractors and subordinates. Papa-in-law might have a much fatter purse if he'd found somebody with Sherbourne's blunt sensibilities to manage his affairs.

"Applicable law is never a detail." Sherbourne held the door. "I look forward to showing you the works soon. When can I expect your bank draft?"

"My business partner is a barbarian," Brantford marveled, as his host escorted him down the main staircase. "One doesn't mention money directly, Sherbourne. You'll have the mine producing before Christmas if you're always so fixed on your objectives."

"We're not partners yet." Sherbourne passed Brantford his hat and walking stick.

But they soon would be, and Brantford had a good feeling about that. Sherbourne wasn't afraid to get his hands dirty, to ask the rude questions upon which the whole transaction hinged. Mining ventures weren't for the faint of heart—Brantford avoided touring his more than once a year, if he could help it, and he never went below the surface—but they could be wonderfully profitable.

"I'll have my man bring around the funds tomorrow," Brantford said.

He waited a moment for Sherbourne to pontificate about the hazards of entrusting a man of business with an actual bank draft, but Mr. Sherbourne only held the door open, like a footman, or one of the large fellows hired to eject unruly persons from taverns.

"Best wishes on your upcoming nuptials, Sherbourne, and safe journey to Wales. May your union be both happy and fruitful."

Brantford trotted down the steps, entirely in charity with

life. He was paying a call on a comely mistress, he'd just secured a significant interest in a new mine, and his business partner had a Midas touch.

Brantford did wish his own union could be fruitful though, not that he'd given up hope. As for the happy part, who needed a happy marriage when life was otherwise humming along to such a cheerful tune?

* * *

Charlotte had tried counting turnpikes, posting inns, cows, even trees. She'd read, she'd played solitary card games, she'd penned a trio of letters from a nonexistent deceased husband—Mr. Wesley Cowper this time—until the rocking of the coach gave her a headache.

The journey to Wales was taking forever.

Sherbourne left her to the joys of his traveling coach, a monstrosity of a vehicle pulled by teams of gigantic horses. The size of the conveyance meant speed was sacrificed to comfort, and the state of the king's highway ensured comfort was a lost cause.

Charlotte's constant companion was worry, about the wedding night, about marriage to a man she didn't know well, about Maggie's contention that Sherbourne could become financially overextended.

Charlotte worried about the unknown unfortunates in London whom she might have helped, and she resolved to continue offering aid wherever it was needed in Wales. Somehow, she'd send out her bank notes to the Mrs. Wesleys, and find a way to broach the matter with Sherbourne when the time was right.

Though the time might not be right for years.

The route was somewhat familiar, because Charlotte had

visited Wales frequently as a child, and because she'd attended a house party at Haverford Castle only a few months earlier. A cold, sleety rain began to fall as they prepared to leave the final inn before reaching their destination.

That Charlotte should bring bad weather with her to her new home was appropriate, for her mood was less than sunny.

The coach door opened without warning.

"Might I join you?" Sherbourne stood outside, waiting for Charlotte's permission to enter his own conveyance.

"You'll catch your death loitering in a downpour. Get in here this instant."

He climbed in, rocking the vehicle and bringing with him the scents of wet wool, horse, and leather.

"Sit with me," Charlotte said, when he hesitated to choose a bench. "We'll share a lap robe."

They were married. They could share everything, in theory. At the inns, they'd taken meals together in private dining rooms, then retired to separate quarters. Sherbourne had been a conscientious escort, but he'd offered little conversation and less companionship.

"Are you cold?" he asked.

Charlotte was swathed in a velvet-lined cloak, and the inn had supplied hot bricks for the coach's floor, and yet, the damp had crept into her bones.

"A trifle chilly," she said. "A result of inactivity and fatigue no doubt. Strange beds, however commodious, don't offer the best sleep."

Sherbourne withdrew a wool blanket from under the opposite bench and spread it over their knees. Without warning his arm came around Charlotte's shoulders.

"I could sleep for a week," he groused. "Every time I make the journey to London, I vow it will be my last."

"You ride for miles without tiring." Hour after hour, he

had ridden before the coach, changing horses when the coachman swapped teams.

"At twenty, I rode for miles without tiring. Now I merely want to be home. I've sent word ahead to your sister, though if she's on hand to welcome us, that means Haverford will be about as well."

He tugged at Charlotte's shoulder, urging her against his side. She complied, though such proximity to an adult male was novel.

Also warm. "You invited Elizabeth and her duke to your home?"

Sherbourne stuffed his riding gloves into a pocket of his greatcoat and tucked the blanket more closely around Charlotte's legs.

"To *our* home. Our wedding was small, and any fuss your family can make to excuse their absence at the ceremony ought to be encouraged."

Charlotte refused to lament the nature of her wedding. No St. George's at Hanover Square for her, no assembling all of the cousins or reading of the banns. She'd spoken her vows in the Moreland formal parlor, with Aunt, Uncle, Westhaven and his countess, and Maggie and her earl in attendance.

Everybody else was off domesticating or gestating in the country, and Mama and Papa had been visiting family in Scotland.

"Mama sent an express," Charlotte said. "She'll visit Elizabeth and me at Christmas."

"I look forward to meeting her and your father."

No, Sherbourne clearly did not, and Charlotte had her doubts that Mama would have visited at all, but for Elizabeth duchessing nearby in nothing less than a genuine crenelated castle.

"Mama will lecture your ear off in Welsh," Charlotte said. "I love to hear her speak in her native tongue, love the music of her scolds. Papa barely gets along in Welsh, but he insisted his offspring be proficient."

"My servants all speak English and Welsh both. You may address them as you please."

Our servants. Sherbourne was warm and solid, and a good deal more pleasant to lean against than the coach squabs. But what to talk about? What to talk about for the next half century?

"Would you like to have friends pay us a visit, Charlotte?"

"No, thank you. I'm sure we'll have a steady parade of family over the years. They'll want to look in on us, and Elizabeth is right next door. Mama loves her homeland, and traveling here by sea isn't that difficult for those closer to the coast."

The coach hit a spectacular pothole, tossing Charlotte nearly into her husband's lap.

"I assure you, Sherbourne Hall is appointed as elegantly as any Mayfair mansion," he said. "You needn't worry that your friends will pity you for your domicile."

Charlotte unlooped his arm from her shoulders. "Your home was once a ducal dower house, from what I understand. Of course it will be commodious." In his way, Sherbourne was *trying*. Charlotte's conscience compelled her to extend an olive branch. "The fact is, I can think of nobody to invite."

The dratted coach chose then to sway around a curve, all but shoving Charlotte against her husband.

"Not a single soul?" Sherbourne asked. "No friends from finishing school, ladies who made their come out with you, former governesses, that sort of thing?"

Charlotte had wondered similarly about her husband:

Who were his friends? "Most of the women I made my come out with have long since married and started families. Finishing school was years ago, and I have a wealth of sisters and cousins. One young lady who was like a sister to me has gone to her reward."

Saying the words hurt. Charlotte thought often of Fern Porter, but she almost never spoke of her.

"A good friend?" Sherbourne asked.

Outside the rain pounded down, and the countryside went by in a dreary brown blur. Autumn was more advanced here, not a benevolent easing of summer's heat, but a harbinger of winter's dark and cold.

"She was a best friend," Charlotte said softly. "Fern and I were inseparable from the first day we met at the age of eleven. We shared a room at school, we shared hopes and fears, and got into such mischief. When we had to separate over holidays, we'd write to each other daily. I had hoped she'd marry one of my cousins, though she was a mere minister's daughter."

Sherbourne's arm had found its way around Charlotte's shoulders again. Maybe husbands and wives traveled like this, all snuggled up and informal despite the potholes.

"Fern became enamored of a handsome bounder after we finished school," Charlotte went on. "She couldn't afford London seasons, but her family scraped together some means, and we sewed her dresses ourselves. When she came to town, she went everywhere with me. Then I realized she'd stopped joining me on many of our outings."

"She was smitten?"

Sherbourne's tone was indulgent, the mature male making a tolerant allowance for the follies of young women. Charlotte could leave him to his ignorance, but Fern's memory deserved honesty.

"She was smitten, then she was ruined, then she was dead."

Sherbourne took Charlotte's hand. "I'm sorry. I hope she did not take her own life."

This was the hardest part, the part that still had the power to make Charlotte's throat ache. "She had a child, a little boy. She wrote to me, said she was happy despite all because she loved that child more than life. She did not recover from her lying in. The child's father—a lord's son—never acknowledged her letters, never so much as apologized for her ruin."

Charlotte braced herself for a platitude, which she would somehow manage to endure without tossing Sherbourne from the coach.

These things happen.

A cautionary tale.

Where was the girl's family when she was going so badly astray?

Such a pity.

And the one she dreaded most: *You were her friend. Why couldn't you talk sense into her?*

Why did nobody ever talk sense into the *man* who caused such tragedies? Why wasn't he at least deprived of the ability to wreck another young woman's life and leave another child to be raised in poverty and disgrace?

"Who was the father?" Sherbourne asked.

"I don't know. I have a likeness of him that Fern sent me to save for the child lest her family destroy it, but I have no idea of his name. He frequented Mayfair ballrooms, so he had means as well as family connections. He also had a fiancée with fat settlements, though he didn't bother to tell Fern that until it was too late. If I ever find out who he is, I won't answer for the consequences."

Sherbourne propped a boot on the opposite bench. "If

you do find out, I might be able to ruin him. I'm part owner of a bank that holds many mortgages for the Mayfair set, and I have some influence in Parliament. If his family is titled, so much the better. We can make an example of him and ensure all and sundry know why his debts are being called in."

Charlotte ought to scold her husband for putting his boot on the opposite bench, but she was too stunned by his response.

"You would take the part of my late friend against a lord's son?"

Sherbourne kissed her knuckles. "With pleasure. What foolish young people get up to when chaperones are lax is not my business, but there's a child involved. If it were your child, the father would have been held responsible, and probably forced to marry you, regardless of a fiancée or breach of promise suit. The mother was relatively poor, and thus the bounder suffered no consequences. He probably knew that as he was charming his way under her skirts."

"Thank you," Charlotte said, subsiding against him.

Sherbourne's motivations were his own—he was apparently critical of a class system based on arbitrary ancestry rather than merit—but he shared Charlotte's sense of outrage. If, some fine day, she found out who had destroyed Fern's good name, Sherbourne would make a thorough job of that man's downfall.

A lovely wedding present, did Sherbourne but know it. The loveliest.

Chapter Seven

"Leave the ladies alone," Haverford said. "They have much to discuss, and you owe me a drink."

His Grace had been Sherbourne's neighbor since birth. Their parents and grandparents had been at outs, and thus he and Haverford had been raised to nod curtly at each other in the churchyard—and then only if the vicar was watching.

"Did I, or did I not recently enter into the state of holy matrimony?" Sherbourne countered. "As such, does it not fall to *you* to offer *me* a drink, Your Grace?"

Sherbourne felt entitled to grouse, for Haverford and his duchess had deprived the new bride of the honor of being carried over the threshold by her husband. As soon as the horses had halted, the duchess had flown down the steps of Sherbourne Hall and enveloped Sherbourne in a hug, while Haverford had stood smirking on the terrace. Then Her Grace had swept Charlotte into an equally indecorous embrace and bustled her into the house.

The senior staff had been lined up in the foyer, ready to greet their new lady, and Sherbourne had been relegated to making introductions rather than grand gestures.

"I'll overlook your poor hospitality," Haverford said, pouring two glasses of brandy, "because you are road weary and a traveling coach is nowhere to spend a honeymoon. What were you thinking, whisking the lady from town like that?" He passed Sherbourne a glass, then raised his own. "To wedded bliss."

Sherbourne drank to that. "I was thinking to escape London before I went mad."

"You wanted to see how the mine is progressing." An accusation, from Haverford, who was skeptical of all industries not mentioned approvingly in the Old Testament.

Sherbourne had wanted to get Charlotte home before autumn turned to winter. "The lady's family specifically asked that we wed by special license. If they couldn't be bothered to gather for the nuptials, then why linger in town?"

Haverford tossed another square of peat onto the fire in the library's hearth. "Did you perhaps anticipate the vows? I'm told that's something of a Windham tradition."

"That is none of Your Grace's bloody business, but no, we did not anticipate our vows. I'll thank you to stop wasting my peat."

"Said the man who's mad to dig a coal mine, and we're family now." Haverford was smirking again. "Your business is my business."

Haverford used the cast iron poker to fuss with the fire, and Sherbourne wrestled an urge to toss the duke into the corridor. Haverford was a healthy specimen, dark-haired, tall, and fit, but Sherbourne was an expert on the proper use of the element of surprise.

"I come home," Sherbourne said, "my new bride at my side, and then she's not at my side. She's disappeared to do God knows what with a sister she's had nearly three decades to gossip and conspire with. They saw each other at your own wedding, mere weeks ago, and when I asked Her Grace to oversee a bit of tidying up here at Sherbourne Hall, I did not expect her to kidnap my bride on my very doorstep."

Haverford put down the poker and lounged against the mantel as if he owned the house, the grounds, its fixtures, outbuildings, and livestock. "Been going short of sleep have you? Tending conscientiously to your marital duties?"

"I have escorted my lady wife more than one hundred fifty miles along the king's highway in less than favorable weather. You will please collect your wife and don't allow her back on this property for a week. Perpetual absence on your part would be a singularly insightful wedding gift."

Sherbourne took another sip of his brandy—only the best quality graced his decanters—when he wanted to hurl his drink at the wall. Was a quiet meal with his new wife too much to ask? A little privacy to show her about her new home?

A chance to think through her disclosures in the coach? Charlotte's tale of illicit love gone awry was significant. Whoever authored the downfall of Charlotte's friend had in a sense ruined Charlotte as well, for much of her innocence had died with her friend.

"That is not the expression of a man contemplating marital bliss," Haverford said, wandering away from the fireplace. "Give the ladies time to visit over a pot of tea. Elizabeth was ecstatic to learn of your engagement to Charlotte, and my duchess should be allowed a chance to interrogate her sister."

Sherbourne settled himself onto a sofa that had learned his exact contours years ago. "Sisters interrogate each other?" Charlotte certainly hadn't had many questions for her new husband.

Haverford appropriated the middle of the same sofa, which caused the cushions to bounce. "Are matters off to an acceptable start between you and Mrs. Sherbourne?"

"Again, this is none of your business, but because you will pester me without mercy until I gratify your vulgar curiosity: I hardly know if matters with Charlotte are off to an adequate start."

Haverford propped his boots on a hassock. "Then they are not. If a woman is pleased with her new spouse, he'll know it until he's sore and exhausted."

Sherbourne was sore and exhausted. "You have been married a mere handful of weeks, Your Nosiness. You are hardly an expert on holy matrimony, much less on Charlotte Sherbourne."

The name pleased him. He hoped that someday it pleased his wife.

"I am becoming an expert on how to make my duchess happy. I suggest you apply yourself to the same subject regarding your own spouse."

"The wife who agreed to marry me only after we'd been found in a compromising position by Their Graces of Moreland? The same wife who, five minutes previous to Their Graces' untimely interruption, had been telling me I did her a great honor, but to take myself the hell off? That wife?"

Haverford rose and brought the bottle to the sofa. "Dear me, Sherbourne. How does a woman who's refused your suit manage to be in a compromising situation with you five minutes later? That's like no sort of refusal I've heard of."

A comforting thought that had kept Sherbourne company in an otherwise unforgiving saddle. He held up his glass, and Haverford obliged with another half inch of his host's brandy.

"You don't accuse me of forcing her."

"I'm not stupid, and Charlotte Windham would have had your tallywags in a knot before you'd so much as kissed her, had she been unwilling."

"Consenting to a kiss isn't the same as consenting to marriage." Which thought had also kept Sherbourne company in that unforgiving saddle.

"She did consent to the marriage too, didn't she? This is excellent brandy, if I do say so myself."

"I sent a case over to the castle to remark the occasion of your marriage. Do you have any bastards, Haverford?"

Haverford set his drink aside. "I beg your pardon?"

"We're family now, God help us. Your business is my business."

"I have no illegitimate offspring. What about you?"

"None. Why doesn't a duke of nearly ancient years have any by-blows? Polite society hasn't grown that priggish, has it?"

"Sherbourne," the duke said gently, "you are married to the granddaughter of a duke, the sister of two duchesses, the cousin of countless titles. *You* are now polite society, which ought to restore anybody's faith in miracles. I haven't any children born out of wedlock because they and their mamas cost money and create complications. I'm none too wealthy and prefer to avoid needless drama."

"So by-blows are still acceptable, and turning one's back on them is not?"

"You've become a quick study. Moreland himself raised a pair of by-blows with the ducal herd. If a man takes responsibility for his actions, society tolerates the results. If he doesn't, he's no gentleman."

Then society must know nothing of the *affaire* that had resulted in the ruin of Charlotte's friend.

"I assume you've looked in on the colliery," Sherbourne said. "How do matters stand there?"

Haverford took that bait. The duke had resisted allowing any mines in the valley, until he and Sherbourne had reached a compromise: one mine, developed along Haverford's notions of the valley's best interests. The duke refused to own shares in the venture, which made his informal oversight disinterested.

Ninety minutes later, Sherbourne was finally escorting Haverford and his duchess to the front door. Charlotte did look a bit more the thing for having been closeted with her sister.

"Did you have a peek at your bedchamber?" Her Grace asked as she kissed Sherbourne on the cheek.

"I'm sure it's lovely," he replied.

Haverford held out Her Grace's gloves. "Stop whispering to my duchess."

"We're family now," the duchess said. "Whispering is part of the fun. Come along, Haverford, I've a few things to whisper in your ear as well."

They wafted down the steps on a cloud of connubial damned joy, leaving behind a profoundly welcome quiet.

Sherbourne both closed and locked the door, feeling as if he'd repelled a siege.

"They're always like that," Charlotte said, a little forlornly. "They were that way in town too. I don't think they knew anybody else was at the church when they spoke their vows."

"I've banished them for a week. Have you ordered a bath?"

"That is a splendid notion."

"Let's have a tray in the library, and by the time your bath is ready, we'll have eaten."

Sherbourne's library was a mere gesture compared to the collection at Haverford Castle, which meant the room was cozy. They ate in companionable informality, though Sherbourne marveled to think he could discuss ordering a bath with a female, and she regarded the idea as splendid rather than scandalous.

Charlotte excused herself to enjoy her bath, and Sherbourne used the time to go through the correspondence stacked in date order on his desk. He gave Charlotte an hour—fifty-two minutes—to soak, then made his way to the ground floor suite now serving as the master bedroom.

He found the new Mrs. Sherbourne swaddled in his favorite dressing gown, fast asleep in a chair by the fire.

"Thus begins the wedding night," he murmured.

Mrs. Sherbourne slumbered on.

After he'd warmed the sheets and pillows, Sherbourne scooped her up and deposited her on the bed, dressing gown and all. He tucked the covers around her, blew out the candles, banked the fire, and went back to the correspondence waiting for him in the library.

* * *

Charlotte slept like a debutante after her court presentation, felled by profound fatigue and relentless worry. Her first thought, before she'd entirely awakened, was that she was near the ground, the safest place to be.

She opened her eyes and was greeted by unfamiliar surroundings, and yet the sense of being anchored rather than one or two floors higher than she preferred would not leave her.

"Mr. Sherbourne said to let you have your rest, ma'am. I've kept the tea hot, and there's chocolate too, if you prefer."

The voice belonged to a giantess of a maid, and she'd spoken in Welsh.

I'm in Wales, in my husband's house. In my new house. "We're on the ground floor, aren't we?" Charlotte could hardly recall arriving, though Elizabeth had been on hand, and then there had been enormous trays in the library, to which Sherbourne had done swift justice. Charlotte had enjoyed a lovely, hot, bath...

"Right you are, ma'am. The footmen had a time moving the furniture downstairs, but Her Grace got us organized. Would you like breakfast in bed?"

The bed was huge and singularly lacking in evidence of another occupant. "I'll use the table by the window. What's your name?"

The girl—for she was quite young, despite her grand proportions—popped a curtsy. "Heulwen Jones, ma'am. Most at Sherbourne Hall call me Heulwen, because half the staff are Joneses."

Heulwen meant sunshine, and the name suited her. She was plain and freckled with bright red hair peeking from beneath a white cap.

Charlotte struggled from the bed, and Heulwen held up a dressing gown Charlotte hadn't seen since she'd left London.

"You unpacked for me?"

"Mr. Sherbourne said we were to see to your *every* comfort. When he uses *that* tone, even lazy Owen Jenkins pays heed. Owen is ever so handsome to hear his mama tell it.

Handsome is as handsome does, I always say. Chocolate or tea, ma'am?"

"Let's start with chocolate. Owen is the first footman, if I recall correctly?"

Heulwen made the bed and freely discussed her coworkers while Charlotte munched on fluffy eggs and buttered toast. Most-call-me-Heulwen was not by any standard a London house servant.

Thank the heavenly intercessors for that mercy.

"What did you mean, that the footmen had to move furniture about?" Charlotte asked, when the maid had laced her into a comfortable day dress.

Heulwen tidied up the tea cart, making enough racket to mortify any Mayfair housemaid. "Mr. Sherbourne sent word to the duchess that the master bedroom was to be moved to the ground floor. Himself takes an occasional queer start, and Her Grace says newlyweds must be indulged. Her being newly wed to His Grace, she must know what she's about. And she's your sister, and a duchess, so we did as we were told."

Sherbourne had moved his bedroom to the ground floor?

"Heulwen, you have made my first morning in my new home comfortable, and for that I thank you. Have you any idea where Mr. Sherbourne might be?"

Town servants didn't expect thanks, and town employers would not ask the maid where the master had got off to. Town was one hundred and fifty miles away, and for the first time, Charlotte was glad.

"Mr. Sherbourne has gone down to the works, ma'am, and best he does that while the rain has let up. I'd rather it snow, though Mrs. Moss says I'm daft, but I'm not. We've had nothing but rain for the past fortnight, and enough is enough. Snow is much prettier than mud, I always say."

The day outside had a sunny, blustery look that presaged changeable weather and swift-moving clouds. Like friendly servants, fresh air was another rarity in London, especially as the coal fires heated up in colder weather.

"Please ask Mrs. Moss to meet me in the library," Charlotte said, opening one of two large wardrobes. She was greeted with an assortment of waistcoats, shirts, and morning coats.

One question answered. The second wardrobe held Charlotte's effects. She wrapped her favorite plain wool shawl about her shoulders.

"Tomorrow, you needn't bring both tea and chocolate for me. Chocolate will do."

Heulwen gave her a curious look. "Yes, ma'am."

Last night's glimpses of the house had left an impression of luxury on a tasteful scale. Sherbourne Hall wasn't a castle, but neither was it a manor house with bare, narrow corridors and more pantries than bedrooms. The appointments were spotless, the carpets bright, the corners free of cobwebs.

The staff valued either their master or their wages, and the housekeeper was competent. The master of the house apparently set little store by his own life, however, for he failed to appear for either luncheon or dinner.

The clock was chiming ten when Charlotte gave up pretending to embroider in the library, and returned to the bedroom. She dismissed the maid, built up the fire for the night, and started rehearsing her first proper rant as Mrs. Lucas Sherbourne.

The unforgivably neglected, furiously impatient, anxious-beyond-all-bearing Mrs. Lucas Sherbourne.

* * *

Thus far, Sherbourne did not like being married. He liked his wife well enough, what he knew of her, but he did not like his household having been put at sixes and sevens by the addition of a female. His valet was nowhere to be found, when by rights, Turnbull ought to have been dozing in a handy dressing closet.

Sherbourne's sleeping arrangements, his staff, his schedule, his everything was changing because he'd taken a wife.

And there she slept, in the same chair by the fire where he'd found her the previous night.

Sherbourne washed as thoroughly and quietly as he could, and decided against shaving. As tired as he was, he'd probably cut his own throat and not notice until Charlotte scolded him for the resulting mess.

Another night in the library beckoned, lest he waken at some ungodly hour and reach for his wife uninvited.

"Mr. Sherbourne." Charlotte hadn't moved, though she had opened her eyes. Cats did that, went from restful contemplation to poised alertness merely by opening their eyes.

"Madam, I apologize for waking you." Apologizing was a skill smart husbands doubtless perfected in the first week of marriage.

"Where have you been, sir?"

Charlotte's tone—one he'd not heard since he'd been in leading strings—rather woke him up. "At the colliery, where apparently nothing can go forward without my hand on the figurative plough. If you want to tear a strip off me for abandoning you the livelong day, now is a good time to do so, because I'll sleep through most of your lecture."

He dared not admit that he'd been so overset by the state of works that he'd lost track of the time.

Charlotte rose and came closer, bringing with her the floral scent of French soap. She wore a dressing gown that covered her from neck to toes, but the way she moved told him that beneath the satin finery, she wore no stays or bindings.

"You had the master bedroom moved to the ground floor. Why?"

Because my wife shouldn't have to be afraid even as she dreams. "Because you'll sleep better in a room without a balcony. If you sleep better, so will I."

His honesty earned him a small smile. "What's amiss at the mine?"

"Everything, and it's not even a mine yet. My engineer claims he was laid low by an ague, but I suspect he overimbibes, which was why I could hire him away from the works at Waxter. If something seems too good to be true, it *is* too good to be true."

"What about last night?" Charlotte smoothed the lapels of his dressing gown. "Were you at the works last night too?"

In his nightmares. "I fell asleep at my desk in the library."

"Ah, but *why* did you fall asleep at your desk in the library? Are you having second thoughts about this marriage?"

And third and fourth thoughts. Also *married* thoughts about the woman standing barefoot before him.

"I spoke vows, Charlotte. Second thoughts don't come into it."

She gave him a disappointed look. Too late Sherbourne realized he'd blundered into a verbal trap. If he'd answered honestly—yes, this hasty, expedient union had left him with many reservations—Charlotte would be hurt, even if she'd been harboring similar doubts.

If he professed a false enthusiasm for their marriage, she'd be disappointed in him for dissembling.

"If you have no second thoughts, Mr. Sherbourne, you are the first newlywed in the history of marriage to enjoy certainty about nuptial obligations entered into under dubious circumstances. I have second thoughts."

After firing off that round of marital artillery, Charlotte marched to the bed, unbelted her robe, and climbed beneath the covers.

Sherbourne considered another night on the library sofa, another retreat into a bachelor's privileges, and rejected the notion. The library was chilly, the sofa lumpy, and the whole room smelled of peat smoke and books.

Charlotte smelled much nicer, and she was his wife.

Sherbourne blew out the candles, banked the fire, draped his dressing gown over Charlotte's at the foot of the bed—a metaphor, that—and appropriated the opposite side of the mattress. Some fool had forgotten to warm the sheets, which was probably a blessing.

"Tell me of your second thoughts, Mrs. Sherbourne."

A gusty sigh greeted his invitation.

"Madam wife, I'd like to hear your second thoughts, if you're inclined to share them."

On the other side of the bed, a good yard from where Sherbourne lay, Charlotte shifted. "I was prepared to endure you."

Likewise, I'm sure. "We are man and wife. I'm confident a fair amount of enduring will be necessary all around."

She stirred about some more. "I meant..."

Sherbourne waited. He was not up to this conversation

at this hour, but the alternative was sleeping in the library, possibly for the next thirty-seven years.

"I *worried* about you," Charlotte said. "The weather was fickle, you were gone for hours, and you didn't send a note. Men are pigheaded, and mines can be dangerous."

"You worried about me." The unhappy former bachelor part of Sherbourne wanted to resent her worry, to see it as yet another burden, more proof that marriage was an undeserved penance.

Except... nobody worried over Lucas Sherbourne. They worried that he'd call in their debts, accelerate a promissory note, reveal the state of their finances.

They did not worry *about him*.

"I'll send a note next time I'm delayed. We haven't even dug our main shaft yet and won't until spring at the rate we're *not* progressing. I'll show you around the premises tomorrow, if the weather's fair."

"Thank you."

He didn't want her thanks. He wanted to get to sleep, to forget this whole miserable, bloody day, and wake up with his life back as it had been before he'd gone to London.

And he wanted to wrap himself around his wife and know that he was welcome in her embrace.

Sherbourne pondered that insight for several long minutes.

"Charlotte?"

A soft sigh, and then, "'Night, Bethan."

Now, she was drifting off? "We have only the one tub that's large enough to accommodate me, the one you were using last night. I wanted to bathe but couldn't, and then it was too late to wake the staff. One shouldn't come to one's new bride in all one's dirt when consummating a marriage."

Sherbourne delivered a few sincere blows to his pillow. His explanation had sounded like Haverford giving a Boxing Day speech at the punch bowl. Sherbourne had bathed thoroughly before leaving the house that morning, and in the normal course would have bathed again before retiring.

He was married now, and the normal course was nothing but a fond memory.

* * *

"I know you're awake," Sherbourne said, stretching his chin up and scraping a razor along his throat.

"I'm admiring the view," Charlotte replied, from the cozy haven of the bed. Some of the leaden fatigue of travel had eased, and she'd shared a bed with her husband for the first time. She was also getting her first look at him naked from the waist up. "You don't use a valet in the morning?"

Sherbourne tapped the razor against a porcelain basin and took another smooth swipe over his throat and jaw.

"I did without a manservant for years, and Turnbull has enough to do seeing to my wardrobe. You don't snore."

"Neither do you, though you talk in your sleep."

He shot her an amused look in the mirror, as near as she could tell. His left cheek was still covered with lather. "I do not."

"You mutter about timbers, ventilation, and hoses. Very romantic."

"Very profitable, I hope. Would you like to see the colliery today?"

Charlotte would like to see her husband without his breeches. She was reassured to learn that she found him attractive in a semi-undressed state. Very attractive.

"I would, if it's not too much bother."

"No bother at all." He was soon finished shaving, and donning a shirt and waistcoat.

Charlotte climbed out of bed to tie his cravat, and from a tray on his vanity she chose a simple silver pin to secure it.

"This is the most subdued waistcoat you own." Plain black, though silk-lined and well made. He had several more like it in the wardrobe—dark green, grey, brown. Charlotte had gone through his clothes press as well, finding that fewer than half of his waistcoats adhered to the peacock style of his London attire.

"A colliery is a monument to dirt, or mud depending on the season. You'll take a chill without your dressing gown."

Charlotte was wearing a lawn nightgown that fell below her knees. Before she could assure Sherbourne that she was warm enough, he'd draped her night robe over her shoulders, though she caught him glancing down and then fixing his gaze over her head.

Oh. *Oh.* "Do we ride or drive to the colliery?" Charlotte asked, finding the robe's sleeves.

"Drive, given the dampness."

Heulwen interrupted with the tea cart, and an awkward moment arose as Sherbourne grumbled about the kitchen forgetting his damned tea in their haste to impress the lady of the house.

"Share my chocolate," Charlotte suggested, taking a seat at the table by the window. "I'm sure the teapot will be on the tray tomorrow."

"It had better be," Sherbourne muttered, taking the opposite chair. "How soon can you be ready to leave?"

Charlotte set down her chocolate and threw caution to the wind. "If you'll lace me up, fifteen minutes after we finish our meal." Husbands did that. Charlotte had been assured of same by no less than three sisters and five cousins.

The look Sherbourne gave her was wary and intrigued. "Lace you up."

"If you insist that we share a bedchamber, then you'd best be prepared to make yourself useful. I tied your cravat, and I assume you're capable of dealing with my stays. They're not complicated."

Sherbourne applied strawberry jam to a triangle of toast and set it on Charlotte's plate. "I can manage your stays. Wear boots. The colliery will be a swamp given all the rain here lately."

Charlotte served him eggs, they shared the pot of chocolate, and the meal progressed in domestic tranquility. Sherbourne excused himself to let the stables know to hitch up the landau, and Charlotte chose an older carriage dress that was more comfortable than stylish.

As it happened, Heulwen came back to collect the tea cart, so Charlotte prevailed on the maid for assistance with her stays. When Sherbourne returned, Charlotte was putting the finishing touches on her coiffure, a simple knot secured with pins.

"You managed without me," he said.

"I gather time is of the essence," Charlotte replied, rising. "Shall we be off?"

He held the door, and Charlotte could read nothing in his gaze. Not relief, but not disappointment either.

Chapter Eight

Somewhere between pummeling the pillow, staring at the bed canopy by the hour, falling asleep to the sound of Charlotte's sighs, and waking in a state of procreative readiness well before dawn, Sherbourne had had a brilliant insight.

He was a married man.

As Charlotte had said, no sensible person arrived to the married state free of all misgivings. His misgivings were the sort that would abate with time or grow worse. He couldn't think himself into trusting Charlotte's regard for him, and he couldn't talk himself out of his regard for her.

He'd offered for her because he was convinced they'd suit. She'd refused him, and then she'd *changed her mind.* Women changed their minds all the time, as did men.

Charlotte had put up with being hauled away from her family on her very wedding day.

She'd barely scolded Sherbourne for neglecting her on her first day in her new home.

She'd *worried* about him.

The image that stayed with Sherbourne on the chilly drive to the colliery was Charlotte, barefoot, her nightgown dipping low across her bosom, while she tied a neat Mathematical knot in his cravat. She'd fashioned it perfectly the first time, though even Turnbull occasionally resorted to fresh linen to get the look just so.

The confluence of emotions assailing Sherbourne as Charlotte had knotted his cravat had been uncomfortable: desire, affection, protectiveness, tenderness, joy, and some messy, inconvenient yearning that blended all of the above. Maybe Haverford had a word for it, not that Sherbourne would inquire.

"Can we see the works from the house?" Charlotte asked.

"Yes, though only from the upper floors of the east wing. By the lanes, the distance is nearly a mile and a half. Across the fields, it's less than a mile."

"I read about coal mining yesterday. You have many books on the subject."

Was that a rebuke for leaving her unattended? "Feel free to add to the library so the collection reflects your interests as well as mine."

"Elizabeth is the bookworm. Has she driven you daft with her lending library scheme?"

"Yes." Daft and somewhat short of coin. Sherbourne had agreed to finance Her Grace's charitable libraries in part as consideration for Haverford's acceptance of the mine.

"Then you must assign the library project duties to me," Charlotte said. "Elizabeth means well, but I won't allow her to ride roughshod over common sense. She'd turn every schoolchild into a literary critic and leave the nation devoid of farmers, laundresses, and other useful people."

"You have no interest in libraries."

"Neither do you."

A gentleman didn't argue with a lady when she was right. Instead Sherbourne handed his wife down from the landau carefully, making quite certain she had her footing before he dropped his hands from her waist.

As she linked arms with him, he came to another brilliant insight, this one not half so cheering: Their marriage would best be consummated at the time and place of *Charlotte's* choosing. For both of their sakes, she should not merely endure his attentions, but welcome them.

"You're constructing houses of stone?" Charlotte asked, as he guided her along a gravel path. "That has to be costing a fortune."

The "works" were a warren of cart tracks, stacked supplies, excavations, and tents. Heavy machinery sat under tarps, and some of the property was staked with ropes and cords. An enormous pile of building stone lay in a great, grey heap beyond the tents.

Why on earth had he thought she might be interested in any of it?

"We have lumber here in Wales," Sherbourne said, "unlike most of England, but we have stone in greater abundance. Stone dwellings will last, whereas anything constructed of wood falls prey to the elements. Besides, stonemasons are easier to find locally than carpenters, and local craftsmen will do a better job than itinerants."

"You've even accounted for kitchen gardens." Tidy rectangles had been laid out with twine behind where the long rows of houses would stand.

"Haverford's idea, and we're to have hogs, sheep, and chickens, also a few dairy cows. The colliery will be an estate of sorts, an experiment."

A young man trotted forth from one of the tents. "Beg pardon, Mr. Sherbourne, Mr. Hannibal Jones would like a moment, if you can spare the time."

"Tell Mr. Jones—" Sherbourne began.

"Tell Mr. Jones that Mr. Sherbourne will be along directly," Charlotte said.

The lad tugged his cap and darted back the way he'd come.

"I spent all of yesterday with Mr. Jones," Sherbourne said, "and I left him with a list of tasks that's so long, he ought not have the time to bother me today."

"You could hire a manager."

Well, no, Sherbourne could not. The basic idea—dig a hole, haul out the coal—was complicated by issues of drainage, ventilation, safe accumulation of the slag, and safe construction of the shafts. Miners—women and children included—died every year as a result of tunnels collapsing, flooding, or catching fire. Slag heaps in the wrong position caused landslides, and abandoned shafts filled with water that then flooded the working portions of the mine.

Even the housing area had a substantial retaining wall behind it, reinforcing the steep rise of a hillside.

"I will not hire a manager," Sherbourne said. "Not yet. Managers have a way of creating more problems than they solve when an undertaking is getting started. They make independent decisions when they should consult me and fail to show initiative about trivial matters. When the mine is producing a profit, then I'll find somebody trustworthy to oversee daily operations."

Above all else, managers cost money.

"Deal with Mr. Jones," Charlotte said. "I'll be fine on my own."

Sherbourne would not be fine. "Rescue me in about five minutes, please. Jones likes to spout numbers for the sake of impressing his audience."

"I'll count the timbers in yonder stack," Charlotte said. "Or pace off the distance between the last house and the first garden. I like how geometrical this place is and I can't wait to see it when it's a working mine. Where will you put the schoolhouse?"

What schoolhouse? "Haven't decided yet. Perhaps you'll have some ideas."

She smiled at him, Sherbourne smiled back, and then— because a newly married man should be allowed to express a bit of affection for his wife when on his own property— he brushed a kiss to her cheek.

"Five minutes, madam." He moved off toward the main tent, though something—perhaps a lady's gloved hand— brushed softly over his fundament before he'd taken the first step.

* * *

Charlotte saw a side of her husband at the colliery she would never have glimpsed in the library or the bedroom: Sherbourne was passionate about his mining venture.

All the fire and focus he could bring to a kiss expressed itself just as eloquently when he waxed poetical about cables, steam power, tram tracks, and drainage. His vision went on for miles and decades, to the point that his works would someday have a private dock for loading coal directly onto coastal barges.

The mine was still mostly equipment and raw materials stacked under tarps, but Charlotte could smell that watchword of commerce in the air—*progress*.

She slipped into the tent perhaps fifteen minutes after parting from her husband and eavesdropped on an argument between Sherbourne and a white-haired, red-faced terrier of a man who seemed irate about the masons' schedule.

The tent was ringed with tables, and on every available surface lay maps, graphs, bills of lading, and technical drawings. All quite lovely—quite *numerical*.

"The damned miners can sleep in tents," the smaller man was saying, as Charlotte perched on a stool. "They're accustomed to dwelling in the very bowels of the earth. Put the masons to building the tram now, so you'll have it ready to go in the spring."

Charlotte ran her finger down a timber merchant's bill. "Language, Mr. Jones."

Both men looked up sharply, as if she'd materialized from the celestial beyond.

"Beg your pardon, ma'am. Humbly beg your pardon."

Charlotte rose. "Mr. Sherbourne, won't you introduce us?"

Her husband obliged and stood by silently while Charlotte asked Mr. Jones a few questions. How had he chosen the scale upon which to draw his elevations? What had first interested him in engineering and how had he been trained? Was there a Mrs. Hannibal Jones?

"Gone these five years, God rest her soul."

Sherbourne took out a gold pocket watch, flicked it open, then snapped it closed.

"You must miss her very much," Charlotte said.

"I miss her smiles, her cooking, her—well, yes, ma'am. After twenty-two years of marriage, I miss my Florrie powerfully."

"So you understand why the masons really ought to finish at least a portion of the houses before they start on your tram, don't you? The men will be happier if they're not pining for their families, and I'm sure Mrs. Jones would have agreed with me that happy fellows do better work. Of course, a temporary dormitory for the bachelors could be erected fairly quickly, but I'm sure Mr. Sherbourne has discussed that with you."

Mr. Sherbourne was staring at his closed watch, though Charlotte knew he was listening.

"Right," Mr. Jones said. "A dormitory for the bachelors, who are always the first to come around looking for work, and usually the least skilled, which means they are exactly the fellows to build my tram line."

"We'll discuss it later." Sherbourne shoved his watch into its pocket. "I've promised my wife a tour of the premises, and unless I want her to get a soaking in the process, I'd best be about keeping my word."

Charlotte sent a wistful look at all the figures, charts, and tabulations. "A pleasure, Mr. Jones."

Sherbourne had her out of the tent in the next three seconds. "A bachelor's dormitory isn't in the budget."

"You expected all of your employees to be married?"

"I'm guilty of an oversight. A budgetary oversight."

Budgetary oversights apparently numbered among the deadly sins. "This is your first mine. How can you expect to get every detail right?"

This was Charlotte's first marriage, but she suffered the same need to appear competent that plagued her husband.

"Because it's not my first business, and all businesses require labor. Did I think the men would sleep in the trees?" He paced along in silence for some twenty yards. "This is why I should have taken on a partner sooner."

A partner—not a wife. "I beg your pardon?"

"A partner, somebody who knows mining, as Lord Brantford does. I don't bother with tenant farms because I know little about farming. What to plant where and in what order, when to fallow, when to graze sheep in the valley, when to move them up to the hillsides. I have no interest in such undertakings, so I rent out my acres year-to-year to those who know what they're about."

"You do have an interest in mining?" Charlotte did, and she'd been at the colliery less than an hour.

"I thought I did, but what sort of mine owner forgets that his men need a warm place to sleep between shifts?"

Charlotte let her imagination roam over the heavy carts stacked upside down in a neat bank, huge spools of cable sitting under an open-sided tent, the small mountain of gravel piled at the top of a grade where houses would someday sit. The site was muddy and deserted on this bleak autumn day, but in six months, it would be bustling with people and productivity.

"Might I have a look at your site plan, Mr. Sherbourne? If the children are using your schoolhouse during the day, the bachelors can set up cots and make a dormitory of it overnight."

"My schoolhouse," he muttered, gazing off at the pile of gravel. "I suppose my lending library will be housed in the same palatial edifice?"

"A lending library can be a few shelves of books to be-gin with," Charlotte said, taking his arm, "just as a mine can be a few sketches and some ambition. Do you have un-occupied tenant cottages on your land?"

"Three. My last tenants left a year ago."

"Then use one of those tenant cottages for your school-house dormitory, or demolish the largest cottage and put the materials to use here."

Sherbourne looped his arms around Charlotte's shoulders and drew her against him. Nobody was about, though Mr. Jones was shouting in the tent thirty yards away.

Charlotte held her husband, the experience novel, for all she'd done it before. They stood in the middle of a muddy, unattractive work site, under a grey, forbidding sky, and nothing of desire colored their embrace.

But something of marriage did, something of hope.

"I have a set of site plans at the house," Sherbourne said. "I'll be happy to show them to you. The best view of the works is from the top of that hill. Shall we have a look?"

He kept her hand in his all the way up to the summit. The trek wasn't steep, but the way was wet and the wind became sharper the higher they climbed. When they reached the hilltop, Sherbourne spoke for a long time, about his reasons for choosing the site and for laying it out as he had.

When he pointed over Charlotte's shoulder to indicate where the tram tracks would run, Charlotte relaxed back against him.

His arm came around her waist, and he fell silent, a warm, solid wall of husband at her back.

"When I considered marriage at all," Charlotte said, "I saw myself stuck in a cheerful, tidy parlor, pouring tea for an endless procession of gossiping women. My husband would be off until all hours being fitted for a new pair of boots or playing cards with his friends. Children would come along just as I was about to suffer strong hysterics from sheer boredom."

Sherbourne turned her gently by the shoulders, and another embrace ensued as the wind whipped at Charlotte's skirts, and a fine mist threatened to turn to rain.

"It won't be like that," she said, wanting to laugh and

cry at the same time. Laugh for sheer joy, and cry for the young woman who'd spent years dreading a dismal fate. "With us, it won't be like that."

Sherbourne kissed her with a restrained hunger that matched the rising wind. "Our marriage will never be like that. Not for either one of us."

She expected he'd turn loose of her, and they'd hurry down the hill ahead of the next downpour, but Sherbourne instead wrapped her close.

"I've changed my mind about something, Mrs. Sherbourne."

Lord, he was warm. "You don't want the schoolhouse and the dormitory to be in the same building?"

"Hang the blasted schoolhouse. I told you that we'd consummate our vows at the time and place of our choosing."

What had once filled Charlotte with trepidation now interested her mightily. "Ours will not be a white marriage, Mr. Sherbourne. You promised me the full menu of husbandly attentions."

The rain started, a soft shower—for now.

"I will keep my promise, but not at the time and place of our choosing."

Thinking was difficult when a husband turned such blue, blue eyes on his wife. "And now?"

"We will consummate our vows at the time and place of *your* choosing, and I pray to the almighty powers that you choose to avail yourself of my intimate favors soon and often."

* * *

Charlotte's hems were a mess by the time Sherbourne returned her to Sherbourne Hall, but she didn't seem to notice, much less mind. When he handed her down from the landau, he and his wife stood for a moment nearly embracing, *regarding* each other.

He wanted her—he'd shown her that before they'd become engaged—but he also wanted her to want him back, and—*mirabile dictu*—she apparently did.

Despite the difference in their stations, despite the dubious beginning of their union, Charlotte was willing to go forward in good faith.

Or so she'd have him believe. She beamed up at him as if he'd promised to buy her an entire jewelry establishment on Ludgate Hill.

Minx. "Shall we go inside, Mrs. Sherbourne?"

She twined her arm with his. "I asked Cook to make us a proper lunch. Hot soup, beef and ham with all the trimmings. She said you eat whatever she puts in front of you, but that will have to stop."

"You'd starve me?" Now that Charlotte had mentioned food, Sherbourne realized he was famished.

"I'd pamper you. The menus should reflect your likes and dislikes. Because you are so invariably appreciative, Cook isn't sure what those are."

And here, he'd thought sending his regular compliments to the kitchen was simply good manners.

As the groom led the carriage horses away, the front door of the house swung open, revealing the butler, standing militarily straight in the foyer. Sherbourne considered carrying Charlotte over the threshold, then discarded that daft notion, but did set about removing her bonnet and cloak once he'd escorted her inside.

A husband performed those courtesies, and now Sherbourne understood why: They were an excuse to stand close to his wife and to touch her.

"I like hot food to come to the table hot," Sherbourne said, untying Charlotte's bonnet ribbons, "and Cook excels at that miracle. I like meat well cooked, but not burned, which she also invariably manages. I like good wine, which Crandall here has a knack for choosing."

Crandall gave Charlotte's bonnet a shake, sending water droplets all over the carpet. "My thanks, sir."

Sherbourne passed the butler Charlotte's cloak, and Charlotte began unbuttoning her husband's greatcoat.

"I like some flowers on the table," she said. "Nothing elaborate. One shouldn't have to peer around a centerpiece as if one were wildlife in the hedge."

She gave Sherbourne a shove. He turned and she slid the garment from his shoulders. Turnbull had done likewise numerous times—minus the shove—but the gesture had felt entirely different.

Charlotte handed the coat to Crandall, then took Sherbourne's top hat.

"Rotten weather." Sherbourne eyed himself in the mirror, and swiped at his hair to erase the creases left by his hat.

"Let me." Charlotte ran her fingers through his hair, as Crandall took an inordinately long time to hang their outer apparel on the hooks opposite the porter's nook.

Amusement and frustrated desire were an interesting combination. Sherbourne clasped his wife's wrists. "That will be quite enough, madam."

She merely wrapped herself about his arm again. "Did you know that the Windhams are great believers in naps in the middle of the day?"

"If you bestow any more such helpful insights regarding your family's domestic habits, I will not survive until sundown."

"Yes, you will." Charlotte went up on her toes to kiss his cheek. "It's tonight for which you must fortify yourself."

And for the next forty-seven years. Sherbourne had always enjoyed a challenge. "Will you rest after lunch? I promised Jones I'd go back to the works. The old boy frets if I don't spend at least half my day arguing with him."

"Does he have an assistant?"

"He has boys to order about. They are less expensive than an assistant engineer."

Why werc there no fresh flowers at Sherbourne Hall? Autumn was advancing, but surely the conservatory had a few blooms yet.

"If Mr. Jones should go visit family," Charlotte said, "or if he falls prey to another ague, who can find anything amid all the maps, papers, bills, and estimates littering that tent?"

An extraordinary thought assailed Sherbourne as he seated his wife at the table in the breakfast parlor: Charlotte would make an excellent assistant to Hannibal Jones. Her air of feminine authority would accomplish more than Sherbourne's orders ever had.

But then, if Charlotte were on site at the works, Sherbourne would be distracted by his wife bustling about and smelling of flowers the livelong day.

"Prior to my London trip, I had a fair sense of where Jones had stacked which documents." Sherbourne took his own seat and sent the footman at the sideboard a glance. "In my absence, Jones has become disorganized." Or possibly a tornado had touched down inside the engineer's tent.

The footman remained at his post, gloved hands folded, gaze straight ahead.

"We'll start with the soup," Charlotte said, offering the

servant a smile. "A small portion for me, though I suspect Mr. Sherbourne is in *good appetite*."

That salvo could not go unanswered. Sherbourne lifted his wife's hand to his lips. "I'm famished."

"Of course, ma'am." The footman, Ninian Morgan by name, refused to meet Sherbourne's gaze while the soup was served, but Sherbourne's loyal servant was clearly amused.

Charlotte used their first proper meal as husband and wife to interrogate Sherbourne about the mine. When would it be operational? How much ore would it ship? What quality? How many men would be employed? Her appetite for information matched Sherbourne's apprecia-tion for the food on the table. She consumed facts and figures at a great rate, all the while asking how Sherbourne liked this dish or that cut of meat.

And to think he'd worried that they'd have nothing to talk about.

"Will you rest this afternoon?" he asked, as the plates were cleared. As soon as the question was out of his mouth, he realized he'd put it to her once before.

"Rest? From what?"

"From running all over the works with me this morning. Hiking to the summit, braving the elements." *Kissing me witless.*

"This morning's outing, while interesting and enjoy-able, was hardly taxing. I have lists to make, and I might pay a call on my sister."

Sherbourne rose to hold Charlotte's chair, and debated whether to steal a kiss now that the room was free of ser-vants. "Am I to accompany you on this call?"

"Asked the condemned man of his jailer? Do you truly dislike Haverford that much?"

"I resent him," Sherbourne said. "He was born into wealth and consequence he did nothing to earn."

Charlotte patted Sherbourne's cheek. "So were you, so was I, which is why we must use our resources responsibly and not squander them on fleeting indulgences."

Sherbourne stopped with her at the door to the corridor. "I'm not a damned duke, and if I have nineteen generations of sons, none of them will be dukes, either."

"But the twenty-first might, Mr. Sherbourne, while if I have a thousand generations of daughters, none of them will ever be a duke. Women are half the population, but once we marry, we legally cease to exist, simply because we had the great misfortune to be born female. The highest ambition my daughters might have is to marry a duke and bear his children. Perhaps you'd like to trade places with me? I'm told childbirth is the most painful privilege known to . . . well, not man, because men never have to endure it."

She blinked up at him, as if this were a serious debate.

"I will concede that I was born to significant privilege," he said. "I also work my arse off."

Charlotte withdrew the pin from Sherbourne's cravat, rearranged the linen folds, and fastened them again. "Haverford spends his days lounging about on velvet pillows, then? I must take Elizabeth to task for allowing such sloth."

Good God, she was dauntless. "Maybe that's why I resent Haverford—because he's so blasted saintly. Farmers name their children after him, old women gossip with him in the churchyard, and he actually listens to them."

"Dastardly of him. What's the real reason you and he don't get on well?"

The morning spent hiking around the work site had left Sherbourne hungry. This exchange with Charlotte taxed him in a different sense. His wife made him *think*, and not about the expenses involved in establishing a working colliery.

"Haverford owed me a substantial sum."

Charlotte made a "yes, yes, and?" motion with her hand. "Now he owes you much less."

"Now he owes me nothing, because I forgave him the balance of the loan as a wedding present. Tore up the promissory notes and sent them to him with a signed release. For years, though, he took it upon himself to improve this tenant farm, or import that new strain of sheep. He employed half the valley in his great, crumbling castle, and he kept the shops in the village in custom feeding and clothing his army of servants."

"And?"

"And he could manage all of that because I forbore to collect on the debts he owed me. In a sense, all of his commerce and charity, every bit of it, was undertaken with my money. He's well loved and respected, while I'm the modern-day Grendel, laying waste to a paradise of Haverford's making. I want to sink this mine, Charlotte, not because it will make me rich—it won't, though I expect it to be profitable—but because the land can't support all the families who dwell here."

She was listening, which was more than Haverford seemed to do.

"Haverford means well," Sherbourne went on, "but he lacks vision. I can employ a hundred men at that mine, while Haverford would have to come up with at least twenty farms to keep them in work. We aren't making any new farms, and unless we take to the Dutch habit of reclaiming land from the sea, we never will. Corn prices fluctuate wildly, but the world will always, always need to keep warm."

Why couldn't Haverford, a reasonably intelligent man, see that?

Charlotte slipped her arms around Sherbourne's waist and gave him her weight.

What sort of reply was this? Sherbourne stood in the doorway, awkwardly poised to hug her in return, then settling to the embrace for an odd, quiet moment.

"You are a good man," Charlotte said. "I didn't think you were a bad man, but I'm glad to know that your ambition is not merely for yourself. In this, you and Haverford are the same. The welfare of your neighbors concerns you. You know it, and I know it."

For her that seemed to decide the matter. Sherbourne rested his cheek against her temple. Her hair was still damp from the rain and bore the fragrance of gardenias, a sweet, substantial scent that calmed him.

Or perhaps holding his wife did that. She was warm and pliant in his arms, and abruptly, the prospect of an afternoon spent yelling at Mr. Jones in a cold, damp tent held no appeal.

Charlotte nuzzled his cravat. "One of the lists I'll make is of local families upon whom we will call. We are newly married, and thus socializing is required."

They were to converse while holding each other, right in the doorway of the breakfast parlor. Married life was a procession of revelations.

"I will endure the civilities if I must."

"You must. We will also have guests for dinner, and work up to a dinner party or two. At Christmas, we'll have an open house."

All of which would cost money. "I will try to contain my ebullient anticipation of these ordeals."

"We will contain our anticipation together, Mr. Sherbourne. I would rather be setting Mr. Jones's tent to rights than fussing over menus, but in pursuit of cordial relations with the neighbors, sacrifices must be made."

The prospect of a nap appealed—merely a nap, with Charlotte, behind a locked bedroom door. "Must they?"

"You will never be a duke, thank God," Charlotte said, easing away, "but this whole valley will know you for the gentleman you are if I have to dance with every one of their spotty sons to make it so."

A gentleman. More to the point, *her* gentleman.

Maybe that was as good as being duke—or maybe it was better.

Chapter Nine

Charlotte's husband had parted from her at the front door with a maddeningly perfunctory kiss, but then, the butler had stood not six feet away holding Sherbourne's hat and gloves. Mr. Sherbourne, for all his way with a passionate kiss, was dignified—for now.

Marriage to a Windham took a toll on any man excessively attached to decorum.

"Will I do?" Charlotte asked, surveying her reflection in the bedroom's cheval mirror.

"You'll do splendidly, ma'am," Heulwen replied. "That's a very fetching carriage dress. My hair gets all a fright in this damp, but you don't have that problem."

"I do, but one must persevere in the face of challenges." Heulwen's comment brought to mind a missing amber hairpin. Eleven was a bothersome number when, for years, Charlotte had managed with twelve. She'd taken to using her nacre set until she could find the twelfth amber pin.

"Heulwen, where might I safely keep a small sum of money or other form of valuable?"

Charlotte would never have posed that question to a London servant, even a retainer of longstanding, absent exigent circumstances. All of the Mrs. Wesleys' circumstances were exigent, however, and needs must.

Heulwen left off rearranging bed pillows. "Whatever are you asking, ma'am? Nobody on Mr. Sherbourne's staff would steal from him. That would be wicked and stupid." Heulwen's expression bore consternation, also a hint of suspicion.

"I may want to surprise Mr. Sherbourne," Charlotte said, "with a nightgown I've embroidered for his enjoyment, or with a new cravat pin that matches his eyes. For such gifts to be effective, I need a private place to store personal items."

Lying had never been Charlotte's strong suit, and Heulwen's frown said she wasn't convinced. "You could use a hat box. No man troubles himself to look in hat boxes."

"An excellent suggestion, and you remind me that I have the perfect bonnet for this dreary weather."

Charlotte sent her maid into the dressing closet to riffle through the hat boxes. Why had she asked Heulwen such a question? She ought to have solved the dilemma herself, of course, or as a last resort, prevailed upon Elizabeth for help.

The lanes were muddy, so the trip to Haverford Castle was undertaken at a frustratingly decorous pace. The groom driving the gig refused to proceed at anything faster than a walk, lest the mud fly up and ruin madam's cloak.

Sherbourne's servants were either devoted to him or terrified of him—perhaps both.

As the gig rounded a bend, a woman came into view

walking alone beside the road. She wore a plain brown cloak and plain straw bonnet, and carried a covered wicker basket over her arm.

"Give her room," Charlotte said, "or she'll be brushing the mud from her skirts for the next week."

The groom, who'd been introduced to Charlotte as Morgan, attempted to steer the carriage to the side, but the lane was ancient, with high berms both left and right.

"Good day," the woman called in cheerful Welsh. She was young, dark-haired, and sturdily built. Her most striking feature was her friendly blue eyes.

Fern had had such eyes. "Good day," Charlotte replied. "Morgan, a moment please."

The coach rolled to a stop between puddles.

"I'm Clara MacPherson," the woman said. "My father is the vicar. You must be the new Mrs. Sherbourne, and you will doubtless be appalled at my lack of manners."

Civilities in the countryside were vastly less bothersome than elsewhere. "I am Charlotte Sherbourne, Miss MacPherson, and we must contrive when nobody is on hand to make introductions. Are you bound in our direction?"

The groom cleared his throat.

"That depends on where you're going," Miss MacPherson replied. "Oh, don't look all sniffy at me, Hector Morgan. Visiting the less fortunate is our Christian duty."

"If you say so, Miss MacPherson." Morgan's words were deferential, while his ironic tone argued the point.

"I'm bringing honey and tea to a neighbor," Miss MacPherson said. "I've only another mile or so to travel."

"That mile will be muddy going. Morgan, please assist Miss MacPherson into the gig."

The groom heaved a put-upon sigh, wrapped the reins,

and hopped down. Miss MacPherson passed Charlotte her basket—laden with bricks from the weight of it—and climbed onto the bench.

"Very kind of you, Mrs. Sherbourne," Miss MacPherson said. "I've avoided a soaking so far, but the sky promises more rain."

"This is Wales. Without the rain, the land couldn't be so beautifully green."

"With that attitude, you'll get on well here. Everybody's dying to meet you."

Charlotte was not dying to meet *everybody*, though for Sherbourne's sake, she'd become the most gracious hostess in the valley, if need be.

"You must assist me," Charlotte said, for a vicar's daughter knew every household in the parish. "Upon whom should I call first?"

As the horse plodded along, Miss MacPherson verbally sketched a whole rural community. The Duke and Duchess of Haverford sat at the apex of the valley's society, though the Marquess of Radnor and his lady—Haverford's sister—were also much respected and well liked.

Beneath the duke and marquess were squires and farmers, the old feudal pattern in a modern setting. The village included various trades—a blacksmith, carpenter, apothecary, bakery, and the usual assortment of lesser commercial establishments.

"We also have a lending library, of course," Miss MacPherson said. "Her Grace stops in frequently, though she delivers books more often than she borrows them. But then, she's your sister. You'd know that about her."

"Her Grace has made lending libraries a passion, and enlisted my husband's support for her cause."

Charlotte made that comment in hopes Miss MacPherson would pounce upon mention of Sherbourne, for he'd been notably absent from her recitation.

"Her Grace was clever, putting the Sherbourne resources to use in such a fashion," Miss MacPherson said. "We were all pleased to see her pull that off. Hector, I'll get down at the crossroads."

Pull that off. As if Sherbourne's coin was hard to access, despite the fact that he was sinking a fortune into a local mine.

"Miss MacPherson, my husband would like to remark the occasion of our marriage with another charitable endeavor, besides the libraries he's financing all over Wales. Could you suggest a suitable gesture? He wants to undertake a project to benefit the whole community, something in addition to establishing a model colliery."

One he'd said would not make him rich, but would be managed according to enlightened standards established by the damned duke.

The dear duke, rather.

"A charitable endeavor?" Miss MacPherson asked as the gig slowed. "You mean, like purchasing new hymnals?"

"No denizen of Wales over the age of seven needs a hymnal. Something enduring."

As a marriage should be.

"Haverford keeps most of the valley in good trim," Miss MacPherson said. "He sees to the roads and ditches about his estate, which is the majority of the arable land. Lord Radnor's papa bought us an organ not fourteen years ago, so we've no need in that direction. Perhaps you might walk with me for a bit and we can discuss this topic further?"

The crossroad was a quagmire. "If you've only a short way to go, we'll take you."

Morgan apparently knew Miss MacPherson's destination because he took the left turning and drove on in silence for a few hundred yards, then turned again onto a narrow pair of ruts barely deserving of the term *lane*.

He handed Miss MacPherson down at a small stone cottage with a thatched roof and a door bearing a peeling coat of red paint. A waist-high stone wall surrounded the yard, though no chickens were in evidence.

"Who lives here?" Charlotte asked, as Morgan handed her down.

"Maureen Caerdenwal and her mother," Miss MacPherson said. "I'll not be introducing you."

A baby's squall pierced the chilly air. A healthy child, though not at the moment a happy one.

"I see."

Miss MacPherson's gaze was not so friendly now. "She's sixteen, Mrs. Sherbourne, and took her first job in service in Cardiff working as an upstairs maid for a man who owns several ironworks. Somebody has to support Mrs. Caerdenwal, because her husband and son were both killed in the mines over by Swansea. Maureen came home in less than six months, and six months later the baby showed up. That was in spring."

To lose a father and a brother, and one's respectability... "And the child?"

"Half a year old, more or less. A boy."

The baby had stopped crying, and a curtain had twitched.

The household had curtains. The yard was tidy, the steps swept, the roof in good repair. This had been a respectable household until some iron nabob hadn't been able to keep his footman, or himself, or his son, in line.

"Has she told you who the father is?"

"He promised to marry her. A rich man like that, twice her age and more. He was lying, of course. Maureen is a hard worker, not that bright, and too pretty for her own good."

She wouldn't be pretty for long, not trying to eke out an existence with no help and no coin.

"Who owns this land?"

"Griffin St. David, the duke's younger brother. He's..."

"Different, I know. I am fond of Lord Griffin." Some might call Griffin simple, but to Charlotte he was honest, friendly, kind, and decent.

Very decent. He was likely charging the women no rent.

Hector Morgan stood by the horse's head, his expression severe. He might not personally judge Miss Caerdenwal for her fall from grace, but if Sherbourne disapproved of this detour, Morgan could lose his job.

If I weren't married...But Charlotte was married, and Sherbourne's standing in the community mattered to him, as it should.

"I would not want to intrude on the family's privacy without warning," Charlotte said, "because I am a stranger to them. I will send a basket to the vicarage tomorrow, and ask that you see it delivered where it will do the greatest good."

The curtain twitched again.

"I can do that," Miss MacPherson said slowly. "I can do that as often as the need arises, Mrs. Sherbourne." Her gaze was more than friendly now; it was conspiratorial.

"My thanks," Charlotte said, "and you will consider what charitable project my husband might undertake in addition to the libraries?" *And the mine.*

Miss MacPherson set down her basket on the garden wall. "Something enduring? I will think on this, Mrs. Sherbourne, and put the question to my father as well, but Haverford has always taken quite good care of us."

By the grace of Lucas Sherbourne's generosity. "We can discuss charitable projects further when my husband and I call at the vicarage. Please give my neighbors my regards."

Miss MacPherson beamed at Charlotte, a blessing of a smile that turned a dreary day sunny, and reminded Charlotte very much of Fern Porter.

"I will do that. Good day, Mrs. Sherbourne, and thank you."

"One does what one can, Miss MacPherson. My husband and I will call at the vicarage in the near future." Not a word of the Caerdenwals' situation would be discussed at that visit, all would be tea and shortbread, the weather, and the latest local wedding.

Miss MacPherson waited by the gate while Morgan assisted Charlotte back into the gig.

"We put Miss MacPherson down at the crossroads," Charlotte said. "She insisted."

Morgan's expression eased. "If you say so, ma'am."

"I do, and Miss MacPherson will say so too."

They rattled along in silence all the way to the castle drive. The sun made occasional attempts to poke through the clouds, but the overcast soon swallowed up errant sunbeams.

"I won't be long, Morgan. Two cups of tea for you in the kitchen, and I should be ready to go."

"Very good, ma'am."

Charlotte wanted to spend time with her sister, of course, but she also wanted to get back to Sherbourne Hall, where she would find the biggest basket on the premises and set about filling it before her husband came home from the colliery.

* * *

"I'm sorry," Sherbourne said, closing the front door on a sharp gust of wind. "I should have asked you when you'd scheduled dinner."

Charlotte did not look happy to see her husband, and Sherbourne was guessing at the reason. Darkness had fallen before he'd left off tramping about the works, Hannibal Jones jabbering at his elbow.

Charlotte whisked Sherbourne's top hat from his head. "Your apology is not accepted. I should have asked when you planned to return from the colliery." She passed the hat to Crandall, then started on the buttons of Sherbourne's greatcoat. "You are soaked to the skin, sir. Might I suggest a hot bath before we dine?"

He'd fall asleep in the tub, had done so on many occasions and awakened all the more stiff and cold, because Turnbull allowed foolish employers to reap the results of their decisions.

"My horse slipped in the mud and came up lame," Sherbourne said, as Charlotte worked her way down the front of his greatcoat. "I had to walk him most of the way back." In the dark, in the cold, in the pouring rain, cursing like a schoolboy given extra sums to do in detention. "I'm more interested in food than a bath at present."

"Thank goodness the beast didn't send you into the ditch. Crandall, you'll need to hang Mr. Sherbourne's coat in the kitchen if it's to dry by morning."

"Of course, ma'am."

"And please have Mr. Sherbourne's warmest dressing gown brought to the library. We'll take trays there, and a toddy wouldn't go amiss."

"I'll see to it, ma'am."

She peeled Sherbourne's sodden coat from his shoulders, and the chill of the unheated foyer penetrated to his bones.

"The fire in the bedroom must be built up as well," Charlotte went on, "for Mr. Sherbourne will have a bath after we've eaten."

"Very good, ma'am."

"Don't just stand about looking dignified, Crandall. Please take Mr. Sherbourne's coat to the kitchen this instant."

Crandall bowed and withdrew, the sopping coat leaving a damp trail on the carpet.

"What are you grinning at," Charlotte asked, fussing with Sherbourne's hair. "You'd think he had nothing better to do than eavesdrop."

"He doesn't. I don't believe anybody has ever scolded Crandall for looking dignified."

Charlotte kissed Sherbourne's cheek. "Gracious, you're cold. I've been wanting to do that since you walked in the door, but didn't know if—"

Sherbourne kissed her on the mouth. "I've been wanting to do that since you knocked my arrow from its path at Haverford's house party this summer."

They stood smiling at each other until a shiver passed over Sherbourne.

"To the library with you," Charlotte said, taking his hand in a warm grasp. "What did you and Mr. Jones get up to this afternoon?"

Sherbourne cast back over hours spent arguing, explaining, and insisting. Haverford had given grudging support to the mine on condition that it meet high standards for safety, while Jones, veteran of years in the coalfields, knew every corner there was to cut.

"I'll be curious to see what Brantford makes of some of Jones's reasoning," Sherbourne said.

Charlotte had taken Sherbourne's green dressing gown from the footman, held the garment to the fire screen, then wrapped it around Sherbourne in place of his coat. The bliss of finally being warm, of having soft cushions to sink into, was exceeded only by the pleasure of hot soup and fresh, generously buttered bread consumed while regaling Charlotte with the day's efforts at the works.

"Who is this Brantford?" Charlotte passed over another slice of bread. "You've mentioned him, though I can't place the name—or is Brantford a title?"

"The Earl of Brantford has become a junior partner in the mine." Sherbourne dipped his bread into the soup, then realized his wife was watching him. "Sorry."

"Mr. Sherbourne, we are private, and you are famished. I'd rather you get some food into you than impress me with your manners. I like to dip shortbread in my tea."

"I'd like, given the circumstances, for you to call me Lucas." Two hours from now, they would be in bed, and he desperately hoped Charlotte had decided the occasion was right to consummate their vows.

She'd threatened as much. Mrs. Lucas Sherbourne was not a woman who made threats lightly.

"Were you named for Luke the Physician?"

"I was nearly named for the Fiend. I arrived to this world at the start of a new day. When I was placed in my mother's arms, she gazed out the window to behold the dawn star on the far horizon, and decided I should be Lucifer. My father persuaded her that a saint would be a more fitting namesake than a fallen angel. What of you?"

"Nothing so colorful as a biblical debate. I was named for the late queen, of course. Tell me about this partner of yours."

"He's forward-thinking, he agreed to my terms, and he

has coin to invest. I won't make him enormously wealthy, but neither will I squander his money and disappear on the next packet for Calais. If you don't care to finish your soup, I'll see that it doesn't go to waste."

Another breach of manners, though Charlotte passed over her bowl.

"I wonder why I haven't heard much about Lord Brantford. Is his seat in the north?"

"It is, which is why he has experience with mines. God help me if he decides to pay us a call before I get Jones sorted out."

Charlotte tore a slice of bread in half. "*Pay us a call?* We're to have a visitor?"

Shabby table manners hadn't caused her to blink, and she'd taken in stride a husband who'd twice neglected to appear on time for dinner. The prospect of a visitor had her sitting up very straight.

"He'll probably stay with Haverford, being titled, but I do respect when a man takes an interest in his investments."

"Does Lord Brantford have a countess? Children? If he's thinking to visit soon, I must have details, Mr. Sherbourne. Guest rooms must be prepared, the wine cellar put in order, menus decided, a dinner party or two planned. Guests are not a small matter, sir."

Mr. Sherbourne, spoken in that tone, did not bode well for the balance of the evening. "You're nervous about having company?"

"We are newly married, and first impressions matter, as I suspect you know. Am I a good hostess? Do I set a fine table? Can I assemble a group of guests who are both lively and congenial even when I'm new to the shire myself? You don't undertake an investment without significant planning, and my role as your wife is similar. I will be scrutinized by Lord Brantford, and he will carry a report to his countess. She will have correspondents, and thus my reputation as a hostess will be established or doomed."

Sherbourne had taken Brantford on as an investor without thorough investigation—he'd had time for only the usual inquiries—and now, more than a week later, that decision resulted in unease.

"You think Brantford will carry tales because we married in haste?" Sherbourne asked.

Charlotte took a nibble of her bread. "We did not marry in haste, as far as anybody knows. I met you this summer, and many couples in polite society marry by special license after a short courtship."

Their marriage would be subject to greater scrutiny because Charlotte Windham had married down. Just when Sherbourne had convinced himself that the difference in their stations didn't matter, doubt reared its ugly head.

"Don't fret," Sherbourne said, cutting into a serving of steak. "If the weather stays this nasty, the roads alone will prevent anybody from journeying into the wilds of Wales. Did you visit your sister today?"

Charlotte recounted her visit to Haverford Castle, most of which she'd spent listening to Elizabeth discuss the infernal lending libraries. The moment had shifted however, from a husband and wife enjoying a private meal at the end of the day, to a wife humoring her thoughtless husband.

Again.

"Shall I see to your bath?" Charlotte asked, taking the trays to the sideboard. "The water should be hot by now."

Sherbourne was warm and fed, and had he been a bachelor, he would have stretched out on the sofa, and drifted off after a long and tiring day.

"A bath would be appreciated." Particularly if Charlotte was offering to attend him. Spouses did that for each other in some marriages.

"I'll let Turnbull know," she said, "and have the footman take these trays. Would you like another toddy?"

He'd like his wife to sit in his lap and kiss him until his eyes crossed. "No, thank you."

"Good night, then. Enjoy your bath, Mr. Sherbourne." She withdrew on a soft click of the door latch, probably off to drag Crandall into the wine cellar for a late night inventory of the clarets.

"My name is Lucas," he muttered to the empty room. "Not Mr. Sherbourne, not husband, not sir. To my wife, when we're alone, late at night, I'd like to be Lucas."

* * *

"Good evening." Brantford offered the greeting with a slight smile, which his wife returned. They avoided one another socially, though occasional encounters happened.

"My lord. I hope you're enjoying the music."

Veronica was still pretty, still lovely even, but she was no longer *dewy*.

"I am very partial to a well-played pianoforte," Brantford said. "And you, my dear?"

Around them polite society gossiped, laughed, and watched. Brantford and his countess were known to be cordially bored with each other. Her ladyship had failed to produce offspring, and thus her diversions were limited to the insipid variety.

Poor thing.

"I thought the violinist was superb," Veronica said. "Would you like to sit with us?"

Across the room, her second cousin, Tremont, Viscount Enderly, nodded politely. Doubtless his mama, the viscountess, was at the punch bowl mentally assessing the settlements of any young lady who offered her son so much as a simper.

"I'd enjoy visiting with your family," Brantford replied, "but I'm promised elsewhere and won't be staying for the vocalists. Did I mention to you that I'm leaving for Wales next week?" The notion had just popped into Brantford's head, and being a decisive person, now was as good a time as any to announce his plan. He and Veronica saw each other infrequently of late, and keeping her apprised of his whereabouts was only courteous.

Veronica studied her fan, which bore a painted image of pink roses, blue butterflies, and stylized greenery. She was a talented artist and might have created the artwork herself.

"Shooting?" she asked.

"Some shooting, and I thought I'd look in on a colliery in which I've secured an interest. You'll manage without me, I'm sure."

She waved her fan gently. "How long will you be gone?"

"A few weeks. I'll leave my direction, of course."

Enderly was in conversation with Lady Ophelia Durant. She dined on young bachelors at every opportunity, sometimes several at once, if rumor was to be believed. And yet, Enderly, while giving every appearance of attending to Lady Ophelia, was also casting discreet glances in Veronica's direction.

"I might travel with Aunt and Cousin down to Enderly House for a visit," she said. "The opening hunt is next week."

Veronica was happiest in the saddle. Perhaps equestrian

pursuits had affected her ability to bear children. The quack had also mentioned that a bout of the French disease could impair a man's ability to sire offspring, but Brantford had gone more than three years without any symptoms of that indignity, and he'd been careful to keep a distance from his wife when she might have suspected he was ailing.

"Autumn in the country has many charms," he observed. Was Tremont's company among those charms for Veronica? She and her handsome cousin had grown up together. Perhaps she regretted choosing the earl over the viscount, or perhaps she hadn't had a choice.

Brantford had had a choice, and like any sensible man, he'd chosen enormous settlements at the first opportunity. He should have realized that Veronica's settlements were the last, desperate show of bravado by a family that hadn't a clue how to manage their fortune.

"You wouldn't object to my leaving town for a time, my lord?"

Did she think he'd drag her along to *Wales*? "Your happiness will ever concern me, my dear. I'm sure the viscountess will be a congenial hostess. Why would I object?"

"No reason."

Must she sound so plaintive? Brantford saw to her every comfort, was never less than gracious in public, and only bothered her once a week for conjugal favors that by right were his any time he chose.

"I see our hostess over by the dessert table," Brantford said. "She looks determined to end this intermission. Enjoy the vocalists." He brushed a kiss to Veronica's cheek, a gesture of loyalty before the gossips lurking in every corner. "Until Sunday, my lady."

Sunday night being their standing appointment in her ladyship's bed.

"I'll leave on Saturday."

Veronica was asserting her independence. She'd begun this amusing habit about a year ago, when she'd turned five-and-twenty. Sometimes, her tantrums manifested in bills from the milliner, sometimes they took the form of Sunday night megrims, though not often.

The lack of a child was his sorrow but her shame, after all.

"Then I'll see you on Friday," Brantford said.

Because if Veronica was inclined to dally with her cousin, any resulting child must at least in theory be Brantford's. To support that theory, Brantford would do his wife the courtesy of swiving her before they went their separate ways.

And if Tremont could get her with child, so much better, for Brantford would soon weary of trying.

Chapter Ten

Charlotte left her spouse privacy to bathe in their bed-chamber because Sherbourne had not indicated that her assistance was needed or welcome. Perhaps Turnbull had been summoned, or perhaps Sherbourne had bathed himself, shaved himself, washed his own hair...

A procession of footfalls outside the door of Charlotte's private parlor suggested the footmen were wheeling the tub away.

She forced herself to concoct another week's worth of menus, then tidied up her desk, banked the fire, blew out the candles, and prepared to consummate her wedding vows.

She stopped with her hand on the bedroom door latch and chose not to knock.

Please let this go well.

The bedroom was warm, humid, and perfumed with the scent of floral soap. Few candles were lit, and thus

Sherbourne made a contemplative picture, wrapped in his dressing gown in a chair by the fire.

"Are you waiting for your hair to dry?" Charlotte asked.

"I'm waiting for my wife to come to bed."

Well. He'd apparently eschewed a nightshirt, for the V of the dressing gown revealed the bare flesh of his throat and sternum.

She took two steps into the room, abruptly feeling uncertain and resentful. "Shall we see to the consummation, Mr. Sherbourne?"

He rose, which made the dressing gown gape open farther. "Perhaps you're too tired?"

"I am weary of the anticipation. These intimacies are a normal part of married life, and we've yet to tend to them."

He raised a hand to cradle her cheek, and Charlotte had to steel herself not to shrink away, which made no sense. She *liked* to touch her husband, liked knowing the feel of him, liked that she had the right to be affectionate with him.

Perhaps that was the problem: She liked taking the initiative.

Sherbourne stepped closer, bringing Charlotte the fragrance of freshly bathed male. "I have a suggestion, madam."

Now, she wished he'd toss a few orders at her: Undress, come to bed, hold still—though surely there was more to it than that?

"I'd be pleased to hear your suggestion."

"Feel free to revisit your decision at any point, that's my suggestion. Married couples do, if they're lucky, have regular occasions of intimacy, but we've yet to establish the habit. Perhaps approaching the challenge in steps will serve us better than attempting the whole endeavor at one go."

The challenge. Making love to his wife was a challenge? Charlotte wasn't sure whether to be flattered or appalled, but Sherbourne was right: The next step was to change into nightclothes, which she had been doing every night of her adult life.

She turned her back and swept her hair off her nape. "If you'd oblige?"

His hands settled on her shoulders, shifting her so the fire's light would illuminate her hooks. Sherbourne's breath brushed at the back of her neck, a curious sensation.

"Was this why you paid a call on your sister today?" he asked.

This...? Oh, *this*. "Elizabeth maundered on about what she calls her basic collection, a few books every library ought to have. One could not distract her from the topic."

One had tried, but raising the topic of...*the topic*, had proved impossible.

Sherbourne continued right down to the bottom-most hooks, which wasn't necessary. The sensation of his fingers fiddling with Charlotte's dress even over the swell of her derriere was unnerving.

"Haverford can probably distract your sister from her lending libraries with a single glance. One suspects they are in anticipation of a happy event."

Had Sherbourne kissed Charlotte's nape? "You said you like children. Their Graces will make you an uncle."

"I subscribe to the philosophy that a woman should thoroughly recover from a lying in before conception is risked again, though I do like children."

Do you like me? He desired her, which was of no moment. Charlotte believed that men, young men anyway, could probably work up a case of desire for any comely woman.

Her stays eased, and Charlotte turned to face her husband. This was, by any other name, their wedding night, and she wasn't making the least effort to behave like a bride.

"I like you, Mr. Sherbourne. I like that you are hardworking, patient, considerate, and not one to tax a lame horse merely to preserve your boots. I like that you don't waste food, and I admire that you have been so generous with your neighbors, despite their lack of appreciation. I like that you say thank you to the servants, and I am pleased beyond all telling that your staff respects you. That speaks volumes, particularly where the maids are concerned."

Sherbourne's reply to her babbling was to take her in his arms.

This embrace was different. Charlotte felt no circular bump where his pocket watch would have been. Her stays were loose about her middle and thus her breasts were unconfined. She felt Sherbourne's heartbeat, not as a dull concussion through layers of clothing, but as the palpable ebb and flow of life.

He wasn't nervous, which was doubtless good.

"I like that you are fierce," he said. "That you don't suffer fools, ever. I admire your marksmanship with a bow and arrow."

Charlotte waited for more—she was very good at sums, competent at the pianoforte, fairly well read—but Sherbourne didn't know these aspects of her. He was left to compliment the traits that others considered her shortcomings.

"Don't be anxious, Charlotte. Just be yourself. Scold and fuss, give orders. Be blunt. What follows might not be wonderful in the first few instances, but it will at least be pleasant. We'll manage."

That he knew she needed reassurance should have been embarrassing, but Sherbourne was *her husband*. The firelight brought out a wealth of fatigue in his face, also patience and affection.

He was not nervous, he was determined that their wedding night go well, and thus it would.

"I'll get into my nightgown." Charlotte would have moved to the dressing screen, but Sherbournc stopped her with a hand around her wrist.

He kissed her, a slow tasting that promised pleasure and yet more patience. Charlotte borrowed his patience when she wanted to dive beneath the quilts and pull the covers over her head. Crossing the room with her dress unbound was another new experience, and knowing that Sherbourne watched her gave her the resolve to walk away slowly.

"Warm the sheets, please," she said. "Your hair is still damp, and I can't have you taking a chill."

He laughed, though she'd been perfectly in earnest.

Charlotte made a thorough job of her ablutions, left her hair in a single braid, and donned her nightgown. The room was warm, and the bed was eight feet away. She emerged from the dressing screen without the benefit of a dressing gown, and without any sort of plan for the next hour.

Sherbourne was also without benefit of dressing gown, and once again sitting in his chair by the fire.

"Ready for bed, Mr. Sherbourne?"

He rose, his silk trousers riding low on his hips. "I'm ready, Charlotte."

Ye gods, he was fit. His musculature formed a landscape, like a patchwork of rectangular fields on either side of the slight indentation down the middle of his belly. Chest, shoulders, arms...all were wrapped in sleek muscle and shamelessly on view.

"You look larger without your clothes," Charlotte said. "Why is that?"

He snorted. "Maybe because part of me *is* larger when I'm about to be intimate with my wife."

"You are naughty."

Fatigue made his features sharper, and his smile more piratical. "Not naughty, *married*. Come be married with me, Charlotte Sherbourne."

He held out his hand, and Charlotte took it. "Does one undertake this aspect of married life with or without one's bedtime attire?"

For if she enjoyed looking at him, perhaps he might . . . that thought was beyond *married*.

Sherbourne paused with her by the bed. "Do you have a preference?"

"I've never done this before. How could I have a preference?" Except . . . she did have a preference.

Sherbourne took a step back, drew off his trousers, and tossed them over the privacy screen. "Now, do you have a preference?"

Charlotte couldn't help but peek, then stare, then gawk. Sherbourne was all of a rugged, healthy piece. The taut geometry of his belly flowed into long flanks and defined calves, everywhere lean, smooth, and male.

And there, where the dusting of golden hair became a dense thicket . . . very male.

"You promise me we'll manage *pleasantly*?" Charlotte asked.

"I promised to worship you with my body. Being worshipped should be pleasant, Charlotte."

Valid point. "Then let's to bed, Mr. Sherbourne."

"Lucas," he said, scowling down at her. "When I'm being worshipful, you will please call me Lucas."

Charlotte considered rejecting that order—but, no. He was actually making a request, and a reasonable one under the circumstances.

"Lucas, dearest husband, please come to bed."

In the complete, glorious altogether, he made a circuit of the room, blowing out candles one by one. Charlotte regretted the loss of illumination, but appreciated her husband's respect for fire hazards.

"Shall I untie the bed curtains?" he asked.

"Yes, please, and then you can untie the bows of this nightgown."

* * *

Sherbourne had fallen asleep in the tub, almost as soon as he'd sunk into the hot water. He'd woken in time to wash before the water had cooled too much, but fatigue still wrapped around him like wet towels.

Which was good. A husband consummating his nuptial vows ought not to be in a frantic rush. He should be relaxed, calm, and prepared to delay his own pleasure. Sherbourne was as calm as possible, considering he had a cockstand at full salute and a willing wife parading around in a single layer of linen.

"Let's get comfortable beneath the covers," he said. "We can see to your nightgown later."

Charlotte shot him an exasperated look as she bounced onto the bed.

Wrong suggestion, then. She'd offered to bare her treasures, and he'd bungled his response in aid of his self-restraint. Sherbourne climbed in beside her and found another dose of cold. Some fool by the name of Lucas Sherbourne had again forgotten to warm the sheets.

"Too much inspiration," Sherbourne said, "and my self-discipline will fail us when most needed."

Charlotte scooted down and flopped to her side facing him. "Inspiration?"

"You." Sherbourne said, kissing her on the lips. "Without your clothes. Inspiration."

She smiled against his mouth. "Like you without yours."

Charlotte was not a prude. She'd given him a thorough inspection as he'd strutted around the room, which had been the point of the exercise. That, and a moment to think, to concoct a strategy.

The only helpful notion to form in Sherbourne's tired brain was an admonition from his grandfather, who'd been something of a rogue in his youth: The lady's pleasure must come before all else, or a fellow wasn't likely to get a second chance to impress her.

So Sherbourne devoted himself to kissing his wife. Charlotte was inexperienced rather than reticent, and she was a fast learner. When Sherbourne slid a hand over her hip, she retaliated by pressing her palm to his heart.

When he eased his tongue across her lips, she scooted closer and ran her toe up his calf. Sherbourne trapped her foot between his legs, and she pulled his hair.

Fatigue fell away, replaced by a compulsion to mount and start thrusting, but this was their wedding night, more or less, and Sherbourne was determined to earn a standing invitation to Charlotte's side of the bed. He rolled to his back, taking Charlotte with him.

She straddled him on all fours, not touching him, and once again looking impatient. "You might have asked."

"Charlotte, darling wife, would you please consider settling over me such that I am surrounded by your abundant glories? I like having both of my hands free to plunder your charms while you kiss me any way you please. I like your weight on me, your warmth pressing on me intimately."

She curled down to his shoulder, not fast enough to hide a smile. "I have married a foolish man."

"An incompetent poet but not a fool."

"Abundant glories, Mr. Sherbourne?"

"These," he said, palming the sides of her breasts. "I'd love to worship these with my body, et cetera, if you're inclined to grant that boon."

Charlotte sat up, expression wary. She still wore her nightgown, though it was bunched at her waist.

Sherbourne lay on his back, hands resting on her hips. For the sake of the next five decades of marriage, he remained relaxed and still, though arousal had become a sharp ache.

Slowly, slowly, Charlotte raised the nightgown over her head, then leaned forward to tuck it under her pillow. Before she straightened, Sherbourne caught her breast in his mouth and slid his hands up her back.

By touch, he suggested she linger in that position and learn the pleasure of her husband's teeth on her nipple. She sank closer, and he rejoiced.

"Pleasant?" he asked, switching breasts. *Warm, sweet, soft, delectable.*

"Married, and pleasant." She sounded a tad breathless.

Erotic impressions piled up—the silky-smooth contours of Charlotte's breasts beneath his fingers, the texture of a puckered nipple in his mouth, the throb of desire. An ambition landed amid all these pleasures, a determination that Charlotte get a taste of the destination before the consummation.

More than a taste. Sherbourne was her husband, very likely the only man whom she'd take as a lover, and he owed her that consideration. In a way that speaking vows or sharing a long journey had not, Charlotte's intimate trust struck Sherbourne with the enormity of the commitment they had made to each other.

They were husband and wife, joined for the rest of their natural lives. She was his and he was hers and by God, he would make certain she was pleased with that bargain.

He slid a hand down to her hip and around to pat her bum. "Time to enjoy a few more abundant glories."

"Must I? I was rather enjoying—"

He kissed her. "Glories, Charlotte. Plural. We have many more to sample."

She slipped to the side, brushing her sex over his rampant cock in the process. The haste with which she scooted away confirmed that the caress had been inadvertent—this time. Give her a week, and with any luck, she'd be driving him mad.

Sherbourne fixed his figurative eye on that prize and began rearranging pillows.

"What are you doing?"

"Embarking on an experiment." He propped himself against the headboard, spread his legs, and patted the mattress. "Let me hold you."

Charlotte had the covers drawn up under her arms. "You want me. . . . ?"

"Between my legs, using me as your personal chaise. Your back to my front." *And my hand between your legs.*

She remained right where she was. "Why?"

"So I can worship you to the utmost."

Her expression turned mulish. "When do I get to worship you? The vows were reciprocal, you know."

"Next time, Charlotte. If you want to worship me by taking a riding crop to my bare bum, or licking every part of me while I'm bound hand and foot, we can negotiate that later. This time is just for you."

She crawled over his leg, her breast brushing his thigh, then curled against his chest on her side. "You say the most outlandish things."

Sherbourne put his lips near her ear. "You're interested in that bit about the riding crop, aren't you?"

"Don't be ridiculous, and I don't see the point of binding you." She flicked her tongue over his nipple. "The licking has possibilities. You taste like lavender."

Rather than let her tangle him up with more words, Sherbourne cupped her chin and kissed her while he used his free hand to caress her breast. Her weight pressed against his erect cock, a sensation he tried to ignore.

By stealth, degrees, and determination, he eventually got Charlotte positioned where he wanted her—sprawled with her back against his chest, arching into his touch as he pleasured her breasts.

"You like this?"

She closed her hands around his, asking for more pressure. "I haven't made up my mind."

"Then I must try harder." He trailed his fingers lower, until he was stroking through her curls. "Relax, Charlotte. We're getting to the interesting part."

"This has all been very—*gracious everlasting powers.*"

He'd found the seat of her pleasure, and possibly a way to have the last word at least some of the time. Charlotte squirmed, she wiggled, she sighed, she spread her legs over his, and reached behind her to grab Sherbourne's hair.

He found a rhythm and a pressure that she could follow, and when Charlotte's hips were urging him faster, he resisted. Pleasure delayed was pleasure intensified.

"Mr. Sherbourne...."

"Lucas."

Silence for a few moments, while she probably fashioned an argument, and he added more pressure without speeding up.

"Mister...oh, ye gods, Lucas. Lucas, Lucas, *Lucas*...."

Sherbourne cupped her breast and drove a finger into her slick heat, giving her some part of him to seize around. Her pleasure was intense and protracted, while Sherbourne's was vicarious and bound in frustration.

When he withdrew his hand, Charlotte curled sideways on his chest, her sigh fanning across his heart. His cock throbbed, his balls ached, his back wasn't exactly comfortable and the room was gradually cooling.

"Charlotte?"

She nuzzled him. "Hmm."

He tucked the covers up over her shoulders, cradling her close. Sherbourne cast around for the right words, the right question.

Charlotte had given him her trust in a way that mattered, and he wanted to tell her...something. When she'd recovered, he'd make sweet, slow love with her, and ease her the last distance down the path to marital intimacy. They'd fall asleep entwined and in the morning, share smug smiles over their tea and toast.

For the rest of their lives.

Tenderness pushed arousal aside an inch or two. "Charlotte? Did you find it...pleasant?"

Her breathing was regular, and she was a warm bundle of wife against his chest. Sherbourne waited for her answer—doubtless something honest, original, and accurate—but still Charlotte remained silent.

"Charlotte? Mrs. Sherbourne?"

Sherbourne fell asleep, waiting for his wife to wake up

and answer a question that mattered to him far more than he'd thought it would. When he did awake, weak sun was filtering through the curtains, he was spooned around his wife, and some fiend was rapping incessantly on the door.

"Sir, you must wake up," Turnbull shouted.

Sherbourne forced himself to awareness, because Turnbull never shouted.

"Sir, you must wake up. There's been an accident at the mine."

* * *

The colliery looked the same from a distance. Only as the landau wheeled closer could Charlotte make out men digging at a huge heap of hillside that had come slouching over the retaining wall. The wall was no more, buried under tons of mud.

The neat rectangles of twine that had marked out the longest row of houses had been obliterated as well, while the rest of the site remained unchanged.

The sun chose now to shine so brightly as to hurt Charlotte's eyes, though the breeze was cold. That chill reinforced a sense that she should not have come, should not have intruded into matters she knew so little about.

"Pull up next to the large white tent," Charlotte said. "The one all the shouting is coming from."

In the privacy of their domiciles, Windhams occasionally raised their voices, though Charlotte did not deal well with being shouted out. Sherbourne had left the house within ten minutes of waking, Turnbull at his side, while Charlotte had stood about in her husband's dressing gown and worried. An hour later, somebody had sent a note: *No fatalities, extensive damage.*

Charlotte thought she recognized Sherbourne's hand-writing, but the only time she'd seen it previously had been when he'd signed documents following the wedding cere-mony.

An hour more of pacing and fretting, and Charlotte had made up her mind to cease dithering and *do* something.

"Heulwen, you and Morgan see to the food."

One of the tent flaps had been tied back. Inside, Mr. Jones was marching about and waving his hands, while Sherbourne stood with one shoulder against the central tent pole. He wore no cravat, no top hat, and his boots were caked with mud.

"Hillsides do as they damned well please," Jones said. "We build walls and God laughs. If I'm tempted to skimp on materials, I'll skimp on the materials for the damned palaces you want to build for your workers, not on the sim-plest wall ever to be overcome by mud."

Sherbourne visually tracked Jones's peregrinations while Charlotte slipped into the tent. The piles of paper she'd tidied and organized on her last visit were once again in disarray, with stacks held down by rocks, a pen tray, an abacus, and other makeshift paperweights.

"If that wall had chosen to give way later this autumn, a dozen households would have been buried in mud," Sher-bourne said. "How can I trust you to build a safe mine when you can't manage a single retaining wall?"

Jones strutted up to him. "I told you when I signed on here that I'm a mining engineer, not a perishing architect. I deal with the insides of the hills, not a lot of bloody land-scaping."

Charlotte let the foul language go unremarked, for at some point in this altercation, Mr. Jones had unearthed the calculations upon which the construction of the wall was based. While Jones ranted about timbers and cross-stabilization, she took a seat and studied the figures she'd found under an unlit carrying candle.

"The men can live in damned tents," Jones went on. "You don't need to build the houses before you sink the shafts. What kind of businessman builds a village before his colliery is making any money?"

"One who wants his mine to attract only the best talent, the hardest workers, the most trustworthy crews in Wales. Why should any competent miner bestir himself to leave his post and join my crew, if I'm offering him less protection from the elements than I expect for my horse?"

"Why should he expect any different?" Jones stuck his nose in Sherbourne's face. "You can find an experienced miner a whole lot more cheaply than you can a well-trained horse. A simpleton can work the mines."

"The men might disagree with you," Sherbourne said with ominous quiet, "though the next thing to a simpleton should have been able to design a retaining wall that held up for more than a few months."

Sherbourne's words lashed the air. For the first time, Charlotte glimpsed why people gave her a husband a wide berth. The view was intimidating.

Also impressive.

Chapter Eleven

To Charlotte's relief, Mr. Jones had the sense to take a step back. "I checked my calculations, Mr. Sherbourne. I don't do shoddy work. I measured the land, did the math, and made allowances for the soil containing a disproportionate share of rocks, and then I used only sound timbers in sufficient quantity for the mass involved."

A silence stretched, as Jones produced a flask and tipped it up to his mouth.

"You did not account for the weight of the water in the soil," Charlotte said. "Your figures for the soil were likely correct, but water weighs on the order of 1,674 pounds per cubic yard. Mr. Sherbourne's treatises all more or less agree on that figure. Your wall held up until the rains came in quantity."

Both men stared at her. Mr. Sherbourne in particular did not look pleased to see her, though if he intended to upbraid her for intruding into his business, he'd apparently do so at home behind a closed door.

Which was in a way worse. Charlotte held the calculations out to Jones. "You made no allowance for the incessant rain."

Jones snatched the papers from her. "The water doesn't stay in the soil. It percolates, drains down deeper into the earth, or evaporates."

"With as much wet weather as we've had," Sherbourne said, pushing away from the support, "the soil hasn't been draining. The lanes and pastures are full of standing water. Mrs. Sherbourne's explanation makes sense, and rain water probably isn't a factor in most of your subterranean calculations."

Jones set the figures aside. "I am a mining engineer, and I stand by my figures. Why have those men stopped digging?"

Across the expanse of supplies sitting under tarps, beyond the muddy lane, the men had jabbed their shovels into the great heap of earth and left their work.

"I brought food," Charlotte said. "Hot soup, bread, butter, cheese, and ale. I suspect you both could use some sustenance."

"I could at that," Jones said, slapping a hat onto his head. "A pint or three of ale won't go amiss either."

He stormed past Charlotte, and she was abruptly alone with her muddy, scowling husband.

"How do you know what a cubic yard of anything weighs?" Sherbourne knelt by a parlor stove at the far end of the tent and tossed more coal onto the flames. "I barely know what a cubic yard of dirt weighs, and I own this colliery. Such as it is."

He wasn't shouting, wasn't castigating her for her presence. He also wasn't convinced by her assessment of the calculations. Charlotte was confident of her explanation, even if her marriage was feeling a bit tentative.

Or more than a bit.

She kept to her seat, a lesson she'd learned from Aunt Esther. Kings and queens ruled from their thrones, not that Sherbourne was Charlotte's subject.

"I like numbers," she said, "and weights and measures don't change. If I have occasion to learn one, it sticks with me. According to the treatises in your library, the weight of soil can vary greatly, depending on rocks, as Mr. Jones noted, or how much sand is in the earth. Water is always water."

Sherbourne shut the parlor stove door and stared at the flames dancing behind the glass. "This entire project turns on Jones being as competent as his reputation suggested. I'm paying him a fortune, though all I do is argue with him, and now this." Sherbourne rose stiffly and stood in the middle of the tent looking weary and lost in the thought.

Brooding, which would not do. This bewildered, angry specimen was the same man who'd been so patient with Charlotte last night, so generous, and *intimate*. She untied the tent flap and put her arms around her husband.

"The rains have been severe," she said. "Mining engineers probably design many retaining walls, but not above ground. Shall I have a look at his other calculations?"

"He'll quit on the spot, and I'm tempted to let him go."

"Then you'll get an undeserved reputation for being difficult to work for," Charlotte said. "May I bring you some lunch?"

Let me help. Let me matter to you. She would not beg, neither would she give up.

Sherbourne smelled of wet earth and coal smoke, a far cry from the freshly bathed, scrubbed, and shaved husband Charlotte had shared a bed with last night. His shape was the same, all lean muscle on long bones.

"You are cosseting me," he groused, propping his chin on her crown. "You need not have come, Charlotte."

As scolds went, that hardly qualified, and relief had Charlotte sagging against her spouse.

"I'm your wife. One wants to be useful." Useful was a reasonable aspiration. Charlotte had long ago given up on many others—popular, liked, accepted. They'd been the pointless longings of an awkward girl. She was good at numbers, she was useful to her various Mrs. Wesleys, and she could learn to be a good wife.

The figures covering half the papers Charlotte saw called to her, though an assistant could check the math. Nobody else could hold Lucas Sherbourne when he was plagued by frustration.

"You took no food with you when you left the house," Charlotte said, "not even a half-full flask. Regular sustenance is not cosseting, it's necessary for survival."

Outside the tent, men laughed and joked as they waited for a turn at the keg of ale. Some teased Heulwen, another asked Morgan if he was handy with a shovel. Spoons scraped against bowls, and somebody complained about another fellow stealing too much cheese.

"Now that I can smell food," Sherbourne said, "I'm hungry."

"Then let's feed you. I'm surprised you're not letting the earth dry out before you set the men to excavating."

Sherbourne peered down at her, his expression disgruntled. "Jones had them digging before I arrived, but you're right, a few days to dry out will make the work go more quickly, assuming the rain is done with us for a while."

Which, in Wales, was not likely. "Food," Charlotte said. "Before the men eat every last crumb."

When she emerged from the tent with Sherbourne, she

found a group of rough, muddy fellows gathered around the back of the landau. Every male present yanked his cap from his head and ceased eating.

"Mrs. Sherbourne, I have the honor of introducing to you my masons. Gentlemen, Mrs. Sherbourne."

Nobody moved. Nobody spoke. One fellow near the keg chewed slowly, then swallowed. The same awkwardness that had plagued Charlotte from childhood threatened to silence her, but Sherbourne apparently expected her to know what to say.

My gracious, that mud does stink.

"A pleasure to meet you all," Charlotte said, trying for the kind of smile Aunt Esther wore so easily and often. "I hope the soup was still hot?"

She was earnestly assured the soup was quite hot and very good.

One youth with white-blond hair aimed a shy grin at Heulwen. "I could do with a bit more in fact, if there's enough."

"We brought plenty," Charlotte said. "Please do save some for Mr. Sherbourne. He's easily annoyed when peckish."

Well, he was. Wasn't everybody?

"Oh, he is that," said the man near the keg. "Meaning no disrespect."

The grinning lad accepted a spoon and steaming bowl of stew. "Perhaps you'd like some bread and butter, Mrs. Sherbourne?"

He got cuffed for his forwardness, but good-naturedly, and Charlotte was soon sitting on a stack of timbers beside her husband, holding his buttered bread while he devoured his stew.

"Is this a serious setback?" she asked.

"Yes and no. This is good cheese."

"You buy it from Haverford."

"On second thought, it's overripe." They shared a smile, though Sherbourne's contribution was wan. "The problem is time, Charlotte. Once the ground freezes, we can't lay foundations. If we can't lay foundations, then we can't raise houses, and we can't bring in full crews. If I can't bring in crews, sinking a shaft is pointless, and this whole exercise has been an example of how to spend a fortune and have nothing to show for it."

Charlotte huddled close to her husband, who made a fine windbreak. "You have three empty tenant cottages. Knock them down and build a dormitory."

Sherbourne finished his soup and set aside the empty bowl. "A fine idea, but the only crew I have now are my masons. Jones wants them to build his tram line, I want them to build houses, now you want them to build a dormitory. If I hire more workers, I spend more money without having any revenue coming in, and at some point, I must show a profit. I took on a partner of sorts, and he expects a return on his investment."

Charlotte passed over the buttered bread. "Brantford?"

"Yes, Brantford. I owe him regular progress reports, and I'm loath to send him word of this development. That retaining wall took weeks of labor, and that was before the hillside decided to relocate itself where front parlors and kitchens were supposed to be."

Seagulls strutted around at the top of the glistening mud heap, pecking the earth, then flapping about to land a few feet away. In the sharp midday light, they put Charlotte in mind of carrion crows, feasting on the remains of some huge mythical beast.

"Why put houses where a retaining wall was required?" she asked.

Sherbourne tore the bread in half and offered her the larger portion. Charlotte took a bite, and got hints of coal and dirt with her bread and butter.

"Jones laid the houses out there because workers should live near the works, one of Haverford's requirements. The men aren't to be tramping three miles each day to and from the colliery, out in all kinds of weather. They are to have decent housing at or near the colliery itself."

Which left many choices besides the lee of a steep hill. Charlotte was about to make that point when another conveyance rattled past the white tent, the Duke of Haverford at the reins.

"What is *he* doing here?" Sherbourne muttered.

"He's our neighbor. Perhaps he came to offer assistance."

Sherbourne gave Charlotte an incredulous look and rose. "Haverford."

The duke brought his trap to a halt. "Anybody hurt?"

"Not a soul."

Haverford remained on the bench, looking very much the properly turned out gentleman. "You had a row of houses planned where that mudslide landed, didn't you?"

"Close to the works," Sherbourne said, crossing his arms. "As required."

A tense silence sprang up. Charlotte rose from the stack of timbers and joined Sherbourne beside the vehicle.

"Your Grace, good day."

If Haverford was surprised to see her, he was too well bred to show it. "Madam." He touched his hat brim. "If you don't mind my asking, Sherbourne, what in blazes happened here? Griffin said you'd had a mudslide. Half the hill has landed on your work site, and I don't see how you'll get it put back where it belongs before winter arrives."

"Rain happened," Sherbourne said. "Tons and tons of rain. We'll manage."

Charlotte wanted to smack her husband. Haverford owned much of the valley, and that meant he might also have an empty cottage or two, or a pensioner's patch to spare.

"Harvest is in," Haverford said, as the men began to wander back to their shovels and picks. "I'll send some of my tenants over, shall I? They don't like to be idle, and if you're putting that hill back where it belongs, you need manpower."

Charlotte squeezed Sherbourne's arm, hard. He shot her a glance that blended annoyance and amusement. A married glance?

"We can use all the help you can spare," Sherbourne said. "Some prayers for a stretch of sunny weather would also be appreciated."

"You'll have to take up the prayer request with Mr. MacPherson," Haverford replied. "I'll see who I can muster for a few days of fresh air and free ale. Don't be surprised if Griffin shows up with a batch of shortbread. Why has the Earl of Brantford decided to impose himself on my hospitality?"

Sherbourne ran a hand through his hair. "Brantford is paying a call on you?"

"I have a passing acquaintance with him from various Parliamentary encounters, and on the strength of that acquaintance, he's asked for the castle's hospitality. His letter mentioned having an interest in a new colliery, and I sent him the appropriate gracious reply. He should be here by the end of next week."

* * *

"Why did you do that?" Sherbourne asked, as he drove Charlotte to the house. Heulwen and Morgan were walking home together, and Sherbourne wished them the joy of their flirtation. Dishes rattled in the back of the vehicle, and the aroma of beef stew blended with the scent of a muddy autumn landscape.

And gardenias.

"Why did I invite Haverford and his duchess to dinner on Friday?"

"That too, but why did you bring food when I hadn't asked you to come to the site?"

Sherbourne had spent a good five minutes staring at a scrap of paper, pencil poised to write a message that would allay Charlotte's fears without conveying any of his own. He'd never once considered that Charlotte would want to be involved.

He'd stuck with the facts: *Extensive damage, no fatalities.*

The project budget had sustained a severe injury, though, as had Sherbourne's confidence in Hannibal Jones.

Two hours later, Sherbourne had looked up and seen his wife, his passionate, shy, blunt wife, perched on a hard chair, spouting off about the weight of a cubic yard of water, and his heart had felt lighter.

"I came to the works because I was worried," Charlotte said, bracing herself as the gig hit a rut. "Your note was cryptic, and when is food a bad idea?"

No more cryptic notes, then. Full sentences, a greeting, a signature. He could do that. "The food was good. The men appreciated it." Sherbourne had appreciated it. He'd told her that, hadn't he?

Good God, when had this lane become so full of potholes?

"You don't have to mince words, Mr. Sherbourne. I should not have stuck my nose in, implying that you were less than equal to the situation. One grows concerned—'no fatalities' can imply grievous injuries—and merely sending a footman with a few sandwiches when I know the colliery has no cooking facilities did not seem..." Charlotte snatched away a bonnet ribbon that the wind insisted on whipping against her mouth. "I'm glad the men enjoyed the soup."

She sounded forlorn rather than glad. Across the valley, clouds were thickening into the pewter-bellied masses that always, always brought rain.

"I had plans for us this morning." What his own declaration had to do with anything, Sherbourne did not know.

"I meant for us to pay a call on the vicar today," Charlotte replied. "One starts with the vicar, and nobody can take offense."

They'd reached the stretch of the lane that wasn't visible from the house or the works. Sherbourne brought the horse to a halt.

"I had hoped to waken you this morning with kisses, Mrs. Sherbourne." He couldn't see Charlotte's expression because of the damned brim of her bonnet.

She ran a gloved fingertip over the padded armrest. "I had hoped to waken you with similar affectionate displays."

Affectionate? Charlotte had come apart in his arms last night like a Catherine wheel whirling over the Thames on a moonless night. For a few moments, she'd been wholly claimed by pleasure. Sherbourne had fallen asleep marveling at the lover whom fate had given him in the person of his wife—and he'd fallen asleep aching.

"We'll have many mornings." Sherbourne hoped that

was so, but he had no illusions: Charlotte expected and deserved to be kept in a style befitting her station. The mine did not have to produce enormous wealth, but it could not continue to lose enormous sums if Sherbourne was to uphold his end of the marital bargain.

"Were you angry with me for going to the works this morning?"

Sherbourne turned Charlotte's chin, so he could see her eyes. "And if I was? What then?"

Charlotte batted his fingers from her face. "The day you strike me is the day we part company permanently, and I don't care what the laws of this benighted realm say about my having become your property. Raise a hand to me and you will never see me again."

Of all the words she could have flung at him, Sherbourne would never have expected to hear those. They reassured him that Charlotte would stand up for herself, but they appalled him too.

"Madam, if you think I would raise a hand to my wife—to any woman—then you should not have married me."

They were surrounded by a veritable marsh, and even the lane was more puddles than pathway, which meant Charlotte could not abandon the vehicle with her dignity intact.

Fortunately for Sherbourne's much abused boots, because he would have gone after her until this discussion was concluded.

"Men do," Charlotte said, hands fisted in her lap. "They strike their wives, some men even strike women they profess to love, and the diabolical church—"

Now, Sherbourne *was* angry, not annoyed, frustrated, irritated, or flummoxed. He was furious. "Charlotte, I would never, ever use my strength against you. Do you think because my antecedents are untitled, that I can't control my temper?"

Her glower turned to confusion. "I beg your pardon?"

"I am common," Sherbourne said. "I am as common as mud, but governing one's temper is not a skill reserved to the aristocracy."

"I never said... I never thought..." She twitched at the lap robe covering her skirts. "You are mistaken. Let's get out of this wind."

Most of Sherbourne wanted to do just that, and yet he didn't take up the reins. "One moment, we're discussing kisses, the next you're threatening to leave me. I feel as if a mudslide has landed on my morning twice. What is this about, Charlotte?"

A man could not apologize if he had no idea what his transgression was. Neither could a woman.

Charlotte glanced back toward the works, though Heulwen and Morgan were apparently returning to the house by way of Scotland.

"I once mentioned to you my late friend," Charlotte said, gaze fixed on the muddy lane curving toward the house.

Foreboding edged aside Sherbourne's ire. "Go on."

"I told you that she got with child. I did not tell you that when she confronted the father, he at first laughed and said the child could not be his. The child could only have been his."

"He was a rutting disgrace to his gender."

"When my friend became insistent—he'd promised her marriage—he struck her and told her not to bother him again. He struck the mother of his child and cast her out."

A single droplet landed on the back of Charlotte's glove. The sky above was still bright, the clouds distant, which meant...

Charlotte swiped at her cheek. "He was in line for a title, Lucas. Fern told me that much about him when she begged me for coach fare to return to her family. If I'm critical of violent men, that has nothing whatsoever to do with your antecedents." Charlotte sat stiffly as two more drops landed on the back of her gloves.

She hadn't referred to any other friends, ever. Was this why?

Sherbourne produced a wrinkled handkerchief. "I'm sorry, Charlotte." He passed over the handkerchief, loathing the sense of helplessness, the useless anger that Charlotte's recitation provoked. Charlotte Windham— Charlotte *Sherbourne*—would hate to cry, and whoever this aristocratic varlet was, he'd made Charlotte cry, among his many other sins.

She pressed her forehead to Sherbourne's shoulder. "I was afraid you'd been injured. I hardly know you, and already, you matter to me. If you were wroth with me, sent me back to my parents…"

She spoke so softly Sherbourne had to bend close to hear her. When her words penetrated, he understood her odd logic. If Charlotte feared rejection for having intruded into a difficult situation at the mine, she must threaten him with the same fate, on any grounds she could use. Give no quarter, and never threaten with an empty gun.

At the negotiating table, she'd be fearless. Sitting on a cold Welsh farm lane, she was still fearless.

Sherbourne held her while she cried, though the horse stomped, and at last, Heulwen's red cape became visible over the rise, along with Morgan—holding her hand. Sherbourne resented the intrusion mightily, for Charlotte might never again cry on his shoulder.

Her tears were brief, which he also resented, because

holding her as a husband held an upset wife was a new and oddly precious experience.

"I'm glad you're safe," she said, straightening. "Please, let's go home."

Home, not back to the hall. Sherbourne took up the reins and set the horse to a brisk walk, because a trot was asking for spinal injury.

"May I ask why you invited Haverford and his duchess to dinner on Friday?"

"I need the practice," she said. "Our staff needs the practice. Haverford and Elizabeth are family, so they won't go bearing tales if the footman drops the tureen or my menu lacks imagination."

Sherbourne's staff was well trained, but Charlotte had a point: They were not well trained when it came to waiting on lofty titles. That Charlotte might doubt her own abilities was hard to believe.

"If you are trying to repair relations between Haverford and me, I appreciate the overture, but it won't work."

"Relations between you and the duke are no concern of mine. I simply want my sister's aid as I acquaint myself with managing your staff."

Our staff.

Sherbourne cast around for a way to keep the conversation afloat. "Haverford's sister married the Marquess of Radnor, whom you know from last summer's house party. You might consider inviting her and her husband." In truth, Sherbourne did need to become more familiar with Radnor, for his lordship sat on the board of directors for the mine.

"A duke and marquess," Charlotte said, as Sherbourne steered the gig up the main drive. "That could be a challenge, though I liked both Radnor and Lady Glenys."

Do you like me? He didn't dare ask. "Why not invite the vicar and his daughter?"

"We haven't called on them yet. I can impose on my sister, and by extension, Lady Glenys—Lady Radnor now—but until I've been introduced to other households, we're limited to family connections."

Dinner parties were usually groups of at least twelve, weren't they? "What about Griffin and Biddy? They're Haverford's family."

"I like Lord Griffin, of course, and Lady Griffin is very dear, but would they be an unusual addition to the gathering? Griffin is..."

"Different," Sherbourne said, turning off the drive to the lane that led to the carriage house. "He's a decent, honest, hard-working soul who isn't half so simple as people claim he is. He's different, so am I, so are you. I like him."

"You don't seem to like many people."

"I like you." *Damnation to any who said honest feelings shared between a husband and wife were unrefined.*

Charlotte smoothed her glove over the lap robe. "One rather hoped that was the case. I'll invite Lord and Lady Griffin. By the time the Earl of Brantford is in the area, the staff will be prepared to entertain him."

That's what this was about? "Thank you."

"For the soup?"

Sherbourne pulled up before the stable, and a groom came out to hold the horse, who'd grown muddy indeed during his morning's labors.

"Oats for our noble Athelstan," Sherbourne said, climbing down and coming around to assist Charlotte. "He's slogged through more mud than Napoleon faced at Waterloo."

Charlotte put her hands on Sherbourne's shoulders and

let him swing her to the ground. "I apologize for my lapse of composure. I am not usually prone to displays of sentiment."

Sherbourne suspected he'd married a woman whose sentimentality was eclipsed only by her vast dignity.

"The topic warranted your ire," he said. "Thank you for all you did this morning. Not for the men, for me. The food was lovely, but you spotted the error Jones himself didn't see, and that will save lives, Charlotte."

Standing in the stable yard, the air redolent of manure, horses, and hay, Charlotte blossomed. The last shadow of her tears disappeared into a wondrously warm and happy smile.

"I like numbers." The sun rose higher in her eyes, to a brilliant zenith. "I like you, Mr. Sherbourne."

He leaned close enough to whisper in her ear. "I like when you call me Lucas."

She brushed a kiss to his cheek and whispered back, "Lucas."

The sun took up residence in Sherbourne's chest, along with a compulsion to smile fatuously at his bride, which would not do.

"I could bring home Jones's calculations," he said, oh-so-casually offering his arm. "Perhaps you might review them for me?"

"That would be my pleasure, and when I ask Mr. Jones the occasional question, I will tell him I'm trying to understand my husband's commercial interests, which will be the truth."

"Thank you." The words got easier with practice, at least when spoken to Charlotte.

"Thank you, *Lucas*."

Chapter Twelve

Haverford's duchess had obligingly conceived a child either on their wedding night or shortly thereafter.

Or possibly shortly therebefore. Elizabeth had informed her duke this was something of a tradition with her family where firstborn children were concerned. Haverford was a great believer in tradition, but in this one case, he had reservations.

"You're certain you don't care for any tea?" Haverford had joined his wife in her tower parlor because a midafternoon tea tray was one of his guilty pleasures—also because her company was infinitely preferable to that of his land steward.

To anybody's.

Elizabeth's knitting needles kept up a steady rhythm. "Julian, unless you want to be the first duke to wear hot tea as a hair tonic, I suggest you put that pot down."

He put the pot down. Last night, after they'd made love, she'd dragged him to the kitchens because a cup of peppermint tea with a dash of honey had become her reason for living. The staff was indulgent regarding such eccentric behavior, while Haverford pretended to be amused.

He and Elizabeth had had a short courtship, and a man wanted *some* time to enjoy his beloved's exclusive company. Elizabeth had not conceived a child on her own initiative, however, so what could a chronically worried duke do but love his wife and pray for the best?

"Charlotte is inviting Griffin and Biddy to this dinner," Elizabeth said, sparing her sister's note a glance. "Radnor and Glenys will join us as well. Charlotte says she wants Sherbourne to be confident of her and his staff when the Earl of Brantford comes to visit."

If Lucas Sherbourne were any more confident, he'd appoint himself Minister Plenipotentiary of the Universe for Life.

"If the company is limited to us, Radnor and Glynis, and your sister and her husband, then Griffin and Biddy should manage well enough."

In the previous century, His Grace of Chandos had bought a hostler's castoff wife at a wife sale and made her his duchess. Compared to that choice, Biddy was a more conventional spouse for a duke's son, but only just. She was a local yeoman's daughter and had been Griffin's housekeeper before joining him in holy matrimony.

Elizabeth's needles went still. "You find even saying Sherbourne's name distasteful. I find him somewhat difficult, but then, Charlotte is short of charm herself. We must commend Mr. Sherbourne for being willing to take on a challenge."

Charlotte Windham was a termagant who at least stood a chance of dealing effectively with Lucas Sherbourne.

"A crooked pot needs a crooked lid," Haverford said.

"They can be uncharming together, and raise up a brood of holy terrors in their nursery. Should I review dinner party etiquette with Griffin?"

Haverford poured himself a third cup of tea. No sense letting it go to waste.

"Griffin has joined us for any number of meals, and his manners are exquisite. What do we know of the Earl of Brantford?"

Griffin's manners were a monument to rote memorization and practice. He had many limitations, but nearly perfect recall, often at the worst times.

"I honestly don't know Brantford well. He says he'll be in the area for some shooting—"

A tap sounded on the door of Her Grace's private parlor.

"Come in," Elizabeth called.

The butler stepped into the room. "Lord Radnor has come to—"

"No need to announce me." The Marquess of Radnor, looking gloriously blond and fit, sidled around the butler. "I'm always welcome, or so I was told before I married into the family. Greetings, all. Duchess, you look radiant. Haverford, you look lucky to have chosen Her Grace for your duchess."

Radnor bowed over Elizabeth's proffered hand, took the place beside her on the sofa, then helped himself to the freshly poured cup of tea.

"I'm told hot tea is the latest fashion in hair tonics," Haverford said. "Particularly when applied directly to the coiffure of a presuming caller."

Radnor appropriated a piece of shortbread from Elizabeth's plate. "Do your worst, Haverford, for my good spirits are beyond even your ability to dim. I bring joyous news."

"You're moving to France. Excellent, provided Glenys visits us often."

Radnor balanced the cup and saucer on one knee and affected a concerned expression. "My, my. Is somebody going short of sleep?"

What an obnoxious...Well, yes. Somebody also missed the sister who'd shared his castle until recently. Glenys did visit, but she was thriving as Radnor's marchioness, almost as if leaving Haverford Castle had been a relief.

"Your Grace," Radnor said, addressing Elizabeth, "we must forgive Haverford his testy mood. He's worried about you, and soon you will have to forgive me similarly, for Glenys is with child."

Radnor's sunny bonhomie faltered, and a rare shyness took its place.

"Congratulations," Haverford said. "Take good care of my sister or I'll kill you."

Elizabeth resumed knitting. "You two gentlemen will take good care of each other, or Glenys and I will send you both to darkest Peru for a repairing lease. Please give Glenys my most sincere good wishes, and know that we're ready to stand as godparents if that suits."

This was part of the reason Haverford adored his wife. Elizabeth knew what to say, she knew what to do, and she went about saying and doing the appropriate things with no need to draw attention to herself.

"This is good news," Haverford said. "If you're to be the favorite uncle who spoils my children rotten, then I should have a chance to fulfill the reciprocal role. Will you leave us any shortbread?"

"Yours is better than ours," Radnor said. "I must admit, the thought of becoming a father appeals. The idea of what Glenys must endure to become a mother, though...one worries."

Elizabeth was watching Haverford as she deftly added stitches to her knitting.

"One does," Haverford said slowly. "Incessantly. I suppose it's good training for raising children."

Radnor finished his first cup of tea—or Haverford's third. "I'm told peppermint tea is soothing to the nerves. I shall doubtless become a peppermint tea drunk. I'm off to pass along my good news to the vicar. Prayers, you know. Can't hurt."

The bashfulness was back, while a lone piece of shortbread remained on Elizabeth's plate.

Radnor was friendly by nature, though he was no fool. Once his temper was provoked, he was every bit as thunderous as he could be sanguine. He knew everybody and was universally liked, and also respected.

"Radnor, are you familiar with the Earl of Brantford?" Haverford asked.

"Quinton Bramley. He's a few years younger than we are, family seat in Northumbria or the West Riding. Somewhere dreadfully bleak. Has an interest in coal mines. Indulges in the usual vices."

The usual vices being a mistress, and moderate drinking and gambling.

"Sherbourne has sold him an interest in the colliery," Haverford said. "Brantford is dropping around next week to inspect the progress of the works. Her Grace and I are to host the visit."

Elizabeth whipped the bulk of whatever she was making aside and started on a new row. "The same works that suffered a mudslide earlier today."

Radnor rose. "Those works. I heard that nobody was injured despite considerable damage to the grounds."

"The damned hill decided to move itself a good thirty

yards to the east," Haverford said. "Sherbourne seems undaunted, but I've asked my tenants to lend a hand putting things to rights."

"Sherbourne excels at seeming undaunted," Radnor said. "Duchess, a pleasure as always. I'm off to the vicarage. Haverford, be a dear and see a man off, would you?"

Elizabeth remained serenely knitting on her sofa, though she doubtless knew Radnor was asking for some privacy with a friend.

"Away with you both," she said. "Though if you could have a pot of China black sent up, I'd appreciate it. Somebody seems to have drunk all of mine."

Radnor paused with one glove on, the other in his hand. "But Haverford told me last week—"

"A fresh pot," Haverford said, "along with another plate of shortbread. No bother at all. Radnor, come along."

Radnor kissed Elizabeth's cheek, and came along like a good marquess who didn't want to return home sporting a black eye.

"Glenys claims it's early days," Radnor said, once they'd gained the corridor. "I reckon that means another seven months of fretting and fussing before the real worry sets in. Do you know how large the newborn human is, Haverford?"

"I'm several months ahead of you pondering that alarming topic. Gives a man pause."

"Gives a man a bilious stomach. The ladies marry us, knowing what the likely consequences will be. One can only marvel at such fortitude."

Haverford paused at the top of the main staircase, for this was not a conversation to be overheard by servants.

"Why," he asked, "does one marvel at such fortitude only after one has fallen arse over ears in love, married, and got a woman with child? We see babies everywhere, hear them squalling at every church service, and yet..."

"And yet, our babies will be different," Radnor said. "Our entire worlds will be different, because we're to become fathers. I'm scared witless. You will please tell me I'm being ridiculous, and never mention this discussion again."

They would have this discussion regularly for the next thirty years. "If you weren't concerned for Glenys, I'd have to call you out, but then there'd be nobody to talk sense to me when Elizabeth's travail begins."

"Is your digestion upset?" Radnor asked, lowering his voice. "I vow, Haverford, I'm in worse condition than Glenys in the morning."

"You're simply worried. The dyspepsia will pass."

"Not for months. Months, this ordeal goes on. I already told Glennie we're having an only child. Fat George can have the marquessate. My nerves are too delicate for more than one lying-in."

"You were an only child. You need heirs."

Radnor started down the steps. "If that's your idea of cheering a fellow up, you can forget about being anybody's godfather. I'll prevail on Sherbourne and his new bride."

Like hell. "Radnor, has impending fatherhood addled you that badly?"

"No, actually," Radnor said, rounding the landing. "I will be a competent father because Glenys will see that I am. It's the other part, which might cost me my wife less than a year after I married her, that bothers me. The part that could cause Glenys endless, awful suffering, and consign her to a lingering death. The part where she bleeds—"

Haverford joined his friend at the foot of the steps. "Radnor, get hold of yourself, or have Glenys get hold of you."

"She does, frequently. This delightful discussion reminds me why I asked you to walk me to my horse."

"It's damned chilly outside, and I already braved the elements to make sure Sherbourne hadn't been buried under tons of mud. Say what you have to say."

"You asked about Brantford." Radnor used the mirror above the foyer's sideboard and donned his top hat just so. "I recall some talk, years ago. My mother passed it along, and her sources were extensive."

"What sort of talk?"

"Brantford ruined a young lady. Got her with child and threw her over for the present countess."

"You don't mean he set up an opera dancer as his ladybird?"

"Of course not. Nobody would have thought twice about an arrangement like that. He all but courted a decent young woman of humble origins, then dropped her flat when the inevitable occurred. The lady was packed off to the countryside and not heard from again, but there was a child."

"Many a squire regrets letting his daughter have a season in town." And many a duke too?

"She wasn't a squire's daughter," Radnor said, hand on the door latch. "Her papa was a minister, and she was his only daughter. A man who'll ruin a minister's daughter bears watching."

This was Sherbourne's idea of a business partner? "I appreciate the warning. My regards to Mr. MacPherson."

Radnor went jaunting on his way, while Haverford went in search of two pots of tea. China black for the duchess, though she'd probably not drink a single cup.

Peppermint for him, and for his nerves.

* * *

"Heulwen, can you take some letters to the posting inn for me tomorrow?"

"Aye, ma'am," the maid replied as she unlaced Charlotte's stays. "You could just as well leave anything for the post on the sideboard in the foyer, though. Crandall will see to them."

"I'd rather not chance these letters sitting about until the next groom or gardener wanders into the village."

Charlotte's back ached, possibly from the journey to and from the works on the horrendously muddy lane. The relief of being unlaced was exquisite.

"As you like, ma'am. Shall I brush out your hair?"

"No, thank you. I'll bid you goodnight, Heulwen. I'll have several letters for you to post in the morning. My thanks for all your help today at the colliery."

"That's a lot of mud what came down that hill. Will we be taking the nooning out to the works tomorrow?"

Heulwen was clearly eager for any opportunity to consort with the groom, Morgan, but Charlotte hadn't thought that far ahead.

"I don't know. I'll ask Mr. Sherbourne." *If he ever comes to bed.* "Goodnight, Heulwen."

Charlotte's husband had gone back to the works, his saddle bags bulging with sandwiches and a flask. He'd told Charlotte not to wait up for him. Married life thus far had too much of waiting and worrying, and not enough of anything else.

Though last night had been...splendid.

Heulwen tarried, refolding clothing already folded, smoothing covers that hadn't a single wrinkle.

"Heulwen, I'd like some solitude." Charlotte also wanted

to throw something fragile and use foul language, because her husband should have been here with her, settling in at the end of the day. The intimacies they'd shared the previous night had been wondrous beyond imagining, and then she'd had that disagreement with him on the lane...

Though even that hadn't ended awfully. They'd managed. They'd been civil and brought the conversation to a friendly conclusion.

"Goodnight, then, ma'am. Ring if you need anything, such as a bath for Mr. Sherbourne, for example. Or a tray. Some chocolate. A fresh bucket of coal. Anything."

"I've already told the kitchen to keep bath water heating." Charlotte jabbed a finger in the direction of the door, and finally Heulwen left.

Charlotte found her sketch pad and drawing pencils and pulled a chair closer to the fire. The colliery sat between three hills. To the south, the land fell away in the direction of the sea. The retaining wall had been built along the eastern boundary of the planned village, though the slope rising to the west was less steep.

She was still rearranging the work site on paper an hour later when Sherbourne walked into the bedroom without knocking.

"Haverford sent a dozen men." No greeting, no kiss to Charlotte's cheek. "Radnor came trotting by and said he'd do likewise. He's on my board of directors, and of course must poke his nose into the works."

Charlotte yanked the bell pull three times. "You resent their support?"

Sherbourne took some time divesting himself of papers, two pencil stubs, and a folding knife. Next came a signet ring, his watch, his cravat pin. He shrugged out of his coat and arched his back, hands braced at the base of his spine.

Should Charlotte assist him? Leave him in peace? *Ask?* Why, if polite society must hold marriage out as the apex of a woman's ambitions, was so little done to explain how she was to go on once the great prize had been won?

"I resent everything," Sherbourne said. "Ignore me. A goddamned mountain of mud sits where my tenant cottages should be, and I have no faith another wall won't give way just as easily."

Charlotte knew exactly the mood he was in, because it visited her frequently. "So don't build another wall. Clear enough mud to make the lane passable and well drained, then put the houses elsewhere."

Fatigue grooved Sherbourne's mouth and ringed his eyes—fatigue and frustration. "I can't put the damned houses in the sea, though I'd like to."

A tap sounded on the door.

"Your bath," Charlotte said, admitting one footman wheeling in the copper monstrosity, and a half dozen more bearing steaming buckets.

Sherbourne's expression said he did not want to be-damned bathe, he did not want to be blasted reasonable, and he did not want to dratted deal with a wife who also wasn't feeling entirely reasonable herself.

Turnbull brought up the rear, laying out a shaving kit, then bowing and retreating with the parade of footmen. Two full buckets sat steaming on the hearth.

Charlotte advanced on her husband. "The water is hot, you are doubtless chilled to the bone. Your clothing is filthy, while you are by nature fastidious. I'm sorry if the notion of soaking in warm, fragrant water and scrubbing yourself from head to toe annoys you, but in all the lending libraries in the world, there is no manual on how to cosset a contrary husband. Please get into the water."

He remained silent while Charlotte untied his cravat and collected his sleeve buttons.

"Where would you put the houses?" he asked, as she started on his waistcoat.

"Not now, Mr. Sherbourne. Shirt off."

Long ago, Fern Porter had said that her papa's mistress was the church. The congregation made endless demands, at all hours, regardless of the inconvenience. Aunt Esther had once remarked that Parliament was a jealous mistress, and Papa had muttered that he competed with all of Wales for pride of place in Mama's heart.

Charlotte was jealous of a muddy patch of ground that didn't even qualify as a colliery yet.

Sherbourne sat by the fire to take off his boots, which were a disgrace in progress. He set them outside the door and passed Charlotte his waistcoat.

"Your expression, madam, would have inspired Napoleon to blow retreat at Waterloo before the first shot was fired."

Another tap sounded on the door. Charlotte took a tray from a footman, and shut and locked the door.

"You'd best make use of the water while it's hot, sir."

Sherbourne's shirt and breeches came off, and Charlotte was appalled to see a long, dark bruising rising along one hip.

"You're hurt."

"I'm clumsy," he said, lowering himself into the water. "Slipped and landed on a disobliging rock. God, this feels heavenly."

Not quite a thank-you, but gratifying nonetheless. "Shall I wash your hair?"

"Please, and don't let me fall asleep. What's on the tray?"

"Meat pastries, ale, apple tarts. Shall you wash before I tend to your hair?" *And are you the same man who was so patient and understanding with me earlier today?*

Sherbourne lifted a pastry and sniffed it. "I am famished. My hands will taste of soap if I wash myself. Perhaps you'd assist?"

He was disappointingly nonchalant about this request, more interested in his viands than in flirting with his wife.

Charlotte knelt by the tub. "Give me your foot."

She became better acquainted with her husband's person part by part. Large feet, the arches somewhat high, the second toe longer than the first. Two toes on the left foot were crooked, which Sherbourne explained as the result of having been stepped on by a fractious horse in his youth.

One ankle was larger than the other—a broken ankle having occurred when he'd been tripped at supper his first term at public school.

Sherbourne had muscular calves and thighs, though Charlotte had known that. His hands were in proportion to the rest of him and not the hands of a gentleman for all their elegance. Calluses covered his palms, suggesting he often indulged in manual labor.

Long arms, one of which had been broken in a schoolyard melee, broad shoulders, hair a bit in need of a trim at the back. Charlotte rinsed the soap from that hair.

"Shall I shave you?" Not that she'd ever shaved a man before.

"Perhaps in the morning."

She took the tray—not a crumb of food left—and set it outside the door. While she relocked the door, Sherbourne lounged in the tub, one foot propped on the rim, the tankard of ale in his hand.

"You're not to fall asleep, Mr. Sherbourne."

He saluted with his ale. "Yes, ma'am. Why is your hair still up?"

Charlotte put a hand to her head. "I became distracted." By a tired, naked husband. "I'll see to it."

Sherbourne rose and set his ale on the mantel, water cascading off of him. "If you'd pass me the linen, I'll take down your hair when I'm dried off."

Triton in all his glory was not as magnificent a specimen as Lucas Sherbourne fresh from his bath. But for the bruise on his hip, he was male perfection, and though he was standing naked right before Charlotte, he was also still tromping around his bedamned, blasted, dratted colliery.

Charlotte passed him the linen...slowly.

"Thank you, madam wife. It occurs to me that a mudslide is not much of an introduction to married life." He scrubbed his face first, then his chest and arms, then dragged the towel over his hair. "In spring, we'll nip off to Paris or Lisbon if the colliery is coming along. I owe you a wedding journey."

Doubtless the colliery would not be *coming along* for years, and then there would be a new colliery, or a shipping venture, a canal, something. This realization was daunting, but then, Charlotte didn't want a husband who idled away the day, or worse, lay about underfoot, expecting her to entertain him.

"I've never seen the Lakes," she said. "If we traveled there instead, you could also visit various mining operations in the north and show me your hotel."

Sherbourne paused, the towel bunched to his chest, his hair in damp disarray. His expression was intrigued and then guilty. "I owe you a wedding journey, and coal mines are hardly scenic."

Much less romantic. "Mr. Sherbourne, don't you think

you owe me a wedding *night* before you make too many plans involving a wedding journey?"

He lowered the towel, obscuring any evidence of his interest in said wedding night. "I do owe you a wedding night. Have you any particular night in mind?"

"Tonight will do splendidly."

Chapter Thirteen

Sherbourne pitched the damp towel onto the hamper and reached for the dressing gown his wife had spread over the fire screen. A new husband needed a few fig leaves when discussing his wedding night.

"I thought you might want to recover from last night's exertions." He'd also thought of every undemanding way he could make love with his wife, until his inattention had landed him arse-first in the mud.

Charlotte took a seat at her vanity. "I'm recovered."

Well, I'm not. "Delighted to hear it." Also relieved.

She made a lovely picture at the vanity, candle light reflected in the glass, her hair shimmering with garnet highlights. Her dressing gown was...actually, she was wearing one of Sherbourne's dressing gowns.

He took the place behind her, resting his hands on her shoulders. "Is tonight your preference, Charlotte, or are you being accommodating?"

"I am seldom accommodating, Mr. Sherbourne, but I am married. To you. We could put off the consummation yet again, though I suspect mudslides of one sort or another will be frequent in this marriage. Tomorrow night is a possibility, but then Friday we have company. The house must be put in readiness for guests the following week, even if Brantford stays at Haverford Castle. Other predictable inconveniences will intrude as well."

Sherbourne studied her coiffure which appeared to affix itself to her head by magic. Tentative exploration revealed a few nacre-tipped hairpins.

He eased them free one by one. "Haverford is a predictable inconvenience. I suppose we'll have to call upon him and upon Radnor."

He found more pins, and put each one in the tray on the vanity, twelve in all. Charlotte's braid came down, a thick skein of russet and gold in the firelight.

"We will pay calls. That is not the predictable inconvenience to which I refer."

He had her braid half-undone before he realized why the nape of her neck had turned pink. Awkwardness and tenderness assailed him, just as they had when Charlotte had become so upset on the lane.

Sherbourne wrapped his arms around her shoulders. "Is it much of a bother? I haven't any sisters, and one doesn't ask one's mother. What the university boys had to say on the subject was ridiculous."

Charlotte's cheek against his arm was hot. "*Must* we discuss this?"

He straightened and went back to undoing her hair. "You could leave me to guess. Does her back pain her? Does her womb trouble her at such a time? Should I sleep elsewhere? Should I order her a pot of some concoction from the herbal? Shall I bide in a tent at the works for the next week? Shall I rub her back?"

He demonstrated, pressing firmly low on Charlotte's back, and she made a sound much like a tired hound settling to a cozy rug before a blazing hearth.

"I become easily annoyed," she said. "Just before. Prone to displays of temper and sentiment. That feels good."

Twenty-four hours ago, Sherbourne had been ready to make love with his new wife as enthusiastically as a considerate husband could. Then a hundred tons of mud had intruded into his plans, toppling his carefully balanced budget and putting an element of risk into his future that left him uneasy.

Marrying Charlotte Windham was to have been a prudent, even shrewd, business decision. Day by day, she was less a matter of business, and more a *person* who dragged, lectured, and surprised Sherbourne into emotions that hadn't been part of his plans.

"If having your back rubbed feels good," Sherbourne said, "then you ask it of me when I'm too dunderheaded to offer on my own initiative, agreed?"

Charlotte leaned forward, resting her head on her folded arms. "One doesn't know when to presume, when to ask, when to wait patiently to be asked. I had not foreseen that marriage would be much like learning a foreign language without a dictionary."

Apt analogy. So... "Shall I braid your hair?"

"Please. One braid will do."

Tending to her hair soothed Sherbourne and gave him time to think. Perhaps they'd make it part of their nightly ritual, on those occasions when the colliery didn't demand his presence even after dark.

"I didn't want to rush you," he said, drawing the brush

down the length of her hair. "About the wedding night." About anything, but he'd been uniformly precipitous where his wife was concerned. He'd rushed the proposal, whisked her from her family on the very day of the ceremony, and now she was to entertain guests not a week after arriving at their home.

Charlotte sighed sleepily as Sherbourne plied the brush. Her hair was thick and soft, a pleasure to touch. His braiding skills had been learned in the stables, though that seemed adequate for the occasion.

What had he been saying? "I wanted our wedding night to be memorable." Perhaps this aspiration was a symptom of the first incidence of financial uncertainty Sherbourne had ever faced. He'd spend tomorrow with his ledgers, reassessing his situation, but a woman who enjoyed her husband's attentions would be less likely to abandon him if finances became constrained.

Or perhaps Sherbourne was becoming attached to his wife.

Which made no sense at all. Fondness was acceptable, but *attached*?

"I want our wedding night to be memorable too," Charlotte said, sitting up. "Last night was very memorable."

Sherbourne's cock heard that bit of encouragement. "Would you like to do again what we did last night?" How casual he sounded, and yet, he couldn't get the damned hair ribbon wrapped around her braid, much less secured into a proper knot.

"No, thank you."

Well, hell. He'd been fairly certain his wife had enjoyed herself. With women, though, a man never—

"I want to see your face," Charlotte said. "I want to touch you too. I want to see your eyes."

He finished with her braid, though his bow was lop-sided. "I want to see all of you."

She smiled at him over her shoulder. "Said the man who just spent the better part of an hour lounging about in the altogether. I'm glad you're not overly shy."

"I was overly in need of a bath. One usually bathes in the altogether."

Charlotte rose and disappeared behind the privacy screen. "Would you mind warming the sheets? The foot-men can deal with the tub in the morning."

When filled with cold, less than pristine water, the tub was not a fixture in any erotic fantasy Sherbourne could conjure. He pushed the whole business into the corridor, which exertion reminded him that his hip was sore, and likely to be downright painful in a day or two. He set the empty buckets outside the door as well, and gave himself up to a moment of resentment.

He resented being married. Resented having to think of a wife, share a room with a wife, consider her social prior-ities, and send her notes. Listening to Charlotte humming softly behind the privacy screen, Sherbourne resented all the servants who knew he'd abandoned the lady of the manor for dinner more often than he'd joined her.

He resented the weather, which would go from bad to worse to awful.

He resented Brantford, who couldn't be bothered to spend a night under the roof of a business associate, but must instead prevail on His Grace of Have-A-Title for ac-commodations.

"Your turn," Charlotte said, emerging from the privacy screen. "I left you some warm water, though you hardly need it."

"The sheets..."

"No matter." She unbelted her robe, and damned if the woman wasn't naked. "I'm sure we'll be quite cozy in no time."

She climbed under the covers, depriving him of an opportunity to gawk—for now—but he'd glimpsed a slim haunch, the curve of her breast.

Sherbourne used his tooth powder and blew out the candles, but he didn't bank the fire. Charlotte had said she wanted to see his eyes, or some damned nonsense to that effect, so a little illumination was basic husbandly consideration.

He shrugged out of his dressing gown and draped it over a chair. "My hair is still damp."

"All the more reason for you to get under the covers lest you take a chill. You seem to have the constitution of a bull, but tempting fate is for fools."

Sherbourne got under the covers, the sheets cool rather than frigid. He considered waiting until morning to make love with his wife—they were both tired, the hour was late, he wasn't at his best—but in the morning, he'd be off to the colliery, arguing with Jones about moving a row of houses that should probably never have been laid out at the foot of the hill.

"Lucas?"

He found Charlotte's hand beneath the covers and brought her fingers to his lips. "You're sure?"

She tucked herself along his side. "I'm more sure by the moment."

Sherbourne draped himself over his wife and kissed her. His hip hurt, which was good, because a little pain would offer a distraction when a distraction was needed. Charlotte kissed him back, which was very good.

He needed her kisses. He needed the pleasure he could share with her while he forgot, for one blessed, private hour, the tons of mud that had destroyed his schedule, his budget, and some of his confidence.

As Charlotte took his hand and tucked it over her breast, Sherbourne spared one last thought for his commercial undertakings: He, who thrived on a challenge and had schemed for years to bring mining into the valley, resented his colliery.

He resented his colliery mightily.

* * *

Charlotte considered letting Sherbourne drift off to sleep, or—more likely—lie beside her, fretting over his tenant houses, tram lines, and business associations. Two thoughts stopped her from pursuing that course. First, she refused to yield the very consummation of her vows to the press of business. Beginning as she intended to go on in the marriage meant that in this instance, she was owed her husband's attention at the time and place of her choosing, exactly as he'd promised.

The second thought that weighed against allowing Sherbourne his rest was the growing realization of how alone he was, and how much responsibility he carried.

Finding a set of widow's weeds for a ruined laundress or scraping together a few pounds for coach fare had been significant accomplishments in Charlotte's eyes. Sherbourne sought to employ scores of people, to provide sustenance for many families, and this was only one of his ventures.

He deserved a respite from his obligations. He deserved one place where business could not intrude and where his satisfaction mattered.

"You make a lovely quilt," Charlotte said. "All warm and friendly."

Sherbourne nuzzled her ear, which tickled. "I don't be-lieve I've ever been accused of friendliness."

The texture of his chest hairs against Charlotte's bare skin was peculiar, his beard slightly abrasive. Blunt warmth nudged against her thigh.

"Should I be doing something?"

Sherbourne rested his forehead against her shoulder. "You and I are alike in this regard. We worry less when we're busy. You should be enjoying yourself."

Difficult to do, when uncertainty and arousal were evenly matched. "I liked it when you..." Charlotte could not say the words. She was naked in bed with her husband, and she could not say the words.

"Show me."

She took his hand and closed his fingers around her nip-ple. Not too hard, but not too lightly either.

"As it happens," Sherbourne said, "we both enjoy that. Let's try something."

In the next moment, he had her atop him, which meant Charlotte was more or less sitting on a particularly tumid part of his anatomy, and her *abundant glories* were on dis-play.

And Sherbourne was admiring them. He smoothed his hands over her breasts, filling his palms, and curling up to press his face between them, rough beard and all.

Charlotte wrapped a hand around his head, his hair warm and damp where it had been against the pillow, cool where it grazed her breasts.

"Shall I use my mouth?" Sherbourne asked. "Did you like that too?"

"This is not an interview, Mr. Sherbourne."

He laughed and hugged her, the sensation of bare skin tightly pressed to bare skin a lovely shock.

"You are modest and passionate," he said. "An inconvenient combination for you, I'm sure. What if I bumble along as best I can, and you let me know if I've chosen the wrong direction?"

Charlotte put his hand back on her breast. "That will suit."

His bumbling was an entrancing progression of kisses, caresses, and suggestions. Charlotte was to touch him too, apparently, for he used her third finger to draw light circles around his nipple, and when she added a slight pinch and a scrape of her fingernail, he arched into her touch.

All the while, his arousal was evident against her sex, a hot, hard, intimate promise all its own.

Charlotte cast about for how to form a question, but "Shall we get on with it, Mr. Sherbourne?" struck her as ridiculous. "When do we...?" wasn't much better, but she hoped it was soon.

Very soon.

"You make me ache," Sherbourne said, flexing his hips. "You make me ache and rejoice."

He rearranged himself so Charlotte lay on her back beneath him as he slid *that* part of himself against her sex.

His slow caress sent need clamoring through her. "Again, please."

A silent conversation took place, between his body and hers. He teased, he dared, he hesitated, and Charlotte moaned against his neck. All else fell away as Sherbourne shifted the angle of his hips and positioned himself to join with her.

The act was strange, physical, and unrelentingly intimate. Sherbourne eased his way into her body, and the yearning that had swamped Charlotte tangled up with tenderness for the man in her arms.

"Don't be so careful," she murmured. "Be passionate with me."

He brushed her hair back from her forehead. "You're managing?"

How odd, to trade words when nothing separated them. "I want to worship you with my body too, Lucas."

He hitched closer, and pleasure welled from where they were joined. "Move with me, Charlotte."

How could they move when—? Oh. *Oh.* He set a tempo like war drums, slow, resonate, full of leashed power and unwavering focus. Charlotte matched him, scooting down to lock her ankles at the small of his back. Her touch wandered everywhere, the span of his shoulders, the taper of his waist, the slightly warm, raised bruise along his hip.

As close as they were, she wanted to be closer, to be inside him the way he was inside her. Desire became a madness, obliterating all else—fears, worries, dignity, even dreams fell beneath Sherbourne's passion—until Charlotte lost her very self in pleasure.

Her awareness clung to one reality: Sherbourne was with her. With her in pleasure, and with her in the panting, thunderstruck aftermath, as she curled beneath him, and his heartbeat reverberated with her own.

Puzzle pieces fell into place: *This* was what lay behind a thousand glances passed between Charlotte's cousins and their spouses.

This closeness was where families began, where every marriage was both the same and unique.

This was what a ruined woman sacrificed her future for. Not the bodily sensations, amazing though they were, but the tenderness and cherishing, the oneness.

Sherbourne's breathing slowed, and though he remained close, he braced his weight on his elbows. Charlotte wanted to hold him tightly, because on the heels of all these revelations came a tide of gratitude toward her husband.

She might have missed this. She might have spent the rest of her days shooting arrows through the hats of randy bachelors and turning down proposals from fortune hunters. She might have never known this wonder, never experienced the profound relief of putting aside every burden and hope to be one with her spouse for a few moments.

She kissed his biceps. "What does one say after that?"

He traced her eyebrow with his nose. "One says, 'Lucas, fetch me a glass of water, please.'"

No, one did not. "I'm glad I married you."

He went still, mid-nuzzle. "I'll bring you a flannel."

Perhaps one didn't admit to being glad to be married either. Charlotte would ponder that puzzle later, when she didn't feel so relaxed or—had marriage made her barmy?—cheerful.

Sherbourne brought her a damp cloth, then disappeared behind the privacy screen. Charlotte tended to herself, tossed the cloth over the privacy screen, and pulled up the covers.

"Come back to bed, Lucas."

By the light of the dying fire, he emerged from the privacy screen in his dressing gown. "I'm off to the library for a bit. Thought I'd read over some correspondence, let you get to sleep."

Charlotte's first reaction to Sherbourne's plan was hurt, that he'd be *capable* of rising from their bed and turning his attention to...what? Ledgers? Reports from the solicitors?

After making love with her *like that*?

But another theory presented itself, one having to do with the privacy necessary to contemplate a marriage he might be reevaluating even as Charlotte was.

"Mr. Sherbourne, for once, you will ignore the siren call of your commercial ventures and get some rest. You've earned it, and you will need your strength in the coming days and nights."

He stared at his bare feet. "I will?"

"Most assuredly. Come to bed, Lucas."

He came to bed.

* * *

Sherbourne waited until Charlotte dropped off to sleep to spoon himself around her. He should be in the library, making calculations, revising estimates, figuring the cost of the extra labor Radnor and Haverford were providing.

He should be searching for a replacement for Hannibal Jones or for a competent assistant, though that would be another extra expense.

He should be finding more investors.

He should be—

"Lucas?" Charlotte murmured.

"I thought you were asleep."

She rolled over to face him. "I was. I dreamed of you. Can't you sleep?"

He was exhausted, and yet he could not reach for sleep, so he'd reached for her. "I don't need much rest."

Charlotte came to him, burrowing closer, tangling her legs with his. "You will need more rest in the coming months. Marriage will take a toll on your energies."

"Bold talk, Mrs. Sherbourne."

"I like it when you call me Mrs. Sherbourne."

He really ought to be in the library, not wasting half the night cuddling around his warm, gardenia-scented, curved-in-all-the-right places wife.

"I cannot neglect my business, Charlotte, not for anything. If the mine doesn't soon get on its feet..."

She commenced drawing slow circles on his chest with her index finger. "Then the mine fails. This valley has never had a mine, so nobody is any worse off than if the mine had never been attempted."

Nobody but me and my investors—and you. "Haverford will never cease gloating if the mine isn't thriving by this time next year."

"So this determination where the colliery is concerned is about your pride?"

The success of the mine was purely about pence and quid now. "A man should always take pride in his endeavors."

"What about a woman? Is she allotted any pride?"

Sherbourne kissed her, because he wasn't equal to a debate on gender differences at this hour. Charlotte returned the kiss, and then lay on her back, urging him to settle against her side. The position was novel, with Sherbourne's cheek pillowed on her breast, her fingers playing with the hair at his nape.

"We must find a balance, Lucas, between your infernal obsession with immediate business and the long-term endeavors that will aid your interests over the course of a lifetime."

Her touch was so sweet, so soothing—and yet she was speaking to him in imperatives. "Hard work aids my business endeavors."

She kissed his temple. "Was it hard work that inspired Haverford to relent regarding the mine? No, it was not. You attended his house party, comported yourself like a perfect gentleman, rescued that hopeless Miss Twit from the lake, entertained me when I was bored, and flirted with a few wallflowers. Haverford had to see you as something other than his vexatious creditor."

Charlotte traced the curve of Sherbourne's ear, then used her thumb and forefinger to pull gently on his earlobe. The sensation was exquisitely relaxing, which was no help at all when she was already befuddling him with her pillow talk.

"I attended that house party on the barest pretense of an invitation because I was considering offering for Lady Glenys."

Charlotte's grip on his earlobe became quite firm. "Are you besotted with her? She is a duke's daughter, and the sister of a duke. You lose your common sense in the presence of titles, Lucas. I'll not have you pining for thy neighbor's marchioness."

"I was besotted with the idea that Haverford would have to choose between economic ruin or approving of me as a match for his sister. You have not married a saint, Charlotte."

Her grip eased. "I have not married the scourge of the high toby. Haverford is a duke, and they can leave a trail of aggravation that stretches for miles, one which they seldom notice. Elizabeth will have her hands full with Haverford. You mustn't be too hard on him, though. He hasn't had family about in any quantity to help him go on."

And Sherbourne had?

"That tickles," Charlotte said. "When you flutter your eyelashes like that."

"I do not flutter my eyelashes."

"And yet, you tickled me. We should call on the vicar."

Calling on the vicar would not clear the mud from what was to have been the high street at the works. Calling on the vicar would not revise the project estimates waiting for Sherbourne in the library. Calling on the vicar would not do a damned thing to solve any relevant problem, though it would give Sherbourne another hour in his wife's company.

"Why take tea with the vicar? He comes to Sherbourne Hall annually, to secure my donation to whatever fund he pretends to manage for the widows and orphans."

Charlotte traced her fingertip over Sherbourne's lips. "If you don't like how the funds are managed, you pay a visit to the vicar and indicate that your lady wife is in want of charitable projects. I insinuate myself onto the committee that oversees the money and take matters in hand. This is part of why you married me."

Sherbourne let his eyes drift closed, because he could think just as well that way as with them open. "What is part of why I married you? To run the local parish?"

"To be your eyes and ears in places you do not or cannot frequent. To add to the store of intelligence with which you make decisions."

"You'd spy for me? Hardly honorable, Mrs. Sherbourne." Though Charlotte had a point. He had offered for her because she'd open doors previously closed to him. He hadn't considered that one of those doors would lead to the church committee room.

"I would be mindful of my husband's interests, because I vowed to honor him. That means giving the dear fellow the benefit of my insights from time to time."

"You're putting the dear fellow to sleep." Sending him into the loveliest, most relaxed doze, better even than the sweet, sleepy postcoital stupor he'd wallowed in earlier for two entire minutes.

And she'd called him dear, albeit half in jest.

"I'm enjoying my marital privileges. You need your rest, Lucas."

He needed to be in the library. "We can visit the vicar soon, after Brantford has worked his mischief, and the colliery is no longer at sixes and sevens."

Charlotte said something he didn't quite catch, about being patient with great lummoxes stuck in the mud of their own making—could she have said that?—and then he was dreaming of a red velvet sofa, one without lumps, that could accommodate a newly married couple in all their intimate enthusiasms.

Chapter Fourteen

Heulwen was particularly subdued as she laced Charlotte up. Perhaps the housekeeper had had a word with the maid about proper decorum where handsome young grooms were concerned.

"This is a very fetching carriage dress," Heulwen said. "That shade of velvet makes me think of melted chocolate."

"Velvet is marvelous for keeping warm," Charlotte replied.

Sherbourne was accomplished at keeping Charlotte warm, moving with her in a cozy rhythm throughout the night. He'd left in the morning before she'd risen, the wretch. At least she needn't guess where he'd got off to.

Heulwen tied off the laces. "Shall I ask Morgan to bring the dog cart around, ma'am?"

"I'll send a footman to the stables."

"It wouldn't be any trouble at all to pop out to the carriage house, and tell him—"

Did Morgan know how devoted Heulwen was? "You and Morgan can bring the bread and soup around at midday. Dress warmly, Heulwen, for I don't trust that sun to keep shining."

"Aye, ma'am."

Heulwen had taken to wearing a shawl, which might simply be an accommodation the maids were permitted as winter approached, though Charlotte hadn't seen any of the other maids wearing shawls. Charlotte took a chill easily, which Papa claimed was generally true of redheads.

"The letters on my vanity should go out with today's post. If you could take them into the village for me, I'd appreciate it."

"I'll just leave them on the sideboard in the front hall, shall I? Whoever goes into the village to pick up the post usually drops off whatever mail we're sending."

The girl was either feather-brained or outrageously smitten with her swain. "We have discussed this, Heulwen. I want those letters taken straight to the posting inn. I do not want them lying about on the sideboard visible to any passing servant or caller."

Or husband.

"Aye, ma'am." Heulwen withdrew a brown wool cloak from the wardrobe. "The kitchen is all in a swither to be entertaining His Grace and his lordship tomorrow. Haven't ever had such fine company here at Sherbourne Hall."

"They are family, Heulwen. They will call frequently. The kitchen needn't take any particular pains."

"We don't have many guests here at all, ma'am. Vicar comes once a year or so, some of the squires who owe Mr. Sherbourne money will join him for a meal. Nobody special."

Charlotte slipped into her cloak and drew a bright red

scarf from the wardrobe. This time of year the slightest breeze could bring a profound chill, even when the sun shone.

"You must never discuss the family's finances, Heulwen. Not with Morgan, not with anybody. I'm sure you wouldn't mention a neighbor's indebtedness before anybody but me, and Mr. Sherbourne is owed your utmost discretion otherwise."

Heulwen looked as if Charlotte had threatened to turn her off without a character. "I beg your pardon. I would never talk out of turn."

Now there was a complete work of fiction. "I'll be back this afternoon. Bring lunch to the site promptly at noon."

"If I'm to go with Morgan, and he's driving you there, then how—?"

"I'm driving myself."

Rather than allow the maid to interrogate her—for Heulwen would at least make an attempt—Charlotte swept from the room. She stopped by the kitchen to collect some buttered bread, cheese, and a flask of hot tea, then made her way to the carriage house.

"Wouldn't be any trouble at all to drive you, ma'am," Morgan said, as Charlotte took the reins. "Mr. Sherbourne might rather I did."

"Thank you, Morgan, but I need you to help Heulwen bring lunch to the works again. I'm a competent whip and will inform Mr. Sherbourne of that fact should he raise a question."

She clucked to the horse, who set off at a businesslike walk down the lane. The road was far from dry, but it was no longer a glorified marsh, and thus Charlotte was shortly at the colliery, where for once, nobody was shouting. The men were making rapid progress clearing the lane, picks and shovels raising a racket, and in Mr. Jones's white tent, Charlotte found only the Duke of Haverford seated by the parlor stove.

"Your Grace, good day."

He rose and bowed. "Mrs. Sherbourne."

"You must call me Charlotte, for we're family. I don't suppose you have seen my husband?"

Haverford was a good-looking devil, though a bit too full of his consequence for Charlotte's taste. Elizabeth was smitten with him, though, so the duke had Charlotte's approval too.

Up to a point.

"Jones and Sherbourne marched off to argue about relocating the workers' housing, and Radnor went along to referee. I'm reviewing progress reports, such as they are."

"With only the masons on site and much to be done, I am sure progress has been slow."

Haverford brought a second chair over to the parlor stove. "Perhaps you'd like to have a seat? Why have only masons on site, I ask myself? Why not hire laborers as well?"

"The masons brought their apprentices and hod carriers, from what I saw, and laborers cost money. Are you hoping my husband will fail, Your Grace?"

The question was combative, but Charlotte had had a wonderfully cozy night's rest, and somebody had to take Haverford in hand if he was intent on sabotaging the mine.

"Elizabeth warned me you are fierce."

"Elizabeth was being polite, Your Grace. I am unrelenting when it comes to protecting those I care about. Mr. Sherbourne is at these works in all weather, up until all hours with his schedules and budgets. He and I have had no wedding journey because he could not leave the works unattended any longer, and now his dratted business partner must arrive like the bad fairy at the christening and make a challenging situation worse. If you intend anything less than the best of good faith and neighborly goodwill toward these works, say so now."

Haverford's expression had gone blank, but what had Charlotte expected? That a duke, doubtless among those named to succeed to the British throne, would scurry off like a chastened schoolboy?

"He's here at all hours?" Haverford asked, hands behind his back.

"And then up for yet more hours in the library, poring over ledgers and correspondence. If you think Mr. Sherbourne an idle wastrel, you are much mistaken."

"I never thought him idle. In fact, he's a bit too industrious. He has his fingers in every pie from the coaching inn to mortgages on half the farms in this valley."

This bothered Haverford, who doubtless had tenants on the other half.

"Do you want the mine to fail?" Charlotte asked.

"That would be ungentlemanly."

"So you *do* want the mine to fail. Why?"

Haverford gestured again to the chair, and Charlotte realized that his gentlemanliness also prevented him from sitting when a lady stood, or paced, or tidied up stacks of paper that admitted of no order whatsoever.

She sat.

"I have placed my trust in Sherbourne," Haverford said. "I hope he does not disappoint me. Others in this valley expect to find employment at this mine, but what I've seen so far is not encouraging. Then there's this Lord Brantford getting involved when he has his own collieries to tend to in the north. I've also...well. Let's leave it at that, shall we? I have reservations."

Haverford had been poking about, in other words. Gathering intelligence on Charlotte's spouse. "Then you owe it to Mr. Sherbourne to share those reservations. He has not undertaken this mine because he needs another distraction or is in want of coin. He's opened the mine because without it, this valley will become another forgotten Welsh backwater remembered only in London pub songs."

That was going too far. No corner of the realm that boasted a ducal family seat would ever be entirely forgotten.

"You'd have me attribute charitable impulses to *Lucas Sherbourne*?"

And that was going beyond too far. "Need I remind you, Your Grace, that my own sister's determination to put a lending library in every Welsh coal town is funded by no less a person than Lucas Sherbourne?"

Charlotte pulled off her gloves, and stopped short of smacking them across the duke's handsome cheeks. Sherbourne had been a very lenient creditor to the St. David family, which was probably why Haverford's support of the mine was so grudging.

"You need not remind me of Elizabeth's lending libraries *ever*. I have wondered if she married me simply to get her hands on my books."

"Surely you jest, Haverford. She has more or less given your books away, while she seems quite attached to you."

One corner of his mouth kicked up, and he crossed his boots at the ankle. "As I am attached to her. Elizabeth is very pleased to have you for a neighbor. I've suggested you might want some time to settle in before she becomes a regular fixture in your parlor."

Charlotte did not know Haverford well, but this conversation was encouraging. He was just another healthy, busy, besotted man, and the Windham family boasted a surfeit of same.

"I will no sooner be settled in than dear Mama will arrive for the winter holidays, a month or two early. She loves Wales, and now she has two more reasons to spend time here."

"Soon to be three," Haverford said, looking smug.

Oh, yes, he was family. Title or no title, Julian St. David had become family.

The tent flap was thrown open to admit Lord Radnor and Sherbourne, with Hannibal Jones bringing up the rear.

"Mrs. Sherbourne, good day." Sherbourne offered a bow, and Charlotte decided the moment wasn't right to kiss his cheek. He looked delectably windblown and thoroughly annoyed.

With her?

"Ma'am." Radnor bowed as well. "A pleasure to see you. My lady and I are looking forward to your hospitality tomorrow evening."

"You are my rehearsal audience," Charlotte said. "I appreciate your courage, and I'm sure your company will be lovely too. So where are we putting these houses?"

All four men exchanged glances.

"I say, put them where they were," Mr. Jones replied. "The retaining wall won't give way a second time if it's properly reinforced, and putting the houses there saves us having to build any more dratted roads."

"First, you'll have to move all that mud," Radnor retorted. "Tons and tons, and that's effort that could be spent laying foundations, sinking a shaft, or building the tram line."

Jones took a deep breath, clearly filling his sails to defend his position.

"I'd like to hear my wife's suggestion," Sherbourne said. "Women bring a different perspective to the whole matter of domestication."

Now the other three men looked at him—Jones incredulous, Radnor amused, and Haverford politely agog—while Sherbourne regarded Charlotte calmly.

"My suggestion would be along the top of the north ridge."

"Then we can't excavate any levels up there," Jones began, referring to mines dug laterally into the side of a hill. "Need I remind you that the purpose of these works is to extract coal from the—"

"We aren't planning on digging any levels," Radnor retorted. "Not for at least the next five years, and we have hills to the east and west if levels for some reason become imperative."

"Nothing about this mine is imperative," Haverford growled. "Not one damn—single thing, but the miners must have decent housing if this project goes forward. Mrs. Sherbourne, can you show us where you have in mind?"

With disagreement from all sides, no wonder Sherbourne was worried, and that was before Haverford had started making unpleasant innuendos about the mine's sole investor. Charlotte abruptly wanted to trot back to the house and spend the day writing letters to her sisters in Scotland.

"Of course, she can show us where she'd like to see the houses built," Sherbourne said. "Madam?"

He gestured to the tent flap, and Charlotte preceded the men into the brisk sunshine.

"Up there," she said, shading her eyes and pointing. "Two rows of houses will fit easily without encroaching on the pasture. One can see the ocean from that hilltop, and drainage won't be a problem."

Neither would failed retaining walls or a contaminated well.

Jones sputtered about having to build a track up the side of the hill, for the houses wouldn't raise themselves, and Radnor countered with an observation that nothing was being built anywhere as long as certain people insisted on arguing away half the morning.

"Let's have a look," Haverford said, striding away in the direction of the path up the hill. "Using skilled masons to move mud is an abomination against the natural order and damned slow work."

"You're right, of course," Sherbourne said. "No mason has ever had to do a spot digging, square up a foundation trench, or deal with mud and mortar." Sherbourne went off with the duke, arguing all the while, and Jones and Radnor followed, bickering like a pair of tipsy washerwomen.

Charlotte trailed along behind the men, grateful that she'd worn sturdy boots and resentful that her husband had to defend himself from accusations flung by a duke who'd probably never lifted a shovel in his titled life.

Halfway up the hill, Charlotte realized that she had landed herself in a pickle. The last time she'd traveled this path, she'd had her husband's entire focus and held hands with him. She hadn't given the height a thought, a miracle she'd consider *later*. Now Sherbourne was remonstrating with Haverford thirty yards ahead, closer to the summit.

To Charlotte's left, the hillside rose steeply, while to her right... "Do not look," she muttered. "Do not look. You are safe. The ground is solid beneath your feet, you have been this way before, and Sherbourne is counting on you."

She looked, and—no surprise—the works appeared tiny at the foot of the hill. The men were miniature figures digging through the great mass of earth that had obliterated the planned housing site. The stacks of equipment were so many toys strewn about, and the white tent sat in the middle, much, much too distant.

Charlotte forced herself to gaze up the path, though now Sherbourne was forty yards away. Her heartbeat became painful and her breathing inadequate to fill her lungs. If she fell...

"Mister..." Her voice came out barely above a whisper, and vertigo threatened her balance. "Mr. Sherbourne."

He couldn't hear her, not with the distance and wind. He'd soon round the last curve of the path and be lost to sight. Charlotte would die, lifted off the hillside by a gust of wind, and dropped onto the hard ground far below.

Panic threatened.

"Lucas, please help—" The ground lurched, though of course it hadn't really. "Do not look. Sit down," Charlotte lectured herself. "Sit down right here, right now, and the men will find you when they are finished arguing, or when spring comes, or when...I can't do this."

Those four men would never cease arguing, and when they found her, Sherbourne would be mortified that his wife couldn't even traverse a Welsh hillside without turning into a blithering ninny. Charlotte could not move, could not turn her head, could not figure out how to sink to her knees without toppling down the incline to her right.

She could only gaze up the path, at her husband's retreating form, hating her weakness and wishing she'd never thought to intrude into matters beyond her ken.

Though building the houses in the middle of the colliery itself had been a truly daft idea.

"Charlotte!"

Sherbourne's voice. He was jogging back down the path, coming nearer with each step. "Charlotte, are you well?"

She closed her eyes. He might misstep, he might go plummeting over the side of the hill, he might twist his ankle on a loose rock, he might—

"I've got you," Sherbourne said, wrapping her in his arms. "Say something. You're pale as the angel Gabriel's wings. Please say something."

Hold me, which came out as "Meep." He was warm, he was solid, and Charlotte could breathe. She tried again. "I am being ridiculous."

"I should not have left you without an escort. The height is bothering you, isn't it? Damn it, what was I thinking. I'll have you down the hill in a trice."

Charlotte shook her head. "I should be able to do this. This is merely a hill."

"It's a damned high hill, with a good drop if you take a wrong step. Damn it, damn it, blast and damn it."

Charlotte gradually realized that Sherbourne was more upset than she was. For him, she could muster some calm, provided he kept his arms around her.

"I have been up this hill before," she said. "If your miners are to dwell on the summit, I will be here frequently. Shall we proceed?"

"Are you sure?"

She loved him—*loved him*—for asking that, for the concern in his voice, for the earnest regard in his blue eyes. He'd asked her the same question in bed last night, but this time seemed even more significant.

"I am quite sure. Hold my hand, and we shall contrive."

He not only held her hand, he walked on the outer side of the path, talked to her about Radnor's argument earlier with Jones regarding the tram line, and step by step got her to the hilltop.

Every inch of the way, Charlotte held her husband's

hand, until she was at the summit, pacing off a row of houses, and mentally laying out gardens and chicken coops, while trying to ignore the burning revelation that *she loved her husband*.

* * *

"I didn't think they were a love match," Radnor said, as Sherbourne and his lady sauntered down the hill hand in hand.

"Why do you conclude they are?" Haverford countered.

"When was the last time you remained hand in hand with your duchess in public for a good half hour?"

"You ask a very personal question, Radnor. You're newly married yourself. Draw your own conclusions."

The wind at the top of the hill was brisk, which Charlotte had pointed out would dry laundry quickly. The breeze was also likely to be free of coal dust, given that the prevailing direction was from land toward the sea. Fresh air was healthier for all concerned, and the air where the houses had originally been laid out would not have been fresh at all.

Even Sherbourne hadn't seen that, but neither had Haverford, Radnor, or Jones.

"I hold hands with my marchioness with lovely frequency," Radnor said, "though seldom in public. Sherbourne has fallen for that red-haired dragoness."

Haverford felt an odd affection for Charlotte Windham. She was bold, awkward, and—most unexpected—ferociously protective of her new husband. What had Lucas Sherbourne done to deserve such a champion, much less a woman bristling with intelligence and sense?

"That red-haired dragoness is my sister by marriage, Radnor. She and Sherbourne do seem to suit."

"Unlike Sherbourne and Jones. Did Sherbourne explain to you Jones's error with the retaining wall?"

Sherbourne and his bride, still hand in hand, disappeared around a bend in the path.

"No explanation yet, and one doesn't want to ask. Sherbourne is devilish prickly where I am concerned."

Radnor had been friends with Haverford since they'd been breeched, and now, having married Haverford's sister, Radnor was family. They had few secrets, though Haverford was prepared for marriage to change their friendship.

"*You* are devilish prickly where *Sherbourne* is concerned," Radnor retorted. "You haven't any coin invested in this venture, you have no expertise with mining, so what exactly do you think your hovering about accomplishes?"

"I can't hover about my duchess every hour of the day. The lady needs her rest."

Radnor punched him on the arm. "Admit you are worried for Sherbourne. Jones isn't the engineering paragon he presents himself to be, not if he forgets to calculate the weight of rainwater in topsoil when designing a retaining wall."

Good God. "Is that what went wrong?"

"Charlotte Sherbourne figured it out, and thank the angelic choruses, Sherbourne listens to her. She has good ideas."

She was also pretty, in a robust, severe way. Elizabeth was prettier, of course. "Mrs. Sherbourne knows as much about mining as I do. If Jones is incompetent, he'll have to be replaced."

"He's probably a decent mining engineer, but no sort of architect. I've dabbled in the occasional design project, enough to draw a few elevations."

"Jones hasn't?"

Radnor gazed down at the great heap of earth lying atop the planned street. Whole trees had come along with the side of the hill, and were now standing upright a hundred yards from where they'd been last week.

"Jones has never designed a dwelling, or a surface structure of any kind, and did not admit his limitations until they were obvious. He needs this post, I suspect, and I'm making inquiries in Swansea and Cardiff regarding his work history. I also consulted with Glenys regarding Lord Brantford."

Radnor had been busy, in other words, while Haverford had been... not much help at all. "What did Glenys have to say?"

"Brantford married an heiress, or so he thought. Turns out the woman's family had put every available groat into her settlements, and their fortunes have continued to decline since she married Brantford."

These things happened. They'd happened to Haverford's own family for the past hundred years. "Is Sherbourne supposed to send coin pouring into the earl's family coffers?"

Radnor's gaze dropped to his boots, which were wet from tromping about the hilltop. "Sherbourne has a fine grasp of finances, Haverford. I invested in this mine because I've made money with him on two previous projects, though I resorted to intermediaries to handle the details."

"You're not suggesting *I* invest in the mine?"

"If you're not an investor, and you know nothing about mining, then what in blazes are you doing here?" Radnor's tone was mild, but then, his tone was always mild when he was delivering a *coup de grace*. Only fools underestimated Cedric Radnor.

Fools and, occasionally, best friends.

"I don't know, but sometimes a disinterested third party has a useful perspective, witness Charlotte's opinions about the houses. What do we do about Jones?"

"We watch him closely. Find somebody to review all of his calculations, let Sherbourne know that engineers are employees, not dictators."

"I can help with that last part. Where has Jones got off to?"

"The coaching inn. Griffin says he's there rather a lot."

Griffin had passed that along to Radnor, rather than to his own brother? "I'm off to have a word with Griffin, and I'll see you tomorrow night. Elizabeth will probably inveigle Glenys into helping with the lending library scheme."

"Glenys will have to dodge that fire on her own, for Her Grace has already sent out the press gangs after my handsome self."

Haverford started down the hill. "Do you suppose the climb truly winded Charlotte? She seems a healthy woman."

"Who knows? Perhaps she was laced too tightly. Sherbourne's concern was real."

True, and seeing Lucas Sherbourne in a flat panic over a woman who could literally shoot a man's arrows out of the sky had relieved an anxiety Haverford didn't entirely understand.

"Elizabeth loves those lending libraries," Haverford said, "and they are being established largely because of Sherbourne. If anything happens to him or his fortunes, my duchess will take it amiss."

Radnor kept right on walking. "Oh, of course. The lending libraries. If anything happens to Her Grace's little sister, your duchess will take it much worse than *amiss*, and Her Grace's little sister seems much taken with Sherbourne."

"Ergo, nothing awful must happen to Sherbourne. As distasteful as the duty to safeguard his venture will be, you have the right of it. For the sake of my duchess, Sherbourne's interests must be guarded."

That logic worked as well as any, though Elizabeth would see right through it.

Chapter Fifteen

Charlotte was poised and relaxed—to appearances—as her dinner guests moved from the formal parlor into the dining room. As hostess, she took Haverford's arm, leaving Sherbourne to escort the duchess.

"Is Charlotte as happy as she seems?" Her Grace murmured.

"You should ask her," Sherbourne replied. "I pray she'll answer in the affirmative."

"She's your wife, sir. I hope you'll trouble yourself to read her moods."

Sherbourne allowed the duchess her scold, because she spoke as a concerned sister, not as Her Grace of Haverford.

"We have been married barely a fortnight, and we had no courtship, at the insistence of the bride's family. If I do not presume to speak for my wife's happiness, I am acknowledging my ignorance as a new husband, not my indifference."

"You'll suit," the duchess said, patting his arm. "Charlotte thrives on confrontation and challenge."

No, she does not. Charlotte thrived on solving problems, on being of use, though her talents were not those a lady typically cultivated—thank God.

Griffin St. David, escorting his sister Lady Radnor, nearly collided with them at the door to the dining room. He grinned, bowed, and let Sherbourne escort the duchess to her seat. Lady Griffin was on Radnor's arm, though in this company Charlotte had decided the couple would be addressed as Griffin and Biddy.

By extension, they were Sherbourne's family now, too, the pick of the lot in his estimation.

The dining room was large enough to hold thirty at supper, though Charlotte had had all the extra leaves removed from the table. Bowls of heartsease served as centerpieces, and two footmen stood by the sideboard. The meal would be informal, and thus conversation could fly in all directions.

Sherbourne suspected this was how the Windham family typically dined.

His correspondence that morning had included letters from two of Charlotte's titled cousins—both earls—while Charlotte had received letters from one sister and yet another cousin—a duchess and a marchioness.

"Now we all sit down," Griffin announced, "and we have witty conversation." He beamed at the company, as if pleased to instruct them.

"Exactly so," Sherbourne said, "and we enjoy good food as well. Haverford, I nominate you, as the ranking title, to lead the witty repartee."

The duke left off goggling at his duchess long enough to deliver a pointed stare in Sherbourne's direction. "Surely that is mine host's privilege?"

"We had a lovely visit with the vicar yesterday," Charlotte said. "Miss MacPherson is a delightful young lady. Very dedicated to supporting her papa's work."

The lovely visit had consisted of tepid, weak tea, served with small, stale cakes and not many of them. Charlotte had finagled an invitation to join the lady's charitable committee while Sherbourne had endured Mr. MacPherson's innuendos about christenings that followed too soon after weddings.

"We should find Miss MacPherson a fellow," the duchess said, "or she'll be her father's unpaid curate for the rest of her days."

"Maybe she likes life at the vicarage," Charlotte countered. "Not every woe is solved by marriage."

"My every woe has been solved by marriage." Griffin was in complete earnest, and his comment earned smiles and laughter. Biddy blew him a kiss across the table—most unladylike behavior, but then, why not let a husband know he was appreciated?

"If we're looking for spouses," Griffin went on, "couldn't we find one for Maureen Caerdenwal? She has a baby, so she should have a husband."

Haverford, Radnor, Lady Radnor, and the duchess all reached for their wineglasses simultaneously.

"A fine notion," Charlotte said, "one that speaks well of your kind-heartedness, Griffin. If we can't find the young woman a husband, perhaps you could spare her some chickens?"

"We have lots of chickens," Griffin replied. "Biddy and I will take Miss Caerdenwal some hens. Then the baby can have eggs. We'll bring a big basket, as big as the one Miss Charlotte sent, and just as full of good things."

"We'll do it tomorrow," Biddy said, "unless it rains."

"If it rains, we'll go the day after tomorrow."

Griffin and Biddy shared a gaze of such mutual approval, Sherbourne could not look away. They were a couple completely without artifice, entirely besotted, and entirely unconcerned what anybody thought of them.

Though when had Charlotte had time to send a basket to the local fallen woman?

"Would anybody like more wine?" Radnor asked. "At the mention of rain this time of year, all I can think is, snow would be worse."

The weather served its usual purpose, and various courses were presented and removed, until the ladies abandoned the menfolk. Sherbourne, having been instructed by Charlotte previously, escorted the women to the family parlor, which private moment gave him a chance to receive fresh orders from his wife.

"I trust you will manage without us men for a short time," Sherbourne said, "and I won't allow the gentlemen to tarry too long with their port." He bowed over Charlotte's hand and would have returned to the dining room, but Charlotte kept his fingers clasped in hers.

"Kiss my cheek," she muttered. Her back was to the ladies. Nobody else would have heard her quiet words.

Sherbourne did as she bid, which had the other three ladies smiling at him. He kissed Charlotte's other cheek as well—one good kiss deserving another—and then left the women to their tea and talk.

He passed through the foyer on his way back to the dining room and noticed correspondence sitting in the salver on the sideboard. Charlotte—for the direction was in her hand—had written to a Harold Porter, who had the great misfortune to dwell in a godforsaken corner of Brecknockshire. Three other letters lay beneath the epistle to Mr. Porter.

One to Mrs. Wesley Smythe, one to Mrs. Scott Wesley, a third Mrs. Morton Wesley.

Interesting. Charlotte wrote only to family that Sherbourne knew of, and no Windhams rusticated in Brecknockshire.

He was tempted to pocket the letters and study them further, but Griffin poked his head out of the dining room at that moment and motioned Sherbourne down the corridor. He rejoined the gentlemen, who were looking more forlorn than relieved to have parted company with their ladies.

"Shall we to the decanter?" Sherbourne asked. "I'm under strict orders from Mrs. Sherbourne not to tarry over the port for more than thirty minutes."

His guests brightened, Griffin launched into an earnest panegyric to the Welsh laying hen, and Sherbourne breathed a sigh of relief. His first dinner as host to multiple titles—even Griffin was a courtesy lord—was going well. Charlotte knew what she was about, and tomorrow Sherbourne could get back to creating a mine where even nature seemed determined that he should not build one.

"You are quiet," Griffin observed. "Do you miss your wife? I miss Biddy."

"Might as well admit the truth," Radnor said. "We miss our ladies, don't we, Haverford?"

Haverford's smile was less than dignified. "Terribly. Eight minutes to go, though. Courage, lads."

Sherbourne was not a lad. "Nothing says we must wait the full thirty minutes. This is an informal gathering of family, and we've discussed the weather enough to last us until spring. If the rest of you are too domesticated to storm the tea tray, I am not."

The three other men rose as one, and Radnor finished his drink in a single swallow. "Lay on, MacDuff, and damned be him that first cries, 'Hold, for I'm too domesticated to storm a teapot.'"

"Is Radnor sozzled?" Griffin asked. "He'll have a sore head in the morning if he is."

"He's in love," Haverford said, heading for the door. "He'll be fine in the morning, if Glenys lets him out of bed."

Griffin's beatific smile was back. "Biddy sometimes won't let me—"

"To the parlor," Sherbourne said. "I expect each of you to compliment my wife effusively on her hospitality."

"Right," Radnor said.

"Of course," Haverford added.

Griffin was already out the door.

Sherbourne followed, mostly pleased with the evening. Charlotte had been right—they'd needed a dress rehearsal, a family-only gathering for practice. That Haverford and Radnor were family still boggled Sherbourne's mind.

And yet, the evening had been disquieting as well. Charlotte had made no mention of sending a basket to the Caerdenwal household, and she was writing to some man in Brecknockshire whom she'd also never raised in conversation with her husband.

Also to several women who'd married men named Wesley.

Charlotte had kept her fear of heights from her family's notice for years.

What was she hiding from her husband, and why?

* * *

The Earl of Brantford was a fine specimen of English nobility, blond, above average height, with the pale blue eyes of the typical Saxon. Every instinct Haverford possessed told him Elizabeth had disliked the earl on sight, though her manner had remained gracious throughout the introductions and ensuing small talk.

"If you gentlemen will excuse me," she said, rising, "I'll let the housekeeper know our guest has arrived."

Haverford bowed. "Until dinner, my dear."

The housekeeper had doubtless known the instant Brantford's coach had turned up the drive. Elizabeth was simply abandoning ship, doubtless off to enjoy a solitary nap, while Haverford was left to make yet more small talk with Sherbourne's pet earl.

Brantford offered the duchess a bow as well, then resumed decimating the tea tray.

"I hadn't realized you'd married such a beauty, Haverford. Never hurts when the wife is easy on the eyes, eh?"

The remark rankled. Exceedingly. "I beg your pardon?"

"Wait until you've been married a few years. The early days can be lively, but after that, boredom sets in, particularly if your best efforts don't result in a full nursery. You're a duke. I needn't spell out the obvious." Brantford wiggled his eyebrows while he munched a beef sandwich.

"Will you be staying with us long?" Haverford asked, for the past hour had been among the longest he could recall.

"Dear me, of course not. Wales in winter? You must be daft, but then, you are newly married. One and the same for some. I'm guessing Sherbourne's nuptials were an entirely mercenary undertaking. I don't know the man well, but I've heard a few *on dits* regarding the new Mrs. Sherbourne."

Haverford got up to toss more peat onto the fire, for the afternoon was growing chilly. "Such as?"

"You married into the same family. The Windhams are well connected, but they aren't all as, shall we say, genteel as your lovely duchess. Her sister is known to be outspoken, or so I've heard."

Haverford used the wrought iron poker to rearrange the peat and coals. He put the poker back on the hearth stand, though delivering a stout blow to Brantford's thick sense of his own consequence appealed strongly.

"I delight in Mrs. Sherbourne's outspokenness," Haverford said. "She's a refreshing change from the toadies and flirts who have nothing better to do than gossip about the same people they attempt to flatter."

Brantford saluted with a silver flask and tipped it to his lips. "Just so, just so. I've been asked why I invested in Sherbourne's little project by those same people. Why entangle my affairs with *such as him*? He's part owner of a bank, you know. One of the other partners is the grandson of a Ludgate jeweler."

Which had exactly nothing to do with anything.

"I'll tell you why I'm investing with Sherbourne," Brantford went on. "I'll never begrudge a man's efforts to better his situation if those same efforts also better *my* situation. Everything Sherbourne touches turns to gold. He's shrewd, has a knack for knowing when to step in and when to step out. As distasteful as coin might be to those of us raised with refined sensibilities, the lack of coin is more distasteful still."

A lack of couth ranked even higher on Haverford's list of disagreeable qualities. "And yet, you clearly had sufficient means to invest. One hopes your own situation prospers adequately, irrespective of Sherbourne's projects."

Brantford emptied his flask. "Was that a warning, Haverford? Have I backed the wrong horse? That's why

I'm wandering about the wilds of Wales, you see. Sherbourne himself challenged me to inspect the colliery, more or less. Likened solicitors and men of business to meddlers. He doubtless never expected to see me here in person. I have better things to do than ruin my boots and court a case of lung fever."

Haverford had better things to do than listen to this braying ass. "Though here you are, in the wilds of Wales after all."

Brantford rose, a bit unsteadily. "So I am. I need for Sherbourne's little project to show a handsome profit. He has odd notions about providing housing for the miners, no children employed below the surface—no women, either, and that's just the start of his daft fancies. I'll set him straight, and a word from you would be helpful too. One cannot coddle the brutes who labor for their bread or they simply take advantage."

His lordship wandered over to the sideboard and lifted a glass stopper from a crystal decanter. "Mind if I refill my flask?"

"Help yourself, of course. We keep country hours, and if you'd like to rest before changing for dinner, I can send a footman to waken you."

Brantford made a mess and wasted good brandy refilling his flask. "Don't send me a footman, for heaven's sake. Send me a hot bath and a comely little chambermaid to assist me. I like blondes and prefer a woman with good hips. A tray of viands wouldn't go amiss, and none of this peat, please. Coal will do for me, and I'll need some clothing pressed if I'm to be properly attired for dinner."

"I'm sure the staff will be happy to meet your every need." Though Her Grace had already warned the butler and housekeeper that only men were to wait on his lordship. "If Sherbourne is not amenable to your ideas regarding management of the colliery, will you withdraw your support for the project?"

"I ought to," Brantford said, snatching the last biscuit from the tea tray. "That would serve him right. He got quite above himself with me. I admire ambition, but will not tolerate disrespect." Brantford ate his biscuit as the fresh peat caught and the lovely, tangy scent of a blazing fire filled the parlor. "Here's the thing, Haverford. I have been beset lately by something of a premonition."

He ran a hand through thinning hair, and for a moment, Brantford was not the arrogant, confident aristocrat, but rather, a man who could see middle age bearing down upon him, much sooner than expected. He was weary and worried, though he probably didn't admit that even to himself.

"My in-laws are in dun territory," Brantford said. "Their situation is not common knowledge yet. They put every spare farthing into the marriage settlements, and I've done what I could with those funds. My countess has yet to oblige me with an heir, though not for lack of trying on my part. I have it in my mind—you will think me addled—that if I can replenish her family coffers, then she might conceive."

To make that admission, Brantford had to be nearly drunk or very preoccupied with his lack of children.

"A titular succession can be a terrible weight," Haverford said. "Have you no indirect heirs?"

"Some bantling second cousin in Scotland. I'd rather see the estate revert to the crown than fall into the hands of a barbarian."

Two of Elizabeth's sisters had married Scotsmen. "I can't promise that Sherbourne will be amenable to your suggestions. He's developing this colliery in part to provide employment beyond what's available on the valley's smallholdings and tenant farms. Excessive profit isn't his aim."

Which had surprised Haverford, and it apparently surprised Brantford.

"Excessive profit is a contradiction in terms. I'll sort him out easily enough, Your Grace. If he ever wants to attract another titled investor, he'll see reason. About that bath?"

"Right," Haverford said. "Your bath, a tray of viands, somebody to see to your wardrobe and lay out your evening clothes. Anything else?"

"Coal on the bedroom hearth. Peat has its charm, but not while a man is trying to sleep." Brantford started for the door. "I'm partial to French wines, if you were wondering what to send along with the tray. I prefer the reds, as long as they aren't too dry."

"Our staff will be happy to oblige."

Brantford took himself off, while Haverford recited the earl's list of required amenities to the first footman.

"Mind you don't let the maids near him," Haverford said. "He's our guest, but Her Grace will skewer him with a rusty sword if he disrespects any member of her household."

Not, of course, that food and wine in abundance, a hot bath on demand, footmen stepping and fetching in all directions, and a hearth kept blazing was *coddling* his lordship.

Haverford used the footmen's staircase to join the duchess in the ducal apartment and found his wife awake, though beneath the covers with a book.

"I'd hate him," Haverford said, "except I pity the man."

"Brantford?"

"Of course, Brantford. You thought I meant Sherbourne?"

"Come to bed," Elizabeth said. "Our guest has put you out of sorts."

"He's put me in a quandary." Haverford did not need to be invited to bed twice. He peeled out of his clothes—all of them—and climbed in beside his wife. "Brantford is greedy, which is probably to be expected, but he's also in want of an heir. He refers to Sherbourne as having a Midas touch, and yet the legend of Midas seems to apply to the earl."

"Midas turned his daughter to gold, didn't he?"

"And realized too late that all the coin and consequence in the world mean nothing without somebody to love. I could have been Brantford." He'd made the last admission quickly, before self-consciousness could snatch the words back.

Elizabeth wrapped herself along his side. "You could never he Brantford, else you would have sunk a mine ten years ago and ignored all the agricultural interests in the valley. You would never have married me, either. You would have married some giggling heiress who left you to molder away with your books. Sherbourne will deal easily with Brantford."

"If Sherbourne fails to impress Brantford, the earl will try to withdraw his money." Why did the scent of Elizabeth, the simple feel of her body, soothe Haverford when nothing else could?

"Can Brantford renege like that? Lucas Sherbourne strikes me as a man who'd tidy up all the legalities before coin changed hands."

Haverford pulled the covers over his wife's shoulders. "Doubtless Sherbourne has dotted i's and crossed t's in triplicate, but Brantford will slander Sherbourne in the clubs if Sherbourne doesn't give the money back, or manage the project according to Brantford's rules. That will be the end of Sherbourne's ventures with titled investors."

Sherbourne, for reasons Haverford only dimly grasped, wanted to move among titles as an equal.

"Then you and Radnor and various Windhams will simply unslander him," Elizabeth said. "Brantford is a minor northern earl with airs above his station. Sherbourne is ours now, and we protect our own."

"Spoken like a duchess." Also like a Windham *and* a St. David. "Is it very rude for a host and hostess to be late for dinner?"

"I haven't yet told the kitchen when dinner is to be served."

"Nor will you be telling them for at least another hour."

"Spoken like a duke," Elizabeth said, drawing her leg over his thighs. "Like a very wise duke."

* * *

"He's here." Sherbourne might have been speaking of Old Scratch, so grim was his tone.

"Lord Brantford has arrived?" Charlotte asked.

They were in the library after a quiet supper. Rain pelted the windows in icy torrents and darkness had fallen hours ago. While her husband had clicked away at an abacus and penciled figures on sheets of foolscap, Charlotte had read Mr. William Sharp's treatise on coal mining, which was more interesting than any edition of *La Belle Assemblée*.

Mining was an endeavor made possible by tons of mathematics as well as tons of ore. Without a quantity of careful calculations, the whole business was little more than digging in the dirt while relentlessly praying to remain alive. To construct a tunnel that would not collapse, flood, subside, or lack for ventilation was a puzzle of numbers, and until those numbers came right, lives were in peril.

Sherbourne pitched a crumpled-up note into the fireplace behind his desk. A second fireplace before Charlotte's perch on the sofa burned just as a brightly.

"Haverford welcomed Brantford shortly before sunset," he said. "The weather will prevent us from touring the site tomorrow."

"If his lordship is so keen to inspect his investment, then he ought to brave the elements," Charlotte said. "You certainly haven't let rain, cold, wind, hail, or dark of night stop you from being there."

Sherbourne rose, braced his hands on the mantel, and arched his back. "Have you missed me, Mrs. Sherbourne?" The question was more weary than flirtatious.

Perhaps even a trifle annoyed?

"Ever since last week's dinner party, you have been preoccupied." Charlotte patted the cushion next to her. "Come sit with me."

Sherbourne cast a longing glance at his calculations, though Charlotte knew they did not call to him the way they did to her. Sherbourne was worried, and his fretting required him to *do* something, not simply sit and read a week-old London newspaper to keep up with the gossip.

He took the place beside her. "You have made a nest on my sofa. If you've bided here to keep me company, you needn't."

Charlotte pushed her quilts aside, rose, and stood before her husband. "Boots off, Mr. Sherbourne."

He extended his left foot, expression wary. His boots were worn, though this pair lacked any evidence of mud.

Charlotte took off first one, then the other, and set them in the corridor. She pulled up a hassock, and put her husband's feet in her lap.

"Has it occurred to you, sir, that you might have been keeping me company?" She wrapped her arms around his feet. "My aunt likes to have her feet rubbed. This is a family secret. Are your feet cold?"

Sherbourne's manner had been colder lately. Preoccupied, quiet, reserved—worried, very likely.

"My feet are tired," Sherbourne said, leaning his head back against the cushions. "Shall we to bed?"

"Soon. Have you had a look at Debrett's?" Charlotte had suggested that exercise over breakfast yesterday.

"I have, and can tell you that Brantford is the eighth earl of that title, the viscountcy having been raised to an earldom by Charles II. The present earl is married to the former Miss Veronica Carruthers, of the Carruthers family of East Anglia, and her father is a baron. No children have yet graced Brantford's nursery, which means I had less to memorize."

"No children will be gracing our nursery yet either." Heat flooded Charlotte's cheeks as soon as she'd made that announcement.

Sherbourne regarded her for a stern moment, then his brows rose. "The inevitable inconvenience troubles you?"

She peeled off his stockings. "These things happen in the ordinary course." Though how did couples discuss them?

"Shall I sleep elsewhere?"

"You needn't." Sherbourne often began the night stretched out on his side of the bed, staring at the canopy, arms crossed behind his head. When Charlotte woke in the middle of the night, she was invariably wrapped in his embrace.

And he in hers.

"You're sure?" he asked. "It wouldn't be any bother."

Charlotte had a nagging suspicion her husband would rather sleep elsewhere, but that for him to establish his own quarters on some higher floor of the house was the wrong direction to go at this point in their marriage.

"I'd miss you, Mr. Sherbourne. You are a lovely bed-fellow."

A week ago, he might have returned that compliment. Now the fire hissed and popped at Charlotte's back, and the silence grew.

She rubbed his feet, taking time to learn more of him, and casting around for a topic that did not involve the mine, the Earl of Brantford, or immediate family.

"Does your ankle ever pain you?"

"The memory of sprawling on my face before the entire dining hall of boys pains me."

"Was that mishap courtesy of the same helpful soul who broke your nose?" His nose had been broken at public school, though it had healed almost undetectably.

"One of his loyal henchman, and a different one broke my arm. They ran around in a pack, laughed at one another's jokes, got drunk together. Typical younger sons and lordlings. That feels good."

She'd ventured to the thick muscles of his calf. "With whom did you run around and get drunk?"

"Nobody, and I learned not to excel at my studies, either."

"But you're quite bright."

A smile quirked and was gone. "Coming from you, that's high praise. At school, if I did poorly, I was an ignorant mushroom, trying to get above my station. If I did well, I was a presuming upstart who needed to be put in his place. I was beaten for mumbling, for a disrespectful tone of voice, for not reciting quickly enough, for rushing through my recitations, for failing to respect my betters when the other boys made up all manner of lies about me. My father laughed and told me I was getting exactly the education I needed."

Charlotte hugged his feet. "Is that the education you envision for our sons?" An education in prejudice, isolation, brutality, and snobbery?

"We haven't any sons yet and apparently none on the way."

Charlotte was tempted to shove his feet off her lap, storm out, and lock the bedroom door. She didn't, because in casual admissions and pensive silences, she was coming to understand how much courage Sherbourne had displayed when he'd married her.

Those young fools breaking his bones for sport had been from "the best" families. The instructors and headmasters seizing on any pretext to beat him had been beholden to those same families. Brantford, who expected a handsome return on his investment, acted as if he were doing Sherbourne a favor by adding to Sherbourne's burdens.

The very neighbors who'd boxed Sherbourne into turning a profit from an exorbitantly expensive new venture were titled aristocrats held in high regard throughout the realm—and thanks to Charlotte, they were also Sherbourne's family.

She was his wife. He'd have her loyal support, and others could learn from her example.

"Tomorrow morning," Charlotte said, "you send a cheerful note over to Haverford Castle, welcoming Brantford to the neighborhood. You inform him that your lady wife is eager to entertain him as the first official guest following our nuptials, and that all at the colliery is in readiness for a tour on the first available fine day."

The past few days had seen a flurry of busyness at the works, with string pegged out to mark the houses atop the hill, the first of the tram tracks laid, and laborers from both the Haverford and Radnor holdings swelling the ranks of the masons.

"I'm to be cheerful?" Sherbourne lifted his feet from Charlotte's lap and pulled on a stocking. "Perhaps you ought to send this note. Cheerfulness eludes me lately."

She picked up the other stocking. "I can draft the note, but it must be written in your hand. Where is Debrett's?"

"You don't have it memorized?"

Charlotte balled up the stocking and pitched it at Sherbourne's head. "Written correspondence requires different forms of address than greetings offered in person. What is Brantford's Christian name?"

Sherbourne donned the second stocking and rose. "Quinton, the family name is Bramley, if I recall his signature. Charlotte, may I ask you something?"

"Of course."

"How do you know a Harold Porter, from rural Brecknockshire?"

Sherbourne stood above her, looking tall, tired, and unreadable by the firelight.

Charlotte rose and kissed him while her mind whirled. "An old, old friend. I went to school with his sister."

"Young ladies do not correspond with single gentlemen," Sherbourne said. "I may not have taken any firsts at university or spent much time with my nose in Debrett's, but I know that much."

"Mr. Porter is married, as am I." And Heulwen was in for a severe talking to, for Charlotte had asked that the letter to Mr. Porter be taken directly to the posting inn. "Are you reading my correspondence now, Mr. Sherbourne?"

He looped his arms around Charlotte's shoulders. "I need for this mine to succeed, Charlotte."

What did that have to do with letters to old friends and Mrs. Wesleys? "Then I need for it to succeed as well."

They would have remained thus, touching but not exactly embracing before the fire, except Charlotte took the initiative and stepped closer, resting her cheek against Sherbourne's chest. They had not had a pleasant evening together, though neither had it been unpleasant.

Charlotte mentally began composing a note to his lordship, Quinton, Earl of Brantford—a cheerful note—though it puzzled her that an eighth earl would be named Quinton. A fifth earl might have such a name, while an eighth would more likely be Octavius.

She fell asleep beside Sherbourne an hour later and dreamed of calligraphy written in twine, his lordship's initials all tangled up with the colliery, the tram tracks, and Sherbourne's stockings. When she woke in the middle of the night, she was not entwined with her husband.

He was not, in fact, even in the bed.

Chapter Sixteen

"I'm reduced to delivering notes," Radnor said, passing along Haverford's epistle to Sherbourne. "If you ever sought revenge on Haverford for past slights, he's suffering mightily now."

Sherbourne broke the seal and read what Radnor probably already knew:

Sherbourne,

Brantford will join you for a tour of the works tomorrow at three of the clock, rain or shine. If you were to invite him to dinner thereafter, my duchess would be ever in your debt.

As would I.

Haverford

PS: Her Grace expects to be struck down—even

bedridden—by a terrible megrim no later than sundown tomorrow. She will, alas, decline any invitation to join your household for supper. I will remain loyally by my duchess's side, offering what comfort I can.

Brantford had spent three days underfoot at Haverford Castle, three days during which Sherbourne had rehearsed optimistic speeches, refined detailed estimates, and watched the rain dribble down the library window panes.

"His lordship is not good company?" Sherbourne asked.

"Unlike you, Haverford has probably been troubling himself to be a decent host." Radnor lifted a glass from the tray on the sideboard. "May I?"

"Of course, but the noon hour has passed. I was about to ask if you'd prefer tea or a tray before the fire."

Sherbourne hadn't been about to ask any such thing. Failing to offer a guest libation was a gross oversight, and he could not afford to be making gross oversights. Making *more* gross oversights.

"I am a bit peckish," Radnor said. "You aren't joining your lady wife for a midday meal?"

"Mrs. Sherbourne is off to the vicarage." Or avoiding her husband. "She and Miss MacPherson are hatching up some plot or other involving the widows of the parish."

Radnor tossed back a nip of excellent French brandy. "Will you order us lunch, or will it appear with a lift of your eyebrow?"

Sherbourne went to the door and gave the footman instructions. "If you'd also like to dictate the specific menu, Radnor, I'll send for the housekeeper, who will relay your wishes to Cook. Did Haverford have anything else to say regarding Brantford?"

And would it have been too much to ask that the ducal

fundament grace a saddle to pay a call on nearby family to convey that information in person?

"His Grace had much to say." Radnor poured another glass of spirits and brought it to Sherbourne. "None of it fit for polite ears. He's a newlywed, and yet he takes his duties as a host seriously. I expect the duchess has had to ambush him in the conservatory a time or two."

Sherbourne accepted the drink and set it aside. "His Grace is not newly wed, Radnor. He's recently married, relatively. The only gentleman in this valley who is yet enjoying his honey month is myself."

Radnor took a sip of his brandy, smallest finger extended. "You have a point, as usual. How is married life?"

"Married life is lovely." The problem was, married life with Charlotte truly *could be* lovely. She was both a well-bred lady and a restless mind that enjoyed challenges unbefitting of her station.

Such as being married to Sherbourne, for example.

"Your tone leaves me to question your veracity, Sherbourne. Early days can be trying."

Though Sherbourne rarely partook of strong spirits during daylight hours, he allowed himself to sample the brandy.

"You are such a *lord*, Radnor. You've been married only a handful of weeks yourself, and you're already an expert on the institution. You must point out to me that Haverford too is newly married when I attended the ceremony myself. You come bearing a note that tells me little, except that I've incurred a debt to Haverford, and I'm supposed to thank you for the courtesy. Why are you really here?"

Radnor set his glass on the mantel. "If you exhibit such faultless hospitality to Brantford, he'll withdraw his funds from the mine before Monday next. Is that what you want?"

Maybe. "If he withdraws, I'll be hard pressed to move forward at all. Is that what *you* want?"

"You'll abandon the project you fought for years to bring into this valley?"

Sherbourne could not abandon the mine, not if he expected to support his wife and eventual children in the style they deserved.

"I'm part owner of a bank," Sherbourne said. "The bank has recently come into some difficulties."

"A bank in difficulties is not good."

"Your lordly acumen is raining down like manna from heaven today." While outside, the sun was attempting to pierce the clouds. For Charlotte's sake, Sherbourne was happy to see some decent weather. For his own sake, the longer he could put Brantford off, the better.

Radnor stalked away from the mantel to stick his nose in Sherbourne's face. "Permit me to visit upon you a short history lesson. I am a marquess."

"My condolences on your misfortune."

"The marquessate of Radnor, like most marquessates, was established to honor the contribution of a lord of the marches, one granted many privileges beyond those given to mere earls and barons."

"Long-windedness among those privileges, obviously."

"The marquesses of Radnor *keep the peace*," Radnor said, jabbing a finger at Sherbourne's chest. "I want your damned mine to succeed, you idiot, just as I want Haverford's flocks and farms to flourish. Why is your bank failing?"

"The bank is not failing," Sherbourne said. "It's in difficulties. Five years ago, the other directors insisted on lending money to a canal scheme. I was against it."

"Why? Canals can be quite profitable."

"We have enough canals, and steam power will soon connect what few canals need connecting. The mines have already started using steam to haul ore from the collieries to the iron works, and that trend will only continue."

Radnor smoothed his fingers over Sherbourne's cravat and stepped away. "Is that why you're so hell-bent on this damned mine? You want to see our horses put to pasture by steam locomotives? Nasty odoriferous things, if you ask me."

Sherbourne *hadn't* asked Radnor. "Your horse's fragrance is unfailingly delightful? Perhaps he's an equine marquess."

Radnor fetched his glass. "I sold off my last canal shares when Wellington got Boney buttoned up. Steam interests me. Can't deny that. I gather it doesn't interest your bank."

"If I can make good use at the colliery of current science where steam is concerned, the other directors will get their minds out of the past. A great deal of money is to be made by facing forward, but my directors are almost as bad as Haverford, clinging to—"

A tap on the door heralded lunch. Three footmen brought in a procession of trays, setting them down on the low table before the sofa. They bowed quite properly and withdrew.

"The bowing is new," Sherbourne said. "My wife has taken the staff in hand." The staff was thriving under the direction of a lady of the house who knew all the rules and when to bend them.

"Is Mrs. Sherbourne taking *you* in hand?" Radnor asked, seating himself before a tray. "This is quite a feast. Do sit down. Running the world is hungry work. What will it take to bring your bank right?"

"Time," Sherbourne said. "I'm a conservative investor. I choose projects that will yield a sure, steady return. Better than the cent per cents, and unlikely to fail. The mine was supposed to be such a project."

"This soup is delicious. Has your mine fallen into difficulties already?"

"You know about the mudslide." The beef and vegetable soup was comforting and so, in an odd way, was this discussion with Radnor. He was no fool, despite having Haverford for a best friend.

"I know of no mudslide," Radnor said, around a mouthful of buttered bread. "Haverford has heard nothing about a mudslide, and I have it on good authority none of our laborers or masons will mention a mudslide in Lord Brantford's hearing."

Hannibal Jones had been instructed at length on the same topic. "My thanks. You haven't told me why you've graced me with your presence, Radnor."

His lordship rose and brought Sherbourne his drink. "My marchioness thought I needed to get out and socialize."

"You were driving the poor woman addle-pated." Sherbourne had likely driven Charlotte addle-pated. "Does your wife correspond with any old friends of the male gender?"

Radnor dipped his bread in his soup, the same as any yeoman might have. "I should say not. She might tuck a note in with my own correspondence, add a few lines to a letter of mine, that sort of thing. Why?"

"No reason. What can you tell me about the Caerdenwal woman's situation?"

"The who—? Oh, her. Poor creature went into service in Cardiff or Swansea, I forget which. She got with child and that was that. As Griffin so baldly put it, she has a baby but no husband. Is that burgundy in this soup? I do fancy it."

How had Charlotte become aware of a fallen woman

among Griffin's tenants, and why would she make a neighborly gesture in that direction before she'd even called on the vicar?

"The recipe is French," Sherbourne said. "Mrs. Sherbourne brought many recipes with her, and the kitchen has been in constant readiness for a visit from Lord Brantford."

"Does he know about your situation at the bank?"

"I only found out the day following our little dinner party. The post brought all manner of disappointing news." Would Mr. Porter write back to Charlotte, and would Sherbourne intercept that letter if he did? When had Charlotte crossed the path of Mrs. Wesley Smythe of East Anglia or Mrs. Wesley Scott in Liverpool?

"Brantford won't hear about your bank from me," Radnor said. "Nobody will."

"My thanks."

"I doubt you'll thank me for what I'm about to tell you now."

"Another mudslide?" Whatever it was, Radnor had done a good job of keeping his own counsel, while Sherbourne had prattled on about soup recipes and steam.

"Haverford and I are agreed that Hannibal Jones was negligent in his design of your retaining wall."

Charlotte felt the same. "And?"

"And I did a bit of corresponding with friends, and I think you have a problem on your hands."

The soup was no longer hot enough. Sherbourne set his bowl aside and tore a slice of bread in half. "Truly, your insightfulness astounds me, Radnor. I do, indeed, have problems on my hands." Problems he'd like to discuss with Charlotte, if she ever came home.

"Hannibal Jones is a very competent engineer."

"Considering what I'm paying him, he should be a

damned genius, but he apparently forgot that water weighs sixty-two pounds per cubic foot." An inch of rain falling on a square foot of land weighed slightly more than five pounds, another fact Charlotte had passed along.

"He drinks," Radnor said gently, "possibly to excess. The last mine he worked for suffered a tunnel collapse due to flooding. If the collapse had happened any day but the Sabbath, dozens of men, women, and children would have been trapped below the surface. The mine owners kept it quiet, because they didn't want their misfortunes to become public."

"Tunnels collapse," Sherbourne said, though the very words left him queasy. "Mining is a hazardous undertaking."

"The miners warned him that water was leaching into the tunnel, warned him that his trusses were too far apart. He ignored them, and after the accident, his drinking grew appreciably worse. If his drinking is still a problem, you will have to replace him as soon as Brantford is done strutting about. I say that not only as a member of your board of directors, but as one who wants your venture to succeed."

The queasiness in Sherbourne's belly became a burning that pushed up into his chest. Charlotte had offered to check Jones's calculations, and Sherbourne had smiled and done nothing to provide her the figures.

"Have you any more cheering news to report?" Sherbourne asked.

"Glenys assures me we're to have rain tomorrow. Her left knee aches, and she claims that's a reliable predictor of bad weather."

"Then Brantford will see the colliery in all its rainy splendor, and once I've subjected my household to his dubious company at dinner, we'll hope the grouse moors lure him away."

Radnor was soon back in the saddle, leaving his best wishes for Mrs. Sherbourne and a promise that he'd join the inspection tomorrow afternoon. Sherbourne watched him ride off, not sure if the call had been friendly, for all it was appreciated.

Charlotte's dog cart came up the drive even as Radnor turned his horse onto the lane, and Sherbourne waited in the chilly wind until he could assist his wife to alight from her vehicle. Morgan appeared from the stables to lead the horse away, and Sherbourne abandoned all decorum to kiss his wife's rosy cheek.

"Mr. Sherbourne, good day. The vicarage sends greetings. I hope you and Lord Radnor had a pleasant chat?"

"His lordship spread a pall of gloom thicker than the foul miasmas wafting off the Thames in July."

Charlotte took Sherbourne by the arm. "This sounds serious, even for you. You must tell me all about it, and I shall explain how thrilled Vicar was that you have agreed to repair the church steeple."

Sherbourne stopped halfway up the front steps. "Charlotte, I cannot spare a single mason to repair a steeple that hasn't gone anywhere for nearly three hundred years."

She peered up at him, nothing but concern in her eyes despite how sharply he'd spoken. "I was standing in the churchyard, visiting with Miss MacPherson, and a stone fell and nearly struck me on the head. I thought it was a sign from on high that I'd found the most public, charitable project for you to undertake. I'm sorry."

Many more such signs from on high, and Sherbourne would be the one drinking to excess. He made it as far as the foyer and even got the door closed before drawing Charlotte into his arms.

"I'll see to the steeple repairs, I promise, just as soon

as Lord Brantford has pranced off on his merry way. He's coming to dinner tomorrow night and will tour the works in the afternoon."

Charlotte stepped back to untie her bonnet ribbons. "Shall I join this tour of the works? He will behave himself if I am on hand."

Sherbourne undid the frogs of her cloak. "You mean, I'll behave myself. I'd rather let him do his worst, then get rid of him once for all."

"What is the worst he could do?"

Ruin me. "Withdraw his funds because I've misrepresented the state of the project, in which case I'll find another investor." A near impossibility if Brantford spoke ill of what he'd seen.

Charlotte kissed Sherbourne's cheek, treating him to a soothing hint of gardenia. "As long as his lordship can do nothing serious, we shall contrive." The same phrase she'd used when nearly in a swoon from her fear of heights.

"Shall we contrive with a shared midday nap, Mrs. Sherbourne?" The suggestion arrived to Sherbourne's mouth without having given any notice to his brain. He had much to do, not enough time to do it, and canoodling with his wife wouldn't help one bit.

Though it wouldn't hurt, either.

"Tomorrow," Charlotte said, going up on her toes to whisper in his ear. "I am yet plagued by my inconvenience, but tomorrow I will be better able to share naps with you."

Share a nap with me anyway. Sherbourne kept that sentiment to himself, for he didn't know what he'd be asking of her. Simple affection? A quiet respite from his worries? Rest?

"Another time, then. I'm sure you'll want to confer with Cook regarding tomorrow night's menu."

Charlotte slipped her arms around his waist. The butler had found someplace else to be, and thus Sherbourne had a private moment with his wife. She simply hugged him, and before he could reciprocate the embrace, she was bustling off in the direction of her personal parlor.

* * *

"I am growing to dislike Quinton, Earl of Brantford," Charlotte said. "How does a man develop a head cold when he has not stirred from Haverford Castle for three days?"

His lordship had waited until early afternoon to send along a note postponing the tour of the works, and Charlotte had dispatched Morgan straightaway to inform Sherbourne at the colliery.

The weather was beautiful, of course—mild, sunny, not much of a breeze. Gulls strutted around on the terrace, while Sherbourne's expression across the small table beneath the maples put Charlotte in mind of sea cliffs.

Stoic and endlessly beset by the tides.

"You received this an hour past?" Sherbourne asked, studying the note she'd had taken to the colliery.

"Not even that. Will you eat something if I order you luncheon?"

Sherbourne had been gone since dawn and had come stalking across the garden's carpet of fallen leaves only five minutes ago. His hair was windblown, but he'd taken care with his wardrobe, even to wearing a gold cravat pin tipped with a small emerald.

One didn't wear jewels during the day, but on Sherbourne the effect was a dash of daring amid casual elegance.

"Brantford is toying with me," Sherbourne said, gazing

off toward the colliery. "He's rapping me on the nose with his newspaper, as if I'm a naughty puppy who piddled on the carpet."

Like the younger sons and lordlings, who'd broken a young boy's nose, ankle, and arm for sport?

"I suspect he is simply enjoying ducal hospitality for as long as he can. Haverford was notably reclusive until this summer's house party. Brantford wants bragging rights, wants to be able to say that he was the first guest Their Graces of Haverford welcomed after their nuptials. He doubtless hopes that Haverford will take him shooting, and if he attends services, he will delight in sitting in the ducal pew."

Sherbourne set the note aside. "They're like that, the titled snobs. They play those inane games. Haverford will kill me." This last was said with a slight smile.

"Haverford is the one who accepted the earl's request for hospitality," Charlotte replied. "He doubtless did so with the duchess's blessing." Also without consulting Sherbourne, upon whom the earl had come to spy.

Sherbourne's smile was gone, and he was again studying the lane that wound across the fields to the works. "I should get back to the colliery. I thought I'd bring you some calculations to review, but I left them amid Mr. Jones's mess when I got your note."

Charlotte hadn't wanted to pester him for those figures. "As it happens, I am not interested in calculations at present."

That got his attention. "Are you well, Charlotte?"

"I am well. A midday respite with my husband would put me in the very pink." Her ears had doubtless turned pink at that wifely boldness.

Some carfuffle among the seagulls sent them all winging upward, leaving Charlotte and her husband the only living creatures in the garden.

"As it happens, Mrs. Sherbourne, I've been short of sleep myself lately."

Sherbourne came to bed with Charlotte most evenings, but then he disappeared until all hours before snatching some rest before dawn. Truly, the Earl of Brantford had much to answer for.

"Give me a minute to have word with the housekeeper," Charlotte said, "and I'll join you in the bedroom shortly."

The staff graciously accepted the news that the company dinner was postponed, despite preparations having been under way for hours. Charlotte let none of her own frustration show, though she didn't much care whether she made a good impression on his lordship or not.

Sherbourne cared, and thus Charlotte would do her utmost to be a charming hostess.

She let herself into the bedroom, expecting to find her husband at the table, poring over one of his endless reports or estimates. Sherbourne was face down on the mattress, naked and snoring gently, one foot hanging over the edge of the bed.

He looked at once utterly immovable and vulnerable. A solid, sizeable male, and a fallen warrior.

"I love you," Charlotte said softly. "I know not how or when this sentiment arose, but I love you, and the Earl of Brantford will have to deal with that if he thinks to strut about your colliery and treat you with anything less than respect."

She sat on the bed to remove her boots, while Sherbourne slept on undisturbed.

* * *

Conflicting impressions too hazy to qualify as thoughts woke Sherbourne. The first had become as familiar as his own heartbeat: He must away to the colliery. Jones might have a drinking problem—something bedeviled the old man—the masons were squabbling with the yeomanry provided by Radnor and Haverford, and for reasons that Sherbourne's tired brain refused to enumerate, a sense of dread made these problems pressing.

Something else was pressing. Charlotte was tucked against Sherbourne's side, her hand drifting along his chest and belly. Her touch was slow and sweet, and she tempted his attention away from anything having to do with the dratted mine. She was exploring him, even while she might have been trying to let him rest.

Sherbourne kept his eyes closed until Charlotte's expedition ventured south of his waist. He was more than half aroused, which state of affairs provoked her to cupping his stones and running a single finger around the tip of his cock.

"My wife has grown bold."

She sleeved him with her grip. "I have always been bold in some regards. The wife part is new. I was nobody's wife before."

Sherbourne had been nobody's husband, nobody's family, even. He'd been a disliked neighbor, a resented creditor, a ridiculed classmate. Long ago, he'd been a disappointing son.

What did Charlotte see in him, besides wealth that was growing more imperiled by the day?

"I am your husband and you are my wife until death do us part." Charlotte was stuck with him, regardless of the fate of the mine, the bank, the infernal lending library scheme—regardless of anything.

"I like being your wife," Charlotte said, giving him a gentle squeeze. "You don't bore me. I hope you like being my husband."

She'd carefully not asked him a question. Sherbourne turned on his side, the better to answer her without words.

He kissed her on the mouth, then wrapped his hand around hers and showed her how to tease him. Charlotte delighted in knowledge. She would have puzzled this out on her own eventually, but Sherbourne wanted to give her something—a gesture of trust, perhaps?

"You respond to this," she said, taking another slow, thorough tour of his stones.

"I enjoy it." A vast understatement. Sherbourne's worries and woes were falling away, his plans and estimates drifting into oblivion as his mind focused on one plea: *Don't stop.*

Charlotte took his hand and placed it over her breast.

Her bare breast. Sherbourne matched her tempo, which had accelerated from a dreamy *largo* to a maddeningly placid *andante*. Surely he was losing his reason if the long-ago maunderings of his piano teacher were surfacing?

"I want you inside me," Charlotte said, arching into his hand. "Does that make me wanton?"

His slid his hand up to cup her cheek, and of course, her cheek was hot against his palm. She'd closed the bed curtains, but there was light enough to see that she, too, had offered him a gesture of trust.

"Desiring your husband does not and never will make you wanton. It makes me damned lucky."

Though even as Sherbourne shifted over her, worry nagged him: If he got Charlotte with child, that would be one more mouth to feed, one more set of expectations he could never escape. One more person who might someday—soon—be ashamed of an association with Lucas Sherbourne.

His immediate dependents would never be cast out into the elements, but in some ways, shabby gentility was a worse fate than outright penury.

Sherbourne knew from experience that disgust was easier to endure than pity.

Charlotte laced her fingers with his, as if drawing him away from the gloomy precipice of his thoughts. Such was her way with loving, that Sherbourne's worries fell beneath an onslaught of desire. She bit him on the shoulder at the exact right moment to drive him over the edge, though he had the satisfaction of knowing he'd taken her with him.

She held back nothing, growling softly against his neck as pleasure overtook her, sinking her nails into his hip in a grip that satisfied even as it stung.

"You undo me." Charlotte unwrapped her legs from his flanks some moments later, but kept her arms around him. "You absolutely undo me, Lucas. One has more understanding of why newlyweds are sent away for a month where none of their familiars will observe their adjustment to wedded bliss."

He owed her a wedding journey, another unpaid debt. "When we've dealt with Brantford, I'll take you into Cardiff, if you like, or up to the Lakes. A sea trip to the north might be pleasant."

"Winter approaches," Charlotte said, as Sherbourne slipped from her body. "Worse yet, my mother has threatened to pay a visit. Why can't they leave us alone?"

Her lament was reassuringly grumpy. Perhaps she truly did enjoy being married to him?

Sherbourne rose, wrung out a flannel in the warm water by the hearth, and rinsed himself off.

Charlotte propped herself on her elbows and watched from the bed.

"Keep looking at me like that, Mrs. Sherbourne, and we'll be late for supper."

She flopped to her back. "Will the world come to an

end, because a very tired man and his very new wife were late for supper? You'll have to do better than that, Mr. Sherbourne. We can journey to the Lakes in spring, assuming all goes well at the works, and it will go well."

"Radnor tells me Mr. Jones has a potential drinking problem," Sherbourne—or some befuddled gudgeon—said. "A man who drinks can be fatally careless. Once Brantford is gone, I'll see about replacing Jones."

Charlotte smoothed a palm over the mattress. "Is this why you've been so preoccupied lately? Because you're worried for the works?"

For his whole future—for their whole future. "In part. The bank has been giving me a spot of bother as well."

"I would love to be left alone for hours at a bank," Charlotte said, folding her hands behind her head. "All those lovely, lovely numbers. Pages and pages of them, as far as the eye can see."

She'd not tucked the covers up high enough to hide her breasts, which was as far as Sherbourne's eyes could see at the moment.

"When we're next in London, I'll turn you loose at the bank after business hours. You can prowl the ledgers like a mythical creature, spotting mistakes and inaccuracies and breathing fire upon them."

"I'd like that."

Except if he truly let her loose at the bank, sooner or later she'd learn that one of the investments had gone perilously sour, and Sherbourne hadn't yet found a way to manage the damage. He considered explaining the canal situation to her, but she'd already closed her eyes, a goddess who'd earned her slumbers.

Sherbourne very nearly dressed to return to the works. Hannibal Jones was probably inebriating himself at that very moment, and the temperature was doubtless planning to plunge overnight.

Charlotte sighed—a contented, sweet sound. Who knew how long she'd be content with her choice of husband?

Sherbourne climbed back into bed, wrapped himself around his wife, and tried to set aside thoughts of the bank, the mine, the crumbling steeple, and a nosy earl in delicate health.

They all followed him into sleep anyway. Again.

Chapter Seventeen

Brantford had inherited his mines, and thus had no idea what a colliery should look like before shafts were sunk. He might have peppered Sherbourne with questions, except that the Marquess of Radnor hovered at Sherbourne's elbow like an underfootman new to his livery.

"You are on the board of directors for this undertaking?" Brantford asked Radnor, as they returned to the white tent at the center of the planned works.

"I am the assistant director of the mine's board," Radnor said. "We in the peerage have an obligation to bring progress to our neighbors, don't you agree, Brantford? What's the use of having a family seat if one doesn't take an interest in the surrounding parishes? Can't have all of our best and brightest leaving for the colonies."

"I'm told you have fine hunting on Radnor land," Brantford replied, though Radnor had yet to extend an invitation to either ride to hounds or try a bit of shooting.

Inside the tent, Sherbourne was engaged in conversation with the engineer, Hannibal Jones. Based on a few discreet inquiries, Jones had a prickly reputation, though he'd answered all of Sherbourne's questions readily and with proper deference for the august guest in their midst.

"Hunting hasn't started here yet," Radnor said. "The rain has made the ground too soft, though most of the crops are off. Perhaps later in the season we'll have some sport to offer you."

"Does Sherbourne ride to hounds?"

Sherbourne had collected a pile of papers from the longest table in the tent, and Jones was apparently explaining something to his employer.

"Sherbourne is a very competent horseman," Radnor said. "Why do you ask?"

Because making money off of Sherbourne was all well and good, but too much socializing with him would not do.

"One doesn't want to create awkwardness," Brantford said. "Can't invite the man to ride in my flight if he's likely to tumble at the first fence."

Veronica rode with the first flight, and the dash she cut in the saddle had drawn Brantford's notice even before he'd realized the ambitions her family had held for her. He'd received a letter from her that very morning, and she was having a grand time in the company of her cousins at the family seat.

Without her husband.

"If you're still in the area once the weather settles down," Radnor said, "I'll happily take you out shooting. At least you have the famed Haverford library to entertain you until then."

Brantford had done more reading in the past several days than in the previous five years. Her Grace of Haverford did not believe in allowing a guest to while away an afternoon with a plump, pretty chambermaid when Sir Walter Scott was available instead.

The duke didn't believe in allowing anybody or anything—much less a mere titled house guest—to upset his duchess. Their Graces' mutual devotion was nauseatingly sincere.

Also slightly enviable.

"What can Sherbourne be going on about?" Brantford asked. "Tramping around in the mud has worked up my appetite, and I'd rather not linger in this wind and court another illness."

He'd rather not have come to Wales, and had almost put that in a letter to his wife.

"Sherbourne is at these works in all kinds of weather," Radnor said. "He's here morning, noon, and night, and if you are to profit from his labors, then you can spare him a few minutes with his engineer."

So the handsome marquess wasn't all fine manners and starched linen. "I heartily agree," Brantford said. "Sherbourne is willing to get his hands dirty, but then, that's what the merchant class is for, isn't it? Getting and spending, filling the pews, minding the shops while we mind the business of the nation. He doesn't always keep to his place, but he'll make me a decent sum before too long."

The wind shifted, catching a flap of the tent and ripping it loose from its ties. Radnor captured the canvas and tied it back with a perfect bow.

"You cannot in one breath castigate Sherbourne for tarrying here when there's work to be discussed, and then applaud him for having the ability to earn you substantial coin, Brantford. This mine is not a hobby for him, nor will it be for the people hoping to work here."

Though Brantford had no idea what made a mine thrive or fail, he did perceive that Sherbourne had an ally in Radnor, and Radnor was a marquess who commanded the friendship of a duke.

"I mean Sherbourne no insult," Brantford said. "I remark upon my own frailty. When do you expect this place will start turning a profit?"

Now Jones raised his voice, barking something about bloody damned figures. Sherbourne touched Jones on the arm, and the older man grew quiet.

"Didn't you read Sherbourne's financial plan?" Radnor asked. "Revenue should begin flowing by midsummer. The initial investments will earn out over five to ten years, depending on how quickly the mine repays the initial principal and at what percentage interest."

Sherbourne tucked some papers into a satchel and left Jones to fuss with the parlor stove.

"My apologies for detaining you both," Sherbourne said. "Brantford, any other questions?"

By rights, no commoner ought to have used such familiar address. My lord, your lordship, Lord Brantford were acceptable, but Radnor was two yards away, tying the tent flap closed, so Brantford kept his scold behind his teeth.

"I believe I've seen all there is to see at this point," Brantford said. "I hope you intend to set a fine table this evening, Sherbourne, for hiking about has left me famished."

In fact, the relentless smell of mud had all but obliterated his appetite.

"Then I'll be happy to take you back to Sherbourne Hall. My wife is looking forward to meeting you, and I'm in need of sustenance myself."

Radnor walked with them to Sherbourne's waiting gig,

where a boy stood holding the marquess's horse. Brantford would cheerfully have waved good-bye to the Marquess of Meddling, but his vexatious lordship merely steered his horse to walk along beside the carriage.

"Where is your next destination, Brantford?" Sherbourne asked, giving the reins a shake. "Will you return to London, tarry here in Wales, or repair to your family seat?"

"I haven't decided. The hospitality at Haverford Castle is outstanding, and I'm not anxious to subject myself to another week on the king's highway so soon."

Sherbourne drove well, and he was turned out in the first stare of casual gentlemanly fashion. The beast in the traces was sleek and muscular and the gig well sprung. Resentment welled because a small, irrational part of Brantford had been hoping to see Sherbourne fail.

Why should wealth come to a man who had no great standing, no particular learning, no family of any consequence? Why shouldn't Sherbourne have to struggle a bit, or more than a bit? Though not too much—Brantford did need rather badly for this investment to be profitable.

"That's your home?" Brantford asked as they topped a rise and a stately country house came into view.

"My home, and the former dower house for Haverford Castle. We purchased it from the St. Davids in German George's day, and each generation has kept the house modernized in every particular."

How proud he was of a mere jumped-up manor house, though his residence did have rather a lot of windows. Also a fine formal garden that led to a park, which transitioned to cultivated land and pastures. The outbuildings were nicely placed behind the main house—a carriage house and a sizeable stable, a summer kitchen, laundry, and spring house, among others.

Gravel walks joined the buildings, and trimmed hedges marked off the gardens. The premises were, in fact, about the same size as the Brantford estate in Yorkshire.

"Will you join us for dinner, Radnor?" Brantford asked.

"Alas for me, no. I'm expected to relay a report of the day's business to Haverford before I join my lady wife for supper."

Brantford hadn't exactly made a map of the neighborhood, but surely Radnor's errands took him in the opposite direction—back to Haverford Castle—rather than along this bucolic lane?

"You could send a note," Sherbourne said. "Have Lady Radnor join us. Mrs. Sherbourne would be delighted to have her ladyship share another meal with us."

Another meal…Meaning Sherbourne regularly entertained the marquess.

Radnor had a hand in running the mine, Sherbourne had married the duke of Haverford's sister-in-law, and by escorting Sherbourne back to his home, Radnor was sending a clear signal to any presuming earls: Sherbourne had allies, close at hand, and well placed.

And yet, the duke had not invested in this mine, while Brantford had. Perhaps dinner would afford a tired, hungry earl far from home several opportunities to remind his host of that salient fact.

* * *

"His lordship is a bumpkin," Charlotte said, setting a pot of heartsease on the bedroom mantel. "He talked about nothing save his collieries in Yorkshire and his sporting acquaintances. Was he much of a pest at the works?"

She should have written to her family and gleaned their

opinions of Brantford, for he'd been a disappointment in fine tailoring.

Sherbourne closed and locked the bedroom door. "Radnor nannied us at every turn, which I gather was at Haverford's insistence. My sense is that Brantford knows little of mining, and while he could have interrogated me at length for the benefit of his own education—which would have earned my esteem—he wasn't about to appear ignorant before Radnor or before you."

Charlotte stood in front of her husband and slipped the pin from his cravat. "For his pride, he does not have your esteem. Sleeve buttons, please."

Sherbourne offered her his right hand, then his left, and she slipped the fastenings at his wrists free. "Pride doesn't offend me, Charlotte. I'm proud. I hope I'm not arrogant. I can undress myself."

She undid his pocket watch next, then set his jewelry on the vanity and went after the knot in his cravat.

"I am your wife, and undressing you is my pleasure."

He tipped his chin up. "You mean that."

"I spoke vows, you did too. Shall I order you a bath?" She folded his cravat over the back of a chair.

"No, thank you. I did nothing today that came close to qualifying as physical exertion. My thanks for a fine meal. You have quite the treasure trove of recipes."

"Our cook has recipes too, but she was loath to try them on you without an invitation. Shall you take off your shoes?"

He settled into the chair by the hearth, his sigh redolent of weariness . . . from a man who hadn't exerted himself.

"Are you relieved to have Brantford's visit behind you?" Charlotte certainly was.

"I should be. Might you sit for a moment, Mrs. Sherbourne?"

Charlotte took a seat on the hassock, though sitting still was difficult. Her first true guest beyond family had come to dinner, and nothing had gone wrong...or had it?

"What did you and Brantford talk about over the port?"

Sherbourne bent to remove his shoes. He set them aside and regarded the fire blazing in the hearth.

"Brantford is unhappy with the terms of our agreement. He waited all day to ambush me, until neither you nor Radnor could hear him express dismay at the schedule upon which his investment will be repaid."

Nothing of Brantford's displeasure had been evident when Charlotte had rejoined the men for a final cup of tea before sending Brantford back to Haverford Castle. He'd been the gracious, smiling, lordly guest, bowing with friendly presumption over Charlotte's hand.

"You are unhappy with Brantford," Charlotte said, taking her husband's feet into her lap.

"Have you a fascination with my feet, Mrs. Sherbourne?"

Yes. "You might offer to rub my feet at some point if I bring you pleasure often enough by rubbing yours." *Or you might not be upset with me, when I find a moment to tell you about Fern's son. And the Mrs. Wesleys. All of the Mrs. Wesleys, including the ones I haven't met yet.*

Now that Brantford's visit was behind them, Charlotte meant to find that moment soon. Sherbourne was a reasonable fellow, and he was *her* fellow, and Charlotte detested keeping secrets from him.

Sherbourne scrubbed a hand over his face. "Brantford signed a contract with me, agreeing that repayment of his investment would be on commercially reasonable terms, determined within my discretion as the owner, major investor, and director of the works, but in no event to involve a period of more than ten years, or less than five percent per annum simple interest."

"If he invested ten thousand pounds, then five percent interest per annum on the entire principle over ten years would be another five thousand pounds. Many people go their whole lives without earning five hundred pounds."

Sherbourne leaned his head back against the cushions as Charlotte pressed her thumbs against his left heel. Achilles had lost his life as a result of an arrow to the left heel, though why that snippet of mythology should occur to her, she did not know.

"Some people go their whole lives without entangling a titled snob in their business," Sherbourne said. "I should not have taken what Brantford was offering. That feels good."

Charlotte pressed harder against his callused sole. "Can you untangle yourself from Brantford?"

"Not soon enough. He's in the wrong. He signed a contract that many others have signed regarding similar projects. The agreement is legally sound, but if his lordship takes me to court, alleging a defect because the language was too vague, then he can destroy the colliery before we've brought out our first ton of ore. He'll demand all of his money back, plus damages and costs, and make me look like a presuming incompetent."

"Give him his money back now and tear up the contract. He's not honorable."

Sherbourne remained quiet, while Charlotte worked her thumbs all over the bottom of his foot. If anybody had told her a month ago that she'd enjoy massaging her husband's feet, she'd have pronounced that person unhinged.

The moment was intimate, and she liked being intimate with her spouse.

"Do you suppose Haverford's watchdog was spying on me," he asked, "or keeping Brantford from stepping out of line?"

"Radnor might have been acting on his own initiative. He is one of your directors. Give me your other foot."

"Radnor made it plain he would drop by Haverford Castle to report on the day's doings before returning home. I know the aristocracy is insular and inbred, but if Radnor sought—ouch."

Charlotte eased the pressure. "Radnor and Haverford do not know Brantford any better than you do. I have the sense I might have stood up with him, though I cannot place him. A blond, blue-eyed earl is hardly a rarity. His looks are unremarkable and his conversation uninspired, and yet I do wonder if I met him somewhere previously."

"He bored you at dinner?"

"He bored me within five minutes of the introductions because he can converse regarding only one topic—himself. I like your crooked toes."

"You like my crooked tocs, while a peer of the realm bores you. You are an eccentric female, and eccentric females have ever been my favorite exponents of the gender."

Sherbourne was...he was flirting with her. Charlotte was almost sure of it. "Fatigue has made you daft."

"Marriage has made me happy, Charlotte." He sounded perplexed, and his gaze was on the fire, and yet he sounded pleased, too.

Charlotte set his feet on the floor and appropriated a corner of his seat cushion. "Might you undo my hooks and stays?" she asked, sweeping her hair off her nape.

Sherbourne unfastened her clothing, and Charlotte arranged herself in his lap, rather than hurry away to the privacy screen. He wrapped his arms about her, and she cuddled with him before the fire in a state of half-dressed, cozy fatigue. Charlotte drifted off to sleep wondering where she might have seen Brantford before, and hoping she might never see him again.

* * *

"Your taste in business partners is disgraceful." Haverford passed Sherbourne a glass of brandy. "If ever I owed you more than coin of the realm, my debt to you has been settled in perpetuity."

"Likewise," Radnor said, lifting his glass so it caught the afternoon sun beaming through the windows of Haverford Castle's library. "Here's to an earl seen safely on his way."

Sherbourne took a sip of exquisite brandy—the very vintage he'd sent Haverford as a wedding present, actually.

"Charlotte pronounced Brantford boring," Sherbourne said. "My wife is blessed with keen discernment."

"Though she married you anyway," Radnor murmured.

Charlotte had married him, made passionate love with him, rubbed his feet, entertained his guests, and paraded around the churchyard with him as if she'd happened upon the greatest marital prize of the season.

All quite . . . different from Sherbourne's expectations.

"And my sister," Haverford said, "for reasons which defy mortal comprehension, is now the Marchioness of Radnor. Here's to our ladies."

Sherbourne drank to that, and to the peculiar pleasure of being thanked by the vicar, in public, and within earshot of most of the congregation, for "seeing to our long overdue steeple repairs, and with such unstinting generosity."

With Charlotte preening at Sherbourne's side, he'd been

given odd looks, tentative smiles, and maybe even a few envious glances from the local squires. Then, in full view of the shire's biggest busybodies, Haverford had offered an impromptu invitation to Sunday dinner at the castle.

"How is Her Grace?" Sherbourne asked, as Haverford rolled a ladder along a two-story expanse of bookshelves. "She seemed in good spirits at services."

"She is relieved to be shut of Brantford," Haverford said, climbing the ladder. "What a tedious excuse for a houseguest. He discovered where the maids' stairs were and frequented them at every opportunity, such that Her Grace decreed the maids and footmen were to switch staircases for the duration of Brantford's visit."

"What's different about this room?" Radnor asked, steadying the ladder at the bottom. "Something has changed."

Sherbourne took his drink up the spiral steps with him, to the section of the shelves reserved for cookery and herbals, for surely Haverford had a volume of recipes Charlotte would enjoy.

"What's different," he said, "is that I have paid to ship half the books that used to collect dust on yonder shelves into the hinterlands of Wales. Somewhere, some tavern maid is struggling through *Candide*, while her younger brother fancies himself a Lilliputian or a Yahoo."

Which was progress of a sort Haverford would never have stumbled on without the aid of his duchess *and his neighbor.*

As a result, the library was lighter, airier, less of a cave, more of a gracious retreat. The scent was the same, though—the vanilla fragrance of old books, a tang of peat, and a mellow undertone of beeswax and lemon.

"I can count on my thumb the number of hours Brantford spent in here," Haverford said, taking out a book, pushing it back among its confreres, then taking down another. "We still have one of the finest collections of reading material in the realm, and his lordship was more interested in bothering the help or talking me into taking him to a local hunt meet."

"He wanted to be seen with you." Sherbourne selected a volume on French desserts. "He did not want to be seen with me."

"While you add coin to his coffers," Radnor muttered. "Not well done of him."

"I will make very sure that Brantford and I belong to none of the same clubs," Haverford said, making a slow descent while holding a book in his hand. "The man lacks couth."

Looking down on the duke and the marquess, Sherbourne's first thought was that he was being subtly rebuked for having associated with Brantford. Another hypothesis suggested itself: The duke and the marquess were ashamed of Brantford, ashamed that a peer of the realm had acted so disagreeably.

So dishonorably, to use Charlotte's term.

"I apologize for inflicting Brantford on you both," Sherbourne said, closing the book of recipes. "If I could refund his investment and send him on his way, I would." The apology was as rare as it was sincere, and yet, more words marched forth into the comfortable elegance of the ducal library. "His lordship threatened litigation if I failed to interpret the terms of our contract liberally. He reminded me that his cousin is a judge."

His *dear* cousin.

Her Grace had towed Sherbourne all over this library countless times in recent weeks, but today was different, because he was an invited guest. Ten feet below, Haverford passed Radnor the book. The view from the mezzanine suggested Radnor would go bald before Haverford did—even that indignity apparently respected the order of precedence.

Radnor glanced up from the book. "Brantford *threatened* you with a lawsuit not a month after agreeing to do business with you?"

"The earl was subtle enough to leave a margin of ambiguity," Sherbourne said, descending the steps. "He is not happy with the terms he agreed to, though I've guaranteed him at least as good a return as the cent per cents, and my own investment will be repaid on the same terms. I'm to improve those terms for him or deal with his displeasure. He awaits correspondence from me confirming my renewed understanding of our association."

Haverford took the reading chair by the fireplace and crossed his feet at the ankles. "Does he want his money back?"

"I asked him that, and he laughed. He invested in my works, and now I'm to make him rich."

"Somebody ought to make him humble," Radnor said. "The man's a disgrace."

A lingering residue of self-doubt wafted away with Radnor's words. Sherbourne had confidence in his own commercial abilities and confidence in his grasp of the law. He worked hard and had a fair degree of common sense. Where he'd erred was in assuming that a man born to wealth, title, and standing would also claim the integrity that should accompany such blessings.

Radnor and Haverford confirmed that Sherbourne's expectations had been reasonable, not naïve, not stupid.

"Brantford is my disgrace for now," Sherbourne said. "I

cannot risk litigation or scandal, or even his lordship's enmity in the clubs. I've recently married well above myself, and my liquid resources are at low ebb. If I do as his lordship wishes and make him a fortune, then I benefit as well."

Haverford scowled at his drink. "I could not be that rational, that pragmatic, or mature in the face of such arrogance. He doesn't need another fortune, and investing with you was hardly taking a great risk. I'd be tempted to plant such an audacious creditor a facer."

Haverford was every inch the duke at his leisure. His Sunday attire was pristine, beautifully tailored, and adorned with his signature touches of lace and luxury. Despite his rank, he was merely commiserating with a neighbor and in-law over a turn of bad luck.

A cat leaped into Haverford's lap, inspiring the duke to swear affectionately and set his drink aside. Purring rumbled forth as His Grace scolded the cat and scratched its chin.

I must get my wife a kitten.

That thought—which brought Charlotte to mind—was followed closely by another: *I owe Haverford an apology.*

"I was an ass," Sherbourne said, before caution got the better of him. "As a creditor, I was an ass, Haverford. I am sorry for it. I should have shown you how to restructure your notes when you came into the title, should have written off the old duke's obligation."

Radnor apparently found the view out the corner window fascinating.

"The old duke should not have been such a profligate spendthrift," Haverford said, "and by failing to accelerate delinquent notes, you essentially did restructure them. What do you suppose the ladies are gossiping about?"

"Feminine mysteries," Radnor said, turning from the

window. "Names for babies. Glenys is honestly considering Galahad if it's a boy."

The expectant fathers fretted about odd names that might befall their offspring. When a child was saddled with six or eight names from birth, much nonsense could creep onto the list.

Sherbourne sipped his drink and missed his wife. Charlotte would know if Haverford had accepted Sherbourne's apology, rejected it, or simply been embarrassed by it. Sherbourne didn't particularly care. He'd tendered the apology that honor demanded, and that was what mattered.

Charlotte would be proud of him—which also mattered—and that might give him the courage to rub her feet.

Chapter Eighteen

"Does Mr. Sherbourne know what you're about?"

Miss MacPherson's tone was polite but firm, such as a senior servant used on a child found outside the nursery at an odd hour. She'd come upon Charlotte making a Monday morning call at the Caerdenwal household, and had accepted a ride back to the village.

"Mr. Sherbourne is too busy with the colliery to be bothered with my social schedule," Charlotte replied. "He has his charitable undertakings, and I have mine."

"He's putting the steeple to rights," Miss MacPherson said, retying her bonnet ribbons. "Papa will be very wroth if Mr. Sherbourne withdraws his support from that project."

Old anger stirred, startling in its intensity. "Do you mean that putting a pretty steeple on the church is more important than seeing Maureen Caerdenwal's baby thrive?"

"I mean that we can't have masonry plummeting from the heavens onto parishioner's heads, Mrs. Sherbourne."

For about a quarter mile, the only sound was the hoof-beats of the gelding in the traces, and the crunch of the gig's wheels on the lane. The fine weather had held, perhaps the last of the year. Along the tree lines, each breeze sent more leaves twirling down to join the carpet below. The undergrowth was dying back with brilliant reds and yellows among the somber browns.

The day was beautiful, and Charlotte made up her mind to take her husband a picnic lunch once she'd delivered her passenger.

"You doubtless surprised the Caerdenwals with your generosity," Miss MacPherson said. "I hadn't thought to collect fabric for them."

Infants needed clothing, and even scraps could be stitched together into quilts and dresses. "Winter approaches and the child must be kept warm."

Charlotte had barely set both feet over the cottage threshold, staying only long enough to introduce herself and leave a basket and a bundle. Maureen had been terrified into near speechlessness, while her mother had accepted Charlotte's offerings with quiet dignity. Poverty had been evident, in the household's painful tidiness, threadbare carpets, and empty quarter shelves in the front room.

No cut work, no framed embroidery, no charmingly amateurish sketch of the baby, no embroidery half-finished in a work basket.

But for the half-dozen plump hens in the yard, Charlotte might have started crying. Griffin had kept his word, and in the coming cold weather, his generosity might be all that kept the child healthy.

"You ought to tell Mr. Sherbourne where you've been," Miss MacPherson said as she climbed down from the gig outside the vicarage. "I've no business presuming to give you advice about your marriage, but Mr. Sherbourne isn't the greedy brute some people would believe him to be."

"Miss MacPherson, you insult my husband even as you defend him." And yet, Charlotte was just as outspoken as Miss MacPherson when the need arose.

The vicar's daughter was also right—about honesty between spouses being essential. Anybody who thought Sherbourne a greedy brute was an idiot.

"I insult my papa's congregation," Miss MacPherson said, shaking out her skirts. "The parish enjoys having Mr. Sherbourne to gossip about, but he's the closest thing this valley has to a banker, and he doesn't cheat anybody. Now he's building us a colliery, and that's something Haverford would have prevented to his dying day but for Mr. Sherbourne's persistence."

She really was quite fierce, quite admirable. "Now you insult my brother-in-law?"

"I speak the truth, and mean the duke no insult. He did find us a lovely duchess, and now Mr. Sherbourne has brought you here as well. The valley will benefit from both unions."

She curtsied and came up smiling. Charlotte smiled back and turned the gig for home.

Of course, she would tell her husband where she'd been. She would also tell her sister, and Lady Radnor, and enlist their aid in developing a plan to keep the Caerdenwals in chickens and quilts. Doubtless both titled households could contribute some fabric scraps, send the occasional gardener around to help with the heavier tasks, and spare a ham once a quarter or so.

Charlotte was happily engrossed in charitable plans as she sailed into the library, intent on jotting down a few ideas.

Sherbourne sat at his desk, neither reading nor writing. He rose when Charlotte entered, and she approached with intent to hug him thoroughly—he'd torn himself away from the works at midday after all.

"Mrs. Sherbourne. Good day."

"Mr. Sherbourne. You have foiled my plans. I had intended to kidnap you from the works for a picnic because the weather is so fair."

He propped a hip on the corner of the desk, dropped something from his pocket into the pen tray, and crossed his arms.

"You planned to kidnap me?" he asked.

No warmth shone from his eyes, no welcome. He was again the calculating, self-contained social interloper Charlotte had first encountered months ago at Haverford's house party.

"Have you and Mr. Jones quarreled?" she asked, drawing off her bonnet. A hairpin caught in her bonnet ribbons. She couldn't hold the hat and untangle her hair both, and rather than help her, her husband merely watched from several feet away.

He disdains to touch me. Charlotte rejected that wayward thought almost before it formed. "Might you assist me?"

He waited for two unfathomable seconds, then withdrew a pair of shears from the desk drawer. He approached, held up the shears, and Charlotte resigned herself to finding a new ribbon for her bonnet. She held still, though at the last second she realized he intended to cut off a lock of her hair.

"You're free," he said, holding up the curling strands with the trailing length of ribbon. "Where have you been, Charlotte?" A taunt, not friendly marital small talk.

"I've come from the vicarage."

"Is that where you've spent your morning?"

Charlotte tried to tuck the shortened lock behind her ear, though it refused to stay there. She set her bonnet atop the globe that stood near a tall window.

"Lucas, what's wrong?"

He pulled an object from his breast pocket and held it out to her. "Why would the earl of Brantford have given you his miniature, and signed the back, conveying all of his love, always?"

Charlotte should have laughed, should have refused to touch the object in Sherbourne's hand. She should have snatched it from him and tossed it across the room.

The very sight of the small portrait made her ill. She hadn't forgotten the miniature, quite, but hadn't made it a point to study the image recently, either.

"You searched my jewelry box?"

"No, I did not. I have been remiss as a husband. Among my many failings, I've never presented you with a morning gift. I thought to leave you such a gift among your effects, a few baubles, such as I can afford. I have no idea what you prefer in the way of jewels so I thought to look at what you already own. Instead, I find you've been playing me false with the same man who's trying to all but blackmail me. Did you and Brantford laugh at your cleverness, Charlotte?"

If Sherbourne had abandoned her on the highest peak in the land, Charlotte could not have been more bewildered.

"You accuse me of betraying my vows with *Brantford*?"

"I'm doing you the courtesy of asking you for answers, Charlotte. You had Brantford's miniature secreted where few husbands would ever look. You entertained him with every appearance of gracious good cheer. He's titled, he's *of your ilk*, he's unscrupulous, and he's in a position to ruin everything I've worked for. He approached me only after the Windhams had shown me a cordial welcome to London. What am I to think?"

Charlotte needed to sit down, and the closest available chair was behind Sherbourne's desk. She took it, refusing to so much as glance at the miniature in Sherbourne's hand.

Indignation was trying to push aside other emotions, for Sherbourne had reached the worst judgments about her without even hearing her explanation. She was prepared to tell him so when a glint from the pen tray caught her eye.

A hairpin tipped with amber. Her hairpin, and Sherbourne had had it in his pocket, the rogue.

If he'd carried this token with him since their betrothal, then he was *her* rogue, and he was her husband.

"I can see why you are perplexed," Charlotte said, "but that miniature is not the Earl of Brantford. I've had it for years, and it belonged to my dearest friend. The man who gave Fern that portrait and penned such tender sentiments to her was the complete scoundrel who ruined her and left her to die shortly after bearing his child. I hate him, whoever he might be, and if the opportunity ever arises, I will hold him accountable for his sins."

The clock ticked three times while Sherbourne stared at the small likeness in his hand, then he stalked across the library and slapped it onto the blotter.

"This is Brantford, Charlotte. Younger, thinner, handsomer, but it's him. Don't put me off with some flimsy lie."

"It's not Brantford. It's one of many blond, blue-eyed lordlings whom the portraitists are paid to flatter outrageously. Fern refused to tell me his name because she knew I'd see him ruined if it was the last thing I did on this earth."

Sherbourne's cool façade cracked to reveal a hint of exasperation. "*Charlotte, this is Brantford.* I know his penmanship, and the initials on the back are his. He makes a particularly vain production out of his Q's, and the likeness is him."

A chill passed over Charlotte, leaving a queasy weakness in its wake. "That cannot be Brantford. It's not..."

Sherbourne pushed the little painting closer, so Charlotte had merely to tip her chin down to study it. A blond, bland countenance smiled up at her, though as she'd said, many a young lord was blond-haired and blue-eyed, and every one of them smiled.

The artist had taken the predictable liberties and flattered the subject, though not unduly. The image was years out of date, too, and age was not improving Brantford's looks. His hair was thinner, his cheeks fuller, his eyes colder.

But Charlotte knew that smile. She'd last seen it when he'd bowed his farewells, and offered her fine compliments on a lovely meal.

She rose, though her knees were none too steady. "I need to wash my hands."

She needed to be sick, to toss that devil's painting into the fire, to cling to her husband and cry until she had no more tears left.

"You're not making sense, Charlotte. You always make sense." Concern lurked beneath Sherbourne's terse observation.

"He killed my friend, Lucas. That vile, rutting, smiling, despicable, mortal sin of a man lied to my friend, struck her, and cast her out when she was with child. It was Brantford, and I've entertained him at my own table. I gave him my hand, I curtsied to him, when I should have driven a knife through his heart."

Charlotte pushed away from the desk, needing to put distance between herself and the image of evil on the blotter. Sherbourne caught her before she stumbled, and then Charlotte was weeping uncontrollably against her husband's chest.

"Lucas, he killed my friend. I cannot bear it. He killed my friend, and there was nothing I could do."

Sherbourne swept her up in his arms, settled with her on the sofa, and even produced a much-needed handkerchief, and still Charlotte could not cease weeping.

* * *

All of Charlotte's passion, her magnificent dignity and decency, fueled hot, miserable tears that wet Sherbourne's shirt and broke his heart. She cried for her friend and for her own lost faith in gentlemanly honor. He knew—because this was his wife, the woman he'd been born to partner, the woman who'd frightened him witless when he'd thought she'd played him false—that the last lament was the deepest cut.

There was nothing I could do.

He held her, he rocked her, he stroked her hair, and kissed her brow until she slowly quieted.

"I hate him," Charlotte said, voice raspy and low. "Lucas, I will hate him until the day I leave this earth, and should the Almighty consign me to the Pit, part of me would rejoice, for there I'd see that human plague-rodent and confront him with the evil he's done."

She meant every word, and Old Nick himself would not dare interfere with her vengeance. "Tell me what happened."

"I have told you. Fern was a vicar's daughter. The

sweetest, most mischievous, dear, young woman ever to
help me tie sheets together so we could dance under a full
moon and feel as daring as pagans. We were ridiculous,
and I will never have a friend like that again."

You have me. "She decided to dance with Brantford under the stars instead?"

Charlotte squirmed about and took the place beside
Sherbourne on the sofa. He tucked an arm around her
shoulders, and after a bit of fussing, she scooted down to
rest her head against his thigh. He draped a quilt over her—
her favorite quilt—and wished he'd met his wife before
heartache had made her so indomitable.

"Fern did not *decide* to tryst with Brantford. She knew
he was far above her touch. She was introduced to him only
because a cousin of his attended the same finishing school
we did. I was at Morelands, spending a holiday with my
family while Fern bided at school, and she met Brantford.
He charmed her, then struck up a correspondence with her.
She initiated none of it and didn't answer his letters until
he threatened to cast himself from the nearest sea cliff if
she continued to ignore him."

Would that he had. "I assume you tried to dissuade her?"

"I knew nothing of it—he enjoined Fern to secrecy and
for good reason. If I'd suspected that vile abomination was
sniffing about her skirts, I'd have set my cousins to chas-
ing him off that cliff at gunpoint." A shuddery sigh went
through her. "Hate is a taxing emotion, but Brantford deserves my hatred, Lucas. He deserves to be pilloried for the
rest of his life."

Charlotte was not meant for hatred, but neither could
she tolerate injustice. Sherbourne treasured that about her.
He needed her moral clarity in his life, needed her common
sense—and her affection.

"When did you become aware that your friend was conducting a liaison?"

Charlotte bit his thigh. "Fern did not *conduct a liaison*. She made a poor family's version of a come out, and if I'm to believe her, she avoided Brantford. I certainly didn't see her showing favor to any particular man, though she later admitted she'd danced with him occasionally. Brantford's attentions would have been considered gentlemanly, even generous, given the difference in their stations. All the while, he was stealing kisses and tempting her to clandestine meetings."

Very likely, Brantford's cronies would have known what he was about, for he would have bragged of his progress and joked about his objective. Men did, and other men pretended not to take the boasting seriously, for then no guilt need trouble them, either. The same unspoken rules meant that boys at school could beat Sherbourne without mercy, while other boys pretended not to notice.

"When did you learn that your friend had misstepped?"

Charlotte sat up, though she kept the quilt about her. "She did not misstep. She was seduced by a conscienceless snake, one promising undying love and matrimony. He cozened her consent and her affections with his lies, and then he betrayed her trust."

All true enough, and yet, young ladies were warned almost from birth against such scoundrels. Sherbourne would start warning his daughters from the moment of their conception.

"He offered marriage?"

"He did, on bended knee. I am very glad your proposal wasn't offered from that ridiculous posture. He gave her a ring, which I also have, and he got her with child. Fern turned to me only when her situation was past denying. Her own father wanted nothing to do with her, but her brother agreed to take her in, and he and his wife are raising the child."

Insight lifted a burden from Sherbourne's memory. "Your old friend, Mr. Porter?"

"The very one. He might have been as hypocritical as his father, but I promised him sufficient coin to raise the boy, and in the end, he and his wife were kind to Fern."

Would they have been as kind without Charlotte's money? "You are supporting the child?"

Charlotte shot him a glance over her shoulder. "*You* are now, indirectly. I set aside a sum from my pin money. Do you mind?"

Sherbourne did not dare mind. "I mind that you didn't tell me. I don't begrudge the lad necessities when I was raised with every comfort. Few would come to the aid of a fallen woman as you have, Charlotte. Your loyalty is commendable."

Charlotte rose and folded the quilt over the reading chair. "Is there more you would say? I intend to continue supporting the boy, Lucas. His father's sins are not his fault."

Sherbourne stood and took her hand. Her palm was hot and damp, her cheeks red, and her eyes glittery with spent tears. The lock of hair he'd cut short curled up at an odd angle by her jaw.

His wife was far from composed in her present state, and yet she was dear.

"The failings of the boy's mother are also not of his making. Anybody with human parents should agree with you there. If we're to believe our history books, King William himself was the child of a fallen woman."

Charlotte withdrew her hand. "Fallen woman, Lucas?

You call my friend a fallen woman? Why do you not refer to Brantford as a fallen man? Why is there *never* any such creature as a fallen man?"

Charlotte paced to the hearth, indignation ringing with every footfall. "When did Fern fall from honor? When she rebuked *his lordship* for his inappropriate correspondence? When she avoided him in London? When she believed his lies and trusted his promises? Why call her fallen, when with malice aforethought and a dash of casual violence, Brantford despoiled her, ruined her, got her with child, cast her out, made no provision for his own progeny, and none for the mother of his child, either?"

Skirts swishing, Charlotte paced before the fire. "Tell me again why my friend, my friend who died after delivering Brantford's unclaimed son, is *fallen*, while his lordship is worth all the hours you put in at the colliery, all the late nights, all the careful estimates and hard work. Why should *that man* be allowed to continue to draw breath, much less profit from your efforts while he does?"

Too late, Sherbourne realized he was in the midst of a negotiation. Charlotte had a grievance, in the truest sense of the word—she grieved for her friend, and for the trust any young woman expected to be able to place in male decency. Both were gone, one just as surely as the other.

Which could not be helped.

"Charlotte, my fate has now become entangled with Brantford's. He was in the wrong where Miss Porter was concerned, without doubt he was in the wrong, but we cannot change the past."

Charlotte was sensible, she'd have to accept that reasoning.

She marched up to him, and despite her blotchy complexion, flyaway curls, and red nose, Sherbourne resisted the impulse to step back.

"I do not expect you to change the past, though God knows I've wished I could. I do, however, expect you to change the future. Cut your ties with Brantford, Lucas. He's not worth your time, your coin, or your passing thoughts. Cut him out of our lives, and do what you can to limit his access to anybody from whom he might profit. That much is in your grasp, and I'll content myself with it if I must."

The expectation in her eyes, the righteous certainly that Sherbourne would not fail her made him want to howl.

"What you ask is impossible. I signed a contract, I gave my word, and Brantford has already let it be known I'm to improve on the terms agreed to, not renege on them."

Charlotte's regard shifted to the steady, gimlet gaze he'd seen her turn on a presuming lordling, the same look she'd give a streak of bird droppings on a park bench.

"You don't even like Brantford. You don't trust him, you regret your association with him, and now you know he's dishonored a decent young woman and ignored his own child. Why would you choose his part over the honorable path?"

Charlotte's question confused so many conflicting priorities and emotions. She wasn't wrong for asking, but she was Sherbourne's wife—had taken vows to cleave to him, forsaking all others, even the memory of her departed friend.

"He ruined a young woman," Sherbourne said. "Now he can ruin me. If I let that happen, it will do nothing to right the wrongs of the past, and everything to imperil the future of our own children. Is that what you want?"

"We have no children," Charlotte said, glancing around the library as if unsure how she'd come to be there. "If, for better or for worse, you choose to earn coin for the Earl of Brantford knowing what you do about him, then I can assure you, Mr. Sherbourne, we never will."

He tried to fathom what that ominously calm pronounce-ment meant as Charlotte crossed to the desk and drew some-thing gold from a skirt pocket—his plainest cravat pin.

"I told myself I could keep this with me in case you ever needed a spare." She set the little gold accessory on the blotter beside her hairpin. "What I really wanted was a to-ken to remind me of the decent, dear, worthy man whom some miracle of fate placed at my side."

Sherbourne remained alone by the hearth, angry, sad, resentful—and impressed—while Charlotte quietly left the room.

* * *

"I understand why you didn't tell Mr. Sherbourne," Eliza-beth said, choosing a bench near a window dripping with condensation, "but why not tell me, Charlotte? I'm your sister, and I did notice when your best friend disappeared from London without a word of explanation."

The Haverford conservatory was full of plants brought in from the terraces and gardens in anticipation of cold weather. The greenery should have been soothing, and the fecund, earthy scent comforting.

"Fern was owed my silence," Charlotte said, remaining on her feet. "I feel like ripping apart everything I see. Like smashing every pot. That contemptible, putrid excrescence on the face of manhood bowed over my hand, Elizabeth."

Charlotte had washed her hands, thoroughly, before summoning her gig and departing for the castle. She was hungry, queasy, wrung out from crying, and heartbroken over her discussion with Sherbourne.

And Elizabeth, so serene and composed on her bench, was no help at all.

"Be that as it may, Charl, had you thought to confide in me—in any of your family—regarding Miss Porter's situation we might have been able to help."

"Fern was my friend." Charlotte sank onto a plain wooden chair worn grey with age. "She asked me not to interfere, not to risk tainting my own name with scandal."

"We could have helped with the boy."

Not with ruining Brantford or holding him responsible, *of course*. "My husband is allowing my support of the child. Evander will continue to thrive." Which was something. Sherbourne had not quibbled at that expenditure for an instant. Charlotte plucked a dead bloom from the nearest potted chrysanthemum. "Bethan, what am I to do?"

Weeping was such a lot of bother. It left a woman exhausted, unlovely, and predisposed to repeating the indignity. Sherbourne had been so kind, so patient . . .

Until he'd made Charlotte so angry.

"You must choose your own course, Charlotte. Anyone would find this contretemps vexing."

Charlotte twisted off another spent blossom. "I do find the situation vexing." Terribly and completely, and yet the facts were straightforward: Brantford had not been held accountable. For Sherbourne to enrich the earl was absolutely wrong. For Fern to have been disgraced was wrong.

Everything was wrong.

"I have been so certain for so long that I knew the difference between right and wrong, Bethan. I took vows. The only vows I've spoken in my entire life. I'm supposed to honor my husband, and I do, but Fern was lied to and ruined. Brantford was and is in the wrong."

"Sherbourne would be in the wrong," Elizabeth said, "if

he let Brantford's threats similarly ruin the colliery. I agree, it's complicated."

No help at all.

Charlotte tossed the dead flowers among the pruned roses and pushed to her feet. "I shall be going, then. Thank you for listening."

Elizabeth took up a watering can and gave an enormous, feathery fern a drink. "You are always welcome here, Charlotte. If Sherbourne should prove difficult, or his temper unruly, don't be so proud again. Come here and let him stand outside the castle walls begging you to relent. It might do him good, and Haverford would enjoy the very sight."

That Elizabeth would imply Sherbourne should be humbled for the duke's entertainment was infuriating, and thus Charlotte's resentment latched on to an additional target.

"Haverford's requirements for this mine are a large part of the reason Sherbourne took on a junior investor. The colliery is exorbitantly expensive to set up on Haverford's terms, many of which are more luxury than necessity, from what I've read about mining operations."

Elizabeth's watering can had a slow leak dripping from the bottom. A fat droplet hit the duchesses's ivory satin slipper while she aimed an unreadable look at Charlotte.

"You have ever had the gift of direct speech, Sister, though sometimes your words come close to criticizing a family member. I have always thought you couldn't help it, that you must speak the truth, however flawed your perception of it might be."

Faced with Elizabeth's gracious *understanding*, Charlotte grasped exactly why Sherbourne had no patience with his titled neighbors.

"Haverford knows next to nothing about mines." Charlotte pulled her driving gloves out of her reticule and jerked them on. "That is not an insult, that is a fact. His Grace's ignorance did not stop him from dictating to Sherbourne many details of the colliery's appointments, and they are expensive details. I could lend Haverford some books. Big, heavy, bound books, and then you might believe me."

Drip, drip, drip. *Thunk*. Elizabeth set the watering can on the table, where it would doubtless leak for the next two hours and warp the wood.

Charlotte did not care.

"You are upset," Elizabeth said, sounding very much like their auntie, the Duchess of Moreland. "I will overlook your tone, because when I believed that Haverford and I were to part, I was a wreck."

"Now you tell me I'm a wreck and take on your Older Sister of Doom voice. I am not wrong, Elizabeth. Haverford dictated terms in ignorance, and Brantford is awful, and sometimes, I think not a single adult male should be allowed out without a nanny."

Charlotte set the watering can onto the packed earth floor, batted aside a gauzy frond of foliage, and marched to the door. She jerked on the door latch, but the humidity of the conservatory had made the mechanism unreliable. She was still rattling the door when Elizabeth's arms came around her.

"You love him," she said. "You love Sherbourne, else you'd never be this overwrought. You love that man like you've never loved another."

Charlotte's ire subsided, to the bright, steady flame of indignation she'd carried thanks to Brantford for years.

"Love isn't supposed to hurt, Bethan. Not like this. Never like this."

"You have been hurting for a long time," Elizabeth said,

stepping back. "I didn't see it, probably nobody saw it, but now you can't look away from it. That's good, Charl. We can't heal wounds that remain unacknowledged. I'll say something to Haverford about the mines."

Sherbourne had seen the bewilderment behind Charlotte's exasperation and testiness, and abruptly, all Charlotte wanted was to assure herself that her husband was whole and well. She longed to hear the decisive click of his abacus, to feel the muscular security of his arms about her in the dark.

"I'm sorry for my temper," she said. "You're right. I am terribly overset."

Charlotte saw herself out, and as the horse trotted back to Sherbourne Hall, she admitted that Elizabeth was right about something else too: Charlotte loved her husband, loved him with an abiding respect that had been a significant relief, given how few men she encountered who bothered to earn her esteem. Sherbourne was at the top of that very short list, and if he should tumble, felled by financial pride, Charlotte's heart would never recover.

Chapter Nineteen

A frisson of sympathy for Hannibal Jones stole through Sherbourne's mind as he stared at the figures on the page. Charlotte would delight in deciphering these crabbed calculations—would have delighted in them, had she not stormed off to the safety of her sister's castle, likely never to be seen again.

For the first time in his life, Sherbourne was tempted to consume a quantity of strong drink. Perhaps that was Hannibal Jones's problem. He drank because Mrs. Jones was lost to him forever.

If Sherbourne mourned abandonment by his wife after less than a month of marriage, what must Jones be suffering, and how must that affect his concentration?

The library door clicked open, and Sherbourne tossed down his pen, ready to rebuke any footman who'd failed to knock when the master was intent on brooding away the evening. Brooding and possibly getting drunk.

"I missed luncheon and my sister failed to offer sustenance," Charlotte said. "I've ordered a tray."

The relief that coursed through Sherbourne was undignified and nearly complete, but for a thin vein of resentment running near his pride. He rose and remained behind his desk rather than approach his wife.

"Mrs. Sherbourne. Good afternoon."

"Darkness has fallen. I am sorry for my earlier temper, for I ought not to have spoken to my lawfully wedded husband in anger, and yet I am angry still."

She could be furious, and he'd still rejoice that she hadn't left him—yet—though if she intended to cling to her anger, then Sherbourne could feel less guilty about his own.

Charlotte was no longer in her driving ensemble. She wore a day dress of unrelieved brown, her hair was ruthlessly caught up in chignon, and no trace of her earlier tears remained. She reminded him of the acerbic young woman who'd endured a bumbling proposal from Viscount Neederby.

"Your ire is understandable." Sherbourne was prepared to be gracious but firm, and thus he sidestepped the word "justified."

Charlotte gave the globe a spin. "Then you're willing to cut Brantford loose?"

"Of course not. I've signed a contract with him, and he'll be difficult if I'm anything other than generously accommodating."

"I see."

Sherbourne knew better. He *knew better* than to take that bit of bait, redolent with wifely indignation. "What do you see?"

She spun the globe the opposite direction. "I see that

honor ceases to matter when a man's business interests are at stake. I had thought a gentleman's honor ought to be *more* scrupulously in evidence where coin is apt to tempt him from the path of decency. I see that I was wrong. Profit renders honor null and void."

Her finger trailed along the spinning surface of the globe, a diversion children enjoyed. When the sphere came to a stop, she was touching darkest Peru.

"I esteem you above all others," she went on. "You persist in the face of discouragement. You have a vision for the nation's future that encompasses all walks of life, not simply your own interests. You can admit when you've erred, and that makes the present situation all the more baffling, because Brantford is so very, very wrong. He has no place in your affairs."

Sherbourne would have agreed with her—but for the requirement that an honorable man provide for his dependents and keep his word at all times.

"This gets us nowhere, Charlotte."

"Where do you want us to be?" She spared the desk a glance, where the hairpin and cravat pin lay side by side in the silver pen tray. Sherbourne had tucked the beribboned lock of hair he'd snipped earlier into his breast pocket.

"I would like to be back to the place we occupied before Brantford intruded on our marriage. You are my wife, and I esteem you above all others as well. That hasn't changed."

Her defenses faltered if the downward sweep of her lashes was any indication, but the damned tea tray ruined the moment. The footman set it on the low table before the sofa, bowed, and withdrew.

"Will you join me, Mr. Sherbourne?"

He wasn't hungry, and her invitation wasn't a concession. "One cup."

They sat side by side on the sofa, not touching, while Charlotte poured out. She was pale, and in her very composure, Sherbourne sensed roiling emotion.

If she was preparing to tell him she was bound for the Windham family seat in Kent, he'd smash every piece of porcelain in the library, throw every book into the fire, and drink himself insensate.

Which would *also* get them nowhere, though it might leave him feeling less helpless.

"Sandwich?" Charlotte asked.

"Please."

She set two beef sandwiches on a plate along with a square of shortbread. "You need not wait dinner on me. I'm developing a headache and will retire early."

Not a month into marital bliss, and she'd trotted out the much vaunted wifely headache, though this was Charlotte, and she'd not dissemble about even so minor a detail.

"Would it help if I rubbed your feet?" *Would anything help?*

She set down her teacup, the saucer and spoon rattling against the library's quiet. "That is a very gracious offer, but I'll decline for the present." She rose and moved toward the door. "I'll wish you a good evening, Mr. Sherbourne."

Sherbourne suspected she offered a civility because rote manners and platitudes were all she could manage, which was some consolation.

Not enough. "If I attempt to join you later this evening, will I find my own bedroom door locked?" Sherbourne asked.

He couldn't see her. She stood behind him, while he studied the delicate floral pattern of the china. So pretty, so easily shattered.

"I will never lock that door to you," Charlotte said. "But my earlier words stand as well."

No children, she'd said, though she wasn't to shame him before the servants. Not yet, and he couldn't bear to shame her by setting up his own private apartment so soon after the wedding.

"Good night, Charlotte."

The library door clicked softly, and Sherbourne pitched a pillow as hard as he could at the nearest wall.

He and his wife were having a civil disagreement—for now—but sooner or later, one of them would slip. A harsh word would be said that crossed what lines remained. A look would pass between them in the churchyard that publicly confirmed enmity had found its way into the marriage.

While part of Sherbourne longed to blame his proud, aristocratic wife for her unreasonable ire, another part of him accepted blame for having been arrogant himself. He'd wanted an earl's coin to bolster his budgets. He'd wanted to prove to Haverford that even a fairy-tale version of a colliery could be made profitable provided Lucas Sherbourne was in charge.

He'd wanted polite society to pronounce his marriage a success rather than a mésalliance.

"Charlotte believes I persist in the face of discouragement," he said to the empty room. "She esteems me above all others. She rubs my feet."

He could not speak the rest of the litany aloud: She also broke his heart.

* * *

"Her Grace is off at the village lending library," Haverford said. "Shall I ring for a tray?"

"No, thank you," Charlotte replied.

She stayed within two feet of the parlor door, while Haverford, who'd been raised with a sister, weighed options. He could pretend that a pale, silent Charlotte Sherbourne was a normal occurrence, and convey her regrets to Elizabeth when the duchess returned.

He could insist on observing at least the civilities—a cup of tea would require fifteen minutes of idle chatter from them both. Not too much to ask from family.

Or he could do as he'd done with Glenys, Elizabeth, and any other woman about whom he cared, and drop the ducal posturing.

"Then you can keep me company while I pine for my duchess," Haverford said. "She's been gone long enough that her return becomes more likely by the moment."

Still Charlotte remained by the door. "Elizabeth does love her libraries."

Haverford gave the bell pull a double tug. "And I love my wife, so I put up with endless effusions about bound volumes, children's stories, and shelving decisions. Do have a seat. Was Elizabeth always so taken with public book collections?"

Charlotte advanced three steps into the room, then seemed to realize she hadn't intended to stay. She and Haverford were family and both married, so propriety offered her no excuse to leave.

"Elizabeth has always loved books," Charlotte said. "They have been her sanity in recent years, hence her desire to support lending libraries. I can't stay long."

"Let me guess," Haverford said. "You're meeting Sherbourne at the works for lunch. The crews think those midday meals are quite romantic and have taken to inviting their own ladies to bring them their nooning."

Charlotte winced as if a stray pin had stabbed her in the ribs. "The weather will soon put a stop to that folly."

She seated herself on the sofa, perching on the edge of

the cushion. Haverford took the wing chair, and silently cursed Sherbourne for a fool. Elizabeth had said the new couple had hit a rough patch, but she'd withheld details.

Or Haverford had started kissing her. Something had distracted him. "Charlotte, shall I treat Sherbourne to a bout of fisticuffs?"

She snorted, wan humor, but humor nonetheless. "Do you long to have your nose broken? His classmates at public school did him that honor. They also broke his ankle and his arm."

That was...not usual. "Was Sherbourne particularly given to outbursts of temper?" Sherbourne seemed, if anything, overly self-restrained, always measuring odds, always considering options.

"He was particularly given to not having a title and not being related to anybody who possessed one. He was given to excelling at his studies. He was given to honesty and hard work, and his father was given to training a boy up in the ways of anger and resentment. Engage in fisticuffs with Mr. Sherbourne if you must, Your Grace. He will get the better of the encounter."

Charlotte looked like *she* wanted to engage in a bout of fisticuffs, and Haverford had no doubt he'd get the worst of that encounter as well.

"Is there anything I can do to help?" His offer was partly pragmatic. If Charlotte was miserable, then Elizabeth would be miserable, and if Elizabeth was miserable, Haverford could not be happy.

That cheering Charlotte up might also benefit Sherbourne could not be helped.

She opened a beaded bag and set two large books on the low table. "If you're sincere, then read those. I have more along the same lines. Our library at Sherbourne Hall is full of such practical tomes and treatises, rather than French novels or Shakespearian plays. Mr. Sherbourne even has two books about libraries, which I suspect are recent acquisitions made that he might better assist with Elizabeth's charitable schemes."

Haverford ignored the implied reproach and examined the smaller of the books. "A Thorough Description of the Successful Colliery Dedicated to Development of Mineral Wealth in the Great Coal Field of Southern Wales and Surrounding Environs."

"Elizabeth likes to read," Charlotte said. "I like to understand."

The damned book could have doubled as a doorstop. "You want to understand coal mining?"

"I want to understand my husband. Coal mining is also fascinating."

He put the book aside. "You've read these?"

"Among others. You have set my husband an impossible task, Your Grace. He's to develop raw ground, meet standards of safety and comfort for the miners and their families beyond any established elsewhere in the industry, show an immediate and substantial profit, use primarily the unskilled labor in this valley, and make it look like a lark. I should be going."

Haverford wanted her to leave, because annoyance rolled off of her in waves. Sherbourne frequently bore the same impatient air, as if surrounded by ill-informed idlers who'd never done a day's work in their lives.

"I'm not stupid, Charlotte, and I do not want to see Sherbourne fail."

She rose and jerked the strings of her bag closed. "But do you want him to succeed? I do, and yet..."

Charlotte Sherbourne at a loss for words was a disquieting prospect.

"Stay for tea," Haverford said. "Please stay for tea, rather. There's more I would ask you, and I haven't known how to ask Sherbourne."

She shook her head. "Find a way, then. Read the books, make a list of your questions, and be prepared to listen well. I must be going."

He stopped her at the door when she would have decamped without so much as a curtsy. "Charlotte, is there anything I should tell Elizabeth?" Other than to pay an immediate call on her sister.

"Tell her I love her."

If Charlotte's words hadn't set off alarms in Haverford's heart, the swift hug she treated him to would have. Then she was gone, leaving the duke alone with two of the most boring tomes ever penned by the hand of man.

And leaving him with a guilty conscience as well. He didn't want Sherbourne to fail, but as Charlotte had pointed out, that wasn't the same thing as supporting the mining venture and helping to ensure its success.

Haverford sat and started reading, and was still reading when Elizabeth joined him three hours later.

* * *

A week went by during which benevolent providence sent Sherbourne neither deluges, mudslides, marital cataclysms, nor workplace riots, and yet he was miserable.

Charlotte slept beside him each night, even ended up in his arms sometimes in the darkest hours, but she never rubbed his feet, never kissed him, never arranged him in her embrace such that all his worries floated away on a cloud of marital contentment.

If she missed his lovemaking, her longing for him had

been buried beneath her righteous certainty that Brantford should be ejected from the colliery project on his lordly arse.

"Brantford is biding over in Monmouthshire," Radnor said, as he escorted his guests to his game room. Sunday dinner this week was at Radnor House, another gathering organized in the churchyard before smiling witnesses, several of whom had loudly remarked on the progress of the steeple repairs.

"Why would his lordship's whereabouts concern me?" Sherbourne asked.

"Because turning your back on a serpent is unwise," Radnor said, heading directly for the sideboard. He poured three glasses and passed the first to Haverford, the second to Sherbourne.

The game room was a spacious masculine chamber. The walls were half-paneled in mellow oak, the furniture heavy and comfortably worn. The billiards table stretched like a bowling green down the length of the room, and books and stacks of newspapers lined shelves near the fireplace.

"That's an interesting choice of portrait," Sherbourne said. A painting of a smiling lady in powder and panniers hung over the mantel. She was more handsome than beautiful, though merry eyes and a smile that hinted of secret joys made her attractive.

"My dear mama," Radnor replied. "Papa said of all places, her influence should most be felt here, lest drunkenness, lewd talk, or idleness be mistaken for congenial company. They were not a love match, but affection grew nonetheless."

They had certainly loved their only son, which left Sherbourne with a question: If his own parents had loved him the way Radnor had clearly been treasured by his mama and papa, how would life have been different?

"That scowl will frighten small children," Haverford said. "Is the brandy not to your liking?"

Sherbourne took a taste and once again found the flavor familiar. "The potation is quite fine."

"Haverford won't tell me where he got it," Radnor said, tossing a square of peat onto the fire. "Gave me two bottles as a wedding present. Wants me to think he's had midnight dealings with the coastal trade, when I know he probably got it from his fancy in-laws."

The duke had been given this brandy by an in-law indeed. A recently acquired in-law. Haverford was studying his drink, suggesting Sherbourne and the duke were to share a secret.

A family secret—his first. "Wherever this is from, it's excellent quality."

"So why the thundering frown?" Haverford asked.

"Because my billiards game is rusty." Sherbourne set his drink aside. "Upon whom shall I sharpen my skills?"

"Haverford. He's fretful these days, owing to his duchess's delicate condition, or his nerves, or some repair or other to his castle walls. You can distract him, and I shall cheer you on from the world's most comfortable sofa."

"While you're a rock of spousal imperturbability," Haverford retorted, taking a cue stick from the rack and rolling it across the green felt of the billiards table. "Though my sister, to whom you happen to be married, paints a somewhat different picture of your steely reserve."

The duke and the marquess bickered their way through two games, Sherbourne winning the first, Haverford the second. All the while, Sherbourne wondered why Brantford hadn't returned to England. The weather would become increasingly cold and difficult, excellent hunting was available closer to the earl's seat in the north, and—

Haverford nudged his sleeve with the tip of his cue stick. "Your shot."

"I'm considering options." The table did indeed present several half-decent possibilities.

"You're fretting over Brantford. I wish I could tell you he's not worth the bother, but he was a guest in my home. The man's a gold-plated ass."

Sherbourne neatly potted the red ball off a side bumper. "He met certain criteria that I find useful in an investor."

"What criteria does an investor have to meet, besides having money to spare?" Radnor asked around a yawn.

What to say? Sherbourne replaced the red ball on the black dot. "He should be sufficiently knowledgeable to grasp the risks he faces, but not so expert or meddlesome as to interfere in every detail of project management. When do we rejoin the ladies?"

"Not soon enough." Haverford took aim at the red ball. "Charlotte lent me some books."

"This book lending must be contagious," Radnor offered from the depths of the sofa. "Or perhaps it's inherited. We shall see when you both have some little darlings populating your nurseries."

Sherbourne stifled an urge to bash Radnor over the head with his cue stick. Charlotte had decreed that there would be no babies, and Sherbourne—for reasons he could not have articulated in his most honest hour—wanted very much to raise children with her.

"What manner of tomes did my wife lend the man who until recently owned half the books in Wales?"

"Books on how to establish and manage a coal mine.

She's apparently read them word for word, though my own progress is halting at best."

When had this occurred, and why had Charlotte done it? "Who are the authors?"

Haverford recited titles and authors, while Radnor snored quietly on the couch.

"Those are good basic texts, though they'll soon be out of date. Did Charlotte say why she'd lent them to you?"

"She said I know next to nothing about mines." Haverford put up his cue stick. "She's right."

What to say to that? Haverford hadn't exactly admitted to putting ridiculous conditions on the colliery, but he'd come close.

"Charlotte is almost invariably correct."

"Have you any more such books?"

What was Haverford asking? "Many. I also have some recent treatises on steam power, which will make your head spin with possibilities."

"Does Mrs. Sherbourne read those as well?"

"If she hasn't, she soon will." Though given the state of the marriage, Sherbourne still hadn't asked Charlotte to look over any of Hannibal Jones's calculations.

Haverford took Sherbourne's cue stick and replaced it on the wall rack. "Elizabeth is concerned about her sister."

So was Sherbourne. "I appreciate Her Grace's solicitude, but can assure you that my wife enjoys excellent health."

For now. How would Charlotte fare after another six months of this arms' length misery that their marriage had become? How would Sherbourne? They ate dinner separated by a distance as great as the billiards table, took their baths at opposite ends of the day, and barely spoke in passing. The trip to and from Sunday services was made in awkward silence, though Charlotte was polite and agreeable to anybody they encountered.

"You look gaunt," Haverford said, "and I don't think it's marital devotions robbing you of your sleep."

"Haverford, you will desist, lest I demonstrate my pugilistic skills on your damned ducal nose."

Except that now—years after Sherbourne had beaten respect into every schoolyard bully who'd served him a bad turn—striking the duke held no appeal. Haverford was family, and Sherbourne suspected he was trying to be helpful.

The duke's interrogation felt arrogant and presumptuous, but he was a duke, and nearly everything he turned his hand to would come across as arrogant and presumptuous. Charlotte had been quite clear on that point, and if anybody knew her way around dukes and titles, it was she.

Haverford crossed to the sideboard and poured half a glass of brandy. "Be that way, but if you think I'm difficult, just wait until Charlotte's mama and papa come to visit for the winter holidays. Were I you, I'd get my house in order before the in-laws come to call, or Charlotte might well accompany them back to England in the new year."

Sherbourne managed to remain standing, but Haverford's taunt—or warning—landed on him like so much cold, wet mud.

Charlotte was being unreasonable, and yet, she was *Charlotte*. She would never relent, never give quarter where her sense of justice was concerned. Sherbourne loved that about her.

Loved that about her, too.

"You did know the in-laws are planning to visit?" Haverford asked. "You look as though you've suffered a significant blow to the head."

To the heart, more like. "I am well aware that the in-laws intend to grace us with their presence for the holidays, and I hope they are frequent visitors. Mama-in-law loves her homeland, and Charlotte loves her mother and father."

Did she love her husband? Could she ever love a man who did business with the likes of Brantford? Sherbourne had married expecting that attraction and respect would see him and Charlotte through well enough, but now...

Now he loved his wife, and "well enough" was less than she deserved.

Radnor sat up, his head appearing over the back of the sofa. "Did you trounce Haverford? He benefits from regular trouncing. I've made a career out of keeping His Grace from getting too high in the instep. The job is thankless and tiring, but what are friends for?"

Sherbourne wouldn't know, never having had any. The more pressing question was, what was a husband for, when a woman could simply remove to her parents' household, never to be seen again?

Chapter Twenty

Charlotte did not flatter herself that she was welcome at the Caerdenwal household, but after three weeks of polite distance from her husband, she needed a reason to leave her home, any reason at all.

Besides, she wanted to see how the baby was faring, and what household couldn't use a bag of apples and one of pears? She'd also purloined some oranges from the larder, along with half a wheel of cheese and a tub of butter. A small ham had also fit into her basket. Cook's growing consternation had stopped Charlotte's plundering of the larders after she'd appropriated a loaf of sugar and raided the tea chest.

The lot of it rattled and jostled in the back of Charlotte's gig as she drove over the frozen, rutted lane. Day by day, the sun set earlier and rose later, the temperatures dropped, and the wind became more frigid.

The weather felt like a metaphor for Charlotte's marriage, and for her life. She'd put off socializing beyond family and the vicarage, because Sherbourne ought by rights to pay calls at her side.

Her visits to Haverford Castle were recitations of the correspondence she'd received from family, for Charlotte was quite up to date on her letters.

Quite. Even the rest of the Mrs. Wesleys had been tended to without any comment from Sherbourne.

Charlotte's staff had so quickly accommodated her directions and preferences that the household fairly ran itself, which meant she retreated to the library where treatises on steam power at least helped her pass the time.

"Good day, Charlotte Sherbourne!"

Griffin St. David stood by the side of the lane, his hair windblown, his cheeks ruddy. He cut a handsome figure in his country attire, but what Charlotte liked most about him was his great, cheerful smile.

She drew the gig to a halt. "Good day, Griffin. Are you out taking the air?"

"Biddy chased me from the house. She said I am awful, though she didn't mean it. I like to help in the kitchen, but sometimes... We burned the bread yesterday." His grin said the loaves had been sacrificed for a fine purpose.

"You can keep me company. I'm on my way to pay a call on Maureen Caerdenwal and her mama."

"I will visit the chickens," Griffin said, climbing into the cart. "They are not my chickens, because I gave them away, but I know all of their names. There are six laying hens."

"You were very generous."

"Six chickens is not so many. I told Glenys that she must send over sugar and tea, and Radnor should give them a fall heifer so they'll have milk, cheese, and butter through the winter. I love butter."

Griffin loved life. He had no complicated depths, no guile. His view of life was uncluttered by moral subtleties, and he thrived on simple rules and the love of his family. Charlotte had a wild urge to confide her troubles in him—perhaps he could cleave the Gordian knot that tied up her marriage—but turning to Griffin would not do.

Assuming Charlotte could explain her problem in terms Griffin grasped, he would fret and pass along her worries to Biddy, and even that much talk felt like disloyalty to Sherbourne.

Whom Charlotte missed hour by hour, even when she could gaze upon his tired, handsome countenance down the distance of a beautiful antique cherry dining table.

"Are you cold?" Griffin asked. "Biddy says it will snow soon. I love snow. Snow makes everything pretty and cozy."

The sky was a blue-grey quilt above a landscape of bare trees and brown fields. "Snow would be a change, though it tends to turn to mud." Sherbourne would not welcome snow. His masons had made progress with the tram lines and had laid foundations for a central hall that would serve as a dormitory, school, store, and management office.

Some progress had also been made in setting up the machinery to sink the central shaft, but not enough progress—never enough.

Radnor had drawn up the plans for the central hall, Jones had approved, and Charlotte had been too proud to ask to see a copy. Heulwen's gossip kept her somewhat informed, but lately even the loquacious maid had grown quiet.

"Mud makes Mr. Jones at the colliery use very bad language," Griffin said. "Biddy will have a baby this summer."

Welsh country air was apparently conducive to conception. "Congratulations. I will pay a call on Biddy to wish her well later this week. Are you worried?"

Griffin lounged against the seat, his boot propped on the fender, his elbow braced on the arm rest. "Not yet. Biddy is very healthy, and babies are wonderful."

For Griffin that was enough information to quiet any misgivings.

Babies *were* wonderful. All over again, Charlotte wanted to take back the words she'd flung at Sherbourne in anger, but then... She hadn't been wrong. Brantford was a disgrace who'd never been held accountable for his vile behavior. To enrich him unnecessarily was to collude in his sin.

"You are quiet, Miss Charlotte. Are you doing sums in your head? Biddy says you can. I like sums, but I can only do them on paper."

Charlotte turned the cart down the track that led to the Caerdenwal cottage. "Few people enjoy sums, though I do. I use paper and pencil more often than not, while Mr. Sherbourne uses an abacus."

Griffin studied the fallow fields. "I would like to learn how to use an abacus. Sums must come out right, everything just so. I am often very slow because I want the just-so answer, and with sums there is always a just-so figure that is correct. The other figures are not correct. I like that."

"I do too." He'd put his finger on something worth pondering. Charlotte liked just-so answers too, but Griffin had brushed up against some other insight, some fact Charlotte had been overlooking.

"I will tell Julian to give the Caerdenwal boy a dog," Griffin said. "Next year, when the lad can walk. A nice dog like my Henry Tudor."

Henry Tudor was a canine plough horse, though he was a well-behaved beast and loyal to Griffin.

"You are very kind, Griffin, to prevail on your brother and sister to assist this household."

"They are my tenants and my neighbors. Love thy neighbor, right?"

And love thy husband.

Though Griffin was a courtesy lord and a duke's son, the welcome he received at the cottage suggested he might have been any tenant farmer or neighbor ducking in from the cold for a few minutes of a gossip.

He was even allowed to hold the baby, while Charlotte perched awkwardly on one of two chairs in the parlor and tried to make small talk with Maureen's mother.

After a fifteen-minute eternity, Griffin departed for home, and Mrs. Caerdenwal had barely closed the door behind him before spearing Charlotte with a fierce blue-eyed gaze.

"We are very grateful, Mrs. Sherbourne, for all you've done for us, but you must not trouble yourself to come here again."

Maureen had taken the baby into the other room, though of course she'd overhear every word.

"It's no trouble, ma'am," Charlotte said, rising and dodging around a sheaf of dried basil hanging from the rafter. "I'll be on my way, having accomplished my aims. Lord Griffin predicts snow, and the day does seem to be getting chillier."

She did not respond to the "no trespassing" ordinance flung at her feet, because she was too upset. What was wrong with wanting to see a child preserved from penury and starvation? What was wrong with aiding a victim of injustice?

"It's not what you think," Mrs. Caerdenwal said as she held the door for Charlotte.

"I beg your pardon?"

Mrs. Caerdenwal wedged through the door and closed it behind her, so she and Charlotte stood in the little yard, surrounded by hens clucking and pecking at the dirt.

"Himself sent money," Mrs. Caerdenwal said, putting a bitter emphasis on the word *money*. "The baby's father, that is. His note said running to our wealthy neighbor hadn't been necessary, and a regular sum would come for the boy by post. It's enough and then some. We'll manage, if he keeps his word, and I suspect Mr. Sherbourne will see that he does."

Relief seized Charlotte, despite the cold, despite her troubles. "*Mr. Sherbourne* had something to do with this?"

"The boy's father referred to a wealthy neighbor, not a titled neighbor, and besides, His Grace isn't that wealthy, not compared to many of his rank. We know that, but he's our duke and he does right by us."

"You don't think Lord Radnor—?"

"Radnor is several miles distant and has never laid eyes on the child."

The wind was bitter, and Mrs. Caerdenwal had only a shawl to protect her, and yet, Charlotte had more questions.

"Mr. Sherbourne has seen the baby?"

"Aye. He came here the one time, spoke with Maureen, and not two weeks later, Lord Griffin brings us a letter from the post with money. We'll manage, Mrs. Sherbourne, and you have our thanks for everything."

Charlotte took what she hoped was a polite leave and collected the gelding, who'd got loose from the fence post and stood cropping from a bush along the lane. Before she could climb into the gig, a figure turned off the road down the lane before the cottage.

He moved slowly, his great coat flapping, a scarf obscuring his features. An older man, Charlotte guessed from his gait and diminutive frame.

Hannibal Jones caught sight of Charlotte, paused, then resumed his progress.

Charlotte stepped into the gig, took up the reins, and got the vehicle turned on the verge.

Jones tipped his hat but said nothing. Charlotte nodded, though what on earth was he doing paying a call on this household, in this weather, when he had work to do at the colliery?

And how was she supposed to remain angry with Sherbourne, when he'd resolved the situation for the Caerdenwal family and never said a word about it to his own wife?

She steered the horse in the direction of the colliery, intent on taking advantage of Jones's absence from the work site.

Also intent on confronting her husband.

* * *

The wind played tricks on Sherbourne's hearing, so when wheels rattled outside the tent, he dismissed it as yet another auditory hallucination brought on by marital discord. A hundred times a day, he thought he heard Charlotte's gig pulling up before the tent.

A hundred times an hour, he wished she'd bring him a parcel of sandwiches and a flask of hot tea.

And with an unrelenting ache, he wished he knew a way to meet her demand that Brantford be cast from their lives. His lordship had sent a note by post, inquiring as to when he could expect a revised repayment schedule from Sherbourne and remarking on the beautiful scenery in Monmouthshire.

Sherbourne had considered the budgets, the estimates, the available funds, and every way to rearrange them, but ousting Brantford could too easily create a cascade of nervous investors on other projects, as well as nervous creditors, and nervous employees.

"I was hoping I'd find you here," Charlotte said.

She stood just inside the tent, looking windblown and chilled—also lovely, annoyed, and uncertain.

"Mrs. Sherbourne, come sit by the fire."

She obliged, sitting in the least-battered chair. Sherbourne took the other seat and cast around for something to say that wasn't too trite, too private, too honest, too—

Charlotte pulled off her gloves and held her hands above the little stove. "Hannibal Jones was paying a call on the Caerdenwal household when I left there not thirty minutes past."

"I wasn't aware he and the ladies were acquainted."

"Neither was I, but I thought perhaps you'd sent him to keep an eye on them."

Was that an accusation, a suggestion, or a mere question? "He passes that way when he travels to and from his lodgings in the village. I thought he was up on the hilltop securing the surveyor's stakes in case we get snow."

Charlotte untied her bonnet and set it amid the detritus on the nearest table. Loose papers and a pair of treatises were weighted down with an unlit lamp. A quill pen lay beside the lamp, along with a quizzing glass and a lump of hard, black coal.

"I want to thank you," she said, casting Sherbourne an unreadable glance. "I mean that. I am happy to express my gratitude for what you did for those women and that tiny boy. That was decent of you, and I hadn't thought to ask it of you."

So absorbed was Sherbourne in assessing his wife's mood, that making sense of her words took him a moment.

"I wrote a simple letter, gained permission from the ladies to send it, and that was that. I will cheerfully send another such letter if it becomes necessary."

Charlotte snatched a sheaf of papers from the table and stared at them. "Haverford didn't think to send that letter, and neither did the vicar or Lord Radnor. They've known of Maureen's circumstances for months. Griffin kept a roof over their heads, but that doesn't solve the real problem, does it?"

"For the boy, a roof over his head solves at least one problem. Have you eaten luncheon?"

She slipped the top paper behind the others. "I have not. I have a few pears and some cheese in the gig along with a flask of tea. The tea won't be very hot."

Pears and cheese with lukewarm tea sounded like a feast, provided Sherbourne could share his repast with Charlotte. She typically sat at her end of the dining table, a marital disaster masquerading as a portrait of fine manners.

Sherbourne found an orange rolling about in the back of the gig, along with the parcel Charlotte had described. A snow flurry danced down from above, and the horse—a fat, furry piebald cob named Nelson—blew out a white breath and cocked a hip.

"Thank you for the food," Sherbourne said, passing Charlotte the orange. "If you'd peel that, I'll find a knife and deal with the rest."

Charlotte set aside the figures she'd been studying and rolled the orange between her palms. "I cannot decipher two consecutive lines of those calculations. Either Mr. Jones needs new spectacles, or he's writing in a code known only to mining engineers. Griffin thinks we're in for snow."

That was more than Charlotte had said to Sherbourne at once for nearly three weeks.

"He and Biddy paid a call?"

Charlotte tore off a thick piece of orange rind. "He was out rambling, and accompanied me to the Caerdenwal cottage. I'm not welcome to return there." She took a bite from the rind and chewed for a moment. "I'll send along the occasional basket, though, and Griffin is prevailing on Radnor to provide a fall heifer."

"Griffin is kind." *As I am not.* Why hadn't Sherbourne given his wife a kitten when the gesture would have been seen as something other than manipulation? "How are you, Charlotte?"

She munched another bite of orange rind, which made Sherbourne's teeth ache. "I miss you. I suspect I would miss you regardless, because you work so much, but I miss you here." She tapped her heart. "I hate that you must work so hard. I hate that much of your hard work will go to benefit a monster."

Did she expect him to lounge about on his rosy arse all day? "I cannot abide idleness any more than you can, and my hard work will go mostly to benefit myself and those who depend on me." But he missed her too—in his heart, in his arms, in his dreams. "I've been meaning to bring you Jones's figures to review, but the moment hasn't been right."

Charlotte tore the orange in two and gave him half.

"I can't read his writing, Lucas. A month ago, his hand was crabbed, but legible. This,"—she waved the papers she'd been studying—"it's nonsense."

Sherbourne took the papers from her. Pencil scratchings covered much of the top page. As Charlotte said, the occasional digit was decipherable—a seven, a five, a four—

but nothing like an equation or column of figures emerged from the confusion Jones had wrought.

"Perhaps he wrote this when in his cups." Though Jones hadn't at any point in recent weeks seemed tipsy, despite Radnor's gossip to the contrary.

Charlotte separated a section of orange and ate it. "Mr. Jones wears spectacles. Maybe he wrote it when he couldn't find his eyeglasses. My sister Megan is nearly blind without her eyeglasses, particularly as she grows fatigued."

Nearly blind...

Memories assailed Sherbourne, of Jones rubbing his temples, taking anything he had to read outside into bright sunshine, of Jones taking off his spectacles and holding them several inches away from a treatise Sherbourne cited regarding the optimal elevation of tram lines.

Several of the various stacks of documents were weighted down with quizzing glasses.

"Eyesight wanes as we age," Sherbourne said, though he suspected the reality was worse than that. "Jones might be having difficulty with his vision."

Charlotte looked up from her orange. "That would make sense."

That would make... a disaster. Sherbourne ate his orange, cut the cheese and a pear into slices, and made a trencher out of a book about building terrace homes. Charlotte deserved better, but he hadn't better to offer, which made him perversely annoyed with her.

"I could ask Mr. Jones to reconstruct his calculations." Charlotte took a slice of proffered cheese and got up to pace. "I could ask him to explain the engineering to me. That wouldn't be any bother."

"Then you too would be contributing to the enrichment of the Earl of Brantford. Will you blame me for that as well?"

Charlotte stalked back to her seat, scooped up the orange peels, and tossed the lot into the parlor stove.

"You, sir, are being impossible."

Sherbourne wanted to apologize for ruining the meal, such as it was, but he could not apologize for having taken on an investor whose past had included a quiet scandal years ago. Investing in a mine wasn't an application for ordination.

"Charlotte, if I could find a way to untangle Brantford from this colliery, I'd do it. I simply don't see how. Perhaps he'll untangle himself when he learns I've hired a blind engineer."

In the normal course, Charlotte would have corrected that overstatement—Jones wasn't blind, yet—but she sat two feet away, staring at her hands.

"Griffin said something about sums being pleasing because they have one right answer. He called it a just-so answer. I have considered our situation from every possible angle and have reached such an answer."

Her answer did not make her happy. "What have you concluded?"

"If you could extricate yourself from Brantford's clutches, you would, and it's not a lack of business acumen that prevents you from doing so. The problem is the money, isn't it? You paid too much for me, and now you haven't room to maneuver with Brantford. I'm the reason you cannot act as your conscience dictates, and you have been too decent to point out the obvious to me."

You paid too much for me. Never in Sherbourne's most private self-indulgent rants had he connected Charlotte's settlements with Brantford's greed. Brantford's arrogant sense of entitlement, his conviction that all rules should be rewritten to benefit him was the root of the problem.

Sherbourne mentally stopped short of admitting that, like Charlotte's late friend, he too was a victim of titled hubris.

"Your question has no acceptable answer, Mrs. Sherbourne. If I admit that my finances are overextended, I have failed you as a husband. If I dissemble and expect my wife to accept untruths from me, I'm a failure as a gentleman."

Charlotte regarded him levelly. "We're in dun territory?"

Sherbourne got up to toss a scoop of coal onto the fire dying in the stove. He wanted to march straight out into the bitter air and keep going until he found Quinton, Earl of Brantford, and pounded him to dust.

And he wanted to grab Charlotte by the shoulders and shake her for marrying a man who had nothing to offer but wealth. She deserved better of course, but so did Sherbourne. He'd glimpsed what a real marriage with Charlotte might look like—an intimate partnership full of trust, understanding, and loyalty.

Thanks to sodding Brantford, the marriage would never have a chance to be that.

"I am not in *dun territory*. I am entirely solvent and can pay my bills in the ordinary course, but I underestimated the cost of building out this damned mine. I certainly did not foresee a mudslide, and I did not foresee that my bank would encounter difficulties right at the moment I might have called upon that resource to support this colliery. Neither did I foresee an engineer whose abilities I have cause to doubt."

"You did not foresee that I'd impress two of your masons into working on the steeple, either. I'm sorry."

Two of his best masons, because a steeple was a difficult undertaking. "They're almost finished with the steeple, but you're right. Being short-handed hasn't been helpful, the rain hasn't been helpful, and Brantford prancing around the works wasn't helpful. Now I've reason to question Jones's faculties. That's very unhelpful."

Charlotte rose and pulled on her gloves. Sherbourne thought she'd plunk her bonnet on her head and leave him to his woes, but she instead took the last slice of cheese, nibbled a bite, and passed it back to him.

"I am consoled to know that you are determined to make a success of this colliery for many reasons, not simply to impress Brantford. If *you* are in dun territory, then *we* are in dun territory. Let's be very clear on that."

"*We* are not." Sherbourne finished the cheese because he didn't know what else to do with it. Already the food tasted like coal dust and dirt.

Everything tasted like coal dust and dirt, and now Charlotte was lecturing him about some damned arcane point or other.

"I don't care a rotten fig for Brantford's opinion," Sherbourne said, an oddly liberating truth. Six weeks and several Sunday dinners ago, the cachet of having an earl's money to fund the coal mine had been gratifying. Now Sherbourne wished he'd never met the man.

Charlotte stepped closer. "Can you abandon the works long enough to drive me to the posting inn?"

What was she going on about now? "As long as you're not taking the stage for London."

He'd meant it as a joke, but Charlotte was too astute for that. She patted his lapel. "I blame myself, you see. You can't know how little store I set by your money, because I've done nothing to make that plain to you. You hold my hand, you don't laugh at me when I'm terrified. You have faith in my numbers, and you have settled your differences with Haverford, all because of me, or at least in part because of me."

She grabbed his lapel and glowered up at him. "I do not care *half* a rotten fig for your money, Lucas Sherbourne. It's you I married, and you I love."

Her kiss conveyed a no-nonsense declaration of possession and not a shred of relenting.

But she *had* kissed him, and she had said...the most outlandish words. Sherbourne cast about for a reply, but Charlotte had already moved away.

She had said...

She had said words in the midst of a fraught exchange, and he would not hold her to them. He would consider later what it meant when a woman who never stooped to manipulation or subterfuge let fly with such a sentiment.

"You asked me to drive you to the posting inn?"

Now, when he needed to see Charlotte's eyes, she put her bonnet back on. "If you please. I expect correspondence from various family members, and heaven knows what the weather is about to do."

Sherbourne banked the coals in the stove, grabbed his hat, gloves, and scarf, and left instructions with his foreman to send the crews home until further notice, for by the time Charlotte was sitting in the gig with a thick robe over her lap, the sky was pouring snow.

Chapter Twenty-One

Brantford slapped the maid gently on her bare bottom. "Be off with you. I've correspondence to see to, and then I must be downstairs in time for a hand of cards before dinner."

She tossed him a disgruntled sigh, but left the bed like the well-trained domestic she was. "That's always the way with you lot. You spare your horses more care than you do the ladies."

She was no lady, though nature had endowed her with generous curves, lustrous dark hair, and a wide, *clever* mouth.

"My horse knows better than to give me sassy talk when the ride is over."

She pulled a worn chemise over her head and grinned at him. "Then your lordship can cuddle up with a horse the next time you're in the mood to roger."

Brantford laced her up, gave her a few coins, and let her tarry at the vanity long enough to tidy her hair and don her cap.

"Same time tomorrow, my lord?"

Her tone suggested the question was a matter of complete indifference to her. She'd as soon spend the afternoon on her knees rubbing beeswax into a chair rail as pleasuring him.

"If this weather clears up, I'm sure we'll be out with the hounds." Brantford's host, Sir Cheevers Dalrymple, was hunt mad and pleased beyond telling to count a genuine earl among his sporting guests.

The maid pulled the covers over the bed. "The weather won't clear up. We're in for it. First real winter storm, right on schedule. The grooms are scrubbing down the sleighs, and Cook has out her recipes for syllabubs and toddies. If you're of a mind to roger, let old Harrison know you'd like me to come by with a spare bucket of coal. He's the most discreet butler you'll ever meet."

The bed was quickly made, no sign of an hour spent romping on the mattress, and the maid was soon on her way.

Romping was supposed to be enjoyable, and yet Brantford felt none of the good cheer and lassitude he was entitled to after his exertions. The maid's charms had been insufficient to inspire his passion until she'd used her mouth, and then matters had progressed well enough.

Veronica's weekly letter sat on the mantel, a cheerful recitation of Cousin Henry's latest humorous toast and Cousin Lillian's satirical poetry. Of Cousin Tremont—the best-looking of the lot—there was again no mention.

Brantford cast himself onto the mattress, wrinkling the freshly made up covers. "I miss my wife, which is the outside of too much." The point of this excursion was for Veronica to miss him. She was to long for the pleasure of being escorted around town by her lordly husband and cease pretending that galloping across frozen fields was a boon equal to his company.

Near Veronica's letter was a far less sanguine epistle from her father. The creditors were circling, and Brantford, of course, was to wave them all off.

Which he could do, for a time.

This was all Lucas Sherbourne's fault, of course. If Sherbourne were applying himself in his customary manner, repayments of Brantford's investment—with interest—would start as soon as the first of the year.

Brantford rose and rang for a footman to build up the fire. Sherbourne had yet to reply to a letter sent earlier in the week, or to one sent almost two weeks ago. Another reminder was in order, and then perhaps Brantford would write to dear Veronica and regale her at length regarding the fine hunting and lovely company to be had in Wales.

And tomorrow, if the weather proved disobliging, Brantford would spend two hours with the friendly maid. The fire was roaring merrily, and the earl had fortified himself with a bumper of good brandy when he noted a slight flaw in his plans.

If he sought to romp away his afternoon tomorrow, he was to ask the butler to send the dollymop along with a bucket of coal, except...as Brantford had explored the treasures hiding beneath the maid's skirts, he'd forgotten to ask the woman for her name.

* * *

The gig rode more smoothly when Sherbourne sat beside Charlotte, and the frigid weather wasn't as uncomfortable. He was big, solid, warm, and Charlotte loved him.

Her great declaration hadn't merited any reaction from

him besides a willingness to drive her to the posting inn, but that didn't matter. What mattered was that Sherbourne feared she was on the verge of *leaving* him.

Did he want her to go? Was their present difference of opinion truly insurmountable?

"I have done something I should tell you about," Charlotte said.

"This sounds dire, Mrs. Sherbourne."

The weather was growing dire. The snow had already left a white coating on the grass, bracken, and rooftops, and now it was sticking to the rutted lane as well.

"I don't know if it's dire or not, but I've done it, and there's no undoing it."

The village came into view, a tidy collection of Tudor, stone, and thatch buildings, with the church steeple forming a focal point among the rooflines. The village was pretty in warmer weather, but now the shuttered dwellings and snowy streets looked bleak and empty. A lean tabby cat whose fur was dotted with melting snowflakes skulked along the top of a garden wall, then disappeared over the far side, leaving a trail of paw prints in the dusting of snow.

"You might as well tell me what you've done, Charlotte. We have privacy, and I must remain attentive to the horse rather than shout and pace about in an undignified manner."

"I've written to my family."

He brought the horse to a stop right in the middle of the lane and sat very straight on the bench beside her.

"What God has joined together, Charlotte Sherbourne, no meddling Windhams will be putting asunder. I know we're having a rough patch, but I will deal with Brantford eventually. I'll sell the whole damned mine once it's turning a profit, or I'll liquidate other assets to buy him out. You will keep your family away from our marriage."

Indignation vibrated through every syllable, which warmed Charlotte's heart, despite her hackles rising at Sherbourne's preemptory tone.

"Windhams are born to meddle, which you should have realized before you married one, but I haven't written a word to my cousins about the situation between us."

The snow came down, the wind soughed. The horse gave the harness a shake, sending frigid droplets in all directions.

"If you're not airing your grievances against me, then why write to your family?"

Still he would not spare her a glance.

"I didn't know what else to do. Elizabeth chastised me weeks ago for not confiding in her regarding Fern Porter's situation. It never occurred to me to tell my own sister, never crossed my mind."

Sherbourne peered down at her. He was being the shrewd, inscrutable investor, the self-contained nabob who knew many secrets and shared none.

"You told *me* about your friend before we'd even finished our homeward journey. Whatever does she have to do with this?"

"I tell you everything. You listen to me, you notice me. You are my husband, to have and to hold, and to disagree with." *I love you.*

Charlotte kept that admission behind her teeth. Sherbourne had been none too impressed with it on first mention, so why add insult to his indifference?

He gave the reins a shake and the horse plodded forth. "Your description of holy matrimony is more accurate than the vicar's. So what did you write to your family about?"

"How the mine is progressing, how you envision using steam for the tram and eventually at the mine itself. How

Haverford is watching the whole project closely and Radnor has made a regular pest of himself as well."

She'd said a bit more than that, actually.

The gig passed between the houses at the edge of the village. The posting inn, which sat across from the church, came into view.

"You are taking preemptive measures," Sherbourne said. "If Brantford should slander me in the clubs, you have nocked your familial arrow and are ready to let fly."

Was that what she had done? "I expect Haverford and Radnor will do likewise with their associates. Brantford can go to the courts if he's truly intent on scandal, but in the clubs and committees, he won't get very far."

"Not with a dozen Windhams arrayed against him." Sherbourne brought the horse to a halt in the inn yard, and a boy swaddled to the ears in a wool scarf came to hold the horse. "We are alike in many ways, Mrs. Sherbourne. I would never have thought to enlist your family's aid."

Was that a concession, a flag of truce?

Sherbourne climbed down and came around to Charlotte's side of the gig. He was tall enough that Charlotte was eye to eye with her husband as she sat on the bench.

She tucked the end of his scarf over his shoulders. "I didn't enlist their aid when it would have done Fern some good. They could have given her money for a physician, convinced her parents to take her in so she wasn't banished to a Welsh backwater. I did not ask for help for Fern. I relied only on myself. I was wrong. I see that."

Sherbourne's gaze was bleak. "Now you need to rely on me, and I've disappointed you."

He had disappointed her, but not in the manner he thought. "The problem Brantford poses is one of funds," Charlotte said, "not of integrity. I wish I had reached that conclusion sooner—I do enjoy working with figures—but we will contrive, Mr. Sherbourne."

He stepped back, out of fussing range. "What are you saying, Charlotte? That you married a climbing cit whose actions are driven by greed?"

"Not greed, pride. Didn't I just say as much? I have married the most diabolically stubborn, clodpated, determined, thickheaded—"

A movement against the silently falling snow caught Charlotte's attention. From the belfry in the church steeple, a flash of red fluttered where no bird should be on such a wintry day.

"Somebody's up there," Charlotte said, using Sherbourne's shoulder to steady herself as she clambered from the gig. "Would the masons be working in this weather?"

"Nobody should be in that belfry. The work isn't finished, and until my master mason pronounces the steeple sound again, it's no place for—"

"That's Heulwen," Charlotte said, waving her arm. From high, high above the street, the maid gazed out unseeing, her red cloak a beacon in the falling snow. "Why in the world would she be up there, away from her duties without permission, and in this miserable weather?"

In the next instant, Charlotte knew why: the shawls worn in a house that was warmer than most, the unrelenting preoccupation with a handsome groom, listlessness when the groom's interest faded, then a mood withdrawn to the point of melancholia.

"I've seen this before," Charlotte said, dread choking her. "She's ruined, and he cast her aside, and she's ashamed and angry. I have to stop her."

Charlotte took off across the snowy road, flung open the heavy church door, and charged up the steps leading to the belfry, knowing—knowing, *knowing*—that she'd never get to Heulwen in time to prevent a tragedy.

Another tragedy.

* * *

Sherbourne was exhausted, cold, upset with his wife, and reeling from too many verbal blows: Charlotte claimed she did not care about his money, but what had he to offer her other than money?

She regarded his pride as problematic? What was to sustain him if not pride?

She loved him?

Her other imprecations had pained him, but that salvo had stunned him nearly witless, and she'd tossed it off as a commonplace. I love you—please take me to the posting inn.

Now she'd disappeared into the church and more blows fell on Sherbourne's heart.

Heulwen was up in that steeple and outweighed Charlotte by a good four stone. If the maid was suffering a nervous affliction, she could toss Charlotte from the belfry before Charlotte understood the danger.

Charlotte was terrified of heights, and the steeple was the tallest structure in the village.

She loved him, she was the woman he'd raise his children with, and nothing could be allowed—

Sherbourne's feet started moving without him making a decision to pursue Charlotte into the church. Why would a woman eat orange peels, for God's sake? Why would she fall asleep halfway through a sermon that was neither boring nor lengthy? Why would she call on the Caerdenwal household—home of the chubbiest infant Sherbourne had laid eyes on—and neglect to socialize with any other neighbors?

The stairway wound around inside the bell tower, and Charlotte's steps retreated high above.

"Charlotte! Stop!"

Even if she'd heard him, she'd never obey a direct command. "Charlotte, please wait for me."

Silence, and Sherbourne forced himself to slow down. If Heulwen was upset, Sherbourne barging into the situation like a maddened bull would do nothing to aid matters.

If Heulwen harmed Charlotte, he would not answer for the consequences. He crept up the last two dozen steps, leaned against the wall, and—despite every instinct he possessed—waited in silence, while Charlotte, all on her own, faced yet another demon.

* * *

Heulwen stood silhouetted against the frigid, whitening landscape. She was a pillar of despair, but thank God and bright red cloaks, she was yet safe. The belfry was like a balcony open on three sides, with bell ropes running through a sizeable square opening in the floor.

"Come away from there," Charlotte said, trying for her best imitation of an impatient Aunt Esther. "You'll catch your death in this bitter wind, and then I will be without my eyes and ears among the household staff."

Heulwen remained on the far side of the belfry, the snow dusting her cloak with white. "It's no good, ma'am. You don't spy on the help, and they all know what's afoot with me already."

Her voice was dead, her gaze flat.

"Who will lace me up, then? My husband abandons me

at the crack of doom for the charms of his dratted mine and comes home too tired to do more than fall into his bath, clutching yet another treatise or budget."

This complaint, though honest, merited only a sad ghost of a smile. "You and the master rub along well enough, missus. He should not have allowed you to come up here."

Charlotte stalked around the thick ropes hanging down the middle of the belfry. "Heulwen, Mr. Sherbourne knows better than to approach me with allowing or permitting on his mind. He no more allows me to join you admiring the view here than I allow him to hare off for his mine each morning. You aren't even wearing a scarf."

And the poor woman had been crying. Tears had tracked down her pale, freckled cheeks. She flicked a side-long glance at Charlotte, and the well of hopelessness in the maid's eyes was bottomless.

"This is about Hector Morgan, isn't it?"

"Not anymore. He says he can't marry me or he'll lose his post, and then we'll both be out of work. The whole valley will know why, and he'll be as disgraced as I am."

The groom's reasoning was lamentably sound. Employees in domestic service were not to marry. Their entire allegiance was to be their employers, and their wages weren't adequate to support children in any case.

"That is sheer balderdash," Charlotte said. "The man is never as disgraced as the woman, he never risks his life as a consequence of his folly, and he never spends the rest of his days paying for his pleasures. Did Hector promise you marriage?"

"No." Heulwen swiped bare fingers across her cheek. "He said what we did couldn't get a babe, because he didn't...I should not have conceived."

"He withdrew," Charlotte spat. "Thought himself a great

saint for yielding the last inch of pleasure, without bothering to learn that his sacrifice was likely in vain."

"Oh, ma'am, you must not say such things." A flicker of the old Heulwen showed in her mortification, so Charlotte took two steps closer.

"If we're not to be honest here and now, Heulwen, then what place has honesty in any of our dealings? The child is not to blame for your impetuousness or Hector's stupidity."

"There can't be a child," Heulwen said. "I tried the teas and tisanes, I tried not eating. I thought if I fell down the steps, maybe, but I couldn't make myself..."

Her gaze dropped to the dark, wet cobbles of the churchyard forty feet below.

"I had a friend," Charlotte said. "She was ruined by a fine lord and didn't survive the birth by more than a few weeks. I will not let you die for something as stupid as shame, Heulwen. My family is rife with children who arrived but a few months after the vows, and my uncle is a duke."

Heulwen's consternation was genuine. "Them as has money can marry and do as they please. I haven't any money, and Hector has only his wages."

Charlotte ventured another step closer. "Children cannot eat money. Money does not comfort them when they have nightmares. Money doesn't stay up until dawn singing lullabies to a colicky baby. Money won't explain to a small boy how to tie his shoes or apologize for a harsh word.

"Money is not love," she went on, "money is not joy, money is surely not happiness or a kind heart or a keen mind. London is awash in money and yet beggars abound as well. Money is not the problem, Heulwen. I have money, and you are welcome to it, but if you dash your brains out in a foolish moment, my money is useless."

Charlotte was nearly shouting but she dared take only one more step, and still Heulwen was beyond her reach.

"I can't take your money," Heulwen said, gaze swinging back out to the frozen landscape. "I should not have done what I did."

She was a large woman. If she so much as leaned out over the railing, Charlotte would be unable to stop her fall.

"Are you to die for your mistake? Is that what Hector wants?"

"No, of course not. He wants me to go to a place in Cardiff for women like me and let them have the baby. He has some funds—not a lot, but enough that they might let me stay there when the time comes."

"Then your baby will die," Charlotte said, for that's exactly what happened at such institutions all too often, "because you haven't enough coin to raise the child."

Heulwen's tears ran in silent torrents. "I can't give up my baby, and I can't keep my baby. I don't know what else to do."

Her fingers went to the frogs of her cloak—no sense getting blood on a fine wool garment?—and Charlotte moved, tackling Heulwen headlong and pushing her away from the railing.

Heulwen had both height and size on Charlotte, and refused to budge. She got an elbow to Charlotte's ribs, and a grip on the railing, and all the breath left Charlotte's lungs.

"You cannot die, Heulwen. You cannot die—"

Another elbow, this time clipping Charlotte on the chin. Heulwen's cloak was coming loose, and Charlotte was losing her grip on the maid. A glimpse of the slick, deadly cobbles far below closed a vise around Charlotte's lungs.

"Let go, Missus. Let go, please, just let me go."

Never. Charlotte forced air into her lungs, forced herself to find another handful of Heulwen's clothing to clutch, forced herself to remain upright. Simple physics weighed against Charlotte, but determination tipped the scales back to an even fight.

Almost. Charlotte was determined, she was strong, and she was fast, but she was also cold, tired, and not accustomed to physical combat.

Heulwen had a big, worn, wet boot up on the rail when a pair of strong arms plucked her away.

"You heard your mistress," Sherbourne said. "She asked you to step back, and you will step back."

Heulwen struggled, but she was no match for Lucas Sherbourne intent on a goal. He simply held on, arms lashed about the maid, until she ceased thrashing and hung limply against him.

"Thank you," Charlotte panted. "I would have lost her."

"Miss MacPherson!" Sherbourne bellowed.

The vicar's daughter appeared, no bonnet, no gloves, snow melting in her hair. "I'm here. Heulwen, you will come with me to the manse and have a cup of hot tea."

Heulwen's weeping was audible now, sniffly, brokenhearted crying that would eventually stop. The ache in Charlotte's heart felt eternal by comparison—without beginning or end, like the bleak, leaden sky.

With Sherbourne's arm across her shoulders, Heulwen shuffled to the door of the belfry and let Miss MacPherson take her by the hand. They left, their footsteps and Heulwen's crying fading into the bowels of the church.

"You came," Charlotte said. "You came. Thank God, you came and you brought help. I need a handkerchief, and I left my reticule..." She had no idea where her reticule was or how she'd remain standing one more second. The village and even the countryside stretched out far below, and weakness assailed Charlotte, but not because she was too high above solid ground.

She flew across the belfry into her husband's arms. "You came. She nearly pitched us both over, nearly...but you came."

She burrowed into Sherbourne's embrace, and mashed her face against the soft wool of his coat, and let the tears flow.

* * *

"I can walk," Charlotte said, as Sherbourne carried her up the front steps to their home. "I'm not an invalid."

"You are my wife," he replied as a surprised Crandall opened the door. "Carrying you on occasion is my privilege." Still he did not set her on her feet—could not—but continued straight to the library, doubtless leaving a trail of snow and mud on the carpets.

He'd finally carried his bride across the threshold of their home, and that...that helped.

"Lucas, it was a bad moment, and—" Charlotte fell silent long enough to lift the door latch.

"It was an awful moment," he said, kicking the door closed behind them, "one I'll relive in my nightmares until I'm so old I can't recall my own name."

Sherbourne set her on the sofa, cloak and all. Thank God that Charlotte had given orders the library fire was to be kept roaring at all times, for the room was relatively warm. Sherbourne went no farther from Charlotte's side than the distance to the sideboard, where he poured her a tot of brandy.

"Drink this," he said, setting the glass down so he could unfasten her cloak. He untied her bonnet ribbons next, and put the damned hat on the floor before the fire. Her boot laces were the worse for being wet, and when he finally had her footwear off, he wanted to toss the damned things across the room.

He set them around the end of the sofa, where the fire's heat would do little damage.

"You don't have to drink the brandy," Sherbourne said, "but I need to do something for you to calm my nerves, so you will please at least pretend to take a sip."

Charlotte held the glass beneath her slightly red nose. "I'm well, Lucas. I came to no harm, and Heulwen came to no harm, thanks to you."

He settled on the hassock before her, drew her feet into his lap, and searched beneath her skirts for a garter.

"You were nearly pitched to your death by a maid grown hysterical over a situation that developed under my very nose. All I could do was stand outside that belfry and listen, pray, curse, and hope."

He'd also heard Charlotte's speech about money—and love.

He gathered Charlotte's feet and bent over them. He'd nearly lost her, nearly lost everything that mattered. Inside, he was shaking, but as long as he could touch his wife, the shaking did not overpower him.

"Drink this," Charlotte said, holding the brandy out to him. "The quality is excellent, but at the moment, it might not agree with me."

Did she know she was breeding? Suspect? Something in between? Had he been wrong?

Sherbourne took the brandy, downed half of it, and set it aside. "I've realized something."

"I've realized a few things too. You first."

If she'd realized their marriage was over and that the

rest of her life should be spent under her papa's roof rather than in a household where maids developed fatal passions for stable lads and titled scoundrels got rich off the labor of others, Sherbourne would...

Convince her otherwise.

"Brantford is a disgrace of the first water," Sherbourne said. "The mother of his child—*the mother of his child*—came to him for aid and he all but tossed her from the steeple. Tomcats don't prey on their own young, wolves, snakes...I know of no creature under all of heaven that would behave thus."

"Brantford did, Lucas. Many men do, and some women aren't much better. This matters to me."

"You matter to me."

She brushed her fingers through his hair. "What of our offspring, whom Brantford would see tossed into penury? You exaggerated for the sake of argument, but your point is valid: Brantford can ruin you."

This too had come clear for Sherbourne as he'd listened to his wife trying to reason with a hysterical young woman, as he'd recalled that Charlotte was terrified of heights and had scaled the highest building in the village in hopes of rescuing a flighty maid, as he'd raced to the vicarage next door and shouted for help.

"Brantford can ruin my reputation as a businessman, which reputation is overstated at best. He cannot ruin *me*. I can ruin your respect for me, by choosing what's expedient over what's right. Only you can ruin *me*."

Charlotte scooted closer, emerging from her cloak to climb into Sherbourne's lap. "You say the most gallant, romantic things." She twined her arms about his neck, and the panic that had been building inside Sherbourne for weeks subsided minutely.

He shifted, so he and Charlotte were in her favorite corner of the sofa. She pulled the quilt off the back of the couch and arranged it around them.

"I cannot ruin you," Charlotte said. "That was my great insight. I don't want to ruin you, I don't want to be right at the cost of your regard for me or your self-respect. You should be able to trust that one person—at least one person—will not betray you. We might argue and feud, but we must not ever fear that we'll betray each other."

"You did not want to betray the memory of your friend."

"Or the poor little wretch who has Brantford for a father."

They remained cuddled on the sofa, and though nothing was resolved, Sherbourne's anxiety ebbed yet more, enough that he could focus on Charlotte's words: Brantford had a child, and that child deserved his father's support.

A question threaded through Sherbourne's jumbled thoughts: Radnor had clearly been the apple of his parents' eyes, Haverford a treasured ducal heir. Sherbourne's upbringing had been challenging, but he'd been fed, clothed, housed, and given a name in which he could take pride.

What was life like for that small boy in godforsaken Brecknockshire? What name had his mother given him, and what had he been told about his antecedents?

"What shall we do about Heulwen and Hector?" Charlotte asked. "They have been foolish, but half my family has indulged in the same foolishness without benefit of matrimony. Heulwen says those with money can *be* foolish, and yet, her child will have no money."

"I'm thinking," Sherbourne said, which was a lie. He was wallowing in the pleasure of holding his wife, in the scent of gardenia, and in a blossoming of hope, despite the snow coming down outside.

Charlotte twiddled the damp hair at his nape. "We forgot to pick up the post, Mr. Sherbourne."

"Hang the post. Very likely it will hold another scold from Brantford, threatening dire consequences unless I double his money by Easter."

Charlotte's fingers went still. "He *threatens* you?"

"Politely, but yes. He claims I haven't given him an opportunity to earn a decent sum in a reasonable time, you see. He has instead lent his cachet to a dodgy venture, placed his faith in a man who'd do well to respect his betters when they give him an opportunity to improve his situation."

"You can't call him out," Charlotte said, grabbing Sherbourne by the ears. "There's a code about these things. He's titled and you're not, and that means you cannot blow him to bits."

Sherbourne kissed her nose. "Would ridding the world of Brantford be a disservice? Would the boy be any worse off with no father than he is with Brantford for a father?"

"You have the same look in your eye that you did when you came upon Neederby trying to intimidate me into accepting his proposal. You are vexed."

Exceedingly. "I am determined. I must pay a call on Haverford, and then I'd like to prepare for a confrontation with Brantford. I should be back by tomorrow evening, the next morning at the latest."

Charlotte rose from his lap, bringing the quilt with her, like a queen in an ermine cape. "Haverford Castle is not an hour's journey, even in this weather. What are you about?"

Cold air assailed Sherbourne from all sides. "Brantford has tarried in Wales and threatened to pay another call on us, biding with Radnor if he must. He's intent on revising the terms of the contract so I'm beggared and he's enriched. We can renegotiate that document, but I'd rather my next encounter with him be on my terms and not his."

Charlotte nudged her bonnet away from the fire with a bare toe. "Haverford is a good ally. If you must confront Brantford, you're wise to enlist His Grace's support first, but I still don't want to let you go."

She stepped around the hassock and reclaimed her perch on Sherbourne's lap. This time, she straddled him, the quilt settling around them both like folded wings.

"Charlotte, I'd rather travel in daylight and do feel some urgency—"

"I feel some urgency too, Mr. Sherbourne, and sunset is at least two hours away." She kissed him, and without so much as a glance at the clock, Sherbourne kissed her back.

Chapter Twenty-Two

Charlotte hated the idea that Sherbourne must go haring across half of Wales to track down Brantford, and yet, better the earl be ambushed than Sherbourne.

She was ambushed, by emotions so tender and raw, she hadn't names for all of them. Protectiveness toward her husband figured prominently, and gratitude as well. Sherbourne had fetched her down from the steeple, even when he'd been furious with her, even when she'd been demanding the impossible of him.

She kissed him with all the desperation and relief in her, and all the hope too.

Sherbourne drew back and framed her face in his hands. "At least let me take you to bed."

"If you take me to bed, I won't be able to turn loose of you. This is a taste of what awaits you at home should you lose your way in the wilds of Wales."

She tasted *him*, tasted the determination and sheer

animal vitality that coursed through him even when he was at rest.

"God above, I have missed you, Charlotte Sherbourne."

He could kiss and unbutton her bodice at the same time, clever man; kiss, and untie the bows on both of Charlotte's chemises. She'd not worn stays, for reasons she'd confide in her husband when next they did share a bed.

Some announcements wanted rehearsing.

"I've missed your breasts. I think my brain has gone missing," Sherbourne muttered, burying his nose against Charlotte's chest. "I've missed the scent of you here, gardenias and spice. I've missed your hands on me, anywhere, but especially—"

She sank down against the evidence of his arousal. "Especially on your feet?"

"No, Mrs. Sherbourne, not especially on my feet. Perhaps you'd be good enough to unbutton my falls?"

Charlotte obliged and further moved the proceedings along by freeing him from his underlinen.

"You have missed me wonderfully much, Mr. Sherbourne."

His head fell back against the cushions as Charlotte indulged in caresses she'd dreamed of for weeks.

"I wanted to bring you a kitten," Sherbourne said.

Were his teeth clenched? "Kittens are very dear."

"But then a kitten would have been bribery."

Charlotte arranged her skirts, took him in her hand, and began the joining. "We will talk, Lucas. We will talk later." Not only about kittens.

He sighed and quiet filled the library. Peaceful sounds punctuated the silence—the soft roar of the fire, the whisper of fabric, slow kisses.

Charlotte held off as best as she could, but Sherbourne was

intent on galloping away into the frigid afternoon. She could be selfish only so long, before the passion and longing she'd denied them both in recent weeks demanded satisfaction.

She let herself fall into pleasure, secure in the knowledge that Sherbourne fell with her. She'd made her point— they were married, in every sense of the word, and what she and Sherbourne had joined, no pesky, arrogant earl, misguided wife, or stubborn husband could put asunder.

"This is not enough, Lucas." Her brisk pronouncement came out more like a sigh murmured against his shoulder.

"Not nearly," he replied, stroking her hair. "I need at least another fifty years of moments stolen with you in the library."

"Sixty," Charlotte said. "Windhams are hardy."

Sherbourne used his grip on her hair to gently turn her face to his. "You are a Sherbourne now, madam. I'll thank you to remember that."

She was both, which was why she really must tell him the rest about the letters she'd sent. "Yes, Lucas."

They remained in a quiet embrace for far too few minutes, until Charlotte's eyes grew heavy.

"I cannot indulge you in a nap now," Sherbourne said, "though I can carry you to bed."

Charlotte sat up and let her husband retie her chemises. "There'll be no more of that nonsense when I can stand on my own two feet. While your horse is being saddled, I'll have Cook put together some provisions. We missed our luncheon."

Must he be so proficient at dressing her? All too soon, Charlotte was shaking out the quilt and folding it neatly over the sofa while Sherbourne finished buttoning his falls.

Charlotte caught him in a hug rather than face the world beyond the door. "I don't want you to go."

"I don't want to leave you, but I've a puzzle to solve. Do you trust me to solve it to your satisfaction, Charlotte?"

He was so warm and solid, so dear, and the puzzle—the Earl of Brantford's trail of dishonor—was so difficult. "I trust you. I'm good at sums. Puzzles defeat me."

"The riddle is simple: How do I hold Brantford accountable for his sins, while keeping every single groat of his money?"

"Carefully, Lucas," Charlotte said, stepping back. "You do that very, very carefully."

* * *

Leaving Charlotte ranked among the most difficult tasks Sherbourne had set for himself, and yet, he did just that not thirty minutes after she'd loved him witless in the library. The snow had stopped, and traveling by daylight was imperative if Sherbourne was to travel safely.

Then too, Haverford might take a deal of convincing.

"You choose an odd day to pay a call," His Grace said, as Sherbourne was admitted to an octagonal parlor. "Are you hiding from your wife?"

"I don't see *your* wife hanging on your coattails, Haverford."

"Elizabeth is napping, which ladies in a delicate condition tend to do, and I, being the most considerate of husbands in all of Britain, would no more—"

"Haverford, this is not a social call."

"We're family, may God have mercy on us both. Of course this is a social call. Shall I ring for tea?"

A year ago, Sherbourne would have been delighted to see His Grace of Haverford pouring out for him in one of the castle's private parlors.

"I haven't time for tea, and neither do you."

The duke tugged the bell pull. "One always has time for a civilized cup of tea, regardless of how disagreeable the company one finds upon one's doorstep. Stop pacing a hole in Her Grace's carpets and have a seat."

"Haverford, do not, I pray you, tell me what to do. In my present mood, I might reciprocate your impertinence, and then we'll come to blows, and our respective wives will be wroth with us."

Haverford took up a lean against the mantel. "Something has you in a royal pet."

Sherbourne gazed out the window, to a bleak landscape he must soon traverse. "I am in the presence of a monument to perspicacity."

"Five entire syllables in one word."

"Meaning to count them, you had to use every finger on one hand, but do you know what the word means, Your Grace?"

Haverford's brows rose, and then his lips twitched. "That's very good. I must remember to use it on Radnor."

Sherbourne took the chair closest to the fire. "Brantford was your guest for more than a week. What was your impression of him?"

"He'll not be my guest again," Haverford said. "I've encountered any number of aristocratic ornaments, but the idle and titled usually exert themselves enough to be charming. Even on his best behavior—for my duchess tolerates nothing less than gentlemanly deportment at all times—Brantford had a subtle air of arrogance."

"Charlotte hates him."

Haverford took the second chair. "I would not wish Charlotte Sherbourne's hatred on anybody lightly, but if I had to choose an apt target for her loathing, Brantford would do.

There was talk, a few years ago, that he despoiled an innocent and turned his back on the lady. Radnor's own mama
confirmed that rumor, and thus I accept it as fact. I could not
see that such a scandal bore directly on his commercial ventures, else I would have spoken up sooner."

*Would that he had, instead of poking his nose all over
the colliery at every opportunity.* "It is fact. What must a
guest do in this castle to have some sustenance brought up
from the kitchen?"

Haverford sat back and crossed his ankles. "Now you're
demanding your tea and crumpets? Do we blame your contrary disposition on a lack of proper nutrition?"

"You're the one who'll want to partake. The innocent
whom Brantford despoiled was Charlotte's dearest friend."

Haverford stared at his feet, which were encased in a
pair of worn field boots scuffed at the toes and in want of
polish. "Does Charlotte know this?"

"She does now, and Brantford is threatening me with
slander and worse unless I repay his investment on very favorable accelerated terms."

"Extortion dressed up in lace and satin. I should have
had Radnor take his lordship shooting, and arranged for
someone's gun to misfire. Happens all the time in the
damp."

What a delightful notion—and so simple. "Haverford,
we are not barbarians."

"Brantford is, but I gather you know that. So what
brings you here? I make a very fine second—ducal consequence and all that."

His Grace sounded uncharacteristically enthusiastic.
"I'm touched, but I must decline. Charlotte says that because I am not titled, Brantford would ignore my challenge. There's also the matter of Brantford's son."

A tap sounded on the door, and Haverford got up to admit a footman bearing an enormous silver tray. The offerings included tea with all the trimmings, sandwiches, shortbread, and tea cakes. The footman set the tray on a low table, bowed, and withdrew.

Haverford gestured to food. "If you expect me to pour your tea for you like some spinster auntie with a favorite nephew, you're daft. Feed yourself, and I shall do likewise. By the way, an acquaintance in Swansea tells me that Hannibal Jones's last day at the Waxter operation was the day before the shaft flooded. He'd been demanding that the owners spend the money to reinforce the tunnel, and they refused. The parting of the ways was not amicable, and they've been trying to blame Jones for the accident ever since."

"You made inquiries on my behalf?" Inquiries Sherbourne could not have made himself.

"On behalf of the valley. Spare one beef sandwich for me, and please explain how we're to resolve your contretemps with my least favorite earl."

The relief of having Hannibal Jones exonerated for the tunnel collapse felt to Sherbourne like an omen, an indication that determination and hard work—and some hard riding—would see his problems solved.

Determination, and a bit more help from His Grace.

Over excellent food and piping hot tea, Sherbourne detailed the situation with Brantford. Haverford listened while doing his part by the comestibles and asking the occasional question.

"So you have come here to avail yourself of a handy duke," he said, when the teapot was all but empty.

Haverford had been honest, he'd listened, he'd believed Sherbourne's recitation even when it reflected badly on a peer.

And Haverford was family.

"No, actually," Sherbourne said. "I'll settle for a mere duke if that's the only aid I can find, but I'd hoped my cause might instead merit the support of a friend."

Haverford brushed nonexistent crumbs from his breeches. "A friend. Well." He looked around as if hoping his duchess might rescue him. "A friend, whom you will owe for all eternity, even more than you already do. You do realize it's colder than hell's root cellar out there?"

"The fresh air will put roses in our cheeks. Come along, Haverford, while there's still a sliver of daylight to guide us."

Muttering and cursing, Haverford came along as any friend would.

Any good friend.

* * *

The damned snow had made the footing treacherous enough that Dalrymple had called a halt to the hunting after the morning run. The post had brought no word from Lucas Sherbourne regarding the colliery contract, and the buxom maid hadn't bestirred herself even once the livelong afternoon to see if a guest might want for some female companionship.

Brantford was paying his third call of the evening on the decanter in Dalrymple's library when the door opened, and the maid who'd been least in sight all day appeared with a bucket in each hand.

"Do come in," Brantford said. "Can't have the fires going out when winter has announced its arrival."

The library was empty, every other gentleman having gathered in Dalrymple's game room for another evening of cards, drink, and bawdy jokes. Footmen would attend that company, else the gathering would descend into outright debauchery.

What did it say about Brantford that outright debauchery had lost its appeal?

"Evening, milord," the maid said, setting both buckets before the hearth and bobbing a curtsy. She added a scoop of coal to the blaze and replaced the hearth screen. "Shall I light another candle for you, sir?"

Though her manner was deferential—Dalrymple himself might stumble through the door at any moment—her question held innuendo.

Not invitation, exactly.

"In another half hour, you can bring some extra candles to my bedroom. I'm in the mood to read on this cold and lonely night."

"Won't be any trouble a'tall, sir. Shall I bring a tea tray as well?"

He didn't want tea and biscuits. He wanted to roger the daylights out of the insolent baggage. "Just the candles."

She collected a tray's worth of dirty glasses from the sideboard, bobbed another curtsy, and headed for the door. Before she withdrew, she cast Brantford a look he'd occasionally received from his wife. Exasperation and long-suffering, along with a dash of superiority.

She'd offered to bring a tea tray so that she might end her day with two cups of good China black—none of the reused gunpowder the staff was likely to get—and a plate of shortbread, in addition to the coins Brantford would have given her.

Not a stupid woman, though slyness in a domestic was unattractive.

"What's your name?" Brantford asked, before she was out the door.

She stopped, her back to him, and turned slowly. "My name?" She'd given him a romping good time, but this request made her cautious.

"How are you called?"

"Veronica, sir. My name is Veronica."

Damned if she didn't look like Veronica, too. Good breeding figure, dark hair, and that expression. . . .

"Don't bother coming to my room. Send the footmen up with a bath, and let the stable know I'll need a sound riding horse for tomorrow."

"You'll be leaving us, then?"

Was she relieved? "If I have business to tend to or a call to pay on His Grace of Haverford, that is none of your affair. Be off with you before you let all the warmth out of this room."

She curtsied again, the tray of dirty glasses balanced against her hip, and withdrew.

Swilling Dalrymple's brandy and swiving his help was all well and good for a diversion, but Brantford had come to Wales to do business. Lucas Sherbourne would soon realize that a failed colliery was only the start of the troubles Brantford would cause him, if that business was not satisfactorily concluded.

* * *

"Haverford will prevent matters from degenerating into violence," Elizabeth said, holding her needle up to the light. Yesterday's snowfall gave the afternoon sunshine a brilliant quality, making the landscape beyond the window almost too bright to behold.

And yet, Charlotte had spent most of her day staring out the window.

"I *want* matters to degenerate into violence," Charlotte replied. "Mr. Sherbourne would give an excellent account of himself, having been on the receiving end of many an unfair blow. A pummeling is the least of what Brantford deserves."

Elizabeth dampened a length of red silk thread between her lips and attempted to pass it through the eye of the needle. "You are worried. You sound furious, but you're worried."

How could Elizabeth sit there so serenely when both husbands were off on such a momentous errand? "I'm both. Why aren't they back yet?"

Elizabeth had appeared immediately after breakfast, her workbasket in hand, and she hadn't budged much since. She jabbed the needle into the arm of the sofa and set the thread aside.

"They had some distance to travel if they were to meet with the Earl of Brantford, and that assumes he's still at Dalrymple's hunting party. Might you stop pacing, Charl?"

"Pacing helps me refrain from throwing fragile objects and using foul language. I need a parlor like yours, in a high tower, so I can keep watch over the approach to my castle."

Elizabeth closed the lid of her workbasket. "Your pacing has tired me. I must beg the use of a guest room, for a short respite will soon befall me, whether I find a bed or not."

"The fatigue hits me the same way," Charlotte said, nudging a candlestick to the exact center of the mantel. "One moment I'm fine, my thoughts trotting along where I send them. The next, I can't keep my eyes open, and my mind has turned to a quagmire. I've put a guest room in readiness, because you will please spend the night here if the men aren't back by supper."

Elizabeth rose. "Charlotte? What are you saying?"

Gracious angels. "Nothing, until I've had a certain discussion with Mr. Sherbourne."

Elizabeth hugged her. "As it should be. Then you will have a certain discussion with me. Biddy and Lady Radnor will join us, and we'll be merry and quite frank. Then our menfolk can have a turn cosseting us."

She went on her way, a duchess in love and also a dear sister.

Charlotte took Elizabeth's place on the sofa, threaded the needle with the red silk, and prepared to embroider a damned rosette on a dratted handkerchief, when a knock sounded on the perishing door.

"A visitor, madam," the butler said. "The Earl of Brantford. I beg your pardon. I thought the duchess was with you."

Brantford was here? Then where was Sherbourne?

Charlotte remained seated. "Her Grace will return shortly. You may show his lordship in, but please leave the door open and keep yourself and our two largest footmen within earshot."

"Mr. Sherbourne might not—"

"Mr. Sherbourne is from home, and I am mistress of this household. Show his lordship in, and do not think for one instant to bring us a blasted tea tray."

"Yes, madam."

Charlotte got up, fetched the fireplace poker, and tucked it on the far side of the sofa. The idea of breaking Brantford's arm, his ankle, or his nose was unaccountably cheering.

When Brantford came strutting into the room, she was again seated, embroidery hoop in hand.

"Mrs. Sherbourne, good day." The earl offered her a

perfect bow. "You make quite the fetching picture by the window. May I enquire as to whether your husband will be joining us? I saw no evidence of work whatsoever at the colliery, and I regret that my errand is one of business—mostly business—though a spot of tea would be much appreciated, of course."

He beamed a smile at her. Charlotte smiled back, because she had entrusted justice for the earl to her husband, and while everything in her wanted to bash the poker over Brantford's arrogant nose, she resisted.

She could not on her own hold Brantford accountable, which meant her best option was to make small talk and simper.

I hate to simper. She hated Brantford far more.

"Given the weather, perhaps you'd prefer a tot of brandy," Charlotte said. "When Her Grace of Haverford joins us, I'll order a tray if that would suit."

His lordship marched straight to the sideboard. "Her Grace is here? I did drop in at the castle but was told Their Graces were from home. I'll be in the area for another day or so and must prevail upon Haverford for a bit more hospitality."

The hell you will. "I doubt that will suit, my lord. His Grace is, like you, traveling on business, and the duchess is biding with me here."

He downed an entire glass of brandy and refilled it. "I'll content myself with Radnor's company, then. I hope I'm not overstepping when I say that I was surprised that a Windham would end up married to such as Lucas Sherbourne."

He twinkled at her, sharing a jest between aristocrats.

"Mr. Sherbourne and I are quite enamored of each other," Charlotte said, meaning every word.

Brantford guffawed, then treated Charlotte to an insolent inspection. "Did he tell you that? My dear, he wanted his brats playing with the children of your titled siblings. Two sisters married to dukes, and you think Lucas Sherbourne offered you a love match? Women are such fanciful creatures."

Charlotte's hand slipped down to grasp the poker.

"Insult me all you please, my lord, but malign my husband at your peril. He and I are, most assuredly, a love match."

Brantford studied the portrait over the fireplace, which had been done shortly after Sherbourne's parents married.

"Your husband comes from a long line of shopkeepers and tradesmen, and it's all but established fact that his great-grandmother was not, as they say, Church of England prior to her wedding. You have quite married down, Mrs. Sherbourne. I suppose you know that and are putting a brave face on a mésalliance. I might have to ruin your husband, by the way, socially at least. I doubt I have the patience to ruin him financially. This is very good brandy."

Charlotte rose from the sofa, rage a frigid river in her veins. "You come to Mr. Sherbourne's house, swill his brandy with all the delicacy of a great ape, insult me, insult my family, and insult *my husband*. The only thing that keeps me from doing you a serious injury is the fact that I esteem Mr. Sherbourne too highly to befoul his carpets with your blood."

Brantford chortled, until Charlotte held the poker up like a riding crop.

"I like a woman with some spirit," Brantford said, setting his glass aside. "Perhaps—"

"Perhaps you'll wish to choose your words carefully," Sherbourne said from the doorway, "for you're in the presence of an innocent child."

Charlotte lowered the poker. "Mr. Sherbourne, greetings."

Clinging to Sherbourne's hand was a small blond boy. The child had Fern's chin and her nose, though Brantford's contribution was apparent in the flaxen hair and blue eyes.

Haverford strolled into the room. "Perhaps I should take the boy to the kitchen, where we will ask Cook to make us a pot of chocolate."

The child's gaze bounced from Charlotte to Haverford to Brantford. "I've never had chocolate."

The boy spoke Welsh, so Charlotte replied in the same language. "Chocolate is a very rich drink, so be sure to add a dash of sugar. Your mama always took it with a dash of sugar."

His smile was entirely Fern's. "You knew my mama?"

Charlotte nodded rather than trust her voice.

"Civilized people speak English," Brantford snapped.

Sherbourne knelt so he was eye-level with the boy. "Haverford will steal all the sweets if you let him," he said in Welsh. "He has a very pretty duchess who might join you in the kitchen. She'll make sure you get your fair share of biscuits."

"I heard that," Haverford said—also in Welsh. "And you heard the lady, Sherbourne. Mind the carpets."

"We'll talk later," Charlotte assured the child. "I'll tell you all about your dear mama."

Then they were gone, the boy flicking one mildly curious glance over Brantford before taking the duke's hand and skipping off to the kitchen.

Brantford gulped down the remaining portion of his brandy. "I haven't the least notion what that farce was about, Sherbourne, but you and I will come to terms regarding my investment in your little colliery, or I'll see you ruined down to the nineteenth generation before next year's season begins."

"We'll renegotiate," Sherbourne said, thrusting his hand into a pocket. "Let's start with an explanation for this miniature, given by you to my wife's best friend—her late best friend, who was the mother of your only begotten son."

* * *

How do I hold Brantford accountable for his sins, while keeping every single groat of his money, and denying my darling wife the pleasure of drawing his lordship's cork?

Brantford stared down at the miniature Sherbourne had placed on the sideboard. "You claim that is a likeness of me?" He reached toward the portrait, but withdrew his hand—his shaking hand—without touching it.

"You initialed it," Charlotte said. "Look at the back."

He managed to pick up the miniature and stared at the back, while Charlotte glowered at him. Brantford sank into the chair before the hearth and held the miniature out to Sherbourne.

"Take it. Take it, please. I never want to see it again."

Sherbourne remained beside his wife, lest that good woman start laying about with her iron poker.

"I recognize your penmanship, Brantford, having seen it on the contract you signed. You gave that portrait to one Fern Porter, whom you enticed into a liaison, though she was a vicar's daughter and innocent of men prior to her association with you. After you proposed marriage to her, she conceived a child and informed you of her situation. You struck her, turned your back on her, and married another."

Brantford set the miniature on the low table. "I was young, not much more than a boy."

"You had finished university years earlier," Charlotte spat. "You were an adult, she was just out of the schoolroom, and you ruined her. Promised her undying love, promised her marriage, and played her false."

Brantford took out a lace handkerchief and dabbed at the corners of his mouth. "She should not have—"

"Don't," Sherbourne said.

Charlotte had raised the poker. She shot a quizzical look at her husband.

"I spoke to the earl. You, Mrs. Sherbourne, must do as you see fit. I admonish his lordship not to compound his sins by minimizing his own faults, lying, or casting blame. He ruined a young woman, made no reparation for the harm done, and now she's dead, leaving an innocent child all but orphaned."

"I wasn't sure," Brantford said, using the handkerchief to mop at his brow. "How was I to be certain she wasn't deceiving me? How is a man to know?"

"Mr. Sherbourne," Charlotte said, passing the poker over to Sherbourne. "I cannot trust my self-restraint in the presence of such vile, cowardly, spineless, dishonorable, disgraceful, weak...the entire language lacks enough adjectives to convey my contempt for you, my lord. Your son is lucky that he's growing up without a hint of your presence in his life."

Brantford hunched forward, as if Charlotte had struck him physically.

Sherbourne held his peace, because clearly the lady had more to say.

"Fern suffered," she went on. "She suffered scandal and disgrace, she suffered through a confinement with no physician to attend her. She suffered an awful birth, her pangs going on for days. She suffered yet more knowing she would not live to see her child grow up, knowing nobody—not her, not the miserable coward the child must claim as his father—would love this child the way he deserved to be loved. So much of her suffering is your fault, and I hope you are repaid tenfold for your despicable selfishness."

The winter wind was balmy compared to Charlotte's tone. She sent Sherbourne a look, then made a grand exit from the parlor.

Finish the job, that look said. *Find justice for Fern and for the child.*

"Haverford has offered to aid me in arranging your ruin," Sherbourne said, setting the fireplace poker just so on the hearth stand. "Radnor will want to do his part, and my lady wife counts any number of well-placed relations on her family tree. I suspect she has written of your irresponsibility to every one of them. I cannot put a bullet between your eyes—that would be too easy, and make the boy an orphan in truth—but I can make you regret your treatment of Fern Porter every day of your miserable, titled life."

Brantford sat up and put away his handkerchief. "Might I have some brandy?"

"You came here expecting to all but extort funds from me. I owe you nothing in the way of hospitality, much less fairness."

His lordship studied the miniature on the table, his gaze growing sly. "I'll just collect the lad and go. Keep the damned money. I don't need it."

"And the boy does not need you."

"Now see here, Sherbourne. That child is my blood, my only begotten son, you said it yourself. The likeness is undeniable, and I'll not have you interfering." Brantford drew righteousness around himself like presentation robes, his sense of entitlement so ingrained, not even shame could dislodge it.

"You denied any responsibility for him," Sherbourne said, "and in the face of your callous disregard for the child, my wife provided for him. She convinced an uncle to take in both mother and child, saw to Fern's safe travel from London, and has been sending money for the child since before he arrived into this world. You have no claim on that boy, legally or otherwise."

Brantford rose and jerked down his waistcoat. "He is my son. I am a peer of the realm, and you will not deny me a father's rights."

Thank a merciful God that Charlotte wasn't on hand to witness this hypocrisy. "You are a perfect donkey's arse. Sit, Brantford. Now."

His lordship evidenced a modicum of prudence and sat. "You don't understand, Sherbourne. I haven't any other children."

"*Such* a pity," Sherbourne marshaled his best imitation of Haverford in a genteel rage. "The child had only the one father who might have made his mother's circumstances easier, a father who could have seen to it she had proper care and assistance at her lying in. That same father might have spared a few coins for the child, might have given the child his name. Alas for the boy, the one father responsible for bringing him into the world is too busy being a peer of the realm to be a decent human being."

"Damn it, Sherbourne, there won't be any other children. The physicians don't come right out and say it, but a touch of the French pox can have lasting consequences. That child . . . he'll never have the title, but I could acknowledge him, eventually."

Had Brantford asked anything about the boy—his name, his present state of health, his uncle's financial situation—Sherbourne might have weakened, but Brantford clearly saw his offspring as proof of virility, a social accessory or an ornament.

Truly, young Evander was better off without that version of a father's interest.

"This is how we shall proceed," Sherbourne said. "You will place your shares in the coal mine in trust for the boy now, and sign them over to him at age eighteen if they haven't been liquidated."

Brantford wrinkled his nose. "An illegitimate Welsh pauper has no use for shares in a mine."

"He has no use for a negligent father. The trustee managing those shares will be His Grace of Haverford. If Haverford is for any reason unable to serve as trustee, Radnor will step in. They will further acquaint their ward with the details of his birth at an appropriate time. You will be given quarterly assurances of the child's good health and educational progress."

"*Haverford* is taking a hand in this?"

"And Radnor." *My friends, who will be guided in all particulars by my wife.*

Sherbourne went to the window, where bright sunshine had started to melt the snow. As the sun set, the lanes would freeze anew, and travel would become treacherous.

"At least I'll be supporting my son." Brantford was on his feet again, the miniature in his hand. "Let it not be said that when given an—"

"Do we add larceny to your list of transgressions?" Sherbourne asked. "That painting is not yours, and no one has given it to you."

That portrait was also the primary evidence connecting

the child to the earl, and Brantford's attempt to make off with it was proof positive of inextinguishable self-interest.

"You can't have any use for it," Brantford retorted.

Sherbourne prowled across the parlor, glad that he wasn't holding the iron poker. "Put it down, Brantford, or you will suffer a bad fall on my main staircase. Drink makes any man clumsy, and there's not a servant in this household who will say otherwise."

Brantford set the portrait down slowly.

"You are not supporting the child." Sherbourne had just now made that decision. "I am supporting the child. Haverford and Radnor are overseeing the assets you'll convey to the trust. I want that young man to know that he owes you nothing, not one bent farthing. If he chooses to toss the mining shares back in your face, that will be his decision when he's of age. If he chooses to write to you or visit you in London, that will be his choice. He owes you nothing, and never will."

Brantford huffed, he plucked at the hem of his waistcoat, he looked down his nose, or tried to, despite Sherbourne's superior height.

"And if I should take this matter to the courts?"

What an ass. "Please, take this matter to the courts. My uncle-in-law has lunch with a Lord Justice at least monthly, and I can call upon more barristers and solicitors than you have hounds in your kennel. By the time you stand before a judge, the boy will be through university. But indulge in all the legal dramatics you please."

Sherbourne opened the parlor door and swept a hand toward the corridor. "Just know that your only son will be well cared for, despite your negligence, because my wife stood by her friend even when you—with all your means and consequence—turned your back on a woman in need and her helpless child. Now leave, before I toss you down the jakes like the offal you are."

Brantford stalked out, and Sherbourne followed, waiting at the top of the steps until the earl had quit the premises, and the butler had closed the door behind him.

"Mrs. Sherbourne is in the kitchen, sir," Crandall said. "She said they'd save you a biscuit. Cook is having an apoplexy because His Grace is also in the kitchen, but Mrs. Sherbourne has eyes for only the boy."

"Let's hope she'll have eyes for her husband too. Did you know that Mrs. Sherbourne and I were a love match?"

"One would conclude this, sir."

"I hadn't concluded it, but I've heard it from the lady's own mouth, and a gentleman never argues with a lady."

Sherbourne had heard a good deal of Charlotte's tirade, but rather than the words, the utter conviction in her tone had struck him. They hadn't been a love match, not by any stretch.

But they were now.

Epilogue

"Evander's English and his Latin are both progressing," Charlotte said. "His French is hopeless."

Sherbourne plucked the letter from her hand. "All boys have hopeless French, until they realize that the ladies speak it quite well. Are you recovered from your parents' leave-taking?"

Sherbourne hadn't recovered from his in-laws' holiday visit, but then, one didn't recover from being married into the Windham family. One coped as best one could with good fortune of a magnitude that surpassed description. Charlotte's cousins and in-laws had responded *en masse* to her request for assistance where Brantford had been concerned, and the earl and his countess had taken an indefinite repairing lease in Portugal.

Brantford had requested permission to write to his son, which petition Haverford, Radnor, and Charlotte were considering.

Sherbourne was considering the various queries and hypotheticals her cousins had also posed by letter: Did Sherbourne think steam would render canals obsolete? Was steam a viable means of powering navigable craft? Had he an opinion on the commercial potential of indoor plumbing?

Indoor plumbing, for God's sake? That question had been posed by the ever practical Earl of Westhaven, and Sherbourne had joined him in investing in copper piping. This flurry of correspondence was Charlotte's doing, for even before the whole business with Brantford had been resolved, she'd sung the praises of her husband's commercial genius—her word—to any Windham she'd been able to reach by post.

Charlotte tugged her husband down beside her onto the sofa. She'd made a small chamber on the third floor her personal parlor, claiming that she wanted to be able to see clear to the colliery when she couldn't be there in person. The view was lovely, and if the perspective was elevated, well, that didn't seem to bother her of late.

"Mama and Papa are a force of nature," she said, stroking the kitten in her lap, "but yes, I am recovered from their visit."

The beast's name was Beowulf, and he'd been among Sherbourne's holiday gifts to Charlotte.

"Your parents will be back," Sherbourne said, for he was learning to read Charlotte's moods. "With not one but two grandchildren on the way, we won't be able to keep them from a return visit."

And that was...that was lovely. If half the cousins and sisters and in-laws who threatened to visit showed up, Sherbourne Hall would need an entire wing of guest rooms...Rather like a castle.

The butler rapped on the door jamb.

"Come in," Charlotte said. "I was about to order Mr. Sherbourne a pot of peppermint tea. My parents' departure has left his nerves in a state."

"Another pot of tea. Of course, madam, and His Grace of Haverford has come to call."

Haverford strolled in, his cheeks ruddy from the cold, his hair windblown. "We announce family now? That will prove problematic when the shire is overrun with Windhams at next summer's house party."

"Not another house party," Sherbourne groaned. "Scavenger hunts, kite flying, piquet, and whist until I'm bilious—"

"A house party would be delightful," Charlotte said, rising and kissing the duke on the cheek. "Have a seat, and stay for a cup of tea."

Haverford sent Sherbourne an unreadable look, but he sat beside Charlotte like a good duke. "I come bearing news."

"Who's expecting now?" Sherbourne asked.

"In a sense," Haverford replied, "you are." He placed a folded sheet of vellum on the table before the sofa.

Charlotte picked the paper up and smoothed it out. "This is..." She blinked rapidly. "Oh, Haverford. You didn't."

Was that a happy *you didn't* or an upset *you didn't*?

Charlotte threw her arms around the duke and delivered a crushing hug, while the kitten scampered off with an indignant hiss.

"Oh, you are awful, Haverford," Charlotte said. "You are the worst duke ever, and I will name my firstborn after you."

"We're not naming our firstborn Dunderhead," Sherbourne said, picking up the paper. "This is merely a list of names." Though reading the list sent an odd sensation shivering over Sherbourne's skin.

"That is the New Year's honors list," Haverford said. "Congratulations, Sir Lucas."

Sherbourne's gaze lit on his own name. He dropped the paper on the table and crossed the room to throw himself into the reading chair by the window.

"I have no need of a baronetcy. I don't want a baronetcy." *Sir Lucas Sherbourne.* His father and grandfather were probably dancing a jig in heaven for a baronetcy was hereditary. "I have no need of anything. My colliery is coming along, I have an assistant engineer who can jolly Mr. Jones without offending him *and* keep track of all three pairs of his new spectacles, not that Jones needs jollying now that's he's remarried. I've sold my damned bank shares. My in-laws pronounced me a fine addition to the family. What need have I . . . ?"

Charlotte was regarding him, her eyes shimmering, her gaze enough to set Sherbourne's heart thumping. To the casual observer, she was the same woman who'd shot top hats from randy bachelors. To her husband, she had blossomed as autumn had turned to winter. Her figure was changing, of course, but she'd also gained a sense of true confidence where bravado and sheer courage had been before.

"Besides," Sherbourne went on more softly, "I have my Charlotte. With Charlotte to love, what else in the whole world could I possibly need?"

She blew him a kiss. He pretended to catch it and touched his fingers to his lips.

"You're worse than Griffin and Biddy," Haverford groused. "Sherbourne, think of your lady, who I'm sure wouldn't mind having a lady's title. And don't blame me for this development. Elizabeth set the wheels in motion, and it is to her you will express sincere gratitude. Your library scheme found favor with the sovereign, who, like most worthy people, thoroughly enjoys a good book."

"The dratted libraries," Charlotte said, beaming at her husband. "You could still call me Mrs. Sherbourne when we are private."

"I'm leaving," Haverford said, rising. "If I have to swill another cup of peppermint tea, I will go barking mad. Congratulations, *Sir Lucas*."

The duke was making a good show of irascibility, but Sherbourne knew friendship when he saw it. He shook Haverford's hand, slapped him on the back, and let him escape before the dreaded peppermint teapot made another appearance.

Which in subsequent years, it did regularly.

In later life the baronet became a baron, and the coal mine which he eventually conveyed to Evander Porter was an example of the best, safest, most modern practices. Sherbourne became hopelessly wealthy, in part because his lady wife was a fiend for calculations.

Charlotte established a charitable undertaking of her own, one that found safe havens for young ladies in difficulties. She relied on a vast network of family and friends of means to ensure that every child brought to her attention was well cared for and well loved.

And Sir Lucas considered it his greatest privilege to ensure that Charlotte was also well cared for and well loved—very, very, *very* well loved, indeed.

Keep reading for a peek at the
first book in the Rogues to
Riches series.

Coming in Fall 2018.

Chapter One

"You isn't to be hanged on Monday!" Ned declared. "Old Fletcher's got the bloody flux. Can't stir but two feet from the chamber pot. Warden says no hangings on Monday!"

Joy was the first casualty in the earthly purgatory of Newgate prison. When Ned came bounding into Quinn Wentworth's cell, the boy's rare, angelic smile thus had a greater impact than his words.

An uncomfortable, unfamiliar emotion stirred, something Quinn might once have called hope but now considered a useless reflex.

"You mean I won't be hanged *this* Monday."

Consternation replaced ebullience on the grimy little face. "Old Fletcher might die, sir, and then who would they find to do the business? Your family will get you out, see if they don't."

Quinn had forbidden his siblings to "get him out." Abetting the escape of a convicted felon was itself a hanging felony, as were 219 other crimes, among them stealing anything valued at more than twelve pence.

"Thank you for bringing me the news," Quinn said. "Have you eaten today?"

Ned studied ten dirty little toes. "No so's I'd notice."

Miracles occurred in Newgate. One of the most powerful and feared bankers in London could invite a pickpocket to dine, for example, simply because the banker had learned that company—any company—was a distraction from impending death.

Despite the death warrant dictating Quinn's fate, his cell might have been a successful solicitor's quarters. The floor was carpeted, the bed covered with clean linen, the desk stocked with paper, pen, two pencils, ink, and even—such was the honor expected of a wealthy felon—a penknife. The window let in fresh air and a precious square of sunlight, which Quinn valued more than all of the room's other comforts combined.

The foodstuffs, however, had to be kept in a bag tied to the rafters, lest the rodents help themselves uninvited. The pitcher of ale was covered to prevent flies from drowning themselves along with their sorrows.

"Fetch the ale," Quinn said. "We'll share some bread and cheese."

Ned was stronger and faster than he looked, and more than capable of fetching the ale down from the windowsill without spilling a drop. Quinn was, in his own opinion, weaker than appearances might suggest. The warden had taken one pitying look at him and muttered something about the big ones dying quickest on the end of a rope.

That comment—a casual, not intentionally cruel observation—had made real the fact of execution by order of the crown. Hanged by the neck until dead, as the judge had said. The proper fate of all murderers in the eyes of the law.

Though to be accurate, Quinn's crime was manslaughter rather than murder, else even his coin might have been insufficient to earn him quarters outside the dungeons.

"Shall I get the bread?" Ned asked.

The child was being polite, which ought not to be possible, given his upbringing.

Incarceration had also revealed in Quinn a latent propensity for rumination. What would death by hanging be like? Was the point of the proceeding to end the felon's life, or to subject him to such awful, public indignity that he welcomed his own demise? As a boy, Quinn had once witnessed a hanging. He'd been running the streets as usual, curious about the excitement rippling through a crowd until he'd wiggled his way to the front.

And there he'd stayed, because the crowd wouldn't let him wiggle back until—as the mob cheered madly—the condemned had kicked, gasped, thrashed, and pissed his last.

Quinn had avoided the neighborhood for months thereafter.

"The bread, sir?"

"And the cheese," Quinn said, taking down the sack suspended from the rafter. Cutting the bread required patient use of the penknife. Davies, Quinn's self-appointed man-of-all-work, and Penny, the whore-turned-chambermaid, were privileged to carry knives, but Quinn shuddered to contemplate what improprieties those knives had got up to when their owners had been at liberty.

Quinn set the food on the table, cut two thick slices of bread for the boy, situated cheese between them, and poured the child some ale.

Pewter tankards, no less. That would be his sister

Althea's influence, as was the washstand with the porcelain pitcher and basin. No need to die looking like a ruffian.

"Aren't you hungry, sir?" Ned had wolfed down half his sandwich and spoke with his mouth full.

Quinn took a sip of fine summer ale. "Not particularly."

"But you must keep up your strength. My brother Bob told me that. Said when the magistrate binds you over, the most important thing is to keep up your strength. You durst not go before the judge looking hangdog and defeated. You can't run very far on an empty belly neither."

The boy had lowered his voice on that last observation.

"I'll not be escaping, Ned," Quinn said gently. "I've been found guilty and I must pay the price." Though escape might be possible. It wanted vast sums of money—which Quinn had—and a willingness to live the life of a fugitive, which Quinn lacked.

"Why is the nobs all daft?" Ned muttered around another mouthful of bread and cheese. "You find a bloke what looks half like you and has the consumption. You pay his family enough to get by, more than the poor sod would have earned in his lifetime, and you pike off on Sunday night leaving the bloke in your place. The poor sod ends his suffering Monday morning knowing the wife and kiddies is well set, and you get to live. It's been done."

Everything unspeakable, ingenious, and bold had been done by those enjoying the king's hospitality. That was another lesson Quinn had gleaned from incarceration. He'd seen schemes and bribes and stupid wagers by the score among London's monied classes, but sheer effrontery and true derring-do were the province of the desperate.

He'd also learned, too late, that he wanted to live. He wanted to be a better brother and a lazier banker. He wanted to learn the names of the flowers Althea so loved, and to read a book or two just to have the excuse to sit quietly by a warm fire of a winter night.

He wanted...

What he wanted no longer mattered, if it ever had. The reprieve Ned spoke of was more burden than blessing, because Quinn was fated to die, awfully, publicly, and painfully.

"If you're not going to eat that, guv, it shouldn't go to waste."

Quinn passed over his sandwich. "My appetite seems to have deserted me."

Ned tore the sandwich in two and put half in his pocket. For later, for another boy less enterprising or fortunate than Ned. For the birds—the child loved birds—or a lucky mouse.

Quinn had lost not only his appetite for food, but also his interest in all yearnings. He did not long to see his siblings one last time—what was there to say? He certainly had no desire for a woman, though they were available in quantity even in prison. He had no wish to pen one of those sermonizing, final letters he'd written for six other men in the previous weeks.

They'd faced transportation. Quinn faced the gallows. His affairs were scrupulously in order, and had escaped forfeiture as a result of his forethought.

He wanted...peace, perhaps.

And revenge. That went without saying.

The door banged open—it was unlocked during the day—and the day warden appeared. "Wait in here, miss. You'll be safe enough, and I see that his nibs is enjoying a feast. Perhaps he'll offer you a portion." The jailer flicked a bored glance over Ned, who'd ducked his head and crammed the last of the food into his mouth.

A woman—a lady—entered the cell. She was tall, dark-haired, and her attire was plain to a fault.

Not a criminal. A crusader.

"Bascomb," Quinn said rising. "This is not Newgate's family parlor. The lady can wait elsewhere." He bowed to the woman.

She did not curtsy. "I must wait somewhere," she said. "Papa will be forever among the convicts, and I do not expect to be entertained. I am Jane Winston."

She was bold, as most crusaders were. Also pretty. Her features were Madonna-perfect, from a chin neither receding nor prominent, to exquisitely arched brows, a wide mouth, high forehead, and intelligent dark eyes. The cameo was marred by a nose a trifle on the confident side, which made her face more interesting.

She wore a long, voluminous cloak, bits of straw clinging to the hem.

"As you can see," Quinn replied, "we are a company of gentlemen here, and an unchaperoned lady would not be comfortable in our midst."

The warden snickered. "Wait here or leave the premises, miss. Them's your choices, and you don't get a say, Wentworth."

As long as Quinn drew breath he had a say. "I am convicted of taking an innocent life, Miss Winston. Perhaps you might see fit to excuse yourself now?"

He wanted her to leave, because she was an inconvenient reminder of life beyond a death sentence, where women were pretty, regrets were few, and money meant more than pewter tankards and a useless writing desk.

And Quinn wanted her to stay, because she was pleasing to look at, had the courage of her convictions, and had probably never committed anything approaching a crime.

She'd doubtless sinned in her own eyes—coveting a second rum bun, lingering beneath warm covers for an extra quarter hour on the Sabbath. Heinous transgressions in her world.

He also wanted her to stay because frightening the people around him had stopped amusing him before he'd turned twelve. Even Ned didn't turn his back on Quinn for more than an instant, and Davies remained as close to the unlocked door as possible without giving outright offense. The wardens were careful not to be alone with Quinn, and the whores offered their services with an air of false bravado.

Miss Winston's self-possession wafted on the air like expensive perfume. Confident, subtle, unmistakable.

"If a mere child can break bread with you, then I don't have much to fear," she said, "and my father will expect me to wait for him. Papa is easily vexed. Do you have a name, child?"

Such boldness.

Ned remained silent, sending a questioning glance at Quinn.

"He is Edward, of indeterminant patronymic," Quinn said. "Make your bow, Ned."

Ned had asked Quinn to teach him this nicety, and grinned at a chance to show off his manners. "Pleased to meet you, Miss Winston."

"I'll just be leaving," the guard said. "You can chat about the weather over tea and crumpets until..." He grinned, showing brown, crooked teeth. "Until next Monday."

"Prison humor." Miss Winston stripped off her gloves. Kid, mended around the right index finger. The stitching was almost invisible, but a banker learned to notice details of dress. "I might be here for a good while. Would you like to regale me with a tale about what brought you to this sorry pass, Mr. Wentworth?"

The lady took the seat Ned had vacated, and she looked entirely at ease there, her cloak settling around her like an ermine cape.

"You don't read the papers?" Quinn asked.

"Who has time for such frivolity, Mr. Wentworth? Papa would have apoplexies if he caught me reading that drivel. We have souls to save."

"I don't think I'd like your father. Might I have a seat?" Because now—for reasons known only to the doomed—Quinn wanted an excuse to sit down with her.

"This is your abode. Of course you should have a seat. You need not feed me or offer me drink. I'm sure you can better use your provisions for bribes. I can read to you from the Bible or quote from Fordyce's sermons if you like."

"I do not like," Quinn said, slicing off a portion of cheese. He was a convicted felon, but he was a convicted felon who'd taken pains to learn the manners of his betters. Then too, somebody had to set an example for the boy. Quinn managed to cut off a slice of bread with the penknife and passed the bread and cheese to Miss Winston.

She regarded his offering with a seriousness the moment did not warrant. "You can spare this? You can honestly spare this?"

"I will be grievously offended if you eschew my hospitality," Quinn said. "Had I known you were coming, I'd have ordered the kitchen to use the good silver."

Ned looked at him as if he were daft, but Miss Winston caught the joke. Her smile was utterly unexpected. Instead of a prim, nipfarthing little pinch of the lips, she grinned at Quinn as if he'd inspired her to hilarity in the midst of a bishop's sermon. Her eyes—a soft brown—warmed, her shoulders lifted, her lips curved with glee.

"The everyday will do splendidly," she said, taking a bite of her humble fare. "So whom are you supposed to have killed?"

ABOUT THE AUTHOR

Grace Burrowes grew up in central Pennsylvania and is the sixth out of seven children. She discovered romance novels when in junior high (back when there was such a thing), and has been reading them voraciously ever since. Grace has a bachelor's degree in political science and a bachelor of music in music history (both from Pennsylvania State University), a master's degree in conflict transformation from Eastern Mennonite University, and a juris doctor from the National Law Center at George Washington University.

Grace writes Georgian, Regency, Scottish Victorian, and contemporary romances in both novella and novel lengths. She's a member of Romance Writers of America, and enjoys giving workshops and speaking at writers' conferences. She also loves to hear from her readers, and can be reached through her website, graceburrowes.com.

If you love Grace Burrowes, don't miss Anna Harrington's *As the Devil Dares,* available now!

Whether it's business or pleasure, Lord Robert Carlisle never backs down from a dare. But finding a husband for beautiful, scandalous Mariah Winslow will require all of Robert's connections—and rakish charms. He simply never expected to want her for himself...

FALL IN LOVE WITH FOREVER ROMANCE

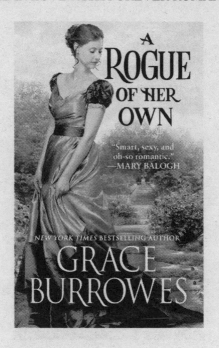

A ROGUE OF HER OWN
By Grace Burrowes

From Grace Burrowes comes the next book in the *New York Times* bestselling Windham Brides series! All Charlotte Windham needs to maintain her independence is a teeny, tiny brush with scandal. What she doesn't count on is that one kiss will lead her straight to the altar with a brash, wealthy upstart she barely knows.

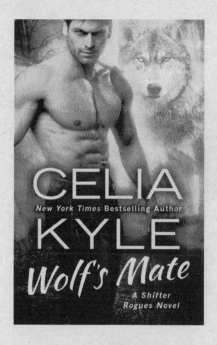

WOLF'S MATE
By Celia Kyle

From *New York Times* bestselling author Celia Kyle comes the first book in the Shifter Rogues series! Cougar shifter Abby Carter *always* plays it safe. That's why she's an accountant—no excitement, no danger, and no cocky alpha males. But when Abby uncovers the shady dealings of an anti-shifter organization, she'll have to trust the too-sexy-for-her-peace-of-mind werewolf Declan Reed... or end up six feet under.

FALL IN LOVE WITH FOREVER ROMANCE

CHANGING THE RULES
By Erin Kern

The next stand-alone novel in Erin Kern's Champion Valley series! Cameron Shaw knows how to coach high school boys on the football field, but caring for his six-year-old niece, Piper, is a whole different ballgame. Audrey Bennett wasn't planning to stick around once she delivered Piper to her new guardian, but the gruff former football star clearly needs help. And the longer she stays—watching Cameron teach Piper to make pancakes and tie her sparkly pink shoelaces—the harder it is to leave.

THE SWEETEST THING
By Jill Shalvis

Now featuring ten bonus recipes never before seen in print! Don't miss this new edition of *The Sweetest Thing*, the second book in *New York Times* bestselling author Jill Shalvis's beloved Lucky Harbor series!